Joss Wood wrote her first book at the age of eight and has never really stopped. Her passion for putting letters on a blank screen is matched only by her love of books and travelling—especially to the wild places of Southern Africa—and possibly by her hatred of ironing and making school lunches.

Fuelled by coffee, when she's not writing or being a hands-on mum, Joss, with her background in business and marketing, works for a non-profit organisation to promote the local economic development and collective business interests of the area where she resides. Happily and chaotically surrounded by books, family and friends, she lives in Kwa-Zulu Natal, South Africa, with her husband, children and their many pets.

A little over a year ago, on the same day that I found out that my dream of becoming published was about to come true, my sister was involved in the most horrendous car accident.

Because she is the bravest, strongest, most incredible person I know, this book is dedicated to her.

Love you, Di.

CHAPTER ONE

'LAPTOP AND MOBILE chargers packed? Did you check the oil in the car?'

Lu Sheppard stood in the east coast early-morning sunshine and, because she knew that throwing her arms around the hairy knees closest to her and hanging on tightly wouldn't be appreciated, jammed her clenched fists into the pockets of her faded denim shorts. Turning her head away, she swallowed furiously before digging deep and yanking out her patented, much practised I'm-OK-you're-OK smile.

'Lu, *you* did,' answered Daniel, the younger of her twin brothers. 'Twice.'

That was right. She had. And she'd ticked it off on the list she'd made for them. Not that either of them had looked at it. Lord, how was she going to *do* this? These boys had been her life and her focus for the past decade. How was she supposed to just let them get into their car and drive across the country to university and, to all intents and purposes, out of her life? She'd yelled at them, cried with them and cried *over* them. She'd provided meals and lifts, helped with homework and bugged them to talk to her. She'd been father, mother, sister and friend.

She was twenty-nine years old and not only was she unable to stare empty nest syndrome in the eye, it was also kicking her non-sexy butt. But, like so many other emotions she'd experienced over the past ten years, the boys didn't have to know that…

Daniel leaned back against the door of his jointly owned car and cleared his throat. Lu saw the look he gave Nate and felt rather than saw the nod Nate gave in reply. Nate moved to stand next to his non-identical twin, equally tall, equally good-looking.

Daniel cleared his throat again. 'Lu, we *are* grateful that you stepped up to be our guardian when Mom and Dad died. If it wasn't for you we would've ended up with some crusty relative who probably would've shipped us off to boarding school and holiday camps.'

Since their parents had both been only children, Daniel's comment wasn't far off the truth. All their relatives were old, crusty, and generally waiting for the light in the tunnel.

'But it's time for a new start…for us and also for you.'

Huh? 'What do you mean?'

Daniel rubbed his jaw. 'We think it's time for you to do all the things you couldn't do because you were raising us.'

Lu frowned. 'Where is this coming from, guys? We talked about this—about you two leaving.'

'Sure—about what uni was like, how we felt about leaving, what we were getting into. But we never spoke about *you*.' Nate chipped in.

Lu's expression was pure confusion. 'Why did we need to? My life isn't changing.'

'It should,' Nate retorted.

'But why?'

'Because nothing about your life is normal for a single woman of your age! When did you last have a date?' Nate demanded.

Lu couldn't remember. It had been a while—six, eight months? She could barely remember the man, just that he hadn't been able to wait to get rid of her after she'd told him that her twin brothers lived with her and she was their guardian. She couldn't blame him; his had been the standard reaction from the very few men she'd dated over the years: shock followed by an immediate desire to find the closest exit.

Add a large house, two dogs, an enormous saltwater fish tank, three corn snakes—no, they'd been moved to a reptile centre when she'd refused to look after them after the boys left—and cats to the pile of her baggage, and it was no wonder her dates belted away.

'We need to talk to you about...*you*,' Nate said.

'Me?' Lu yelped as she pulled a band from her shorts and finger-combed her straight, mouse-brown hair into a stubby pony.

Uh, *no*. She looked after *them*—physically, mentally— they didn't look after her. That was the way their little family worked.

'Look, Lu, we're not only leaving, we're leaving *you*. You know our plans: degrees, then we want to travel. We have no idea where we'll end up but there's a good chance it won't be here,' Nate continued. 'That being said, it would be a lot easier for us if we knew that you were happy and busy and had a full life of your own. Take this house, for instance; we don't want you hanging on to this mansion in the hope that one of us will want it one day. And right now it's a huge house for you to live in by yourself.'

Dan jumped in. 'We're not asking you to sell the house, or anything like that... We just want you to know that we are cool with whatever you want to do with it: sell it, rent it out, start up a commune...'

Lu sat down on the steps leading to the front door and rested her forearms on her thighs. Nate sat down next to her and draped a muscular arm around her shoulder. 'Just please don't become a crazy lady who rattles around here talking to herself and rescuing cats. That was the first thing we wanted to mention...'

There was more? Really? Good grief!

Daniel dropped to his haunches in front of her and pinned her with a look that went far beyond his eighteen years. 'Lu, you are going to be on your own for the first time since you were roughly our age.'

Well, yeah. That was why empty nest syndrome was wiping the floor with her face.

'We want you to have some fun—to live your life.' Daniel raked an agitated hand through his hair, which desperately needed a cut. 'You need to stop being so responsible, to take a breath. To do the things you should've been doing while you were raising us.'

Lu cocked her head. 'Like…?'

'Like clubbing and—' Daniel looked at a point beyond her shoulder and blushed '—hooking up.'

Hooking up? Heavens, if she couldn't remember when last she'd had a date, she'd had absolutely no idea when she last had sex. She suspected she might need a high-pressure cleaner to remove the cobwebs.

'So, here's your "to do" list. We want you to try new things like…skydiving or learning to surf. Pottery classes or dance lessons,' Nate suggested.

Daniel, her brand and fashion-conscious brother, winced at her faded purple T-shirt and battered jeans. 'Some decent clothes would also be a good idea.'

'I *have* decent clothes!' Lu objected.

'Then wear them!' Daniel shot back. 'And your hair needs a cut and you could do with a facial. You need a lifestyle makeover.'

Since their words plucked a chord somewhere deep inside her, she suspected that they might be right. But she certainly didn't have to like it.

Lu growled. 'I hate you.' She glared at Daniel. '*And* you.'

'No, you don't. You love us.'

Nate grinned and her heart flipped over. God, she did. So much. How was she supposed to let them go?

'You *should* go clubbing. Somewhere hip and fun. You'll have to dress up and make an effort.' Nate said. 'Makhosi will take you, Lu.'

Of course he would. Clubbing was her oldest and best friend's favourite way to blow off steam.

'But she has to have a makeover first. I wouldn't be seen with her with that hair!' Daniel added.

'Hey!' Lu protested.

'Haircut, highlights and a makeover,' Daniel stated, and Lu glared at him. 'As Mak has said, more than once, that hair of yours is a disgrace: much better suited to a prissy librarian who doesn't curse, drink wine and who has never had a Big O in her life.'

Well, that sounded like her. Not the wine and the cursing part, but the Big O was definitely true. Could she be so damn emotional because she was sexually frustrated? It would be easy to shift the blame, but the truth was that sex had been scarce—OK, practically non-existent—for most of this past decade, so she couldn't blame her weeping on that.

Empty Nest Syndrome: two. Lu: nil.

And when had her brothers become old enough to mention her orgasms—or lack of them—anyway?

Nate leaned back and put his ankle on his knee. 'But, Lu, more important than anything else…you should get a job.'

Dan shook his head. 'Not that she uses any of it, but there is enough money coming in from the trust. She doesn't have to work if she doesn't want to.'

No, she didn't… If she could bring herself to use the money for anything other than the essentials that kept body and soul together. She had never felt comfortable using her parents' money for anything other than food, shelter and transport.

His brother sent him a you're-a-moron look. 'Not for the money, dude. Because it's something to…to get her teeth into.'

'Oh, right. Good point.'

Lu lifted her fingers and started to tick their demands off. 'So, you two think that if I find a job, go clubbing, have a makeover, learn how to surf—'

'And skydive,' Nate interjected.

'Dream on.' Lu glared at him and continued. 'Go to pottery and dance lessons then I won't have time to mope?'

Two blond heads nodded to some internal twin beat.

Lu stared past their car down the driveway. The thing was they could be right. The distraction of getting out and about might keep her from going off her head worrying about them. It wasn't a bad idea.

Lu nodded slowly. 'I'll think about it.'

'Promise you'll do it.' Nate insisted.

'I promise to think about it.'

'If you do it, we promise to come home in three months' time,' Nate said slyly.

'You're blackmailing me with a promise to come home?' Lu's mouth dropped open. 'You little snot!'

Nate just grinned and looked at his watch. 'We need to get going, Lu.'

She couldn't bear it. She really couldn't. She struggled to find the words and when she did they were muffled with emotion. 'Call me when you get there. Drive carefully.'

Nate pulled her up, cuddled her, and easily lifted her off her feet before placing a kiss on her cheek. 'Love ya, sis.'

When Nate released her, Daniel held her close. 'Take care of yourself. Have fun. Please, *please* have some fun,' he told her. Daniel let her go and hopped into the passenger seat. 'We'll call you when we get there.'

Lu nodded, touched Daniel's arm resting on the windowsill of the car and blew Nate a kiss.

Her boys…driving off to start their new life…

Lu watched their car turn into the road and sat down on the stairs, holding her face in her hands as she watched her two chicks fly from her very large and now very empty nest.

They would be fine, she assured herself. As for herself… she wasn't quite sure.

Two weeks later, in the VIP area of *Go!* on a very busy Friday night, Will Scott placed his elbows on the railing and looked down at the gyrating masses below him. It was nearly midnight and he'd been thinking about leaving the club for the past half-hour. He could walk down the block to the boutique hotel he'd booked into two days ago and in fifteen minutes could be face-down on the monstrous double bed.

That sounded like heaven.

Will felt someone lean on the railing next to him and looked into the battered face of his best friend Kelby, CEO of the Stingrays rugby franchise, who was also his boss for the next three months. Panic swirled in his gut at the thought.

'How is Carter?' Will asked.

The iconic and surly head coach of the Rays had suffered a heart attack a month back, and as the rugby season was fast approaching the team had been left rudderless without a coach.

'Still in hospital. Still doing tests. They're talking about a bypass,' Kelby replied. 'He said to tell you not to mess it up.'

If it was anyone other than Kelby Will would never utter the words he was about to say.

'The chances are good that I will.' Will rubbed the back of his neck. 'I really don't know if I'm doing the right thing, Kels. This isn't some little local team I'll be caretaker coach of. It's one of the top teams in the premier rugby playing world.'

'It is,' Kelby agreed easily. 'So?'

'So I'm thirty-four years old, not old enough to be a coach, and I have no experience at all! I only retired from international rugby last season and I don't want to muck it up!' Will retorted, shoving his hand into his dark brown hair.

Kelby placed his bottle of beer on a high table and sent him a penetrating look. 'It's strange to see you even marginally unhinged. You are probably the calmest, most confident person I know.'

'I don't feel too confident at the moment,' Will admitted.

'You've been unofficial coach of every team you've ever played for.' Kelby replied, his smile wide. 'I remember that first practice you attended as an eighteen-year-old. You were so full of Kiwi confidence that you told—who was it?—that he was breaking from the scrum too soon.'

Will dropped his head in embarrassment. He'd chirped the then Captain of the England squad and his big mouth had propelled him into a series of initiations by the older players that had quickly taught him to keep his head down and his mouth closed. But Kelby did have a point. Even early in his career he'd had an affinity for telling people what to do.

Rugby was as natural to him as breathing…but coaching? He was a player, not a technician. Kelby kept telling him that he had the assistant coaches for that side of things—a support team who were employed to deal with the technical aspects. His job was to train, to motivate, to strategise, to inspire and to lead. To get results and to win.

But, hey, no pressure.

It was a new ballgame, Will told himself. Something new to conquer. Another challenge to meet. A temporary stop-gap while he decided what he wanted to do for the rest of his life.

Kelby looked contemplative. 'You know, when I offered you this job it was more with hope than expectation. I know you've had other job offers, like commentating, and I also know that your business interests in New Zealand are extensive enough to keep you busy. So why did you accept this job halfway across the world, Will?'

Will shrugged and looked down into the mass of people below. There she was again, her long, lean body dressed in tight jeans and a sparkly emerald-green top. Her elfin face was topped by an ultra-short cap of sun-streaked light brown hair and he wished he could see what colour those light eyes actually were. Blue? Grey? She was talking to the guy she'd spent most of the evening dancing with and he couldn't quite work out the relationship between them. There was a lot of touching, but no kissing, and he frequently left her to dance with different women.

Even at a distance he could see that the guy had charm and he used it…and the woman didn't seem to mind. She just perched on her barstool, politely dismissed the guys trying to pick her up and watched the crowd.

'Will?'

Kelby was still expecting an answer so Will jammed his hands into the pockets of his jeans and thought about how to answer his question. 'I just wanted to get out of New Zealand for a while…get away from the constant speculation and conversation about why I retired at the peak of my career. About what I'm going to do, whether I'm ever going to settle down.'

'Why *did* you retire at the peak of your career?'

'Exactly that—because it was the peak. Hopefully when people remember my contribution to New Zealand rugby they'll remember the last seven years—not the years I spent before that, trying to flush my career and my life down a toilet.'

'Did you take this job because you felt you owed me?' Kelby demanded. 'Because if you did I'll kick your ass.'

Of course he had. If it hadn't been for Kelby he wouldn't have had a rugby career—wouldn't have captained the team for the past five years, wouldn't be known as one of the best fullbacks in the sport. Three months of his life spent coaching the Rays wouldn't even come close to paying his debt.

'I do owe you.'

Kelby shook his head. 'You just had your head too far up your own backside and I yanked it out.'

Will shook his head. Only Kelby could describe his self-destructive behaviour so lightly.

'You repaid your debt to me by straightening out your life. But, like with everything else, you, being you, have to take everything to the nth degree,' Kelby added, resting his elbows on the railing that overlooked the heaving club below.

Will's grin faded at Kelby's serious face. 'What are you talking about?'

'Both you and Jo became too successful, too young… and it went to your heads. Jo was the bad girl of professional sports, and because you wanted to get into and stay in her pants she pulled you into her crazy lifestyle.'

'Sex, drugs and rock and roll,' Will said bitterly. 'Then I married her.'

'And, because you're a competitive SOB you thought that whatever she could do you could do better. God, the press loved you two.'

Thanks to their exploits, they'd sold so many newspapers that the holding companies should have offered them shares, Will thought sourly. They'd fallen into bed within an hour of meeting each other, been married within a month. Theirs had been an instant sexual connection, an adrenaline-filled lust that had been as compelling as it was dangerous.

'Jo did walk on the wild side and I loved it. The clubbing, the drinking, dallying with recreational drugs.'

Then had come the hell of trying to juggle their schedules to be together, the massive fights when they did meet up, and his slowly dawning realisation that they didn't have anything keeping them together other than a waning sexual chemistry.

'But what's that got to do with being competitive?'

'After the divorce you wanted to show Jo that you didn't need her to have a good time. The parties got bigger, there were different girls every night, and you were still making the papers for all the wrong reasons.'

'Nearly losing my career by pitching up at practice either drunk or constantly hungover. Yes, I remember! You covered for me that entire season. When the management team threatened to fire me you promised them that you could straighten me out, why?'

'You were too talented to be allowed to mess up your life,' Kelby stated.

Will shuddered. If Kelby hadn't stepped up and fought for him to stay employed by the rugby franchise there would've been no captaincy, no career.

Damn straight he owed him.

'But I didn't think I'd create a Frankenstein! When you finally heard my come-to-the-light talk you went from Mr Wild to Mr Disciplined Control. You hardly drink, you're rabidly anti-drugs, and you never allow yourself to have a relationship that lasts longer than a night. Maybe two.'

'The spark usually only lasts that long,' Will muttered. Bitter experience and a couple of brief affairs had taught him that the hotter the sexual flare of attraction, the quicker the flame died.

'Fires need to be fed, Will. Your problem is that you

think sex fuels a relationship. It doesn't. Not long-term any-way. Love fuels sex. Maybe if you tried getting to know a woman first before taking her to bed you would actually learn this.' Kelby sent him a knowing look. 'Or maybe you *do* know this and that's why you limit yourself to one- or two-night stands. You don't allow yourself to get to know anyone because you don't want to risk falling in love.'

Why would he want to fall in love? Love was the pits! A rollercoaster ride of hot sex, huge fights and total loss of control. Control…he *never* lost it. Not any more. Not on the field, not in relationships, never in the bedroom. It re-minded him of who he'd been and he didn't like it. Didn't want to be reminded of it.

'Have you been taking some of Angie's girl pills?' Will demanded. 'Geez, you sound like one of my sisters!'

Yet Kelby wouldn't shut up. 'Here's an idea…why don't you try being friends with a woman instead?'

'That's not the way it works.'

'On planet Normal it does,' Kelby retorted.

Will couldn't find a clever retort so he fell back on an old, trusted response. 'Shuddup.'

Kelby just snorted into his beer.

Will looked over the railing to see some of his team in the heaving mass of dancers below, surrounded by a lot of nubile, barely dressed female flesh. They were so young and so obvious. He looked right, to the woman at the bar who was the complete opposite of them. Older, but inad-vertently sexy, he mused, fascinated by her. Understated, yet compelling, with her minimal make-up and short, no-fuss hair.

Kelby banged his empty bottle down on the table. 'Let's get out of here.'

Will nodded and drained his beer. His eyes swept over the crowd below and he saw that she was still there, stand-ing by the bar, a long glass of what looked like mineral water in her hand. Unlike the rest of the clubbers she looked completely sober, and when she lifted her arm, and swung her watch-bracelet around her arm, he saw that she was checking the time. Her body language screamed that she wanted to leave and he was momentarily disappointed not to have met her.

You're here for three months only. Sex was important to him, although he was still weary of casual hook-ups. But as the thought of a permanent relationship gave him hives it didn't leave him with a lot of options. What could be worse than being trapped in a relationship with someone after familiarity and boredom had snuffed out all sexual attraction? It had happened with Jo, consistently rated as one of the world's sexiest sportswomen, so it was bound to happen with anyone else.

If he got bored, fell out of lust and couldn't maintain a relationship with someone as hot as *her*, he held out little—actually, *no* hope that he could do it with someone more... normal. He was, he admitted, a dysfunctional ass when it came to women.

As Will and Kelby walked down the steps from the VIP area he debated which exit to use. If he turned right it would take him past the bar and he might see the woman again.

Not that he'd do anything about it when he saw her; he just wanted to satisfy his curiosity about the colour of her eyes.

He traded high-fives with the more sober clubbers and rugby fans who recognised him, and Kelby willingly allowed himself to be pulled into a conversation with a couple of devoted fans. Rugby talk and free beer. Will grinned. Kelby couldn't resist either.

Will dismissed the raucous comments flung his way and flatly ignored the offers from women—and one camp man—to buy him a drink. It took him about fifteen min-

utes to get to where he'd last seen her and he looked around.
She'd disappeared.

Gone.

Later, he couldn't have said why he looked in that direction, what made him glance over his shoulder. But there she
was again. Except this time she was swaying on her feet.
A large man, one whom he hadn't seen before, had put his
arm around her shoulder and pulled her into his side. She
wasn't resisting. She just looked past him with glassy eyes
and her head bobbed on her neck.

She was high as a friggin' satellite.

Will frowned. Fifteen minutes ago she'd been dead sober
and wanting to go home—now she was spaced.

He knew drugs—could spot the signs—but he was convinced she'd been telling her friend that she wanted to go
home. Why take a hit if she wanted to leave? And whatever she'd taken had propelled her into la-la land very,
very quickly.

Will looked at her and his gut instinct screamed that
something was wrong. He really didn't like the look of
the broad, hairy hand that was cupping her ribcage, one
grubby-looking thumb resting just under the curve of her
breast. She'd refused the advances of far better-looking and
better-dressed men than him the whole evening. There was
no way that she'd hook up with that jackass now.

Date-rape drug. The thought slammed into his head
with the force of a rugby scrum.

And where the hell was her friend…boyfriend…date—
whatever he was? Will gnawed his bottom lip and swore,
considering what to do. He was ninety-nine percent sure
that her drink had been spiked, and if it had been, he
couldn't just leave her. Who knew what would happen to
her?

But…what if he was wrong? This could all be consen-
sual and he could be grabbing the wrong end of a very sharp

stick. But it would be far, far worse for her if he was right and he left her on her own.

Oh, well, here goes nothing, he thought as he approached them, pulling a name out of the air. 'Flora? Hey—*hi!* I never expected to bump into you here!'

CHAPTER TWO

DISCONNECTED MEMORIES AND snippets of conversation jumped in and out of her brain as Lu struggled to open her eyes. Eventually she just kept them closed and let herself drift. She remembered a friendly argument with Mak about her new, super-short hair. She didn't think it suited her, and she thought her newly plucked eyebrows were shaped in too thin a line. Mak had snorted that she had the fashion sense of a goat and that she looked fabulous. Rolling backwards in her memories, she saw Mak arriving at her house with skinny jeans, too expensive shoes and a sparkly top, because the boys had been gone two weeks already and he was tired of her moping so he was taking her clubbing.

When was that…? Today? Yesterday?

No, last night she'd been at that club, watching Mak's broad back slink off to the dance floor for one more dance while she waited for him at the bar.

Then…nothing.

Lu forced her eyes open, blinked and rubbed her eyes. When she opened them again they focused on a handsome face lying on the pillow next to her. Her eyes drifted over his long frame, over his muscled arm down to the tanned, broad hand that rested lightly on the top of her much whiter thigh. A masculine hand with a light touch… It felt so right, she thought as her eyelids drooped closed again.

OK, this dream was too awesome to lose by waking up.

Lu had no idea how much time passed before she woke again, but in contrast to the last time this time she didn't feel as if she had cotton candy clouds stuffed in her head. There wouldn't be a man lying next to her.

Lu opened one eye and—*holy mackerel!*—there still was a man. In bed.

With her?

And not just any man. A tall, dark and sexy one, who ticked all her make-me-hum boxes. Broad shoulders—tick. Muscular arms and chest—tick, tick. Long, powerful legs and slim hips. A face that was utterly masculine, a strong jaw and a battered nose that kept him from being over-the-top gorgeous.

Tick, tick, tick, tick, tick…

When he opened his eyes would they be an intense blue or green? They were neither. Just amber…the rich, deep hue of expensive sherry…edged with stubby dark lashes. They blinked once, twice, and then he yawned and she could see excellent teeth and…tonsils.

Tonsils? Seriously?

'Oh, crap!' he said as he rolled off the bed to his feet. He held out his hands as Lu scooted up the bed and wrapped her arms around her knees. 'Don't freak!'

Strangely, she wasn't close to panicking, but he looked as if he was about to.

'How do you feel?' he demanded. 'Are you OK?'

Was she? Lu considered his question. She was in a strange, albeit expensive hotel room, with a man who dinged her personal hotness bell, and she had no idea who he was or how she'd got there.

There was only one logical explanation for waking up in a strange man's bed. *What* was it that she'd tossed down her throat—and how much?—that she couldn't remember having sex with such an attractive man? It had to be the equivalent of an alcoholic bravery pill, because she *never* did casual hook-ups.

Lord, she prayed that he used a condom.

Right—there was only one way to get through this, she thought. *Keep calm. Play it cool. Act your socks off.* After raising two boys she was a master at putting on a 'happy face' to get through any awkward or emotional situation.

She put on a fake smile and met his brilliant eyes. 'So, that was fun. Thanks. I'll just get dressed and get out of your hair.'

Lu forced the words out and held her breath when he placed his hands on hips covered in black low-slung boxers. He topped six feet by a couple of inches and, because the navy T-shirt and boxers left little to the imagination, he radiated physical power. *Why* did he seem so familiar?

Heavy brows lifted before dropping into a frown. 'Fun?'

Oh, good Lord! Hadn't he enjoyed it? Was she *that* out of practice? Lu felt heat creep up her neck and into her cheeks. 'I'm sorry, I'm not very experienced at…' she waved her hand at the crumpled sheets '…this. Look, let me just get out of here and we can both pretend it didn't happen.'

Laughter flashed in his eyes and the corners of his mouth twitched. Lu felt the heat on her cheeks intensify. 'What do you think happened last night?'

Lu stared at her bare knees. 'I'm presuming that we had bad sex.'

'You don't remember?'

'Hence the word *presuming*,' Lu snapped. 'Did we sleep together?'

'Uh, not in the biblical sense.' He crossed his arms across his chest and those spectacular biceps bulged. His mouth flirted with a smile. 'And, for the record, men don't *ever* have bad sex. There's OK sex, blow-your-head-off hot sex and everything in between. But bad sex? Not so much.'

'Thanks for the update,' Lu muttered. 'So, nothing happened?'

'No, nothing happened...sex-wise.'

Damn, was that disappointment she felt? OK, even if she couldn't remember it, re-losing her virginity—and after so long she was pretty sure that she could be reclassified—to such a wonderful-looking man could only have been a fabulous thing.

A headache she hadn't been aware of started pulsing behind her eyes as confusion swirled around her head. 'So, if I didn't sleep with you then why am I half undressed and in your bed? Bra less? Did I say I would and then pass out? Should I start feeling scared?' But she didn't. Not yet. Weird, yes. Confused, definitely. Scared? Not so much.

'I promise that you are safe.' He must have sensed her confusion.

Lu looked into his sincere eyes and nodded. She wasn't sure why but her gut was saying that she could trust him—that despite his size he wouldn't lay a finger on her.

He sat down in the chair to one side of the bed and rested his forearms on his knees. After a short silence he spoke again. 'I'm Will Scott, by the way.'

Will Scott! She'd thought he looked familiar. What on earth was she doing in the hotel room of the new—crackling hot—coach of Durban's super-starry rugby team?

'Ah...'

'Do you want coffee? I need coffee. Actually, I need a drink. But coffee will have to do.' Will stood up and walked over to the phone next to the bed, placed the order with Room Service.

Lu pulled up the neck of the T-shirt that had fallen halfway down her shoulder. His shirt, obviously. Which meant...what? Had he undressed her? And if they hadn't slept together why was she out of her clothes?

'Where are my clothes?' she asked, unable to forget that she wasn't wearing a bra.

'Bathroom. Disgusting,' Will replied. 'You vomited all over yourself.'

Lu winced. OK, gross. Gross to the factor of four hundred. This story just kept getting better…*not!*

'Why did I vomit? I never drink enough to vomit. I don't understand.'

Lu dropped her legs and swung them off the side of the bed. For a moment she thought she saw Will's eyes on them, but when she looked at him again he was staring at the beige carpet beneath his bare feet.

'What happened to me?' Lu questioned as she stood up and his shirt fell to just above her knees. Of course it still revealed most of her shoulder, but better that than her naked breasts…though she suspected he'd already seen those since he'd undressed her.

'I saw you in the club and you looked sober. The next time I saw you—*Lu*—you looked spaced…high. You were also in the arms of a man I hadn't seen you with and he agreed that your name was Flora.'

'Flora? Who is Flora?' Lu demanded. 'And if we've never met before how do you know my name?'

'Oh, you have some business cards in your wallet. After I got you settled I went through it to try and find someone I could contact for you.'

That made sense. She did have business cards in her wallet that she occasionally handed out to promote her photography.

'So, you saw me with this guy…?' Lu prompted.

'I pulled the name Flora out of the air and he went along with it. That was a pretty big clue that something wasn't right. So I grabbed hold of you and tried to figure out a way to attract a bouncer's attention. Then you puked all over him. And yourself. And my shoes,' Will added ruefully.

Lu closed her eyes. 'Oh…hell. Seriously?'

Will nodded. 'Thank God you did. Puking probably saved your life. You got all the rest of that undigested date-rape drug out of your system.'

Lu blinked and held up her hand. '*Whoa!* Date-rape drug? What date rape drug? *What?*'

'It's the only reason why a stone-cold sober person would be reduced to a high, spaced-out, unresponsive robot in fifteen minutes,' Will explained.

Lu felt the pounding in her head increase, followed by an unpleasant whirling sensation. Date-rape drug? Lu staggered to the edge of the bed, dropped down and felt nausea building in her throat. She could have been held hostage, raped repeatedly, subjected to indescribably disgusting acts…

In her head she was screaming, panic was bubbling, and she bit down hard on her bottom lip to keep from whimpering. She would not cry. She would not lose control, she thought as stark images conjured up by her imagination—hard and cruel—slapped her again and again.

She couldn't get any air…she needed air.

Will crouched in front of her, his arm resting on his knee. 'That's quite an impressive show of control. Most girls would be hysterical by now. Right—now, breathe. The important point is to remember that nothing happened. I took you away after you threw up. So just breathe, slow and deep.' It was the voice from her dreams, calm, steady. In control. The images disappeared.

'But…'

'Nothing happened, Lu.'

Will hooked her chin and made her look into his calm face. She could see hot rage bubbling in his eyes…for her? She grabbed his wrist and held onto to him, needing his steadiness, needing the contact, needing to lean, just for a minute, on his strength.

She sucked in more air. 'OK, nothing happened. You're sure?'

'Very sure. A thousand percent sure. You were in my sight the entire time, apart from the fifteen minutes just after your drink was spiked. You've only been alone with me the entire time. Believe me?'

She did.

'Your mobile is dead, so I couldn't contact anyone, but I took you to the closest hospital, they pumped your stomach and you stayed there the night.'

'*What?* I stayed the night in hospital?'

Will nodded, his face grim.

'So today isn't today, it's tomorrow?' Lu cried. 'I lost an entire day?'

Will grimaced. 'Yeah. You came round for a while this afternoon and the doctors thought that you were well enough to be discharged, provided someone kept an eye on you.'

'I don't remember anything!'

'Apparently that's normal.'

'That's your opinion. Nothing is vaguely normal about this. So you brought me back here?' Lu looked around. 'Where *is* here?'

'The Bay—penthouse suite. My temporary quarters until I find a flat to rent. Well, I didn't know who to contact, and I couldn't leave you alone, so I changed you into one of my T-shirts and let you sleep it off.'

Lu looked at the bed they'd shared. 'You slept with me?'

'Just to keep an eye on you,' Will reassured her. 'You were having some nasty dreams. Judging by your quick downhill slide, the hospital doctors think it was GHB, which is very easy to overdose on. You were very lucky. Because you weigh next to nothing, the doctors were worried. An overdose can lead to a coma or death. '

'I never leave my drink unattended,' Lu protested.

'You did. You put it on the bar when your friend came back from the dance floor. You checked the time…' Will cursed.

Lu raised her eyebrows. He'd been watching her? How? From where? And yet she still didn't feel creeped out. Just protected…and safe. As if she had a burly guardian angel looking after her.

Will closed his eyes for a millisecond. 'You were directly below me. I was watching the action from the VIP area above.

'Now I sound like a stalker.' He raked his hand through his short hair and grimaced. 'I'm not, I promise. I saw you. You looked sober. The next time I saw you, you looked high, with someone I hadn't seen you even speak to. Something just didn't seem right.'

Lu believed him. Maybe she was being naïve or dumb, but she knew, to the bottom of her toes, that Will had saved her. Besides, seriously, why would anyone who looked like him need a date-rape drug to get a girl into bed? He was probably beating them off with clubs as it was.

She wasn't a celeb-watcher but his profile was high enough that it was hard *not* to read about him. He was the ex-bad-boy of international rugby who dated supermodels and superstars. His ex-wife was the Golden Princess of women's professional tennis, with a face and body that could launch intergalactic starships. And he was an international rugby god—one of New Zealand's national treasures, Lu thought as she remembered the twins' many conversations about him. He was a multi-capped player and had been instrumental in leading his team to victory in the last World Cup. He'd just retired from international rugby and was in Durban for a few months.

Lu was snapped back to the present by a sharp rap on the suite door. Will smiled and her stomach rolled. *Hooboy!* Mega-attractive man.

'Coffee. It's about time.' Will moved to the door and looked at her over his shoulder. 'My mobile is next to the bed, or use the hotel phone to contact anyone you need to.'

'Thank you. I will…after I use the bathroom. And Will?'

Lu swallowed and lifted her hands when he turned and looked at her.

'Thank you. It sounds inadequate, but I am so, so grateful. For everything. I am forever in your debt.'

Lu washed up and held each side of the free-standing basin, staring down into the expanse of white porcelain. Why did she feel nineteen again? Defenceless, vulnerable, scared… It had to be because, like before, she'd been dumped into this horrible situation without any warning, any time to prepare.

It was a situation she couldn't control and she was propelled back to that black time when she'd felt sick with grief, crippled by the responsibility of her new role as guardian to her brothers, feeling so helpless.

Every insecurity she'd ever had came rushing back— every sadness, every fear. Oh, she knew intellectually that this wasn't her fault, but knowing was different from feeling, and being at the mercy of whoever it was who'd spiked her drink scared her down to her toes. Added to that was the realisation that she'd been in Will's hands, his care… under his power.

She wanted to curl up in a corner and suck her thumb. GHB? Spiked drinks? A high-profile celebrity rescuing her from what might have been a very nasty situation? Incidents like this didn't happen to ordinary girls like her. If she thought about what could have happened…

Lu bumped her hand against her forehead in an effort to clear the cobwebs and realised that her stomach was rebelling again.

Don't think about it. Don't think about it…

Will's face popped into her head and she focused on that as a distraction. He was so much better-looking in real life than in the newspapers and on TV. They didn't capture the intelligence in those topaz-coloured eyes, the flicker of movement in that mobile mouth, the very, very small dimple-type dent that appeared in his cheek when he smiled.

And she wasn't even going to *think* about his body... fit, hard, utterly—shockingly!—masculine. Lu rubbed her thighs together. Strangely, she suddenly felt a pounding pulse in a place where she'd never pulsed before.

Lu raised her head to look at herself in the mirror above the sink and yelped at her reflection. Her brand-new, streaky gold hair that had looked so fabulously chic last night now stood up in tufts on the right side of her head and lay dead flat on the other side. She was sheet-white, her freckles the only bit of colour in her face, and someone had painted the bags under her eyes a bright purple.

No wonder Will Scott had belted out of bed as if the hounds of hell were snapping at his heels. Admittedly her eyes were an unusual colour—sometimes green, sometimes blue—but the spray of freckles across her nose and cheeks were the bane of her life. She was more 'girl next door' than 'I am woman, hear me roar'.

This morning she barely reached 'I am human, hear me whimper'.

So any ideas that he'd been looking at her legs or mouth or any quick flashes of interest she'd thought she'd caught in his eyes was just a very optimistic dose of wishful thinking. *Stupid girl.* Lu pulled a tongue at her reflection, opened the tap and splashed warm water on her face. Stealing a bit of Will's toothpaste, she brushed her teeth with her finger and helped herself to a healthy swig of his mouthwash.

She wet her hands and ran them through her hair in an attempt to look less like a neurotic bantam chicken. She wished she could pull on her clothes, but when she reached for the packet containing them one whiff of the contents had her changing her mind. Will's T-shirt, which barely hit her knees would have to do for now.

Right—she felt marginally human and slightly better able to deal with Will, his smack-you-in-the-face sex appeal and this very weird situation. Lu straightened her spine and opened the bathroom door just as Will walked across from the closet, now dressed in hip hugging faded Levi's, a fire-engine-red T-shirt clutched loosely in his hand.

His chest was lightly covered in dark hair and he had a six-pack that would make a male model jealous. It made her mouth water.

I am woman, see me drool.

'Lu! Lu, where the hell are you?'

Forty-five minutes later a pounding on the suite door and an upset male voice caused Lu to jump in her chair. Will lifted his eyebrows as Lu went to answer the door and the handsome guy from the club pulled her into his arms and whirled her around.

'Bloody hell, Lu. I take you clubbing one frickin' time and you disappear on me! And what the hell were you saying about your drink being spiked? And keep your damned mobile charged, woman!' he bellowed.

Not allowing her to reply, he segued into a barrage of Zulu. While Will didn't understand one individual word, he got the gist. It was the universal tone of you-scared-the-crap-out-of-me.

Lu interrupted him by placing her hand over his mouth. 'Mak Sibaya—Will Scott.'

Mak pushed her hand away, lifted his own hand in a half-greeting and carried on ranting. 'I left you for one dance…I came back and you were gone! I thought you'd done your normal I'm-sick-of-waiting trick and left on your own. When I couldn't get hold of you by yesterday afternoon I went around to the house. When I saw your car was there but you weren't I started to freak. I'm *still* freaking! And what were you saying about a date-rape drug? What the—'

'She's fine,' Will stated, shoving a cup of coffee into Mak's hand and cutting off another barrage of colourful swear words. 'Did you bring clothes?'

Mak sat down and looked around, eventually pointing to the plastic bag he'd dropped by the door. Will stood up and went to retrieve it, understanding that Mak needed a minute to compose himself—that he'd been seriously worried and expressed it by acting like a jerk. He couldn't blame the guy. It was what guys did when they were unhappy. Any man would be jumping the walls if his woman vanished on him and he couldn't get hold of her.

There was another reason not to have a partner or a girl-friend…you couldn't get agitated and upset if there was no one to get agitated and upset about. And he still wasn't impressed that Mak hadn't taken better care of her at the club—kept his eye on Lu instead of leaving her alone at the bar.

Will sat in the chair opposite Mak and poured himself a cup of coffee. They waited in an uneasy silence as Lu dressed in the next room.

Mak lifted his head and his dark eyes looked miserable when they connected with Will's. 'Thanks, by the way. If anything had happened to her…'

Uncomfortable with the level of emotion he heard in the other man's voice, Will shifted in his seat. 'Sure…I'm glad I was there.'

'Me too.' Mak scrubbed his face with his hands. 'Lu is…she's—'

His words were cut off by Lu's return. Will's T-shirt had been replaced by a snug, cropped T-shirt of pale pink, re-vealing an inch of her belly above the band of low-cut white shorts. Long legs ended in a pair of battered flip-flops. She crossed them as she sat down on the couch next to him.

Will handed her a cup of coffee. 'Black. Add what you want to it.' He gestured to the milk and sugar on the tray. Lu, he noticed, took hers black and sweet.

'I hope we're not keeping you from anything?' Lu said after sipping and sighing.

'I have some press interviews scheduled for later, but I'm not in any rush.' Will placed his cup on the tray and leaned forward. 'What do you want to do about the other night? Do you want to press charges?' He watched Lu think.

'I don't know. I feel fine now. A bit of a headache, but that's it.' She dropped her elbows to her knees and rested her face in her hands. 'I'd go to the police but I don't remember a damn thing.'

Will's voice hardened. 'I do. I can give the police an idea of who we're looking for.'

'Except that we can't prove the man you saw me with spiked my drink. He could say that he was helping me,' Lu pointed out.

Will felt his back teeth grind together as the truth of her words registered. 'True, but I still think you should report it.'

Lu placed her thumbnail between her front teeth. 'You're right. It's irresponsible not to.'

'I'll take you, Lu,' said Mak as he placed his empty cup on the coffee table.

He looked calmer, Will thought, less wild-eyed.

Lu angled her head so that she could look at the face of Mak's watch. 'Today *is* Monday, right?'

Mak nodded.

'You can't take me anywhere. You have thirty minutes to get to that preliminary interview at the school. That's all the way across town. '

It took a moment for her words to register, but when they

did Mak shot out of his chair and looked panicked. 'I don't want Deon going to that school.'

'It's a back-up plan, Makhosi. We discussed this. It's just in case he doesn't get into St Clare's.'

'You're right—I know you are right. But I don't have time to take you home, get him, and get across town in time for the interview. Is there any chance you can hang on here until I can get back?' Mak asked.

'Lu and I will go to the police and then I can run her home,' Will suggested.

Mak threw him a relieved smile. 'Thanks, Will. I appreciate it.'

Will stood up to shake Mak's hand. He clenched his jaw as he watched Mak and Lu exchange another tender embrace and then Mak was flying out of the door.

Lu shut the door behind him and shook her head. 'Mak only operates at warp speed.' She flicked her thumbnail against her teeth as she walked back towards him. 'You've already done so much. I couldn't impose on you any more. I'll be fine on my own. I'll go to the police and then I'll find my way home.'

Will resisted the impulse to grab her hand and to tell her to relax, to calm down. 'We'll go together,' he insisted and saw her shoulders drop from around her ears. She'd be fine on her own, his ass. But why did he care?

The girl had had her drink spiked, he reminded himself. If he hadn't interfered she could've been raped, subjected to abuse... Will ground his teeth as his blood pressure spiked. Damn straight he'd go to the police with her.

'Maybe I should just write it off as a bad experience and avoid clubs—no matter what my brothers want me to do,' Lu said, picking up her cup again.

'What do your brothers have to do with you clubbing?' Will asked, intrigued.

'Ah...they think I need to get out more,' Lu explained.

He felt disappointed when she waved her words away.

'It's a long story which you'd probably find boring.'

Strangely, he thought he wouldn't. Sure, she wasn't glamorous or glossy, like the women he normally came into contact with, but he had a feeling that Lu was far more interesting than most of the women he met. There was something settled about her…calm, down to earth…*wise*.

He admired her coolness under pressure. Her assumption that they'd slept together had been funny because she'd had a good excuse to lose it earlier. Instead she'd reined in her emotions and thought the situation through, keeping calm and in control, her emotions in check. He'd been dreading having to deal with a weepy, scared creature and her undramatic reaction had been a very welcome relief.

Impressive. He valued keeping his control and he admired her ability to do the same.

And those eyes, God…a mermaid's eyes, reflecting the greens and blues and aquas of a tropical sea.

Will rested his head against the back of the wingback chair and thought that his brief visit to Durban had started off on a very interesting note.

CHAPTER THREE

WILL TURNED INTO the driveway Lu indicated and parked in front of the huge iron gate as she scrabbled in her bag for her keys. He looked through the bars of the gate to the huge, sprawling house with its deep, wraparound veranda and nodded his approval. With a haphazard garden and pitched roof, it looked as a house should—homely and lived in. Big.

Will looked through the gap between the house and the garage and caught a glimpse of the sea. 'This is home?'

'Yep,' Lu said. 'Thanks for the lift and for coming to the police station with me. You were a lot calmer than Mak would've been.'

'He probably would've shouted at you the whole time,' Will stated calmly.

'He did go a bit berserk, didn't he? Sorry about that.'

Will's fingers tightened around the steering wheel. 'He's crazy about you. How long have you been together?'

Lu sent him a puzzled look. 'We're not. Why would you think that?'

Oh, maybe the fact that he kissed you on your mouth, whirled you around and wouldn't stop touching you! Freaking big clues!

'My mistake,' Will said aloud, but he wasn't convinced. And that wasn't jealousy he felt. It couldn't be. He didn't know what it was, but it wasn't jealousy.

'He used to live next door to us and we remained friends

when he moved. Mak is just…intense. Protective of me. He adores me, but we're only friends,' Lu explained as the gate slid open.

Yeah, and rugby isn't a contact sport, Will thought as he drove up the circular driveway to her front door. She might think they were only friends, but he was a man and he knew how men acted and thought. How could Mak *not* want to sleep with her? She was gorgeous! A natural beauty with those incredible eyes…

'I saw the look on your face…you think that Mak was irresponsible because he lost track of me.'

He couldn't deny it.

Lu sighed. 'He isn't—not really. He just has a lot on his plate, and when he gets time to step away, to socialise, he goes at it full tilt. And I'm not the type of girl that needs to be looked after…Mak knew that I wanted to go home and I knew that he wanted to stay. I've left him behind at many functions, so he wouldn't have thought it unusual. I have taxi companies on speed dial.'

Will just lifted his eyebrows and looked unconvinced.

His mobile rang. He pressed a button on the steering wheel to activate the hands free and greeted his caller. Lu felt that she should give him some privacy to take his call and tried to get out of the car, but his hand on her arm kept her firmly in place.

Through the car speakers somebody whose name she didn't catch was talking about that afternoon's press conference and Lu listened as Will was briefed on the questions he could expect.

'And obviously there will be the usual questions about your ex-wife.'

'Yeah, OK, I'm *so* happy to answer those!' Will barked, obviously frustrated.

She didn't need a degree in sarcasm to realise that he

really *didn't* want to answer any questions on his old life, ex-wife and their marriage.

'Jo's blonde, gorgeous and successful. You're handsome, talented and successful. She's still single. So are you. You were once married and everyone still wants to know what happened to your marriage,' the voice replied calmly. 'The press know there's a story there and they want it.'

'They can all get…' Will shot Lu a look and swallowed the word he wanted to use. 'Stuffed. As per normal, Jo and anything to do with her is off the table, not open for discussion. It was all so long ago you'd think they'd get over it.'

With Will's hand still holding her arm, Lu stayed where she was and thought that they couldn't be more different if they tried. Like Mak, like her parents, even her brothers, Will was a breed apart. One of those successful, innately confident, very-sure-of-their-niche-in-the-world people.

She wanted to be like that.

She didn't have a niche. Her place—her space—had been ripped away when her parents died, and two weeks ago when her brothers had left it had shifted again.

After a decade of the twins being the centre of her world she was alone, and she had to live in this empty house without the daily responsibility of being their guardian. No more suppers to cook, errands to run, parties to keep an eye on. For the first time in her life she wasn't defined by her relationship to her popular parents and her orphaned twin brothers.

Isolation and loneliness kept creeping closer, and she frequently felt ill-equipped to cope with a life that didn't have the twins in it. If she wasn't careful she could slide over the edge into self-pity, and from there it was a slippery slope to depression. She couldn't—refused—to let that happen.

She had to do something about her life, and quickly. After everything that life had thrown at her so far she refused to buckle under because she was alone and feeling at sea. That was why she'd agreed to go clubbing with Mak. She'd realised that she had to get out of the house, out of her own head. The boys were right. She had to start living her life.

Of course getting her drink spiked was an embarrassing start.

It had been a tough decade, she admitted as Will lifted his hand from her arm and carried on with his conversation. She had just started exploring her options for a career when she'd been catapulted without warning into caring for the twins. With the inheritance covering her basic costs she'd run around her brothers, caught up in making their world as secure as she possibility could, determined that they wouldn't feel as lost, as alone and as scared as she did. She'd kept herself and them active and busy in order to keep the grief at bay, and while she'd tried to keep up with her photography she hadn't been able to give it the dedication it required for her to succeed. Somewhere along the way she'd stopped thinking about herself, her place in the world and what excited her.

Who *was* she? Lu was terrified to realise that she hadn't the slightest clue. It was OK, she told herself. She had time to figure it all out. She just needed a plan.

'Sorry about that.' Will's voice pulled her back to the present. 'Lu? Are you OK?'

Lu blinked and focused on his face. Will, so very up close and personal, was even more mouth-wateringly, panty-crumpling, breath-hitchingly gorgeous than any photo anywhere. He wasn't perfect—that would be far too intimidating—and she liked his flaws as much as she liked the rest of the package. Creases at the corner of those warm eyes, and his deep brown hair was, sadly, six inches too short. He had stubby eyelashes and untamed brows and a slash of a nose.

'Do you want me to come in with you? Are you going to be OK?' Will asked.

'I've taken far too much of your time already,' Lu replied, glad to hear that her voice was reasonably steady. 'Thank you for all your help. As I said, I am in your debt.'

Will's eyes tracked over her face. 'If you start remembering anything and you have questions you're welcome to give me a call at the rugby union. They'll make sure that I get the message and I'll get back to you.'

It was a nice offer, Lu thought, noticing that he didn't give her his mobile number. She wasn't that out of practice that she didn't recognise the gentle brush-off. He wouldn't call again and she could live with that.

After all, she had her own life to get back on track. She didn't need the distraction of a super-sexy rugby player.

But, damn, how she wished they *had* had sex. Just one little time and preferably of the blow-your-head-off variety. Just to…you know…clean those cobwebs out…

Two days later Lu sat on the floor between her leather couch and her coffee table, her laptop in front of her. She was updating her website in an effort to attract more photography work and thought she'd made pretty good progress. The site was hipper and brighter than before, and she liked the photos she'd put on the front page. There was the Johnsons' newborn baby, stark naked with a bright blue bow tied around his tummy and a tag that read 'Special Delivery'. Below that was her favourite photograph of a bridal couple, caught in a loving look so profound it made her throat catch every time she looked at it.

She was good at it, she mused. Capable of capturing the essence of the moment. And now that she had the time to devote to it she realised how much she missed being behind a camera. She'd tried to establish herself as a photographer a couple of times over the past decade, but every opportunity had fizzled out. She'd been offered an apprenticeship under one of the better photographers in the city about a year after her parents had died, but when she'd realised that after-hours work and out-of-town shoots were a standard condition of her employment she'd resigned because she had to be at home for the twins.

She'd done small weddings, worked part-time in a photographic studio before it had closed down six months ago, and done some freelance graphic work, but she hadn't, because of her family situation, been able to land her big break. Her fellow students from photography school were flying and she was ten years behind.

It wouldn't take much to kick-start her business. She had a studio already outfitted in the cottage next to the main house: lights, props and backgrounds. She just needed the clients to get back on track; she *had* to make up for all this lost time.

Her mobile buzzed on the floor next to her and she frowned at the unfamiliar number. Debating whether to answer it, she took a sip of wine and wondered whether she felt like speaking to anyone. *You're becoming a hermit,* she chided herself as she pushed the green button. *Six steps away from becoming that self-conversing, crazy cat lady the twins mentioned.*

'Lu? It's Will Scott.'

Lu's eyebrows shot up as her mouth dried up. Of all the people she'd expected to be on the other end of the call Will was last on her list.

'Um…hi…'

'I called to see how you were doing? Whether you had any lasting effects from the drug?'

'No, I'm fine.'

'Nightmares?' Will demanded.

'One or two,' Lu admitted. 'Normally when I let myself think about what could've happened. Uh…how did you get my number?'

Lu swore that she heard his lips pull up into that super-sexy grin. 'I swiped one of your business cards from your wallet. I see that you freelance…how's the photography business?'

'Slow, actually. I was just updating my site and racking my brain about how to get more clients. How's the rugby coaching business?'

Will's sigh was a combination of frustration and weariness. 'Honestly? Right now it's a pain in my ass. I have some squad members who have the maturity of a two-year-old.'

Lu leaned back against the couch and took a sip from her glass of wine, happy to hear his voice sliding over her. Her mouth curved. 'They'll get used to you.'

'They don't have a choice,' Will stated, his tone resolute. 'It's either my way or the highway.'

'So you're a dictator?' Lu teased, and then bit her lip. Lord, what was she saying? She didn't know him nearly well enough to tease him!

'Only in my job. I know what I want and exactly how I intend to get it.'

So sure, so confident. She wished she could rub herself against him and have some of that innate self-assuredness rub off on her. Oh, hell, forget anything else, she just wanted to rub up against him, full-stop. He set her nerve-endings on fire… *This is why you shouldn't go so long between dates, Sheppard! When your hormones are invited to a party they head straight for the tequilas and start doing the Macarena.*

'Well, I'll be rooting for you,' Lu said, after a longer than normal silence.

'Thanks,' Will replied. 'It's nearly seven. I've been here

since six this morning. Any ideas for where I can eat? I can't face Room Service or takeout.'

'Are you going to live in that hotel for three months?' Lu asked.

'Hell, no. I need to find a flat I can rent, but I haven't had any time. I'm planning to look around on the weekend.'

'So…restaurants. What do you feel like eating?'

'Mac and cheese,' Will responded promptly.

'Mac and cheese, huh?' Lu looked towards the kitchen that sat at the other end of her open-plan lounge. Did she dare? What if he said no? She was mad. Of course he'd say no. But there was a chance—a numpty billion-to-one chance—that he might say yes.

And, because her mother had raised her right, she should do something to say thank you. *Yeah, keep telling yourself that's the reason you are about to invite him over. You might convince yourself in a millennia…or two.*

Pull on your brave girl panties, Sheppard.

'If you're interested, I can do one better than mac and cheese. I have a lasagne that I made and froze. I can whip up a salad to go with it if you…well, don't feel obligated… but I feel like dinner is the least I can do for you since you… Um…you'd probably prefer to eat out,' Lu stammered.

'Lu?'

'Mmm? Yes?' He was going to blow her off. She just knew it.

'Homemade lasagne sounds really great.'

'Ah…OK. Good.' Lu closed her eyes. *Eek!* Now she would actually have to defrost the lasagne and make a salad. And have a shower and do something with her hair…

'I could be there in half an hour? That work for you?'

'Sure.' She'd prefer an hour to primp, but that wasn't going to happen. Well, as per usual, make-up would be sacrificed.

'Do you remember how to get here?' she asked, almost

reluctant to let him disconnect even though she'd see him soon.

'I have a pretty good sense of direction, but keep your phone close in case I go off course,' Will told her. 'What is Lu short for, by the way?'

'Um…don't laugh.' Lu blushed. 'Tallulah.'

'Tallulah?'

His tongue caressed her name and Lu shivered.

'Lu suits you better. See you soon.'

As Will pushed the button on the intercom outside Lu's closed gate he thought that the heat and humidity of Durban were obviously frying his brain. What did he think he was going to achieve from this visit apart from, obviously, some homemade pasta? Lu had crossed his mind more than once over the last few days but he'd be lying if he said it was only because he was worried about her, worried that the date-rape drug might have had a side effect that neither of them, nor the hospital doctors, knew about. He'd been thinking about *her* and, unusually, not just as someone he wanted to get into bed.

'Why don't you try being friends with a woman instead?'

Kelby's words from last week kept popping in and out of his head, quickly followed by a flash of Lu's freckled face, her sea-coloured eyes. For the first time in for ever he could see himself being friends with a woman—being friends with Lu. Sure, he was attracted to her. But from the little he'd seen of her he really liked her as well. She seemed unconcerned about who he was and what he did.

She was, he decided, refreshing.

He was in a new country, trying out a new type of job. Maybe he should try something different when it came to the opposite sex too.

Will felt himself relaxing as her gate rolled open and he

steered the SUV up the long driveway. *A change is as good as a holiday*, he thought, pulling to a stop.

Then why did his heart thump when he saw her standing by the open front door, dressed in a similar outfit to the one she'd changed into in his hotel room—a pair of white cotton shorts and a teal tank top with thin straps that showed off an inch of her flat belly? He lifted his hand as he left the car and patted two dogs of indeterminate breed, sliding a hot glance at those long, tanned legs and bare feet tipped with fire red toenails.

Friends. New approach. Don't let your libido distract you. It had, as he well remembered, led him into far too much trouble before.

'Hi.' Lu lifted her glass. 'I started without you. Want one?'

'Hi, back.' Will waved the bottle he held in his hand as he walked up the two stone steps to the door. He brushed past a pot plant and his nose was filled with the scent of sweet lemons. The bigger of the dogs nudged his hand and Lu grinned. 'Harry, stop it!'

'Harry?'

'Potter's behind you. The cat's are Dumbel and Dore.'

Nice place, Will thought as he stepped into a huge hall and Lu closed the door behind him. She took the bottle he held out. He searched her face, happy to see some colour in her cheeks, less blue under her eyes. Lu dropped her eyes from his and Will looked around. A coat rack stood next to the door and a large antique credenza squatted next to the wall, photographs in silver frames crowding its surface. A massive vase of haphazard flowers stood on a narrow high table, and the wall in front of him was dominated by two oversized canvas photographs of two young boys, their faces a chocolate smear.

'My brothers,' Lu explained as he stepped up to look at

the photographs. 'Come through this way. I thought we'd eat on the veranda.'

Will followed Lu through a huge kitchen and his mouth started to water at the smell of garlicky, herby, meaty pasta. The kitchen flowed into a large, messy lounge with battered leather couches, a laptop on a big coffee table and a large screen television. Oversized glass and wooden doors led onto a wraparound veranda, which had its own set of couches, a casual dining table and an incredible view over the city to the Indian Ocean.

'I want to live here,' Will muttered, placing the bottle on the table and dropping his mobile and keys next to it.

'Yeah, the view is pretty impressive.' Lu deftly poured wine into the empty glass on the table and handed it over.

Will sat down in the closest chair and tried to ignore the buzz in his pants when Lu sat down opposite him and folded her legs up under her butt. He pulled his eyes from that expanse of bare leg, looked around and liked what he saw. The house was huge, filled with old, once expensive furniture and eclectic art.

'I love your house,' Will said, after sipping his wine. 'I'm crazy about buildings. Built in the thirties?'

'1931 and inspired by the times: Art Deco rules. It was my grandparents' and then my father's,' Lu explained. 'My grandmother did all the stained-glass panels above the windows and next to the front door. My grandfather collected the furniture.'

He'd noticed the furniture on his walk-through, and now glanced through the open veranda doors into the lounge. He saw another set of canvas photographs: black and white, like the others in the hall, and brimming with emotion and energy. 'Mind if I take a look?'

Lu shrugged. 'Go ahead.'

The first canvas was of a fantastically, lushly beautiful woman, dressed in a corset and fishnet stockings, a walking cane across her ample chest. She had more curves than a mountain pass and, while her face was partially covered by the brim of a top hat, her expression radiated fun and excitement and raw sensuality.

He moved to the other photograph: a long, lanky man, lying in a hammock, a beer bottle in his hand and his eyes— Lu's eyes—half closed. A golfing magazine lay face-down on his stomach.

Sexy, successful, attractive. Everything she wasn't right now, Lu thought as she watched Will take a closer look at the photographs.

Everything she'd ever wanted to be but didn't know how. The embodiment of what a successful life looked like.

His looks were an added bonus, she thought, but his success and the material wealth that came along with it was all his own, created by hard work. *His* hard work and dedication. How she envied him that—envied the fact that whatever he had, and she knew it was a lot, he could say that he'd earned it. Unlike her every possession, including her photography equipment, which came from the massive inheritance her parents had left behind.

An inheritance that would have been non-existent if her parents had died a couple of weeks later than they had. It had been a standard joke between them that there were many millions of reasons to bump the other off…and it was fascinatingly ironic that they'd died together, victims of an out-of-control articulated vehicle.

If they'd lived this house would have been a distant memory for her—sold to pay off the overdraft, the credit cards, the personal loans. At the time of their death they'd been, as Lu had later discovered, living on fresh air and the last couple of thousand on her father's credit cards. The car and credit card payments hadn't been made in months; the utilities bills had been late.

Sorting through the financial mess had been a nightmare on top of the horror of losing them. It was probably the biggest secret she'd kept from the twins: that they wouldn't be enjoying such a privileged lifestyle if their parents had lived.

But her parents' secret remained exactly that; she'd never told a living soul and would never tell the twins. One person feeling guilty and conflicted about the lifestyle of their family was enough. She didn't need to burden them with that information; it was, as she well knew, a heavy load to carry.

The flip and very selfish side of that coin was that if her parents *were* still around they might not have anything like the material wealth surrounding them now, but she'd be supporting herself—working…contributing. She would be on a career path, settled and established. Maybe not rich, like Will, but comfortable, secure. Fulfilled because her security came from the sweat of her own brow and not because her parents had rushed off to a meeting with their bank manager and ended up under the chassis of a ten-ton truck.

So she was ten years behind? It wasn't as if she was old and past her prime. She was young and fit and determined…and she had time. So what if most women her age were thinking about moving onto the next stage of their lives—marriage and babies? That was their life, not hers.

She'd catch up…she *had* to. In the couple of weeks since the boys had left she'd been clubbing—she was deliberately ignoring the issue of the spiked drink—she'd worked on her website, sorted out her studio and looked into dance classes.

She'd even invited a man around for dinner.

That was progress, wasn't it?

Will walked back onto the veranda and leaned against the balcony. 'Your parents?'

Lu nodded and sipped her wine. 'My mother was a cabaret artiste and performer, my father a golf pro.'

'Was?'

'They're dead. Car accident. Ten years ago,' Lu said in a monotone, and she didn't know that pain flickered in and out of her eyes.

Will winced. 'Damn, I'm sorry about that. Did you take the photos?'

Lu nodded. 'I took them shortly before they died; they were supposed to be used in an assignment I had due.'

Lu steeled herself. He'd ask about their death now; people always wanted to know the details.

'And is photography your passion? Your business?'

When Lu recovered from her surprise at his change of subject she focused on the question. Her passion? Absolutely. Her business? She didn't know. Could she even call herself a photographer? She didn't have much of a reputation, didn't have that much of a portfolio, and hardly any experience. Did updating her website and looking for new business mean that she was actually *in* business?

Well, she wasn't a pseudo-mommy any more, so maybe she was.

She touched a camera that sat on the table next to her. 'I always have one close by so I suppose it must be. Is rugby yours?'

'My passion and my business? Absolutely.'

Will placed his ankle on his knee and Lu wondered why he made her skin prickle. Her veranda was spacious, but he made it seem smaller, cosier. Lu tried to put her finger on what he made her feel. *Alive*, she realised with a shock.

He made her feel alive. And that she mattered.

Dangerous thoughts, Lu, you need to switch gears. What had they been talking about? Rugby…

Lu's eyes shot up, sharpened and collided with his. 'Oh, and on the subject of photography and rugby, who took that photo of you for the Rays' webpage?'

'You looked up our webpage?' Will asked, his mouth twitching with amusement.

Lu blushed, caught out. 'I was…it just popped up.' Oh, she was such a rotten liar. 'Anyway…that photo of you? Who took it?'

'What's wrong with the photo?' he asked, amused at her indignation.

'What's *right* with it? It's shocking! The light is wrong, there are shadows, you look older than you are…exhausted. Geez, a ten-year-old with a point-and-shoot could've done a better job,' Lu stated, her embarrassment and awkwardness temporarily banished as she spoke about her work.

'Photography is *so* your passion. Why do you doubt it?'

Lu blinked at him, nonplussed as she thought about his question. Because right now she doubted everything about herself.

Will saved her from making a coherent reply when he continued in his smooth, deep voice, 'Think you can do better?'

Lu's eyes sparked with indignation. 'I *know* I can do better.'

Lu didn't pick up the tongue Will placed in his cheek. 'I think the photographer was one of the most reputable in Durban.'

'Well, I'd demand a refund.' Lu sniffed. 'Shoddy work.'

Will gestured to the camera with his wine glass. 'Prove it.'

'What?'

'I'm a tough subject—the least photogenic person in the world.'

That was like saying that Ryan Reynolds wasn't sexy. 'You?'

'Why do you think I keep endorsement deals and modelling work to a minimum? I suck at camera work.' Will motioned to the camera. 'Do your worst. Actually, do your best. Take a photo of me that's better than the one on the website; God knows I need it.'

Lu narrowed her eyes at him and couldn't resist the challenge in his eyes. Without breaking his stare she reached for her camera, flipped it on by touch and lifted it to her face. She adjusted the light filters, the focus, and fiddled with the settings, and then her finger was on the button and his image flew to the memory card.

There was so much she was unsure of but this she knew. Lighting, framing, capturing, Lu slid into the zone. She knew how to pull an image together, to capture the light on his face, the glint in his eyes, the tiny dimple in his cheek.

She might not know him, but through her camera she caught a glimpse of his soul.

And somehow, very strangely, she felt that she recognised it.

CHAPTER FOUR

'I CAN'T BELIEVE this photo.' Will picked up her camera from the table and looked at his image captured in the view-finder. 'It's really good. I look serious, but approachable.'

Will expected her to say *I told you so*, but she just winged a quick, grateful smile his way as she placed a huge bowl of salad on the table.

Will pulled on his shirt and left his towel wrapped around his hips so that it could soak up the water from the still dripping board shorts she'd found for him to wear. Lu had suggested he take a swim while she got dinner on the table, and since it was muggy and hot he'd quickly agreed.

He gestured to the colourful cushions on the chairs. 'I'm wet.'

'Yours won't be the first wet bum to sit there,' Lu told him, dipping a serving spoon into the lasagne. Behind her back both dogs climbed up onto separate chairs and snuggled into the plump cushions. Lu heard their contented huffs and shook her head.

'You're very relaxed about your house,' Will commented, thinking that his two sisters would have had a hissy fit by now at the thought of dogs on their furniture.

'The furniture is old and the animals are as much a part of this family as we are.'

Will sat down, topped up their glasses with wine and pushed his wet hair back from his forehead. He skimmed a glance over her face as she reached for a plate to dish up onto and wondered what was going on in that very busy head of hers. Not that he cared, he assured himself, he was just being naturally curious.

Will took the plate she held out, put it down in front of him and reached for the salad. He actually groaned his approval as he dumped a mountain on his plate. 'God, this looks so good.'

'Tuck in,' Lu told him as she dished up her own food.

They ate in silence for a couple of minutes—well, she ate and Will inhaled his food. Even at home he wasn't much of a cook, so he mostly ate out or ordered take out, and he'd forgotten the pleasure of a simple home-cooked meal. It reminded him of his family, of feeling relaxed, content.

When his immediate hunger was satisfied Will slowed down and in between bites sipped his wine. Over Lu's head he could see the portraits of her parents, and he frowned as a thought occurred to him.

'So, you have brothers, right? Where are they?'

'They left for university a couple of weeks ago. They're in Cape Town.'

Curiosity turned to intrigue. 'And did you see much of them over the past decade?'

'Sometimes far too much of them.'

Lu's smile bloomed and his heart flip-flopped.

'I became their guardian. We all lived here together.'

Will lowered his wine glass in shock. 'You took on twin boys when you were—how old were you?'

'I'd just turned nineteen.'

'And they were—what?—eight?'

'Thereabouts.'

'But…you were just a baby yourself. They *allowed* you to do that?'

Lu shrugged. 'There wasn't anybody else who could

take them, and I sure as hell wasn't going to put them into care so that I could carry on with my life.'

Will watched her eat as he thought about what *he'd* been doing when he was nineteen. Playing first-class rugby in England, pretending to study, chasing girls, drinking, having a ball. Her sacrifice took his breath away.

'But—'

Lu lifted her hand and he instantly cut off his question.

'It's a bit of a scratchy subject with me at the moment. Do you mind if we don't talk about it?'

'No, that's fine.' It wasn't, of course. He wanted to shove aside those curtains in her eyes and see what she was hiding, thinking…feeling. Unusual, since he never delved deeper than just below the surface; he'd never needed to.

Will cleared his plate and looked at her bent head. If this was any other girl he'd call on years of practice, find a dozen innocuous topics to discuss, but he was finding that he didn't want to skim the surface with Lu. How could he? She'd reluctantly told him about the death of her parents, that she'd raised her twin brothers. And, more unusually, she didn't want to talk about her past… Most women would have given him a blow-by-blow account of her life by now.

She was different, Will thought. And original. And because she was so different he wasn't quite sure how to handle her.

But they couldn't sit here in this awkward silence. He'd have to say something.

'So, do you read?' she asked, at exactly the same time that he asked how often she went clubbing. 'You're kidding, right?' Lu shook her head. 'That was the first time in…um…six, seven—eight?—years. I'd rather hand-wash sweaty rugby kit than go again.'

'That bad, huh? But if you hated it so much why were you there?'

Lu wrinkled her nose in annoyance. 'My brothers.'

Will looked at the lasagne dish and Lu immediately passed it over. He gestured for her to continue explaining.

She sat back in her chair and stared at her plate for a long time. When she lifted her eyes again they were shuttered and guileless. 'It was just a stupid dare between us.'

Will narrowed his eyes at the lie. Why would going to a nightclub be a dare for an adult woman? Nope, there was a lot more to that story than she was saying.

'If that was the best dare they could come up with then they are very uncreative.' Will deliberately kept his voice mild.

Her blush told him that she realised he'd caught her lie. Lu licked her lips and took a sip of her wine as he placed his utensils together on the plate and pushed it away.

'More?'

Will groaned. 'No, I'm stuffed. It was good, thanks. Do you always keep trays of lasagne in your freezer?'

Lu's wide smile flashed. 'With teenage boys in the house you always need extra food for when their mates come home unexpectedly. And I keep a couple of trays in the freezer for Mak to take when he runs out of food—which is often.'

Mak again. Will was very rarely jealous. Clothes and looks didn't concern him, and his success at whatever he chose to do was his to achieve or not, so he never felt envy. However, he did feel something distantly related to jealousy at the very apparent bond Lu shared with Mak.

Will swallowed the last of his wine and thought that if he was at the point of admitting jealousy and frustration then it was definitely time for him to go. He deliberately looked at his watch and was surprised to find that it was later than he'd suspected. 'I should go. We have a gruelling early-morning team run along the beach tomorrow.'

Lu stood up with him. 'You run with the team?'

'I can't expect them to do anything I won't do,' Will

replied, picking up their plates and the lasagne dish. 'In the kitchen?'

'Thanks. I'll stack them in the dishwasher.'

Lu fiddled with her camera, then picked up their wine glasses and the salad bowl and followed him inside.

Will changed from the swimming shorts into his clothes and thought that in his normal life, with a 'normal' girl, he'd just lay it on the line and suggest they spend the night together: big fun, no commitment. That spark of attraction to Lu was there, he admitted to himself. It burned hard and bright and he'd ignored it all night. Whenever he thought about acting on it something held him back.

His conversation the other night with Kelby kept resonating with him and he was forced to admit that Kelby had been bang-on with a lot of his observations. He was Mr Control these days—his life went into a tailspin when he cut loose—and if he had to be totally truthful he admitted that he'd never allowed any of the attraction he felt to a woman to be fanned into a fire. He used sexual attraction to get…well, *sex*. And while he always made sure that both he and his partner had a fun time in bed, he knew that at any time he could walk away. He didn't allow himself to get emotionally involved because he genuinely believed that he couldn't offer a woman anything permanent. Every fire went out eventually.

Yet Kelby's question kept prodding him in the head.

'Why don't you try being friends with a woman instead?'

And Lu—strong, calm and capable—was just the type of woman he could be friends with. Her decision to raise her twin brothers at such a young age told him that she was loyal and determined. He liked those traits in men and they were very attractive in a woman too. He could respect her—another trait he considered essential for a friendship.

And, with her lithe body and quick smile, she was a lot easier on the eye than Kelby and his other mates.

Lu had just started to stack the dishwasher when Will walked back into the room, his car keys dangling from his fingers. 'Thanks, Lu. For dinner and the company.'

'Pleasure.' Lu walked him to the hall and shoved her hand into the pocket of her shorts, pulling out a memory card. She held it between her fingers. 'Change the photo, OK?'

Will's smile was warm and deep as he took the card. 'I'll pass it along. Thank you.'

Will couldn't stop himself from lifting up his hand to touch her cheek. He needed to know whether her skin was as soft as it looked, whether her bottom lip was a plump as he thought it was.

It was all that and more.

Will shook his head as he turned away. He'd never had the urge to touch his mates' faces and thank God. If he did he'd get the snot smacked out of him.

Lu looked up as Mak and Deon walked into her kitchen, courtesy of the set of keys Mak had been given by her father all those years ago, when they'd first become friends. Lu accepted a hug from Mak's high-functioning Down Syndrome son and smiled when Deon headed straight for her cookie jar. He was as at home in her house as the twins were. Lu had been his official babysitter since his mother had left a year after his birth, shortly before her parents' death.

Mak took a seat at the kitchen counter and accepted the glass of iced tea Lu pushed across. 'No wine?'

'It's three in the afternoon, Mak. A bit early.'

'Damn.'

'Tough day?' Lu asked, knowing that it was a battle for Mak to juggle his business and the demands and needs of a highly active special needs child. Deon had an *au-pair* he adored, and numerous aunts and uncle who showered him with attention but Mak was his lifeline, his safety net, his hero.

'How did the interview go at that other school?'

Mak shrugged. 'Fine. They'd take him tomorrow if I wanted, but I'm holding out for St Clare's.'

'You haven't heard yet?'

Mak looked frustrated. 'No.'

Lu bit the inside of her lip. Deon was lonely and needed to get back into school—a school where, unlike at the last one, he wouldn't be incessantly bullied and tormented.

Mak waved his hand in the air. 'I should hear within a couple of weeks. So, have you had any luck picking up work?'

Lu blew air into her cheeks. 'Not a damn thing! I've only had one enquiry on the website and I've visited all the bridal shops and florists and dished out my card, hoping for referrals. I'm thinking of getting another job—'

'Lu, it's only been a month since the boys left. Give yourself some time. Keep plugging at it. Something will come up. So…I saw Will Scott's flashy Range Rover parked in your driveway the other night.'

'Were you spying on me again?' Lu demanded.

'Sure. That's what good friends do,' Mak replied. 'I came around to check on you and saw Will's car, so I left.'

'You should've joined us.'

'And have Deon buzzing on rugby talk for the next week? No, thanks!'

Lu smiled. Deon was completely rugby-obsessed and the Rays were his idols. He would be thoroughly over-excited if he met Will, and he'd nag Mak and her to make Will introduce him to the rest of the team. When Deon got a notion in his head it required a water cannon to dislodge it.

Lu explained that she'd invited Will around for supper to say thank you.

Mak took a sip of his drink. 'So, did he come around

to say it was a pleasure to your thank you? Or did he have other pleasure on his mind?' Mak waggled his eyebrows at her.

Lu glowered at him. 'It wasn't like that, Mak!'

'It's *always* like that, Lu.'

Lu didn't tell him about Will touching her face, about the flare of passion she'd thought she saw in his eyes. She placed her elbows on the counter and grinned at Mak. 'He *is* hot, though.'

Make rolled his eyes. 'So I'm told.'

'So, last night I went to the Botanic Gardens and the Philharmonic Orchestra was playing. I thought that it would be so much fun to have someone to do things with. I mean, I didn't mind being on my own, but—'

Mak looked horrified. 'I am *not* going to any classical concerts.'

Lu laughed. 'Actually, I wasn't thinking about you…this time. I was kind of considering whether to invite Will along the next time. Do you think I could do that?'

'Women have been asking men out for a while now,' Mak pointed out.

Lu slid her bum onto a stool. 'Do you know what I realised this week, Mak?'

'What, honey?'

'That I have been so worried about the boys being independent enough, strong enough to go off on their own, and they are fine. Me—not so much. Of the three of us *I'm* the one who isn't independent. *I'm* the one having the most problems adjusting. Apart from that night with Will I've hated being in this house alone, waking up alone, going to sleep alone. The lack of noise, the tidiness… I miss them so damn much.'

'Of course you do.'

'I desperately need to work, to prove to myself that I am something other than a fake mommy. I want to create again. I want people's eyes to react—good or bad—when then see my photos. I miss it, Mak. I miss being...*productive*. I can take as many photos of the sea, of the dogs, as I want, but it's not the same as creating images for someone else. I miss being...*me*.'

Mak listened and waited for Lu to carry on.

'And...I guess I'm just lonely. I never realised I was until the boys left. Having supper with Will the other night made me realise how much I've missed being with someone... and, sorry, you don't count.'

'You're too skinny and too pale for me anyway.'

Lu reached across the counter to swat his shoulder. 'I thought that Will would be an ideal man to practise on.'

Mak's head snapped up. 'Huh? What?'

'I can use him to get my confidence back, to get back into the whole dating dance again. To help me become— independent. Is that the word I'm looking for?'

'You are making absolutely no sense.'

'I've lost the ability—I'm not even sure I ever *had* the ability—to flirt, to enjoy a man's company, to do the dance. Having a flirtation, a fling with Will, would boost my confidence and in a weird way sort of be a...um...a kick start to this new phase of my life. A way to remind myself that I'm more than what I was—something other than the being the twins' guardian, their housekeeper, their taxi.'

Would Mak understand that she suddenly felt lost and unable to cope now that there was only herself to worry about? She was supposed to feel relieved and free. Instead she felt more insecure and scared than ever before.

That wasn't right. Or fair. And it definitely wasn't acceptable. So she'd do something about it.

Preferably with Will. Could she do it? Was she brave enough?

Mak was quiet for a long time. 'I'm all for you having

some fun—getting your groove back. But there are dangers in this, Lu.'

'Like?'

'You falling for him and getting hurt, for one.'

Lu shook her head. 'Firstly, he's avoided serious relationships for years, and even if I didn't know that he has "No Trespassing" signs all over his heart, so I know that falling for him would be stupid. Secondly, he's only here for three months—less than that now. That's strike number two. He'll be my practice man and when he leaves I'll be fine. I just need someone who's *kind of* in my life to ease me into the rest of my life. Does that make any sense at all?'

'Sort of. If you manage to keep it just fun and games.'

'I won't allow myself to get attached to him.'

'Sometimes you can't help it,' Mak insisted.

'Mak, it's just an idea, and if he says no then it's no harm, no foul. As grateful as I am to him rescuing me from the club, I have no intention of trailing after him, dragging my tongue on the floor, appreciative of any attention he'll give me. I won't beg, I still have my pride. And if he says yes then I'll keep my emotional distance.'

'Mmm. Not sure if you have ever been able to do that, Lu.' Mak stood up and rested his hands on her bare shoulders. He pulled her in for a hug. 'And, talking about clubbing, I am so very, very sorry about the other night, Lu. God, I lie awake thinking...'

Lu shook her head. 'Don't Mak. I'm fine.'

'You're fine because someone else was looking out for you.' Mak rested his chin on the top of her head. 'Your dad would have had my head.'

'I'm a big girl, Mak; I've been looking after myself and the twins for a long time,' Lu told him. 'I don't need you to look after me. I'm taking charge of my life, getting used to being on my own. I've got to get my head, my life, together. I can do it, Mak!'

Mak grinned down at her determined face. 'May I point out that the only person in this room who sounds doubtful about that is *you*, sweetheart?'

'It's taking some practice,' Lu admitted.

'It always does.' Mak stepped away from her and reached across the counter for her mobile. 'So, call him.'

Lu yelped. 'Not now! Um…I need to think about what we can do together.'

'I have double tickets to a cooking demo by that celebrity pastry chef you're so gaga about.'

'Rupert Walker?' Lu squealed. *Oh, wow*! She'd casually mentioned to Mak that she'd like to see the demo, and Mak, good mate that he was, had arranged tickets.

'I was going to go with you, but I think you should take Will. You can torture him instead.'

'I don't think it's his thing. But I'd love to go.' Lu's eyes widened as Mak scrolled through the numbers on her phone, pushed the green button and handed it to her.

'It's ringing. Ask him.'

'Makhosi, you son of a…! What am I supposed…?' Mak thrust the phone in her direction and the next moment Will's deep voice had her toes curling.

'Hey, Lu. What's up?'

'Um…hi. Feel free to say no, because I certainly don't expect you to say yes—'

Will laughed. 'That sounds ominous.'

Lu glared at Mak, who was rolling his finger silently to tell her to get on with it.

'I was given tickets for a celebrity baking demo on Monday night and I was wondering if you'd like to go with me.' Lu expelled the words in a whoosh. She pictured herself jumping into a cavernous pool and finding it empty of water. *Splat!*

'Ah…um…it's really not my thing…but OK. Shall I pick you up?'

Oh, dear Lord, there was water in the pool and she was floating. *Yay!*

Lu pulled a tongue at Mak's satisfied face as they made arrangements. Turning away from his smirky expression she allowed a broad smile to cross her face.

I am woman, hear me roar, she thought. Well, it wasn't quite a roar but it was definitely more than a whimper. *Go me!*

An hour later Lu pulled her SUV into an empty space in the parking lot of the Stingrays' Rugby Union corporate offices. She'd been about to end her conversation with Will when he'd told her he was with Kelby Cotter, the Rays' CEO, and that he wanted to have a word. Kelby had asked her to meet with him to discuss a photography project she might be interested in. *Might* be interested? She *itched* to pick up her camera and get to work!

At this moment she'd walk into the fires of hell if there was photography work there, and any project that had the Rays' name attached to it would be a huge boost to her non-existent career.

Lu got out of the car and looked down at her short black skirt, her tangerine T-shirt and slightly scuffed wedges, and wondered if she should have splurged on another, more businesslike outfit. Heavy silver bracelets ran up her arm and ethnic silver earrings hung halfway to her shoulders. She'd forgotten to put on make-up. Lu sighed. She'd meant to but, as per normal, it had slipped her mind.

Lu was directed to the PR executive's office by a receptionist who looked like a high-class model. Perfect hair, perfect nails…super-slim. Lu resisted the urge to wipe her clammy hands on her skirt and again wondered why she was being shown to an office in the PR and Publicity Department.

She readjusted the strap of her shoulder bag and knocked

on the door. Two seconds later a large, rugged teddy bear of a man opened the door and smiled down at her. He held a sandwich in one hand and shrugged his apologies.

'Lu? Sorry—first moment I've had free to eat lunch,' he explained. 'Kelby Cotter.'

He raised the half-sandwich for another bite and gestured Lu to a seat in front of a very feminine, very messy desk. He swallowed his last bite, took a swig of water from the bottle on his desk and scrabbled amongst the papers.

'Got it.' Kelby flicked the memory card from her camera at her and Lu snapped it out of the air. 'Amazing photos of Will. Can I have them?'

Surely he could have asked her over the phone whether he could use them? She should ask him to pay for them. Her brain whirled. But if she gave them to him and asked for the credit then that would help to raise her profile. 'Uh...sure.'

Kelby tipped his head at her and let out a rumbling laugh. 'You can't just give your work away, Lu!'

'So you'll buy them from me?'

Kelby named a figure that had Lu's eyes widening. It seemed that the Rays paid their photographers very well indeed.

Emboldened by his kind eyes, Lu asked why the CEO was dealing with publicity and PR issues.

'Fair question. My head of PR flew to Cape Town to be with her terminally ill mother. I'm overseeing the department until she returns, and it's easier to work in her office than move all her stuff to mine.' Kelby leaned back in his chair and folded his hands across his portly stomach. 'I have two other offers for you. Both of them involve you getting paid.'

Lu blushed and felt like an idiot. And excited. And nervous if these projects had anything to do with Will Scott. 'OK. That sounds interesting.'

'I browsed through the other photos on the media card

Will gave me and I was blown away by some of your images. They are utterly fantastic.'

'Thank you,' Lu said, her brain racing to remember what images he was talking about. Some photos of the twins and their friends, the baby photo shoot, some beach scenes.

'My partner and I have a six-month-old daughter and we'd love some photographs. Some portrait shots of her and some informal shots of the three of us.'

Yay! A job. 'That's very doable. I have a studio at home with all the props, backdrops and lighting. As for the informal shots, we can do them at your home—whenever it's convenient.'

'Uh…we live in a rather cramped loft at the moment, while our house is being built, so that wouldn't work.' Kelby fiddled with his pen. 'Will says you have a beautiful garden…can we do them there? It'll have to be on a Sunday. I'm swamped during the week.'

'Sure. What about this Sunday morning?'

'Fantastic!' Kelby looked up at a sharp rap on his door. 'Will! She said yes to doing Micki's photos! We're going to do them on Sunday morning at her house.'

'Told you she would.'

Lu's stomach swooped and rolled as she turned in her chair. Dressed in a pair of black athletic shorts, an untucked blue Rays branded T-shirt and trainers, he looked fit and sexy, his hair damp as if he'd just come out of a shower. Will stepped into the room and Lu's eyes widened as he dropped his head to kiss her cheek. Because she pulled back—in surprise—his kiss landed on her temple. Will stood up and his eyes connected with hers. He'd clocked her surprise and those fabulous topaz eyes glinted with amusement.

Will perched himself on the corner of the desk and helped himself to the other half of Kelby's sandwich.

'Hey!' Kelby protested.

'Didn't Angie put you on a diet? No carbs? Salad only?'

Will demanded in between bites. 'I'm stopping you from getting into trouble with your woman, man.'

'But I'm starving!'

'Have a carrot stick or come run with me. Then you can eat shrimp and mayo sandwiches.' Will wiped his mouth with a serviette he'd found next to the sandwich. 'Or get your lard-ass back to the gym.'

'Like I have time for that,' Kelby grumbled.

Will waved the sandwich in Lu's direction. 'Have you asked her yet?'

'I was interrupted by my annoying head coach,' Kelby said, looking longingly at the empty plastic sandwich container. He turned to Lu and his eyes were serious. 'I'm looking for a contracted photographer to work for the Rays—capturing official images of the squad for us to use for various promotional campaigns. I don't have the time to phone around looking for freelance photographers who cost the earth even if they are available. I need *you* to be the official Rays photographer.'

Lu looked from Kelby to Will and realised that neither of them were laughing, so it couldn't be a joke. She thought she'd make doubly sure. 'Sorry—are you being serious?' she asked, her heart racing.

'Yep. You'd have to work flexible hours—work with me, work with the guys.' He sent her a dubious look. 'Can you handle twenty-plus men at a time?'

'She raised twin boys. She's pretty much Superwoman,' Will stated calmly, and Lu shot him a quick grin and tried not to blush at his compliment.

Lu looked at Kelby. 'Wow. Sorry, this is quite overwhelming. Are you sure?'

'If you give me images half as good as the ones on that card I'll be a happy man.'

Lu raised her chin in determination. 'They'll be as good or better.'

Kelby looked at Will and nodded. 'I like her.'

'I thought you would,' he said, and Lu's heart flopped against her ribs.

Kelby's ringing mobile phone broke their look and, after telling his caller that he'd phone him back in five minutes, Kelby reached for a file on his desk. He handed Lu some papers and stood up. 'Look that contract over and start on Monday.' He waved his mobile. 'Sorry, I have to sort something out.'

'Thank you so much.'

Lu noticed Kelby's eyes sliding to his desk drawer and saw that Will had caught the action too.

'What are you hiding, Kelby?' he demanded. Will stood up and walked around the desk, yanked open a drawer. He shook his head as he pulled out an oil stained packet. 'Jelly doughnuts? Seriously? With *your* stress levels and lack of exercise?'

Kelby groaned. 'Who are you? The food police?'

Will opened the packet, pulled one out and bit down. 'These are good.' He looked at Lu and waved the doughnut in the air. 'Want some?'

Lu shook her head. 'No thanks.'

'I hate you so much, Scott. I'll be back in five minutes,' Kelby muttered, looking utterly bereft. 'So are we on for Sunday, Lu.'

Lu felt sorry for him. Being on a diet was the pits. 'Come at ten—for tea. I'll make you some super-healthy beetroot cupcakes that you'll think are laden with fat and calories.'

Kelby brightened immediately. 'You—I like.' He pointed at Will. 'Him—not so much.'

CHAPTER FIVE

LU SWALLOWED AS the door clicked shut and Will resumed his place on the corner of the desk, his knee just inches from hers. He folded his arms across his chest and looked down at her.

He'd thought about her far too much since he'd had supper at her house and had been forcing himself not to call. He'd been surprised by *her* call and even more startled by the relief he'd felt at hearing from her again.

Lu lifted her face and in doing so exposed that fine strip of skin just below her jaw that he wanted to nibble on… He'd spent many nights thinking about her, imagining what he'd do to her if he had her naked and willing. Will gave himself a mental punch to the head.

Lu glanced down at the contract in her hand and he watched as pleasure bloomed in her cheeks. 'I've got a *job*, Will.'

'I know…' He bit his tongue to keep the word *honey* from slipping out. 'Congratulations.'

'I've got to tell the boys.'

Lu shot him an enormous smile before picking up her bag. Dumping it on the desk next to him, she stood up to scrabble in it and eventually yanked out her mobile. Will heard the rumble of a male voice as he stretched out his legs and crossed his feet.

Will listened patiently as she spoke to one brother and

then the other and then, sending him an apologetic look, quickly ran through the news again with Mak. Every time she said the words 'official photographer' she did a hip wiggle that had the blood rushing from his head.

Attraction aside, he was enjoying watching Lu bounce out of her shoes with excitement. When had she last had momentous news of her own to report? He suspected that it had been a long, long time. This was all hers; it had nothing to do with her brothers, Mak or anyone else.

He knew what success felt like—the satisfaction a person felt when the validation of hard work or talent came their way. He'd experienced it most of his life, was probably addicted to it, and had possibly become a bit blasé about his successes. Apart from his 'Stupid Years', failure was rarely—OK, never—an acceptable option.

Lu finished her conversation with Mak and looked up at him, her mermaid eyes excited. 'I'm even deeper in debt to you now. You rescue me *and* you hook me up with a job.'

No, he wasn't going to allow her to shift the credit to him or anyone else. This was her moment. 'All I did was hand Kelby the media card. I didn't say or do anything more. You got this job because you obviously have some wicked skills with a camera.'

Lu rocked on her heels. 'So you didn't hint or suggest that he should—?'

'You're assuming that I have a lot more power than I actually do. I wouldn't tolerate anyone telling *me* how to coach, so I extend the same respect to the publicity division. I wouldn't dare tell them how to promote or publicise. No, Lu, *you* did this,' Will told her, his voice low and serious. She needed to understand that this was her achievement and hers alone.

Lu looked at him for a long minute and then her hips shimmied again in excitement. He really wished she wouldn't. How was he expected not to think about what those hips were made for when she did that?

'Yee-hah!' Lu laughed and did a little pirouette. 'So, what time do you think I should be at work on Monday? What should I wear? And, more importantly, how many lenses should I bring? Maybe I should bring all of them—'

Will's lips quirked. 'How many do you have?'

'Eight? Nine?'

He swallowed his laugh. 'I'm sure you won't need them all. And Kelby will e-mail you what you need to know. Or tell you on Sunday. I'm finally going to see if I can find a temporary flat to move into. I can't stand that hotel a minute longer.'

Will moved to stand in front of her, resting his hand on the desk next to her hip. He saw the heat sliding into her cheeks, caught her motion to lift her hand to touch him and felt disappointed when it fell back to her side.

Will moved closer so that his clothes brushed hers. 'Congratulations on your job, Lu.'

'Thanks.'

'Every new job should be celebrated.'

What was he doing? *It's just a kiss,* he told his inner critic. *No big deal.* He'd kissed lots of woman before and walked away unscathed.

Besides, kissing her wasn't a big deal...he could stop at any time.

Yeah, but you've never kissed a mermaid before.

Will placed his hands on her hips, pulled her towards him...and his mouth had barely brushed hers when the office door opened and Kelby bounced inside.

'Whoops!' Kelby exclaimed.

Will looked over his shoulder to see Kelby back-tracking and cursed, silently and slow, until the door slammed shut again.

Lu pushed one eyebrow up. 'Well, that was awkward.'

Will bunched his fists to keep from reaching for her again. 'Sorry. That wasn't supposed to happen.'

'You didn't even kiss me properly,' Lu pointed out.

She straightened up and lifted those tanned shoulders. She must have seen something in his face because she stormed into the conversation.

'Will, I don't want this to get weird—especially since I asked you out. I don't want you to think that I'm chasing you, or looking for...' Lu bit her lip as her words trailed off. She waved an agitated hand in the air. 'I'm not looking for anything more than a couple of laughs...some fun. I'm not a complete idiot. I know that you're only going to be around for three months and that was just a little bit of getting carried away by the moment. Frankly, I've just come out of a decade-long relationship with two boys and I gave them every last bit of energy I had. I just want to have some fun—some company. I thought maybe you could do with the same.'

Company? What was she offering? *Company* company or *sex* company? 'Does the company involve getting naked?' he asked in his most prosaic voice.

Judging by the shock that jumped into her eyes, she hadn't reached the bedroom. Damn. Then her eyes smoked over and he knew that she wasn't far behind him. Unfortunately, along with I-want-get-you-naked there was a healthy dose of I-don't-know-what–I'm-doing as well.

And anyway, what was *he* thinking? Hadn't he decided to try something different while he was here in Durban? Yet here he was, sliding right back into old patterns and habit reactions.

'Ah...um...well...' Lu stuttered. *Good God.* 'Actually, I *had* thought about it.' Lu eventually got the words out.

Her expression was calm and composed, slightly challenging. and if her eyes had been sending him the same message he would have had her up against the wall and been kissing the hell out of her by now. Unfortunately she had the most expressive eyes in the world and, thanks to living with two sisters, he easily read the trepidation behind the big girl/brave girl look she was giving him.

OK, I'm scared but I'm prepared to try this anyway.

He wasn't sure why but he instinctively knew that he didn't want to be Lu's experiment.

'Will?'

Knock.

'Will?'

Knock.

'Will!'

Kelby knocked again and Will grinned. Saved by his best friend. Again. He definitely owed Kelby for getting him out of a conversational ass-whipping. Because there was no good way of telling a woman *Thanks, but I'll think about it.*

Will yanked open the door to let Kelby inside and sent Lu what he hoped was a reassuring smile. 'I'll leave you to talk with Kelby and I'll see you on Monday night. OK?'

'Sure.'

Hmm, there was more starch in that one-syllable word than there was in a shed-load of potatoes. Maybe Kelby hadn't saved his ass. He'd just delayed it getting flogged.

Whatcha doing?

That was the third, fourth—fifth?—time one of the twins had texted her today and asked the same question. Lu wished they'd stop worrying so much about her! It was like having two over-protective fathers and, while they were happy about her getting a job, they still weren't relinquishing the idea of her social life.

While Will went to the bar to buy them a drink before the show started Lu quickly snapped a photograph of the billboard advertising the trio of pastry chefs and chocolatiers. Attaching the picture to a message, she sent it to her brothers.

As you can see, I'm out and about.

With a man who very obviously doesn't want to sleep with me, Lu thought, but she didn't add that. Daniel replied.

Good for you!

Uh…no…and not for the cobwebs either. Nate's response flashed onto her screen.

Apparently not alone. Was Mak serious when he said you're with Will Scott? THE Will Scott? And what is he doing saying yes to a baking demo?

Who knew? Confusion reigned. And Mak had a whale-sized big mouth! Lu texted back.

Yep. And hey! There are *tons of celebs here. These chefs are BIG news!*

Nate: Bet there aren't any sportsmen there.

Dan: Do you think he could organise for us to meet the squad when we come home?

And when will that be?

When you've taken dance classes, pottery lessons and done a skydive. One date does not a life make.

Yeah! Agreed!

OMG, I'd forgotten how annoying you two can be! :p

Lu shoved her mobile into her bag and looked over to the bar, where Will was easily recognisable in the crush by his broad shoulders in a white shirt worn over a nice pair of jeans. He'd rolled the cuffs back at his wrists and he looked well dressed but casual—relaxed, but as if he'd made a bit of an effort.

And volcano-hot!

She hoped that she'd hit the right note between casual and sexy herself, with a pair of white jeans and a pale green gypsy top falling off one shoulder and belted in at the hips. Strappy heels took her height to Will's shoulder, yet she still felt—like most people, she supposed—dwarfed by him.

Will walked back towards her and Lu saw various sets of eyes following his progress, noticed the nudging elbows, the behind-the-hand comments. The crowd knew exactly who he was.

'Here you go,' Will said, handing her a glass of wine and hanging on to his tall glass.

How exactly was she supposed to act when she'd hinted that she wouldn't say no to a bedroom invitation and he hadn't say anything? Was that a yes? A no? Hang on, I'll think about it?

What she wouldn't do was let him think that she gave a damn—not even for half a second. She'd learnt to hide her emotions, and pride insisted that she do it now.

'What are you drinking?' Lu asked politely. Look—she could do polite

'Coke. I'm driving. I don't drink that much.'

That hadn't been true in his past, Lu thought. She'd internet-searched him to death and it seemed that at one time Will had had a very unhealthy relationship with alcohol. And dope. And his ex-wife. There had been public fights, public displays of over-the-top affection, busted-up hotel rooms. She couldn't reconcile this controlled, calm man with the younger version of himself she'd read about.

She was pretty sure that younger Will would have slept with her!

'So, did you find a place to rent?' Lu asked as people started moving towards the intimate theatre.

'A flat near you, actually. Practically around the corner. It has a hot tub.'

Oh, good grief. Will in a hot tub…bubbles, champagne… She was not going to think about him skin on skin. He wasn't on the same page as her in terms of skin and sex and… Dear Lord, it was hot in this theatre.

Lu handed their tickets over and pulled in a breath when

Will placed his hand on her lower back to guide her down the theatre steps.

'It has a great view,' Will continued as they eventually stopped at the bottom row, dead centre.

Typical Mak to have organised the best seats in the house, Lu thought.

'And it's fully furnished, so I just need to move my clothes across. I'll sign the lease tomorrow. I can also raid your fridge for frozen lasagne when I forget to buy food.'

'I'll make you a tray as a house warming present,' Lu promised him as she sat down. *Maybe.*

'You do love to cook, don't you?' Will shook his head, bemused. 'My skills in the kitchen are limited to making coffee. When you make that tray of lasagne feel free to throw in a couple of those beetroot cupcakes you made for Kelby.'

Lu looked puzzled. 'When did you taste those?'

'You sent some home with Kels and Angie? I ate with them last night.'

'Oh. You liked them, huh?'

'I have a chronic sweet tooth. I'm really hoping that they'll have samples here of what they make tonight.'

Will smiled at her and Lu's stomach flipped over. His smile should be declared a weapon of mass destruction, she thought. How could she remain irritated when he was so charming? So appealing?

'I love the art of baking…decorating. It's so creative.' Lu sighed. 'I wish I could shoot them as they worked…it would be such fun.'

'Talking of photography—Kelby and Angie were over the moon when they received those first couple of photos of Micki you e-mailed them.'

'Good.' Lu crossed her legs and tapped her finger against the wine glass. 'They are a sweet family. Tell me about yours.'

Affection passed across his face. 'I have two sisters—one in London, one in Wellington—and my folks live in Auckland.'

'Do you miss them?'

'Sure. Although I've lived away from them for so long that it's become normal.'

Lu stared at the stage with its three tables and heaps of cooking equipment and felt her throat constrict. 'The boys are having a fantastic time at uni…I already feel like they're slipping away.

'You are one of my brothers' sporting heroes by the way,' Lu told him as the lights flickered.

'Do they play rugby?'

'And cricket and hockey and soccer. And squash. And they surf… If it's called a sport, they'll try it. The one thing I *don't* miss is ferrying them from activity to activity. Kids here only get their freedom at eighteen, and they've only just got their licences.' Lu stared off into space for a moment. 'That's about the only thing I don't miss about them being gone.'

Will heard the tremor in her voice. 'It's been tough, huh?'

Lu managed a quick laugh and waved his concern away. 'Nah, I'm fine.'

'Tell me the truth, Lu,' Will insisted quietly.

Her irritation with him flooded back with his request. He wanted to get into her head but not into her bed? She knew that she was out of practice dating-wise, but she was pretty sure that her complaint was ass-about-face.

She wanted to tell him that she felt as if she'd had her head amputated, that the house was too quiet and that the dogs were pining. How excited she was to be working again. Instead she just turned her head away and stared at the stage.

'It's starting,' she said as a spotlight highlighted the middle table.

'Who is this dude anyway?' Will demanded in a low whisper.

'Rupert Walker is reputed to be the best baker in the world. And Heinz Martine is an amazing chocolatier and another incredible baker,' Lu whispered as Ruper Walker bounced onto the stage and greeted the audience amongst a flurry of clapping and whistling. 'I don't know the third chef.'

When the audience settled down, the chef, dressed in tartan chef's pants and an enormous maroon chef's hat, put his hands on his hips and looked into the audience.

'Thank you for being here! I always ask for audience help and I usually ask for volunteers, but tonight I understand that Will Scott is in the audience. I'm the biggest, gayest fan!' Rupert shuddered delicately and the audience howled with laughter.

Lu heard Will's groan.

'So maybe Will could come up and give me a hand to make sugar baskets? Will, are you...*game*?'

Will muttered a swear word and looked at Lu with panicked eyes. 'Crap, Lu—I burn bloody water!' he whispered.

As Will stood up Lu slapped her hand against her mouth to keep the laughter from tumbling out.

He bent down so that he spoke directly into her ear. 'You might think this is funny, Mermaid, but I *will* get my revenge.'

Lu's laughter, hot and hard, followed Will up onto the stage.

Will bombed at making sugar baskets. He tried so hard, and was such a good sport about it, but he burnt his sugar twice and accidentally knocked Rupert's elaborate half-finished sugar cage to the floor, where it shattered into a million sugar pieces. Rupert eventually, and very good-naturedly, threw in the towel and sent Will back to his seat, where he proceeded to sit so still that Lu was convinced he'd slept through the rest of the show.

As they cleared the theatre Lu looked up at him and lifted her eyebrows. 'Did you enjoy your sleep?'

'It was great. What did I miss?' Will replied cheerfully.

Lu laughed. 'Nothing you want to know. I, however, learned how to make the ganache for a Sacher Torte.'

Will's eyes lit up. 'That Austrian chocolate cake? Cool—thanks in advance.'

'I'm not making you *that*. It takes hours!'

Will placed his big hand at the base of her neck. 'I'll have one because you laughed at me! When I was called up on stage…when I burnt the sugar—'

Lu gurgled. 'Twice.'

'You were rolling in your seat laughing! Sacher Torte—and if you agree I'll buy you an Irish coffee now.'

Lu grinned as he steered her into the theatre bar. 'Oh, all right, then.'

She followed the waiter to a table that looked out onto the bustling city centre street. Will placed their order and shook his head.

'I get to choose what we do next,' he told her, mock-sternly. 'You can't be trusted.'

Lu lifted one eyebrow, remembered that he wasn't that keen on her, and used the don't-mess-with me-expression that normally had her brothers wilting. 'You are presuming a lot, aren't you?'

Will sent her a lazy smile. 'You're irritated with me.'

'Are you asking me or telling me?'

'Telling you. You can keep your face blank, Mermaid, but your eyes are far too expressive. You're annoyed because I didn't give you an answer as to whether I wanted to sleep with you or not.'

Bingo! Give the man a gold star!

Will rested his arms on the table and leaned forward. 'Before I respond to that, I need to ask you if you meant what you said in Kelby's office?' Will asked.

Lu frowned. 'Which part?' she asked, wary.

'About not wanting to get involved with anyone?'

'Yes.' She needed to stand on her own feet before she tried to walk beside someone else. Find out what made her tick, what made her happy.

'OK, so here's what I'm thinking: I can take you to bed—and, yes, I'm alive and breathing, and you're hot, so God knows I want to—and we'll sleep together and have a lot of fun. But I wouldn't see you again. It's not what I do… And that could be weird seeing that we have to work together for the next couple of months.'

'OK…' What was she supposed to say to that? And where was he going with this?

'Or I can *not* take you to bed and see you again.'

Huh?

'Look, Lu, at the risk of sounding like a conceited ass, I can walk into any club in the city and have someone new in my bed every night.'

'You're right—you do sound like a conceited ass,' Lu murmured.

'But I don't have someone to hang with—someone to pass the time with. I enjoy your company…even when you're trying hard to hide your irritation.'

He'd been thinking about it since he'd last seen her— thinking about what Kelby had said. Despite his issues around relationships he genuinely *liked* people and enjoyed being around them. He couldn't foist his after-hours company on his team mates—he was their boss, and who wanted to socialise with their boss? And Kelby had his family and didn't want or need him around. Being single in a foreign city could be lonely, and having someone to hang with would make time go faster, would kill the hours away from the stadium.

Pushing his attraction to her aside—he could do that: he wasn't a hound dog—he genuinely enjoyed her company; she was restful, easy to be with. Lu was real in a way that he hadn't encountered in a woman in long time. When last had he felt so at ease, so relaxed with a woman?

With her, he felt as if he was himself. He curled his lip. Not Will Scott the legendary rugby player. Not the caretaker coach everyone was watching to see what he did with their beloved team. Not Jo Keith's unreliable bad-boy ex-husband.

Just Will. He really liked being just Will.

And he enjoyed the fact that Lu didn't simper or smirk and hang on his every word. That she could call him a conceited ass. Apart from his sisters, who called him far worse, every other woman he'd met only ever complimented him.

It got old very quickly.

He made it sound so easy, so simple, Lu thought. And it *could* be that simple if she didn't overthink this. Sex and walk away, or no sex and a couple of months of hanging together, having fun.

She wanted sex but she *needed* fun. She wanted to laugh like she had earlier, to try new things, to stagger to work bleary-eyed because she'd been out having a blast. She wanted to drink cocktails and wear pretty dresses and try new foods. She wanted to recapture a little of the youth she'd lost, to live life—taste it, feel it, experience it.

And she just knew that she would have more fun with Will than without him.

She'd be mad to pass up this opportunity for one or two nights of hot sex and also—Ding! Ding! Ding! the jackpot bell rang—her brothers would stop messaging her a hundred times a day to see if she was OK.

'OK—and you'd be helping me out at the same time.'

'That's an added incentive…but how?'

Lu waved her hand in the air—a gesture he now realised she used when she didn't want to pursue a subject. Or when she was trying to be brave.

'Would you consider doing things like pottery lessons? Dance classes?'

'I was thinking about dinner and a movie. But I'd consider anything…*if you gave me a reason.*'

Lu shook her head. 'It's not important and….it's silly.'

'Tell me, Lu.'

She heaved in a huge sigh and stared at the table. 'Before they left for uni my brothers told me that they were worried about me being on my own so much and that they wanted me to start getting out more, start doing stuff. They want me to have some fun, to get out and do things.'

Seeing the flash of misery in her eyes, he reached out to comfort her and allowed himself the rare privilege of stroking his hand down her arm from elbow to wrist. Her bare skin was soft and cool under the pads of his fingers.

'What things?'

'Clubbing was one of them…skydiving, surfing, dance lessons. Pottery classes. A job—but that's sorted.' Lu smiled her thanks at the waiter, who placed their drinks on the table. Irish coffee for her, plain coffee for Will. 'I promised I would. And I have been doing some stuff. But it would be so much more fun if I had someone to do it with.'

Judging by the confusion Will saw in her eyes, he suspected that Lu was dealing with a lot more than she was saying. But her expression begged him not to pursue it.

You have been alone and dealing with far too much for far too long, Mermaid, he told her silently. He knew what that felt like.

Pull it back to the surface, Scott. To less dangerous waters.

He groaned theatrically. 'Dance lessons? Pottery? Good

Lord.' Will tapped his finger against the table, his expression thoughtful. 'We could listen to live bands and definitely go skydiving—'

'Uh, *no*!'

'I could teach you to surf.'

'I'd consider that. Ice skating?'

'*Blergh*. Wet and cold. I'd consider pottery lessons if you'd consider dirt bike riding, getting out into the country. I know it's not a girl thing, but you might find it fun.'

Under the table Will's knee brushed Lu's and a bolt of awareness barrelled straight to his groin. Could he do this? Could he ignore this buzz of sexual attraction and be her friend?

Could he stop thinking about the kiss that never was? Stop replaying the way her eyes had half lowered and glinted green, the way her hands had held his hips, the brief taste of that perfect mouth?

He had to…there was no other choice. He was leaving soon and she was too dangerous to be around long-term because he suspected that she could—maybe—make him think about whether sparks could last and keep burning…

'Will? What do you think? Should we do this? *Can* we do this?'

He knew what she was asking… Could they do this without it getting complicated, messy? It was hard to meet her eyes, to see but ignore the corresponding flash of heat he recognised in them. He *had* to dismiss it, he realized. Just as she did. Because she wasn't ready to get involved he wouldn't get involved, so companionship was the only prize that was up for grabs.

'It'll be fine, Lu.'

If we can keep our hands off each other. Because if we can't then all bets are off.

Will sighed. He could really do with a stiff drink.

CHAPTER SIX

As THEY FOLLOWED the signs past the main house to The Pottery Shed Lu flicked her finger against Will's shoulder. 'I thought I said that you should wear old clothes—not a nifty Zoo York T-shirt and cargo shorts.'

She was wearing an ancient shirt, cut-off jeans and flip-flops. Will looked down at his chest and sent her the evil eye. 'When I was packing my clothes in Auckland I didn't think I'd be going to pottery lessons! This is the oldest shirt I have here.'

'I could have lent you one of the twins' old T-shirts.' Lu said as they approached a barn at the back of the property. 'And stop moaning. I've agreed to go dirt bike riding next week.'

'I want to take you skydiving.'

'Not on your life.' Lu shuddered. 'And what do you mean…*take* me?'

'I'm certified to do tandem jumps…we could do one together.'

'Uh, let me think about that.' Lu pretended to peer up at the sky. Two seconds later she spoke again. 'Thought about it…no. Nope. No way. Never.'

'Wuss,' Will said as a long, tall, elderly woman dressed in tie-dyed pants and a glowing caftan drifted from the barn.

Lu stepped forward and held out her hand. 'Hi, I'm Lu. Are you…?'

The woman's eyes drifted across their faces and she sent them a vague look. 'Kate. And I'm stoned.'

Lu looked at Will and lifted her eyebrows. 'You're *stoned*?'

'New supplier. His stuff is wicked good.'

'But our lesson…' Lu wailed, ignoring Will's smile of satisfaction.

Kate's hand wafted somewhere behind her head. 'Go on in—clay's in the bucket next to the wheel. Slap some on the wheel, hit the pedal, move your hands up and down. Make something. Lock up when you leave.'

'But… But…' Lu stuttered.

'*Namaste*,' Kate murmured, and weaved away in the general direction of the house.

Will folded his arms and watched her leave. 'Did you pay her?'

Lu pouted. 'No. I was going to pay her when we were finished.'

'Good. Then let's get out of here,' Will said, his expression a combination of smirky and relieved.

Lu narrowed her eyes at him. 'Uh-uh. You're not getting off that easily. Everything is set up…how hard can it be?'

Will groaned. 'Aw, Lu, come on! Let's go for a walk on the beach, have a beer, watch the sun go down.'

'Nope.' Lu said stubbornly. 'If I have to do dirt bikes then you have to try this.'

Will stepped through the open door to the studio, put his hands on his hips and looked around. Shelves packed with vases, bowls and vessels of every shape and form lined the room, and long tables covered with tools and boxes covered the back half of the shed. In the centre were three triangular-shaped desks with a potter's wheel on each and a bucket with what he presumed was clay next to each wheel.

Will pulled out a stool and sat down in front of one wheel, then looked from the desk to Lu. 'Um…what now?'

Lu's mouth twitched. 'I don't know. I haven't done this either…wait!' She reached across the table and picked up a plastic envelope. 'Instructions!'

Will leaned across and looked at the plastic enclosed paper. He shook his head and pointed to the heading. 'It's printed off the internet, Lu!'

'So?' Lu grinned. 'Let's try it.'

It seemed that he was about to try this thing. He knew that everything that could go wrong would. He didn't have an artistic bone in his body and he suspected that they were about to get dirty.

Really dirty. He looked around. 'Can you see any aprons?'

'Now who's being a wuss? We won't need any,' Lu told him. 'We'll be fine. So, first step… "Gather a small amount of clay—the size of two fists put together is plenty for someone just starting—and form it into a rough ball shape."'

Will dunked his hand in the bucket in front of him and lifted his eyebrows. Kind of the same texture as the mud he'd used to throw at his sisters.

'We need to knead it—get rid of the bubbles.'

'When do we get to play with the wheel thingy?' Will asked, trying to copy Lu's rather expert kneading technique. Which made him think of bread, which made him think of cake, and that reminded him…

'When am I getting my Austrian cake, by the way?'

'When I have time.' Lu peered down at the instructions. 'Maybe. So… "If you think all the air bubbles are out, shape it back into a rough ball."'

Will slapped the clay between his fingers.

'"Put the clay on the centre of the wheel head. The easiest way to do this is by throwing the clay with some force on the centre. Drip some water over it and spin the wheel fairly fast,"' she read.

'OK.' Will threw the clay down and hit the pedal of the wheel with some force. He watched his clay ball shoot across the wheel, skim the rim and fall on the floor. 'Whoops.'

Lu snorted with laughter.

'Think you can do better, Mermaid?'

What Lu didn't realise was that her pedal was next to his left foot . She was so busy trying to get it right that she didn't notice his foot sliding over hers until he pushed down hard. Her wheel spun furiously and her ball skidded across it. Lu yelped, turned in her seat and slipped her clay-covered hand onto his chest, leaving a perfect imprint of her fingers.

Blue-green eyes glinting with mirth met his as she fought to find an innocent expression. 'It could have been worse,' she said on a shrug.

'It could?'

Lu grinned. 'I could've slapped your face.'

Will leaned forward and placed his wet, clay-covered hand on her cheek. 'What? Like this?'

Will kept his hand on her cheek as her mouth opened and closed like a guppy looking for air.

'You…you…'

He didn't think—couldn't think. He just placed his lips and swiped his mouth across hers in a kiss that was as shocking as it was stunning. Lu sighed into his mouth and planted her hands on his chest—intending, he was sure, to push him away. But her fingers curled into his T-shirt and gripped the fabric instead.

She tasted of sunshine and excitement, of cherry lip balm and surprise. Her perfume swirled up from her heated skin and he adored the scent. He yanked her off her stool and whirled her away from the wheel, up against a tall cupboard. He moved into her, needing to get closer, needing to feel her feminine form. Will lifted his hands to hold her face, tipping her head so that he could taste all of her mouth. Lu made a sound of approval that sent all his blood rushing south. She was heat and light, softness and courage, too much and not nearly enough. But he couldn't stop—didn't want to stop.

He knew he had to, because if he didn't he never would.

It took everything in him to lift his mouth from hers, to pull her head to his chest and rest his chin in her hair. 'God, Lu…'

Lu muttered something unintelligible and he thought he felt her lips flutter against his shirt.

'I wasn't going to do this,' he muttered, but the words were barely out of his mouth before he dropped it back to hers.

Her mouth parted to his insistent tongue and his hand drifted over her shirt, palmed her breast. Will felt another wicked flash of lust scuttle through him as she angled her head to allow him deeper access. Moving her hands, she ran her fingers across his taut stomach, let them drift lower before settling them low on his narrow hips.

'Lu, you're not helping!' Will pulled back, gripped her arms and kept her an arm's length away. He tried to inject some assertiveness into his voice. 'We aren't going to do this!'

Lu cocked her head at him. 'Do you always walk away?'

He knew what she meant. 'Yeah. Always.'

'Why?'

Will dragged his hand through his hair, pushing streaks of clay through it. 'Have you ever seen a fire when it's been put out?' he demanded. 'It's a wet, soggy, dirty, disgusting mess.'

'Ah, so you walk before it even gets the chance to become messy?'

Essentially. Some sparks, especially this one between him and Lu, had the potential to become a raging bush fire.

But even bush fires couldn't rage for ever. And the bigger the fire, the bigger the mess. No, it was smarter just to keep this simple, platonic.

Because they had to work together, because he really did have fun with her…but mostly because he hadn't been so tempted to walk into the blaze in a long, long time.

'OK, back up.' Lu wiggled her way out of his grip and leaned back against the cupboard. He looked at his hands. They were now only smeared with clay. She had clay in her hair. It was streaked over her shirt, her hips, down her neck.

'You're filthy,' she said, echoing his thoughts.

Will's finger drifted down her cheek. 'So are you. And, oh, crap…if we hadn't been going straight home we are now.'

Lu frowned. 'Why?'

Will motioned to her chest, where his palm print covered her left breast. 'Kind of a big clue about what we were up to.'

Lu looked down and closed her eyes. 'Pottery lesson a no-no, then?'

Will nodded, his expression rueful. 'It should definitely go on the things not to do list.'

'Along with skydiving,' Lu added quickly.

'Oh, I *will* get you up there.' Will promised.

After work on Friday Lu slipped into Old Joe's, a popular bistro in the middle of Florida Road. Pushing her sunglasses up onto her head, she smiled at Mak before placing her cheek on his and breathing in his scent. His pale pink shirt looked stunning against his skin, his tie was raspberry and his tailored pants were undoubtedly designer.

'I can't stay long. I'm meeting Will to go ten-pin bowling with him and some of the squad,' she told him, hanging her tote bag off a globe chair and sitting on the brightly coloured cushion.

'I don't have that much time either. I just wanted to tell you that Deon got into St Clares!'

Lu let out a delighted whoop before throwing her arms around Mak's neck and kissing his cheek.

'That's such fabulous news, Mak!'

'It is, but now that school is a reality the fear that he's going to be bullied again is back. In him and in me,' Mak admitted, sucking on what looked like a double-thick berry milkshake.

Lu fought temptation, lost, and ordered the chocolate equivalent. She was going for a run along the promenade later. She'd work it off then.

'He'll be fine, Mak. I promise. St Clare's doesn't tolerate any type of bullying.'

'I hope so,' Mak said eventually, leaning back in his chair. 'Anyway, back to you. Does this mean that you and Will are dating?'

Lu shook her head. 'No. Well...*no.*'

'That sounded convincing...not at all.' Mak pushed his empty glass away. 'So, what *is* going on between you?'

'I don't know... I think we're friends, but we have this sexual buzz.'

'So he's shoved his tongue down your throat?'

Lu gasped, blushed, and immediately thought back to that inferno-hot kiss they'd shared in the pottery studio. After holding her for a while he'd pulled back slightly, looked at her, and dived in again. His firm lips, the play of muscles under her hands, the feel of his big hand covering her not-so-big breast... His erection hard against her lower stomach, tenting his shorts...

He touched her and melted her brain. If he hadn't gathered up his car keys and mobile and yanked her to the car she would have let him take her there on that dusty floor.

Since then they'd both pretended it hadn't happened...and they were very, very careful to avoid touching each other.

'Can I get you anything else?'

Mak's eyes didn't leave Lu's face to look at the hovering waiter. 'A fire extinguisher would be helpful. I need to cool her down,' he said in a bone-dry voice.

'Makhosi!' Lu hissed. She blushed as she looked up at the confused waiter. 'Ignore him. Thanks, but we're fine.'

'So, do you want to answer my question now?'

'We kissed. So what? It's not a big deal…' It was *such* a big deal; she'd never had such an extreme reaction to being touched in her life. From nought to take-me-now in ten seconds flat. She heaved in some much needed air. 'I still can't and won't get involved with him, Mak.'

'And why not?'

'Because he is leaving in two months' time. Because he's not interested in anything but a casual friendship, having someone to hang out with.'

'So have a casual hook-up with him,' Mak suggested. 'It's not against the law, Lu.'

Lu closed her eyes. 'I can't, Mak.'

'Why? He's smart, good-looking and successful. Seems like a decent guy. I'm not seeing the problem.'

Lu shoved her fingers into her hair. 'He is strictly a one-night stand kind of guy and I'm not a just-have-sex type of girl. And I work with him. And I have so much fun with him.'

Lu sipped and shrugged. 'After work I work on my photos, or I read, or I exercise. I think, plan. Try not to miss the twins. I need to—am *trying* to—get used to this new life without them, to being on my own. Then, when I feel the walls closing in on me, I call Will and we go out and have an absolute blast. We laugh, Mak—hard. Often. We talk or don't talk…there's no pressure and I like that.' Lu stared at the huge African mask dominating the opposite wall. 'Sure, I'd like sex, but not if it means sacrificing the fun we're having.'

Mak leaned forward and touched her hand. 'Just be careful, Lu. I don't want to mop up your tears, hon.'

'You won't have to, Mak.'

Casual linen three-quarter pants, a funky brown and gold T-shirt, beaded sandals and new jewellery. Will took in Lu's outfit as she moved across the staff dining room towards the table where he sat with the older members of the team. OK, different…he thought.

His gaze travelled up her throat. He remembered that the spot between her ear and her jaw was very tender, and that she'd vibrated in his arms when he'd nibbled her just there. Kissing her had been a mistake, he thought, not for the first time. His pants grew substantially smaller. Mostly because all he thought about was doing it again.

Her mouth had been hot and demanding—and, talking about her mouth…good God. What on earth had she stained her lips with? Mulberries? Will leaned back and looked at her properly: too much blusher, smoky eyes, a bottle of mascara. She looked glossy, but she also looked like every other girl he'd ever dated.

Slick, superficial, sophisticated…*hard*.

He heard the low wolf whistles and the compliments of his two lunch companions: Jabu, the Rays' captain, and Matt Johnson, whom he knew had the hots for Lu. Would he have to have a chat with Matt about keeping his distance from Lu? Maybe.

Matt needed to know that Lu was *way* off-limits.

Will looked at Lu and wished he could pull her off to the showers and wash that make-up off her. He wanted his Lu back: clean skin—her freckles were all but hidden now—clear eyes…normal. He wanted her make-up-free, naturally…*normal*.

Crap.

When a guy started thinking that natural was gorgeously

normal he was neck deep in the brown stuff…or about to fall into the brown stuff. Neither scenario was vaguely attractive.

Lu slid down into the empty chair opposite him and reached for the salt to shake over her chicken salad.

'New look, Lu?' Matt asked.

'Experimenting.'

Lu batted her eyelashes at him and Will felt his stomach contract.

'What do you think?'

'Hot,' Matt answered.

He ran his finger over the tattoo of a naughty angel on her shoulder. Will considered breaking his fingers.

'Cool tat.'

What the hell…? She'd got a tattoo? Not that it had anything to do with him…except he didn't like the idea of ink on that amazing, smooth, clear expanse of skin. Skin he'd all too briefly explored, discovered, wanted to taste again.

Matt tipped his head back to look at her shoulder again. 'Ah, it's just a henna tat—it'll be gone in six weeks.'

'Thank the Lord,' Will muttered under his breath. He ignored Lu's quizzical look, took a healthy sip from his glass of water and pushed his empty plate away. He stretched out his leg and the inside of his calf brushed her bare foot. He felt the bolt of lust shoot up to his groin.

He raised reluctant eyes and saw his desire reflected in hers—along with a solid dose of irritation. She wanted him but didn't want to want him. She wanted him to compliment her on her new look but didn't want him to know that she cared. Will ran his hand along his jaw. This was getting a bit too complicated, a little more intense than he'd bargained for.

And he *still* wanted to take the make-up off her face. Take her back to natural Lu.

'Would you mind signing these for me? I'd be so grateful.' Lu was handing out letter-size photos and dishing out black felt-tipped markers.

'What's going on?' he asked as he took his own photograph and a pen.

Lu rested her forearms on the table. 'You remember that I mentioned Mak has a highly functioning, Down Syndrome son? He's rugby-obsessed and thinks that I am the luckiest girl in the world to know you guys. You're his favourite player, Jabu.'

Jabu's face split into a huge smile. 'Cool.'

Lu wiped her mouth with a paper serviette and Will was grateful to see a lot of the mulberry stain disappear. Three more layers and that gorgeous mouth would be back. 'I've looked after Deon a lot over the years. He's a nice kid. But he's physically small for his age and he's terrified about starting a new school. He was badly bullied at his last school. He's about to start at St Clare's—'

'But that's a mainstream school, not a special needs school,' Matt interrupted. 'I went there; they don't have special needs kids.'

'They introduced a new programme about five years back to integrate kids with special needs into the mainstream school. It's a huge success. I also know the school well. My brothers attended it. Mak is a bundle of nerves for Deon. He's trying to be brave but is scared witless… anyway, I said I'd go with them on his first day.'

'Which is…?' Will asked.

'Tomorrow.' Lu forked up some chicken and waved her fork at the pack of photos. 'I thought that if Deon ran into any bullying he could offer up some signed photos from his Rays heroes to talk his way out of it.'

Will dashed his signature across a photograph and smiled. 'No problem.'

Lu pulled to a stop outside St Clare's and turned in her seat to look backwards. Deon was looking a little grey, his hands were trembling, and his knee bounced up and down. Mak was looking equally nauseous. He might be tough and forthright, but he was a marshmallow when it came to his son.

Lu touched his shoulder before leaning back to pat Deon on the thigh. 'I told you that my brothers went here and that it's a really nice school? Remember that Mr Klimt, the principal, doesn't tolerate bullying.'

'Mr Klimt doesn't go into the boys' bathrooms,' Deon said in his slow, measured voice.

Lu sighed. The child might be challenged but he was not a fool. How was she going to get either of them out of the car and up the steps that led into the school? They were both anxiously watching the streams of laughing, smiling chatty kids mingling on the grass, within the school quad, leaning against walls and doors.

They looked confident and happy…no wonder Deon and Mak were terrified. Even she was feeling a bit intimidated.

'I want to go home,' Deon said, and dropped his chin to his neck.

She couldn't cry. That wouldn't help anyone! Terrified or not, someone had to take charge. 'Right, let's get your stuff together, dude.'

Lu sighed as her mobile rang. She picked it up and sighed at the display. 'It's really not a good time, Will.'

'It's a very good time,.' Will replied, laughter in his voice. 'Tell the kid that his posse has arrived.'

'What?'

'Look in your review mirror, Mermaid.'

Lu slid a glance to her mirror and laughter bubbled up in her throat. Walking down the pavement, dressed in their Rays training uniforms, looking as intimidating as all hell, were Jabu, Matt and three other prominent Rays players. Will and Kelby walked behind them. Will had his mobile in his hand.

Lu swallowed down her emotion and turned to Deon, her face alight with excitement. 'OK, Deon, this is a mega big day for you.' She winked at Mak, who'd just caught sight of the players now coming to a stop outside her car. His jaw fell to his lap. Lu reached over and lifted Deon's chin. 'I know this is scary, but some special people thought that you might need someone to see you into school. Say hello to my friend Jabu.'

Jabu ducked his head inside the car and as long as she lived Lu knew she would never forget the look on the little boy's face when he saw his biggest sporting hero. The back door flew open and Deon tumbled into Jabu's enormous arms. Jabu held him with ease and calmly ignored his shaking as he introduced him to the rest of his team mates.

Lu looked at Mak, whose Adam's apple was bobbing with restrained emotion. 'Did you know about this?' he demanded.

Lu shook her head and sniffed. 'Not a damn thing. Will must have organised it.'

Mak pressed the heels of his hands against his eyes. 'I'm really liking this guy, Lu.'

Will looked at the commotion they were causing and grinned. He'd forgotten the enthusiasm kids could display—that wide eyed excitement. He'd felt exactly the same when he'd met his sporting heroes as a kid.

Then Will looked at Lu's face as she climbed out of her car and grinned at the emotions crossing it. Wonder, amazement, joy. Yeah, this was *so* worth organising.

Kelby jammed him in the ribs. 'Take that goofy look off your face, Scott. You look like a sap.'

'I don't do goofy,' Will said through gritted teeth.

'Well, you sure as hell are doing *something*!' Kelby grinned as they stood a little way off from the rest of the team. 'So what prompted this, mate? I mean, I'm not complaining…' he gestured to a couple of sports photogra-

phers who were walking across the road towards them
'…it's great publicity. But it's way out of your scope as
caretaker coach.'

'Uh…' Will tugged at the collar of his shirt.

'Could it have anything to do with the fact that you are
doing my press photographer, who obviously has a very
special relationship with this kid?'

Will shuffled on his feet. 'I'm not sleeping with her;
we're just friends, Kelby.'

Kelby roared with laughter and slapped Will on the back.
'Yeah, right! You've never done anything like this before.'

Will gritted his teeth. 'Kelby, we're friends…like you
suggested. That's it.'

Kelby's laughter faded, surprise dominated and he shook
his head. 'Oh, my poor, confused young friend!' He grinned
again and slapped Will between his shoulderblades. Again.
'You, dude, are ass-deep in woman trouble. I *love* it!'

Will was thinking about punching him when he felt Lu's
approach. He looked around when a small hand rested on
his bicep.

'You arranged this, didn't you?' Lu asked, tears in her
eyes.

God, he did one nice thing and everyone got soppy!

'Jabu and I had a chat about it. He was bullied at school
so he knows what it's like. The Rays also promote anti-
bullying on their website,' Will replied.

'Thank you. I'm overwhelmed.'

'No worries. It was easy enough to do,' Will said. He
caught Mak's eye and shook his hand, brushed off his gratitude.

It seemed as if a good portion of the school's pupils were
gathered around them when Jabu raised his hand and the
crowd quietened. 'OK—any rugby boys here?'

Hands shot up into the air. 'Who is your favourite team?'

'Rays! Rays! Rays!'

The Rays players smiled and after a minute Jabu lifted his hand again. 'This is Deon. He's a new boy here today and he's our number one fan. We need our fans' support, and sometimes our fans need our support. Deon needs our support today because it's not easy walking into a new school. So, while we might not be here every minute of every day, we're going to be looking out for him. And for when we're not here we're appointing our own boys to make sure he finds his way around OK.'

Jabu bent down and had a quick discussion with Deon.

'Eleven-year-old rugby players, step forward!' he bellowed, and a number of boys belted out of the crowd to stand eagerly in front of Jabu and the rest of the huge players. 'You show Deon the ropes and we'll arrange that your team gets to train with us, at our field, once a month for the next three months. Deal?'

'Deal!' The piping voices bounced back.

Lu lifted her hand to her heart and looked up at Will with shining eyes. 'You'd do that?'

'Apparently Kelby's been asking Carter to do it as part of a community service programme but he wasn't prepared to consider it. Old school. The other clubs do it with different schools all the time.' Will shrugged. 'It's for an hour. It's nothing.'

'It's everything to the kids,' Lu said as the bell rang.

But the children didn't move. They were too busy jostling for the players' attention and demanding autographs.

Will grinned when he saw two boys, obviously St Clare rugby players, standing on either side of Deon to protect him from the crowd. 'I think our work here is done.'

A shrill whistle broke their eye contact and kids and adults all froze as a short, round man bustled down the steps, his face red with what Lu knew was fake annoyance.

'What is going on here? Why aren't you in class?' Mr Klimt roared, but Will saw his face soften as her eyes swept over Deon and his new bodyguards. He placed his hands on his hips. 'What are these big men doing here? Who are they?' he demanded, faking displeasure.

A collective groan rose from the crowd. One brave soul eventually dared to answer him. 'Mr Klimt, they are Rays players! Jabu and Matt.'

'Really? I thought they were ballerinas! Mr Johnson? Is that you?' The crowd fell silent as short Mr Klimt looked up—and up—into Matt's face.

'Yes, sir.' Matt over-exaggerated his grimace and some of the kids snorted with suppressed laughter.

'And what are you doing on Friday afternoon, Mr Johnson?' The principal demanded.

'I don't believe I'm doing anything, Mr Klimt…sir.'

'Good. If I am not mistaken, I believe you still owe me two hours of detention.'

CHAPTER SEVEN

LATER THAT AFTERNOON Lu was in the players' lounge, working on her laptop, when she heard low, masculine laughter
and Will, Jabu, Matt and Kelby walked in. Everyone but
the suited Kelby was now dressed in casual clothes, their
hair wet from the shower.

Lu was getting to know their weekly schedule; it was
Wednesday, so that meant that after they'd returned to the
stadium from St Clare's they'd spent the morning watching a video analysis of their opposition for the weekend's
game and then they'd hit the field. Full-contact rugby and
Will had been in the thick of it.

She could see a scrape on his knee and a bruise forming above his elbow. He did not believe in shouting instructions from the sideline. He put his body on the line
practice after practice. And, judging by the satisfaction she
could see in his eyes, he loved it. Despite their deal to keep
it friendly, he made her heart go flippity-flop every time
he sent her that engaging grin, and with the way his eyes
heated when they settled on her face. Lu closed her laptop
lid as he took the seat opposite her and offered her a taste
of his just-opened soda.

Lu took a sip and handed it back. 'You look like you
took a couple of hits on the field.'

Will rubbed his shoulder. 'I did. Jabu is the human
equivalent of a Sherman tank.'

'Thanks for what you did this morning. Again.'

'No problem. Again,' Will answered as the others sat down around them.

Lu greeted them and asked what their plans were for the evening.

Jabu yawned. 'Nothing more exciting than an early night. Training was brutal this afternoon; Wednesdays are the worst day.'

Will grinned. 'Whiner.'

Jabu lifted a lazy middle finger and yawned again. Looking over Lu's head to the television mounted on the wall, he sat up and reached for the remote control on the table in front of him. 'Hey, Will—your ex is on.'

Unlike the others, who immediately looked at the screen, Lu looked at Will. His face tightened instinctively, his lips thinned and his eyes darkened. Jabu adjusted the volume control and Lu reluctantly looked over her shoulder.

Beautiful. Lean and long, finely muscled. Long blonde hair, big blue eyes, legs that went on for ever. High cheekbones and a quirky mouth completed the package. How and why had Will let her go?

'Do you mind if we watch it, Will?' Matt demanded. 'Your ex is a fox!'

'Knock yourself out,' Will replied, looking for all the world as if he didn't give a damn. Which he *so* did. She could see it in his flattened mouth, in his tapping finger on the side of his thigh.

They listened to Jo talking about her training schedule, her fitness regime. Lu cast the occasional look at Will and sighed every time. His face was a mask of control, his body seemingly relaxed but his eyes radiating tension and frustration.

The interviewer was asking another question. 'So, Jo, you're now ranked at number two in the world, but there was a time when your off-court antics garnered a lot of news.'

Lu saw the flash of panic in Will's eyes but still he didn't react.

'Yeah, it's not a time in my life I'm proud of…'

'Shortly after your divorce you turned your life around. You embraced religion, cleaned up your act. Why do you think it took Will Scott so much longer to do the same thing?'

Everyone else in the room inhaled and Will forced out a laugh. 'Because I was having too much damn fun, jackass.'

His friends laughed, relieved when they heard his jokey tone. Only Kelby, Lu thought, might suspect that he was acting his socks off.

'It was only two years—and I wouldn't presume to talk on Will's behalf,' Jo replied.

'Your marriage was characterised by fighting and making up. When you were happy you were ecstatic—when you were fighting it was obvious. Despite that, the world thought your marriage would survive. So what precipitated your divorce?'

'God, why do people still *care*?' Will demanded. 'Aren't there any twenty-year-olds behaving badly these days?'

'Not as many as we'd like.' Matt shook his head sadly. 'And few of them are as good entertainment as you and Jo were. You two *rocked*!'

'Until I nearly lost my career because I couldn't come to work sober or at the very least not hungover,' Will said, speaking over Jo's reply. 'And talking of that…while I've got the CEO, the Captain and the Vice-Captain here all at the same time, with no other ears listening, you guys need to do something about Campher. He's on something. Drugs, booze, pills, steroids—I don't know what, but it's something.'

Jabu swore. 'It hasn't popped up in the drug tests.'

'I'm telling you he's on something,' Will said. 'I'm only here for another eight weeks. You still have the rest of the season with him. I'll order a comprehensive drug screening, but I wanted to run it past you first.'

Three heads nodded their agreement and then turned back to the television screen.

'Are you proud of what he's done? Achieved?'

The interviewer was still talking about Will.

'Sure. I always knew that Will was destined for great things. We both just took a detour, lost our way for a bit. Why are people still wanting to hear about it?'

'You were good entertainment value. So, let's talk about your sponsorship deals, Jo.'

Matt jabbed his finger upwards. 'You see—he agrees with me! Now you're just old and boring, Scott.'

Will stood up and swatted Matt across the head. 'Funny—you didn't say that when I face-planted you this afternoon. I need to do some paperwork before I leave, so I'm going to head off.'

He hadn't even made eye contact with her, Lu thought as she watched his departing back. Yep, he was good at concealing his emotions—but so was she, and she knew what to look for.

Will had instinctively headed for the far corner of the gym, avoided the fancy equipment and yanked a pair of gloves from the shelf on the far wall. Jamming them between his knees, he pulled off his T-shirt, divested himself of his trainers and socks and left the pile of clothes on the floor next to an exercise mat. Pulling the gloves on, he proceeded to punch and kick the stuffing out of the dangling bag.

Kelby had made him do this years ago. Every time he'd felt out of control and frustrated he'd found a bag and pummelled it. At one time he'd been spending so much time with the punch bag that he signed up for Thai kick-boxing and learnt to do it properly.

He only ever did this now when he was feeling particularly stressed or when…*punch, kick, punch*…he felt out of control.

What was it about watching Jo this evening that had pushed every button he had? She was a prominent personality but he'd learnt how to hear about her, see her on the screen, read about her, with a detachment that came from a decade apart. Why now?

It had nothing to do with Jo, he realised, and everything to do with the life he'd led when he was with her—the person he'd been. Fun, crazy, spontaneous…out of control.

Being with Lu, spending time with her, reminded him of that person he'd once been. Oh, there was no alcohol or drugs involved this time, no dancing on bars and wrecking cars, but like during the best times he'd had back then they *did* have fun. They laughed. They talked.

They *didn't* screw like bunnies.

And they were rapidly becoming friends—proper friends. Instead of just finding her to be a fun person to hang with he was finding that he wanted to tell her things, open up. And that scared him to death. Sex would have been so much easier. This? Not so much.

Being with Lu made him feel like the best version of who he'd been as a young man. Fun. Spontaneous. Curious.

Alive.

He'd been all of that and more. He'd been touted as the most promising young player in a generation—a team man, an amazing talent. Then he'd met Jo and had—oh, so willingly—fallen into the wild life she'd embraced. They'd married on a whim in Bali, and their life together had been fuelled by booze and dope and causing as much chaos as they could. They'd been untouchable, arrogant and superior. He'd started to work less and believe his own press more, had become enamoured of the adulation and adoration of fans and groupies. For a long time he'd thought he was a special person with a talent for rugby. It had taken Kelby to make him realise that he was just an ordinary guy with a special talent for the game.

As for their marriage…he'd been bored with her within three months and hadn't been able to understand why. Sure, she was smoking hot—but she was also bright. Something he'd frequently forgotten. She could be hysterically funny, had superior mattress skills and a personality as big as the sun. There had been no reason to get bored with her. She was everything he'd ever thought he'd wanted but…

The spark had died. Quickly.

Could he be blamed for having doubts about his ability to stay in a relationship, to commit to a relationship? He'd been handed everything any guy anywhere in the world would sell his soul for and he hadn't wanted it. But he'd kept it going—and he suspected she had too—because he'd earned big bragging points for being married to the sexiest woman in the world. And he'd liked the attention.

He hadn't had the balls to break it off…until she did. Apparently there really *wasn't* any good excuse for having an Argentinean woman in your room at three in the morning when you were married.

Will snapped a full round-house kick at the punching bag and followed the kick with an upper-cut when the bag came roaring back towards him. He'd been a yellow-bellied coward and after the divorce, instead of putting up his hand and saying sorry, he had bounced from affair to affair, party to party, bottle to bottle, making more of an ass of himself every month, losing a little more respect for himself every day.

If it hadn't been for Kelby…

Will glanced at his watch. He'd been at it for a half-hour and he hadn't even noticed. Sweat snaked down his bare spine into the back of his shorts and his hair was matted to his head. Using the back of his wrist, he pushed the hair back from his face and hauled air into his lungs. The adrenalin and anger were gone and he realised that he was utterly exhausted, his muscles beyond fatigued. Between the run this morning, the full body contact practice this afternoon and beating the crap out of this bag, he was skating on the edge of physical exhaustion.

Will grabbed the sides of the bag and rested his sticky forehead on the thick plastic. Well, he should sleep well tonight—that was if he didn't start thinking about his crappy past. And Lu. And how much longer he could keep his hands off her…

Will turned on hearing the gentle slap of Lu's sandals as she crossed the gym.

'How long have you been here?' he demanded, pulling off one glove with his teeth, then ridding himself of the other.

Lu tossed him a bottle of water which he caught with his free hand. 'A while. Want to talk about it?'

Will cracked the lid and took a long sip before sinking to sit on an exercise mat. He held Lu's sympathetic eyes as water slid down his throat.

'Nothing to talk about,' he said when he'd lowered the bottle.

Lu tipped her head and shook her head. 'The past loses its power when it's talked about. Secrets too.'

'What would you know about secrets and the power they hold over people, Lu?'

Lu's eyes sharpened and hardened. 'Try clearing out your parents' personal effects on your own at nineteen and say that again, Scott.'

Will winced. '*Ouch*. Did you learn some stuff you'd rather not know?'

Lu folded her arms and tapped her foot. 'Yes. So don't

try and take the high road with me about secrets. I know what I'm talking about.'

Will stretched out his legs and placed his hands on the mat behind him. 'Bet you haven't shared them with your brothers.'

Lu twisted her lips. 'There are some things they don't need to know.'

'And there are some things the world doesn't need to know about *my* life.'

Lu's mouth thinned. 'I'm not talking about the world, Will. I'm suggesting that you talk things through so that you don't have to kick a bag.'

'I like kicking the bag.'

Lu threw up her hands. 'OK, if you're going to be facetious then I give up. I'll just go and leave you to it.'

The words were stiff and staccato and Will sighed at the hurt look that passed over her face. A part of him wished he could tell her, wished he *could* trust enough to talk it over with her, to confess his stupidity. But apart from the fact that he was not in the habit of talking about himself he thought that talking to Lu about it would be akin to slicing himself open and watching himself bleed. He also didn't want to see the look of disgust on her face, to see her disappointment in the man he'd used to be…a man he suspected still lurked under his tightly held cloak of control.

'I'll see you when I see you.'

Lu turned to go but Will's leg shot out, gently catching Lu behind the knees. She tumbled to the mat, landing on her back next to him.

'What the—?'

Before she could say another word Will rolled onto her and covered her mouth with his. Her fist clenched against his shoulder, but as his tongue touched hers her tension disappeared and her hand opened, fingers splaying over him and branding his bare skin.

Will pulled his head back to look down at her, raised his hand so that the tips of his fingers brushed her cheek.

'Lu, if there was anybody I could tell it would be you. I just don't…can't…talk about it.'

She echoed his action, lifting her hand to touch his face. 'You need to talk to somebody about it. You can't kick the hell out of a bag every time you get angry.'

'Actually, I can.' Will's eyes glinted down at her. 'I need to. It's the only way to relieve the tension.'

He knew that Lu felt his erection along her hipbone— could feel his accelerated heartbeat beneath her hand. They both knew it but didn't acknowledge the other, tried and tested way to relieve stress. He liked feeling her under him, but he also liked the fact that she'd noticed that he was out of sorts, that she cared enough to make the effort to comfort him.

Will's eyes collided with hers and underneath the attraction he saw sympathy there, and understanding. Flat-out affection. He could care for this woman. He really could. But when it all went south and the flames died—as they always did—he suspected that he'd be left with third degree burns.

Not an option.

Will reluctantly rolled off her and heard Lu's sweet sigh of exasperation. He knew how she felt. He craved her too. They lay on their backs on the mat for a while, staring at the ceiling.

Lu rolled her head on the mat to look at the bag and couldn't believe she was about to say what she was about to say.

'Does it work for sexual tension too?'

Will sighed. 'Not as good as a cold shower but…yeah.'

'Want to teach me?'

'Are you sexually frustrated, Mermaid?'

Will's hand slid over hers and squeezed. She knew that

he'd been aiming for a jokey tone, but his words had come out pained instead.

And instead of sounding cool and sophisticated *her* words were soft and sad. 'Well, I have this guy that I'm mega-attracted to, and in a fit of madness we agreed that it would be better to just be friends. I'm having the best fun with him, but sometimes I just want to...'

Will pulled in a hot breath. 'Nail him?'

'Yeah.' Lu wrinkled her nose as her rueful eyes met his. Like him, she'd been aiming to lighten the tension, but instead she'd just tumbled them into a miasma of emotion. Lu wanted to look away and couldn't—wanted to make a sassy comment but couldn't find any words to say.

Will's hand contracted around hers. 'God, Lu, I know how you feel.'

'I'm having so much fun with you and I don't want to spoil it, so I'll punch a bag if that helps,' Lu gabbled.

Will rolled to his side and placed his free hand on her face. 'I don't want to spoil it, either so I'll teach you to box,' he said, his voice rough. 'But if we don't get up soon we won't need to punch anything.'

Lu turned her face into his hand and dropped a kiss on his palm. 'OK.'

But they still lay there for a while longer, his one hand holding hers, the other on her face, feeling physically and emotionally connected.

Whoops, Lu thought. That wasn't supposed to happen.

It was late Sunday afternoon and Lu was attempting, unsuccessfully, to make the transition from lying on her surfboard to standing up. Will, standing hip-deep in the Indian Ocean off North Beach, was trying to hide his smile.

'Stop laughing at me, you jerk!' Lu shouted at him as she popped up from under a two-foot wave. 'We weren't all born super co-ordinated!'

'You'll get there,' Will told her, laughing as she rubbed her face.

She would have given up hours ago, but she knew that learning to surf was a way to get some distance from their emotionally charged discussion in the gym the other night.

Constantly looking like an idiot and getting sand in her bikini bottoms was a small price to pay to put the fun and laughter back into their…whatever it was they had.

'I would like to point out, for the record, that we only seem to be doing things *you* like to do.' Lu slapped her hands on her hips. 'We never made it to that art exhibition—and what happened to dance classes?'

'We're going to the photography exhibition,' Will pointed out.

'That's in two weeks' time,' Lu retorted. 'I'm sick of sucking at sport.'

Will laughed. 'Say that again—five times and fast.'

'I'm sip at supping at…*aaargh*!'

Will laughed as he walked through the water to her and took her board from her grasp. 'That's enough for today; Mak and Deon look ready to leave anyway.'

Lu looked towards the beach, where Mak and Deon stood at the water's edge, Deon's head droopy against Mak's arms. The four of them had spent the afternoon there and Will and Mak had spent hours tossing a rugby ball to Deon, much to his delight. They'd all taken turns to swim with him too, and the little guy was utterly, happily exhausted.

Lu scooped him up, gave him a huge kiss and handed him over to Will, who piggy-backed him back to their bags and towels scattered over the still hot sand. Will put Deon on his feet, helped Mak load up their bags and rubbed Deon's head.

'Are you coming to the stadium with the St Clare's kids on Tuesday?'

Deon nodded. 'I'm their main man.'

Will grinned. 'That you are. Later, dude.'

'Later, dude,' Deon echoed and the adults laughed.

After they'd left, Will cocked his head at Lu. 'I'm going back in. You coming?'

Lu nodded and they turned back to the sea, sighing as the warm Indian Ocean crept higher the further in they went.

'School and work day tomorrow,' Lu said, as the waves lapped against her chest.

She wondered what the twins had been up to today…if they'd had as much fun as she had. On days like these— beach days, happy days—she missed them with every cell in her body. She'd been fighting the urge to call them all day, and the couple of messages she'd sent them still, as of ten minutes ago, remained unread. They were never without their phones, so what had they been *doing* all day?

Lu felt Will's thumb brush the space between her eyebrows and she turned her head to look at him. 'Sometimes you drift away and then this frown appears.'

'Sun in my eyes,' Lu replied blithely.

'Yeah, tell me another one.' Will snorted.

Lu snuck a look at his frustrated face. 'How come you want me to talk but you don't…or won't?'

'Because I'm a guy.'

Lu's snort was bigger than his. 'We're really good at having fun and really bad at talking to each other about the things that go deep,' she commented. 'I know that you were seriously upset after seeing your ex on TV—'

'I wasn't.'

'Will.' Just her saying his name had his protest dying on his lips. 'And I'm missing the twins. Yet we still try to pretend that everything is fine.'

'I don't know how to—' Will stopped and automatically reached out to steady her as a large wave broke over them. Using his strength, he planted his feet and kept her upright as water rushed over her head. Lu linked her arms around his neck, droplets of water on her face.

'I wish you'd talk to me, Will,' Lu murmured, frustrated. He was holding back, keeping her at arm's length mentally, and she didn't like it. If he could push *her* out of her comfort zone why couldn't she do the same for him?

The problem was that he just had to look at her with those hot eyes and she forgot about comfort zones and talking and anything else but her need to have his mouth on hers.

Will kissed her shoulder as he whispered, 'I'll tell you that I think you are incredibly beautiful."

Lu hiccupped a laugh. 'Freckly and skinny.'

'Beautifully, gorgeously freckly and skinny,' Will insisted. He looked down into her eyes. 'I don't know how to do this…the other stuff…the talking stuff. I can't do it—haven't the skills. But this…this I know.'

Yes, Lu thought. And it was the perfect end to a wonderful day as Will's tongue slipped into her mouth and his hands pulled her hips into his.

Her stomach pressed against his erection and her breasts were flattened against his chest. She felt uninhibited and free. His actions under the water were hidden from the last few people on the beach, and the surfers were too far away for them to see and too uninterested to give a hoot. Scooting her hand up his hip, she caressed his stomach, feeling the wonder of the warm skin over hard muscles. Will responded by cupping her breast, instinctively seeking her nipple, which instantly bloomed in his hand.

Lu gasped and wrenched her mouth away from his, arching her back as she buried her face in his neck and swiped her tongue across his skin. This was what she'd been missing—this intensity, this flood of lust and emotion that she hadn't experienced with a man in a long, long time.

Will groaned as he snuck his hands under her pink bi-

kini top and tangled her tongue with his. He sensed her
frustration and responded with a silent chuckle. She wasn't
the only one who craved more. But suddenly this wasn't
about him. This was about Lu and the pleasure he could
give her—the pleasure he knew she hadn't experienced in
a long, long time…if ever.

'Wrap your legs around my waist, honey,' he murmured
against her mouth.

Lu, eyes glazed with passion, obliged. Will dropped his
gaze to look down between them. Her thighs were slim and
baby-smooth; he could feel her hipbone under the palm
of his other hand. A beaded ring was hooked through her
belly button.

'Just enjoy, Lu,' Will told her, and saw the soft reply in
her eyes, tasted it in her lifted lips.

She became compliant beneath him, her trust that he
would take care of her blindingly obvious. Will braced himself by pushing his feet into the sand while kissing her—
he couldn't get enough of her luscious mouth. He moved
his hand over her ankle and calf, tracing his way up her
thigh, lingering to knead her bottom. His long fingers slid
under her bikini bottom to stroke lightly between her legs.
He ignored her whimper and felt her intake of breath as
he moved his hand between them and trailed it over her,
bending his head to kiss her again, feeling her throb beneath his fingertips. His fingers—urgent now—slid into
her furrows, automatically finding her nub, causing her to
lift her hips, thrusting into his hand. Astounded at her passionate reaction, by the tension he could feel in her, Will
felt immensely powerful, intensely male.

He felt her orgasm against his hand, saw it in her eyes,
heard it in her whimpered cries.

She made him feel more of a man…

Long, long minutes later she dropped her feet back into
the sand and pushed her hands through her hair. As long

as he lived Will knew that he'd never forget Lu standing chest deep in the sea, tipping her face up to catch the last of the sunshine, looking a lot like the mermaid he sometimes imagined her to be.

'What are we going to do about this, Lu?' he demanded as they walked back towards the beach. 'We're dancing around it and something is going to have to give—soon.'

Lu ran her hands through her hair again, making spikes. 'I don't know, Will! I *don't*! I know that I want you, but I don't want to stop having fun with you either—and that was the deal, remember? Sex and you walk. No sex and you don't.'

'Whose stupid idea was that?' he muttered under his breath. 'Oh, that must have been yours, Scott. Moron.'

It *was* the deal, and he'd thought it made sense all those weeks back, when his life had made sense. Will grabbed a towel off the beach mat and swiped it across his face. He didn't know how much longer he could resist her—resist the temptation to take her to bed, to make her his. But she terrified him. She had the ability to make him lose focus, to do the things, *feel* the things he'd used to when his life had been out of control. Like acting first and thinking later. His life had the potential to spiral out of control when he allowed that side of his personality to rule.

With Lu, his devil-may-care side was demanding a lot more decision making opportunities and—what had Kelby called him?—Mr Disciplined Control was taking a beating.

Either way, he felt as if he was fighting a demonic alien invasion with a water pistol in a desert.

Lu could see all her confusion reflected in Will's eyes. He wanted her—she'd have to be dead not to realise that—but he didn't *want* to want her. As for her, she knew that if they moved from friends to lovers then she would be inviting a whole bunch of complicated craziness into her life. It would be a lot harder to say goodbye to a lover than a friend when he left, and even worse it would be so much more difficult to keep her mind thinking *friends*, her body thinking *lover* and her heart out of the equation if she was sleeping with him.

Lu held his gaze, hating his rigid self-control. He wasn't going to ask her to bed, wasn't going to take that step. If only they could really talk to each other…

What would she say?

I love spending time with you, she told him silently. *But I don't think that I'm ready for a relationship, strings or not. I'm just getting to know myself again, learning to be on my own. I'm finally coming into myself, learning who I am without the responsibility of raising the twins. If we hook up I'll have someone back in my life and I don't know if I'm ready for that. Because you are a strong character, a protector, another alpha personality, and when you go I'll be back to square one, learning to be on my own again.*

It was so hard to resist him, and it would be easy to let him slide into all the empty spaces in her heart and home that the boys had left. But for the first time in her life she had to think about what was best for *her* and, as much as she thought it would be fun, she didn't think it was a smart move long-term. For the first time in a decade she didn't have to worry about someone else—and she liked it.

Lu sighed. 'Will?'

'Yeah?'

'Do you know that neither of us has said anything for ten minutes?'

Will shrugged. 'OK…so?'

'If we need to think about it so much maybe we should leave things the way they are?'

Will twisted his lips. 'Confused and horny?'

Give the man another gold star, Lu thought morosely.

CHAPTER EIGHT

'So, Carter has been cleared to come back to work in a month…'

Will stared at Kelby, nonplussed. 'That means that I can leave Durban in a month or so?'

'We'll pay you out for the full three months.'

He didn't give a toss about the money. It was leaving Lu earlier than he'd bargained for that was threatening to throw him into a tailspin.

'Also, at the director's meeting last night, the board agreed that Carter will retire in six months. I can offer you a position as consultant coach until then and a five-year contract as head coach when he's gone. What do you think?'

Will yanked his thoughts away from Lu. 'Giving control back to Carter sucks. I don't know if I can do it and then work under him.'

'It's for six months, dude! And he's a good coach. You'd learn a lot from him.'

Will placed his hands on Kelby's desk and straightened his arms, thinking it through. 'I've been getting other offers from other teams. Firm consultant and then head coach offers from Melbourne and Auckland.'

Kelby leaned back in his chair. 'Have you talked to Lu about any of this?'

Will frowned at him. 'No.'

'Don't you think you should?'

Will stood up and folded his arms belligerently. Because he was still reeling at the thought of how much he didn't want to leave her, he narrowed his eyes at Kelby's comment. 'She isn't a factor. We're just friends.'

'Friends! Yeah, keep telling yourself that.' Kelby shook his head in disbelief. 'And if you let her go then you're crazier than I gave you credit for.'

Let her go? He hadn't even *had* her yet! He'd spent most of last night tossing and turning, and when he *had* slept his dreams had been super-hot and had involved him taking Lu fifty ways to Sunday.

As a result he was tired, irritable, and still as confused and even hornier than he had been yesterday afternoon. He thought he was either a saint or an idiot to have dropped her off at home after their day on the beach and left her there.

No, he was definitely an idiot.

Will glanced at his watch. 'I've got to go. I'm late as it is.'

Kelby frowned. 'Late for what?'

'Game analysis. It's at four.'

'Do you *ever* read any of the memos I send you? I asked for game analysis to be postponed because Lu is doing that nude calendar shoot with the squad this evening.'

Will turned around very slowly and sent Kelby his death-ray glare. 'What. Did. You. Say?'

Kelby didn't do a very good job of trying to hide his smile. 'Twelve of the franchise clubs are collaborating on a calendar featuring the various teams to raise money for charity. Each franchise is responsible for capturing their own discreet image of the team.'

'And Lu is doing this?'

Kelby looked innocent. 'She *is* our photographer. I don't know why you're looking so surprised about this. I've been mailing you about it all week!'

'I saw the subject heading and thought you were joking.'

'And Lu didn't mention it to you?'

Will frowned. 'I think she did. I said something about it being a stupid-ass idea and that anyone associated with it was stupid…she hasn't mentioned it again.'

'I can't imagine why,' Kelby said dryly.

Will's mouth flattened. 'I'm really not happy about this.'

'Lucky for you that I don't give a toss whether you're happy about it or not. It's her job.'

Right.

'Where are they doing the shoot?' Will demanded.

'In the gym.' Kelby stood up as Will whipped around and headed for the door. 'Will, don't you dare go down there! Don't make things difficult…'

Kelby sank back into his chair as Will ignored his order. *Friends? Yeah, right!* He hoped that Will didn't make the shoot difficult for Lu, but he wouldn't bet money on it. Kelby lumbered to his feet. Maybe he'd wander down to the gym for a little bit of light entertainment…

She needed a fan. She needed a walk-in fridge. She needed to stop blushing, Lu thought as fifteen briefs-clad, buff, super-sexy rugby players streamed into the Rays' gym, their second home. Will was standing off to one side, fully clothed in jeans and a T-shirt, and the scowl on his face was as black as a summer thundercloud.

He'd yet to say a word to her.

Boxers, briefs, even a set of Y-fronts… *Good grief, Lu, you can't look there!* Was the air-con working down here? The team members weren't fazed about lounging around in their underwear. They chatted and joked and insulted each other about the size of their tackle and the state of their underpants.

'We'll let Lu decide,' Matt hooted.

Lu lifted her eyebrows. 'Decide on what?'

'Boxers, briefs or thongs,' Matt explained. 'What do women prefer?'

Lu kept her face blank, knowing that they were trying to get a reaction. She knew boys—they'd push her until they got one. She hadn't raised twin boys and had all their friends using her house as a second home for nothing. But she couldn't look at Will, because then he'd know that she preferred commando.

Actually, just him buck naked would do the trick.

Matt snapped his fingers under her nose. 'Lu! Concentrate, here—this is important research!'

Lu reached up and patted his cheek. 'Sweetie…trust me. If I liked you enough to get to the point of wanting to rip your underwear off I wouldn't really care what you were wearing. Though I'd have second thoughts if you were wearing a red thong with black lace…that's just tacky.'

Matt placed his hand on her cheek and his eyes twinkled with fun. 'But you'd like a leopard print thong, right?'

Lu laughed and played along. 'Absolutely! Who can resist a man in a leopard print thong?'

Matt put his thumbs into his black boxers and shimmied them down his hips. Lu slapped her hands over her face and peeked out through her fingers as Matt did a slow turn, wearing nothing more than the briefest, tackiest, fakest leopard print thong.

Lu dropped her hand and bellowed with laughter as Matt posed in front of her, his hip thrust out in a typical model pose. She clapped before placing the back of one hand on her forehead and pretending to swoon.

The room roared. Matt high-fived her and Lu was still laughing when Will stepped away from the wall and cleared his throat. Cold eyes drilled through her and her laughter died in her throat as the room fell into an uncomfortable silence.

He jerked his head at the gym door. 'Outside.'

Lu frowned. 'Sorry?'

'I want to talk to you…outside,' Will stated, in a biting voice vibrating with anger.

'Lu's in trub-bel,' Matt sang, and then winced when Will walked up to him and slammed his hand against Matt's chest. Matt took two steps backwards.

'If you know what's good for you, you'll shut up,' Will stated calmly, his eyes spitting.

Matt held his hands up. 'Yes, boss.'

'You—outside.'

Will looked at Lu and his furious expression had Lu climbing down from the table and walking towards the door. She heard the door slam behind her and looked up at Will, who was obviously thundercloud angry. What was his problem?

'Stop flirting with Matt,' Will stated through clenched teeth.

Wha-at?

'Jeez, Will, he was just trying to make the situation less awkward,' Lu replied, confused. He couldn't be taking their banter seriously, could he? 'What *is* your problem?'

Will stepped in front of her and pushed her back against the wall. He placed a palm on the wall next to her head and loomed over her. 'My problem? You're about to get fifteen guys naked and the only one I want you to see naked is me. *That's* my problem. I'm frustrated and as horny as hell. That's another problem. I don't care if this is your job. I. Don't. Like. It.'

It was the first time she'd seen Will totally stripped of the cloak of control he constantly wore. His eyes were full of misery and frustration. His body was clenched with tension. He looked almost unhinged.

Over *her* being surrounded by hot, buff men… Well, shoot!

As much as she wanted to smash her mouth against his and be kissed by this out-of-control Will, she had a job to do—a job that was important to her. The other rugby franchises, as Kelby had told her, were hiring big-name photographers to capture their images for the calendar, but he had faith in her that she wouldn't let their side down.

She had no intention of doing that, but she couldn't do it with Will hovering like an angry tornado; he'd make the players tense, they wouldn't relax while he was watching over them, and she wouldn't be able to function. She had to get rid of him. Yet she knew that nothing shy of a dynamite stick would get him to leave.

So Lu stood on her tiptoes, slammed her mouth against his and slid her tongue into his mouth. Her kiss was openmouthed and hot enough to drain all the blood from his brain…just what she needed. It took all her will-power to step away before Will caught her in his grip and wouldn't let her go.

Stepping back quickly, she gave him a quick salute, slipped through the door to the gym, slammed it closed and turned the lock. Ignoring his furious fist pounding against the door, she walked back inside and went to the box she'd carried in earlier and yanked out an i-Pod and external speakers.

'Who wants music?' she asked loudly.

'Yes! But a drink would be better!' Matt responded above a chorus of approval and whistles.

Lu grinned as she pulled two bottles of tequila from the box and waved them in the air. 'I also think this would be a lot easier with a couple of shots. There are quite a few bottles, so don't be shy. But we'd better get slammed *before* Mr Grumpy breaks down the door!'

Lu, dressed in a brief pair of cycling shorts, a crop top and trainers, stood in front of the punching bag in the empty Rays gym and looked down at the small pair of boxing gloves that Will had just tied onto her hands.

'I tried to book a private lesson for you at a Thai kick-boxing school with one of Kelby's mates who is an instructor, but they have a couple of cage fights coming up so he's swamped,' Will told her, dropping her hands. He stepped away from her to get some distance. She was wearing little more than underwear, and his boys weren't making the distinction between gym clothes and lingerie.

It had been a week since he'd held her in his arms, and he'd never be able to look at the sea again without remembering how responsive she'd been to his touch. He'd had a lot of sex over the years, but even the thought of Lu far exceeded the hottest, craziest sex he'd had before.

It was shocking to realise that he, King of Brief Flings, could think like this. He was a rational adult male. He knew that great sex never lasted for ever. It went from great to good, then to OK, and then it faded to *blah* and then to mechanical.

It would happen even with Lu.

Lu interrupted his thoughts. 'Right—gloves on, punch bag waiting.'

Her small hand ploughed into the bag and it drifted ever so slightly. 'That wasn't so good.' She frowned. 'When you hit it, it swings!'

Will grinned. 'That's because I'm lot stronger than you and also because you punch like a girl.'

'Fist into bag. That was a punch,' Lu protested.

'A *girl* punch. You need to put some body weight behind it,' Will told her. 'Stand with your feet shoulder width apart, bend your knees. OK, good. Make a loose fist with each hand and lift, elbows straight out behind you. That's it. Now, push off with your back foot and rotate your wrist and shoulder as you throw the punch.' Will watched as her fist connected with the bag and rocked. 'Better than before.'

'This is hard,' Lu muttered as she tried again.

'Keep your wrist straight. Push off your back foot.' Girl

punching still, Will thought, but, seeing the determined look on her face, he knew that she would get it right if it killed her. Lu, he was coming to realise, had the determination of a dung beetle and the stubbornness of a mule.

'When do I learn to kick?' Lu demanded, huffing.

'When you've learned how to punch,' Will told her. 'Keep your other hand up to guard your face. Don't leave your face vulnerable to attack.'

'Who's going to hit me?' Lu demanded.

'If you are going to learn, then do it properly.'

Lu pulled a tongue at him and rocketed her fist into the bag , making it sway harder than before.

'Better.'

After twenty minutes Lu rested her hands on her thighs and looked up at the bag. 'I could've done with one of these when my folks died.'

It was the first time she'd willingly mentioned their death and Will fought not to react, waiting for her to talk. 'There were days when I was so sad and so angry that I used to punch my bed. This is better.'

Will walked over to the fridge next to the mat, pulled out a bottle of water, cracked the lid and held it to Lu's lips. She drank and sank to the mat, crossing her legs as she sat down.

Will joined her and they sat in silence for a while before he asked another question that he'd been wondering about. 'Who told you? About the accident?'

'Mak. He was our next-door neighbour at the time.'

'How did you cope?' Will asked.

'What do you mean?' Lu asked, giving him a blank look.

'Lu, you were a teenager and suddenly responsible for two kids. How did you deal with your parents' deaths? With having your life splattered against a wall?'

Lu was silent for a long time, her eyes on her shoes. 'Strange…nobody has ever asked me that before.'

'You're kidding?'

She bit her bottom lip. 'Nope. People would ask if I was OK but would barely wait for an answer before demanding to know how the twins were coping, whether they were getting counseling, how sad it was that they were orphaned so young.'

Will's heart cracked at the pain coating her words. 'You were also orphaned.'

'But I wasn't eight and blond and cute,' Lu replied.

'So how did *you* cope?' Will repeated his question.

Lu shrugged. 'I don't know, actually. The first six months were a bit of a blur. We cried a lot. I remember that. I also remember doing a lot of exercise with the boys— playing soccer with them, taking them to the beach, making them as tired as possible so that we could all just sleep without dreaming, trying to avoid the nightmares.'

'The boys had nightmares?'

'Not so much.'

'You?'

'Constantly.'

Will lifted his hand and rubbed his thumb along one prominent cheekbone, then he brushed the violet shadows under her eyes. 'Are the nightmares back, Lu?'

'No.'

'But you're not sleeping?' He could see the start of a lie, an excuse, then saw her pull it back and opt for the truth.

'No, not much.'

Will knew that he wasn't stupid when it came to women; he knew that Lu was thinking. She just wasn't as good at hiding it as he was. He'd noticed the way her eyes lingered on his lips, caught the shudder of attraction when he brushed past her. He suspected that, like him, she lay awake at night remembering the feel of naked skin, the warmth of lips and the heat of hands.

Dangerous thoughts…

Will pulled back and jumped to his feet before reaching down and pulling Lu to her feet. 'Punch that bag for another twenty minutes and I guarantee that you'll sleep well tonight.'

'I don't want to sleep.' The words flew out of her mouth and she didn't know where they'd come from. Maybe it was because she felt so at ease with him, so connected. 'One night. That's it. In the morning we go back to being friends, pretend it didn't happen.'

Will's eyes widened in surprise. He wasn't sure if he was hearing what he thought he was hearing. 'What?'

'You—me—bed. In the morning we go back to normal. What do you think?'

Will's eyes heated. 'I should say no…'

Lu's eyes sparked dangerously. 'I swear, if you say no I will punch you so hard you'll never recover!'

Will threw up his hands. 'Peace! My blood just rushed south. I can't think. Except to say…yes! And thank God.'

'Better,' Lu replied, trying to yank her gloves off with her teeth. 'Get these off me so that I can put my hands on you.'

Will stopped just outside of her reach. 'Do *not* touch me, Lu.'

Lu gaped at him. 'What? Why?'

'You touch me and we won't get outside this room,' Will muttered, then grabbed a glove and started pulling at its strings. 'Seriously, Lu, no touching. Yet.'

Lu flushed. All over.

She waved her hands, agitated. 'Hurry!'

As Will roared up to her gate Lu scrabbled in her bag, looking for the keyring that held the remote control to her electric gate.

'Hurry,' Will whispered, his hand hot and high on her thigh.

'Where *is* the damn thing?' Lu demanded.

'Lu, you're killing me here.' Will grabbed her bag and tipped it upside down so that the contents scattered over her lap. 'You women carry around a lot of junk.'

Lu slapped her hand against her forehead. 'Side pocket!' Fumbling with the bag, she opened the side pocket, yanked out her keys and pointed the remote in the vague direction of the gate. As soon as there was enough space to manoeuvre his Range Rover through the opening Will floored the accelerator and then screeched to a halt and parked the car in a spare space in the garage. The garage door automatically shut behind them and Will groaned as he turned to her.

'I really don't know if I can walk inside.'

Turning, spilling the contents of her bag onto the floor, she clasped his jaw and nipped his mouth, her tongue making tiny forays into his mouth. 'Would it help if I came over there and climbed all over you?' she murmured against his mouth.

Will groaned. 'Yes. Would it help you?'

'So much.'

Will shoved his seat back as Lu scooted across the console and straddled Will's knees.

'Love the fact this is a big car.'

Will pushed a button and his chair flattened out. 'Me too.'

He captured her roving hands and his expression was serious when he looked up at her. 'Lu…stop. Wait…just for a second.'

Lu's hands stilled and then bunched in frustration. 'What?'

'I want you so much, and if you stop this I swear I'll die, but you've got to know…understand. I'm leaving soon—going back to my life in En Zed. I can't get emotionally involved. Love, commitment…us…is not part of the deal. So this would be…'

'A one-time thing. I know. I said that! Suggested it,' Lu said, licking the tendon that ran down the side of his neck. 'I get it, Will. One night… In the morning we go back to…before.'

'One night. Do you want to go inside?'

'I can't wait that long,' Lu muttered, and Will nodded his agreement.

His hand slid under the loose shirt she'd pulled over her cropped exercise top and he pulled all the garments up and over her head, tossing them onto the passenger seat. Then his thumbs slid across her nipples and all hell broke loose.

Their lips collided and they fought for domination of the kiss. Will shoved his fingers down the back of her pants and pushed her over him as he dropped his mouth to her bare breast. Lu forgot where she was as she ground herself onto his steel hard erection, desperate to have him inside her, to be around him.

Will lifted his head from her chest and yanked his shirt over his head. With Lu's help, he slid his shorts out from under him. Lu, deciding they were taking too long, balanced on one foot and shucked her shorts and panties. Barely giving Will time to cover himself with a condom, she climbed back on him, took him in hand and guided him into her. Groaning as he stretched and filled her, she tucked her face into his neck and inhaled, desperate to use every sense to experience the essence of loving him.

She could feel the banked tension in his hand as he gripped her thighs, the urgency in his tongue as he looked for and found her mouth. She felt him quiver inside her. Needing him, she bore down and clenched her internal muscles.

She couldn't slow this down…didn't want to…besides they had all night. They could explore each other later…

Will started to buck beneath her and she grabbed his shoulders so as not to topple off. He bit his lip, lifted his hips and launched himself deeper into her. She pushed down, determined to be the one to make him lose control.

Harder, higher, deeper, faster. Their world receded and the only question of importance was who was going to come first. Lu whimpered and Will shouted as their worlds exploded. Neither could tell where one started or the other ended, yet both claimed the victory of making the other lose control first, for giving their one-night lover as much pleasure as they possibly could in a large but still cramped car in a dark garage at the end of a summer's day.

The next morning Lu felt Will leave her bed and opened one eye to watch him walk, beautifully naked, to her *en-suite* bathroom, picking up yesterday's clothes on his way. She glanced at her bedside clock and saw that it was a quarter to five. She knew that Will had a beach run with his squad scheduled for six.

It was morning and her one spectacularly glorious night with Will was over. Lu buried her head in her pillow as she heard the shower being turned on and tried not to imagine his beautiful body slick with soap. She'd had sex before—not a lot—but nothing could have prepared her for a night spent with Will. He'd turned to her time and again and each time he'd taught her something new about her body. She hadn't known that she had a spot on her ankle which, when he nibbled it, shot sparks up her legs. Or that the backs of her knees were ticklish and that she melted when he dug his strong fingers into the muscles of her butt. He'd been a tender but demanding lover, and she knew that when she stood up she'd discover that she had aches in places she hadn't known had muscles.

Her suggestion of one night had just bubbled out of her, Lu thought. Probably because she'd felt so emotionally connected to him. For the first time she hadn't just discussed her parents' death but *her* reaction to that news—how she'd coped, how she'd felt. Not how Nate and Daniel had felt. It had been all about her—Lu. He'd cared, sympathised and empathised. If she could have crawled into him and curled up inside him she wouldn't have felt safer.

And *boom!* She had known that she didn't want to go one more day without knowing what his skin tasted like, how those long muscles felt under her hands and whether making love with him would be as magical as she imagined it to be.

It had been all that. And so much more.

Lu heard the shower switched off and turned her back to the door. She told herself that it was morning, that she couldn't ask him to come back to bed. That wasn't the deal. Lu bit her bottom lip as the bathroom door opened and minutes later she felt his weight on the bed and his hand on her shoulder.

She'd tucked the sheet up around her arms, so she knew she was decent when she rolled over and looked at him, his face serious in the half-light of morning. She could see that he was looking for words, that he—like her—was fighting temptation. She could see it in the heat of his eyes, in the tension of his jaw.

Lu forced herself to shake her head. 'We can't, Will. This is all we get.'

Will bent down and rested his forehead on her shoulder. Lu got a whiff of soap and toothpaste.

'I—'

Lu permitted herself one brief stroke over his hair before dropping her hand. She forced the words out. 'One night, Will. That was the deal. You're going home in six weeks or so. I'm staying here. We're good friends. Let's not spoil it. Complicate it.'

Will kissed her shoulder before straightening. He cupped her cheek in his hand and shook his head. 'Thank you for the best night of my life. You were magnificent.'

'You weren't so bad yourself,' Lu replied, and then she dropped her eyes and forced herself to be practical. 'There's a spare set of keys with a remote for the gate on the rack of hooks next to the fridge. You can let yourself out and I'll get the keys back from you later…at work.'

Will stood up, put his hands on his hips. His lips twisted. 'Well, that was direct.'

She had to be or she'd cry. Or beg him to stay.

'Before I go…no regrets?'

Lu shook her head. 'None.'

'Are we back to normal?'

'Yes,' Lu replied and watched as he sent her a quick smile before leaving her room. She flopped back onto the pillow and stared at the ceiling.

They were back to normal. Whatever *normal* meant.

CHAPTER NINE

WILL GLANCED ACROSS his car. Lu was curled up in the overlarge passenger seat, her head tucked into the space between the seat and the door. She was fast asleep. He glanced at the red lights of the dashboard clock. It didn't matter that it was eleven on a Sunday morning; he'd learnt that Lu could only keep her eyes open for about thirty minutes in a car before falling asleep.

In only a month, along with learning of her propensity to fall asleep in a car, he'd learnt a lot about her—including the fact that she hated peanut butter, loved any decorating show on TV, and that if she was deeply immersed in a book a nuclear bomb could go off next to her and she wouldn't flinch.

She kept her promises and took the one she'd made to her brothers seriously. She was now—thanks to him—sort of able to surf, and he'd taught her to ride a dirt bike. Of course she'd nearly hit a tree on her first attempt, but she'd tried.

As hard as he'd begged—and he'd begged a lot—she still refused to skydive, and they'd vowed not to go back to pottery lessons.

He still wanted her more than ever. He wanted her in his bed, in his life, in his head. Possibly in his heart. Oh, he knew that it was impossible, but now and again he put aside his fears and resolutions and thought about how good they would be together, imagined a life with her in it. It was his own fairytale—one he knew would never come true.

He liked her—a lot—but he was not emotionally attached to her. He could still walk away.

Lu yawned and stretched and sent him a sleepy look. 'How long have I been asleep?'

'An hour and fifteen,' Will told her.

Lu sat up straight and looked out of the window. 'Where are we? Jeez, I thought we were going to lunch, not travelling halfway up Africa.'

'What is it with you Durbanites? You think that a five-minute drive is too far and you slept for most of the trip. Besides, you'll thank me,' Will replied, switching lanes so that he could take the exit.

Lu pulled her bag onto her lap and took out a small toiletry purse which she quickly opened. Slicking some nude lipstick onto her fabulous mouth, she smacked her lips and Will groaned. He wished she wouldn't do things like that.

Knowing that he might have little time left with her, he wanted to have as much of her as possible. He should warn Lu that he might be leaving sooner than had been planned, but he was unsure what to say. He was also seriously considering Kelby's offer of another six months and then the head coach position. That being said, he owed the other teams a face-to-face meeting, to listen to their offers, which meant a trip back home and soon.

And if he stayed in Durban what would he do about Lu? Would he want to continue this knowing that he was falling deeper into...*something*...every week he spent with her?

Maybe it was better to keep quiet about his plans until he knew exactly what he was doing and where he was going.

Lu flicked him a small frown. 'Are you OK?'

'Sure...just horny.'

Will almost laughed at the shocked look on her face, but he felt as if there was a boa constrictor wrapped around his hips. He was so *over* being around her and not being able to touch her.

'Wha…?'

'Just because we don't touch or kiss doesn't mean that I don't want you. And when you push your chest out like you were doing and fiddle with your lips it makes me hot.' Will shrugged and looked at his GPS, grateful to have something else to focus on besides his straining shorts. 'We're turning off onto a dirt road coming up on the right. Keep your eyes open for it.'

'Ah…OK.'

Will smiled to himself. She looked flushed and bothered and not nearly as composed as she had been five minutes ago. *Good.* It was about time that someone else in this car felt hot and flustered and on edge. *Welcome to my world, Mermaid.*

Enjoying himself, Will thought he'd push her buttons a little more.

'Of course whatever you do makes me hot,' he said as he pulled off the secondary road onto the dirt road.

'You still want to sleep with me?' Lu said in a choked voice.

'Sleep? Hell, no, I don't want to *sleep* with you. Kiss you everywhere, touch you everywhere, be inside you…yes.' Will pulled into a makeshift parking lot under some large tropical trees and switched off the engine. He lifted his hand from the gear stick to close Lu's open mouth gently.

'But I thought we weren't…'

'I agreed to one night—not to stop wanting you, Lu. Do you think I heard *one night only* and turned into a eunuch?' Will rolled his eyes. 'Don't look so shocked.'

'I'm not sure what to say,' Lu said as he jumped down to the sandy, grass-splattered ground.

She sat statue-still in the passenger seat as he walked around the car to open her door for her. He'd floored her.

He could see that. She hopped down from the high cab with a dazed look on her face, and the devil sitting on his shoulder urged him to give her even more to think about.

There was nothing but dense bush on the passenger side, and the Range Rover's over-large body would screen them from arriving cars or anyone walking back to their car.

Grabbing her hand, he jerked her towards him. She opened her mouth to protest and he swooped inside, his tongue finding hers in a long, slow, wet, sexy slide. He felt her murmur into his mouth, a little feminine sound of approval, and he pressed her back against the car door.

'Do you know how much I want you?'

Will grabbed her hand, opened her fingers and placed her open palm on his erection, sinking back towards her mouth. As her thumb brushed over his tip he slipped his hand down her hip and up and under the short, flouncy, sexy sundress she was wearing. His hand smoothed over her bare butt and traced the line of her thong. He stroked her intimately before pulling back to place his hands under her bottom, lifting her up so that he rubbed her intimately, possessively.

Lu let out a yelp that was part surprise and mostly desire as he thrust against her, only a couple of layers separating him from utter perfection.

'God…' Will muttered against her neck, tasting the dent in her collarbone. 'I could take you right here, right now.'

Lu nipped his lower lip and then licked the bite of pain away. 'And I'd let you.'

Will rested his forehead against hers. 'You're driving me insane, Lu. We're going to have to do something about this, Mermaid, before I explode from sexual frustration. We're adult enough to have this—do this—without getting our fingers burnt.'

In his head, *spontaneous* was currently wiping the floor with *control's* face and Will didn't really care.

'We both know what this is—a short-term, big-fun fling. Let's take the risk!'

'Jeez, Will. What happened to sex and I walk, etcetera, etcetera?'

Will shrugged and looked at her with eyes of liquid gold. 'C'mon, Lu, let's live a little.'

Lu's mermaid eyes widened in shock. *'Now?'*

Will grinned as he let her slide to her feet. 'No, not now. I'd prefer to do it without an audience.'

'What?' Lu screeched whipping around in shock to see who was watching them.

Will shouted his laughter and gestured to his left with his thumb. A small troupe of monkeys sat in a grassy clearing, watching them, heads cocked and seemingly fascinated by their antics.

Lu let out an enormous sigh of relief and put her hand on her chest. 'You skunk, Will! I nearly had heart failure!'

Will grinned and leaned his shoulder into the car door as he watched the monkeys scamper back into the bush.

In the ladies' bathroom—in Lu's opinion very conveniently situated at the entrance of whatever this place was—Lu splashed cold water on her face in order to bring down the ferocious colour in her cheeks.

In the mirror above the sink her wide, wild eyes blazed back at her, and she thought that anyone with half a brain would realise that if she didn't get Will into bed again soon she would spontaneously combust.

She'd never, ever experienced such heat and passion before. Every time she and Will touched they went from friends to frenetic in a heartbeat. She wanted him, and he very obviously wanted her, and he was right. They were going to have to do something about it soon.

They were kidding themselves if they thought they could continue this farce about friendship. They'd tried hard, but this compulsion to get naked was too big for both of them. Forget one night—she'd take all the nights she could get, and there weren't that many of them left.

But she had to try and be sensible too—think through how she could be his lover and still wave him goodbye in the not so distant future. He could have her body, do what he wanted with it, but she had to find a way to make sure that when he left her behind he didn't take her heart and soul with him.

Who knew how she was actually going to achieve that? But she'd survived her parents' death, raising her brothers, and she'd damn well do this too. Because—as she was coming to realize—independence wasn't just about a career and learning to live on her own. It was also about making decisions, sticking with them and dealing with the consequences of those choices.

That was independence of thought, a liberation of her spirit, a choice that was all hers. And she was choosing Will, for as long as she could have him.

She didn't know what the cost of this decision would be, but she'd pay the price life demanded and she'd be fine.

Because she was, if nothing else, a survivor.

Lu downed half a glass of icy wine, caught Will's eye and blushed again. She placed the palm of her hand on her forehead and closed her eyes against his wicked, laughing amber eyes. 'You are a bad man, Will Scott.'

Will leaned forward and dropped his voice. 'A *very* bad man.'

Lu blushed again and groaned. 'Will you stop now? Please? I am *so* embarrassed!'

Will just grinned and sipped his beer.

Lu picked up her glass again, took another reviving sip and looked around. She felt beach sand under her sandals, slipped her feet out of them and dug her toes in. There were about ten rickety tables planted in the sandy dune, a rough-looking bar, and a lot of people were either seated at the tables or hanging around the bar. Some were sitting in enormous baskets hanging from a massive wild fig tree, others were seated on beach blankets. Everyone was barefoot, some women wore bikinis, and a lot of the men were shirtless.

'OK, so where are we?'

Will sipped his beer directly from an icy bottle. 'The Beach Shack. Fresh seafood, caught this morning…'

Lu's grin was wide. 'I've always wanted to come here. This is great! It really does look like a shack.'

'But it has the best seafood anywhere, or so I am told,' Will said, leaning so far back in his chair that its front legs lifted off the sand. 'Kelby told me about this place.'

'It reminds me of some of the places my parents used to whip us off to when I was a kid. Sunday lunches were something we always did…fancy hotels, rickety restaurants, diners, dives. We visited them all. My parents always knew where the best food was.' Lu's eyes clouded over and her voice dropped. She was back in that place of tough memories and spiky pain. She shook it off. 'We had our last lunch with them about three weeks before they died. A really expensive lunch. I remember that my mom tried to pay with her credit card and there was a problem. Dad used three cards before the charge went through. That should've been a big clue.'

Will's chair hit the ground. He leaned forward and his eyes were sympathetic when they met hers. 'They were struggling? Financially?'

'Struggling? No. They were to all intents and purposes bankrupt.' Lu drained her glass and tried to change the subject. He didn't need to know this. She shouldn't share it. Sex was one thing, but connecting with him over her very emotional past was just stupid—especially since she was trying to keep her emotional distance. 'The sea is just over this dune, I take it?'

'Down that path.' Will nodded to a thin track that snaked over the dune and reached for her hand. He rubbed his thumb over her wrist. 'Talk to me, Lu.'

'Can we take a walk? Would they keep our table?' Lu asked as she stood up. Will followed her to his feet and nodded. 'I'm sure they will. Let's go.'

Will took her hand in his and led her up and over the dune, not pressuring her to talk—which she appreciated. The sea pounded the beach and washed over their feet. Will just held her hand in his big one.

'After they died I never gave finances another thought,' Lu said eventually, lifting her face up to the hot sun. 'The insurance policies paid out really quickly and there was so much money; the policies were *huge*. The irony is that my parents wouldn't have been able to afford the premiums the next month.'

Lu stopped, bent down to pick up a cowry shell and absently handed it to Will, placing it into the palm of his free hand. She didn't notice when Will slipped it into the pocket of his cargo shorts.

'I hired a financial advisor and he moved the money around—put it into high-interest-bearing funds and accounts. My focus was on the boys, so I was so grateful for his help. Still am.'

'How did you find out that they were broke?' Will asked.

'About six months after they died I finally had enough distance, enough strength, to clean out their closets, the study, sort through their personal stuff.'

'I keep forgetting that you were still a teenager when you did all this,' Will said, and Lu heard the pain in his voice…for *her*.

'There were boxes of unpaid, unopened bills. Boxes and boxes of papers that they should have paid attention to. I opened them all and I felt…devastated all over again. And so, so guilty.'

Will squeezed her hand and the pain and guilt took a step back. 'Why guilty, Lu?'

'Because my parents died in order for us to live this very comfortable life.' Lu stared down at her bare feet. 'If they'd lived our lives would've been very different. No fancy schools or university for the boys. Now there's enough money for them to start a business or buy a house later on.'

'Did they leave the money to your brothers?'

'No. It was equally divided.'

'Then why do you talk as if this is the twins' inheritance and not yours?'

Good question. She *did* do that—think that. 'I don't know. Maybe it's because I was an adult—legally, at least—when they died, and therefore had had the benefit of a life with them. They hadn't.'

'You were also the one who put your entire life on hold to look after them. You are as entitled to your share of the money as they are.'

'They lost their parents, Will,' she objected.

'Sweetheart, so did you.' Will placed his hands on her shoulders and squeezed. 'They only had to deal with their grief. You had to deal with a lot more.'

'My parents must have been so incredibly scared—desperate about what they were going to do. How they were going to look after the boys. Where they were going to live. And even more scary the loss of their image and lifestyle and friends.' Lu dug her toes into the wet sand and blinked furiously. 'Accommodation, food, car, petrol…all my big expenses are paid for by the trust, but I feel like I can't use any of the money on me, on things I'd like.'

'Why not?'

Lu linked her hands behind her head and looked at Will with huge, haunted eyes.

Will touched her cheek with the tips of his fingers. 'Lu, you can't punish yourself for something they did or didn't do. They made the decision not to look after their finances, not you,' Will insisted. 'As for using the money—let's look at the situation another way, Lu. If just one of your parents had died the other would've have had to hire an *au pair* to help with the twins. Am I right?'

'Yes.'

'And that *au pair* would've been paid?'

'Yes.'

'It's a basic analogy, and nowhere near what you did for the boys, but my point is still the same. Use the money, Lu. No guilt attached.' Will slung an arm around her shoulders and hauled her to his side. He dropped a kiss on her temple. 'If you used your share of the money now, would it change the fact that they were broke?'

'No.'

'Would it bring them back?'

'No.' Lu put her hand around Will's broad back and held on tight.

Will looked down at her and touched her chin with the tips of his fingers. 'Then use the money, sweetheart.' He pulled off his cap and placed it over Lu's head. 'I think it's time we got that gorgeous face of yours out of the sun. I can see the freckles forming as we speak.'

Lu yelped, slapped a hand over her nose.

Will laughed. 'I'm joking, Mermaid. When is it going to sink into your head that I *like* your freckles?'

Will shut and locked the front door behind him, and Lu dropped her bag onto the floor in the hall and kicked off her sandals. Their lunch at The Beach Shack had rolled on into the afternoon and early evening. Like a lot of the other patrons they'd gone back to the beach and watched the sun set over the Indian Ocean, and it had been fully dark when they'd finally made the long trip home.

She'd fallen asleep in the car on the way back. Again.

Lu walked into the kitchen, opened the fridge door and pulled out two bottles of water. She tossed one to Will, who caught it with one hand. He cracked the lid and watched her with hooded eyes as he downed half the contents in one long swallow. The entire day had been one long foreplay session, starting with that sexy interplay against the car door. While he had been careful to keep his hands off her all day—most of the patrons at the restaurant had known exactly who he was, and a couple of mobile cameras had been used—she'd seen the heat in his gaze and his whispered words had had her blood bubbling.

'I love the veins on the inside of your wrist. Can you feel my lips on them?'

'I'm imagining you in my bed, all long legs and a sexy smile.'

Lu ran the icy bottle down her neck and watched Will's eyes flare.

A muscle jumped in his jaw as he replaced the cap on the water bottle. 'Hot, Lu?'

'It's summer in Durban,' Lu replied, and couldn't believe her voice could sound so raspy, so sexy. Emboldened, she rolled the bottle against her chest, let it drift across her nipples.

'If you're that hot, then I have an idea.'

Will grabbed her hand, yanked her towards the veranda doors and quickly unlocked them. Pulling her into the still hot night, he led her down the veranda steps to the dark pool. He lifted his hands and held her slim neck.

'Making out with you in the pool has been a big fantasy of mine.'

'Making out? Is that all we're going to do?' Lu asked as he used his thumbs on her jaw to tip her head up.

'I hope not,' Will groaned, just before his mouth fell onto hers.

Lu had expected hot and crazy, but she got slow and sexy—a deliberate, tantalising exploration of every inch of her mouth: a lick here, a nip there. His hands drifted down to her back, deftly unzipping the small zip that held her sundress together. The dress fell in a frothy pile at her feet and she stood in her strapless bra and tiny thong in the moonlight, her body his for the taking.

His big hands smoothed a path down her spine, over her bare buttocks, over the tops of her thighs. They traced her ribcage and slid from her shoulders to her fingers, leaving her nerve-endings quivering.

'So beautiful,' Will muttered.

Right now, she actually believed him. Lu pushed her hands up and under his T-shirt, urging him to take it off. Will lifted his hand, grabbed the back of the shirt behind his neck and yanked it off in that very masculine way of his. Lu groaned as she felt those long muscles vibrating with tension under her hands. Why had she waited so long to touch him again, to taste his skin, to experience the utter wonder of Will?

Lu gasped as his fingers unsnapped the buttons of his shorts and he pushed them and his boxers down his hips. He stood in front of her, bare-ass naked. In the low light spilling from the house he looked like every woman's fantasy. Strong and tall and proud, broad shoulders, rippled stomach, lean hips, and she couldn't ignore his obvious and very large erection.

It was just for her, and she couldn't wait to play with him.

'That's a very naughty smile, Lu,' Will said softly, his hands going to her hips.

'I was having a very naughty thought, Will,' Lu responded.

'I like naughty thoughts.' Will put his finger on her skin and pulled at the fabric between her breasts. 'As much as I like this, I'd prefer it off.'

Lu spun around and offered him her back. 'Feel free.'

Will unhooked her bra, dropped it to the ground and placed his mouth at the top of her spine as his hands cupped both her breasts. His thumbs rubbed her nipples, pulling them up into hard pebbles as his erection nestled into her butt.

'Walk,' he whispered in her ear. 'Into the pool. I have a fantasy to make true.'

Lu settled down into the corner of her couch to watch the Saturday night movie, a bowl of popcorn in her lap, Dore tucked in behind her knees. This was the first night she'd spent alone for more than a week and the house felt empty without Will.

She'd loved every second of having him around.

Every. Second.

He sang in the shower—mushy Nineties songs, off-key and totally out of tune. It made every day an adventure in 'Guess the Tune'. He'd watched her make red velvet cupcakes and eaten three while she'd waited for them to cool, swiping pieces of cake through the cream cheese icing instead of waiting for her to ice them. They'd gone to the photography exhibition and he had staunchly but erroneously insisted that her work was better.

She'd rewarded him handsomely for that.

And they'd had sex. Lots and lots of lovely, lovely sex.

And because she loved being with him she'd deliberately encouraged him to accept Mak's invitation to a soccer match at the stadium in the city.

She frequently reminded herself that he was just someone she was having fun with—someone who would be leaving soon. A man who'd arrived in her life at a time when she needed a friend—someone to make her laugh, to help her play.

And because it was becoming harder and harder to remember that he was leaving she'd thought a night apart wasn't a bad thing. It would help her to gain some much needed distance, perspective, being a reminder that this insane happiness wasn't permanent.

It was make-believe, pretend…a little romantic escape from real life. If she started to think it was anything else she was setting herself up for a fall.

Ooh, movie starting, Lu thought. Hot hero…not nearly as sexy as Will…but then again who was?

Her mobile rang and she scowled down at it when she saw an unfamiliar number on the screen. She just wanted some time out.

'Hello?'

'Hold for a call please,' a crisp voice instructed her, and she frowned.

'Lu? God, Lu…'

Nate's voice broke and Lu shot up, dislodging the cat as her heart belted up into her throat.

'Nate! What's wrong?' she demanded, her voice croaky with fear.

'We went to a music festival and as we were leaving Daniel and I and a couple of other guys got ambushed. There were about eight guys and they roughed us up. Stole our phones…wallets.'

'Are you hurt? How's Daniel?'

'I'm phoning from the hospital…they admitted him. He got kicked in the head and he won't wake up—'

Nate's voice broke again and she heard the tears in his stutter.

'They say he should. Maybe in a day or so. But, Lu, can you come?'

Lu felt the scream forming in her throat, swallowed it down and looked for the rigid calm that she knew he needed to hear from her. 'Of course. I'll catch the first plane I can. Where are you? Where is *he*?'

'Constantia General. Casualty. I don't have any money... a friend of mine is bringing me a phone, so I'll text you the number when I get it.'

'OK. Keep in touch,' Lu stated, idly noticing that her knee was bouncing and that her hand was shaking. 'And Nate...?'

'Yeah?'

'He will be fine. I promise.'

'Just come, Lu. I'm scared.'

'I know, Nate.' She was terrified beyond belief too, but she had to be strong. For him and for Daniel. 'Hang tough.'

Lu disconnected and stared down at her mobile. Instinctively she dialled Will's number and wrapped her arm around her middle as she waited for him to answer.

'If this is a booty call, I'm your man...' Will answered on a laugh.

Lu closed her eyes as an involuntary sob escaped.

'Lu...honey? What's wrong? Are you ok?'

'No...' Lu answered, and as if from miles away heard the breath he sucked in. 'I'm fine. Daniel my brother isn't. I need a lift to the airport. I have to get to Cape Town as soon as possible. Can you take me to the airport? I'm shaking too much to drive and I need to try to get a flight... and information from the hospital about his condition...'

'I'm on my way. Leaving now. Hold on, baby. I'm coming.'

Lu rested her mobile against her forehead as tears rolled

down her face. She'd known that he'd drop everything, that he'd come running. Just this one time she didn't have to be alone.

CHAPTER TEN

ON THE LATE-AFTERNOON flight back from Cape Town a week later, Lu rested her head against the window and stared at the clouds below. She was barely aware of the minor turbulence. Her thoughts were too full of this past week and the knowledge that she was finally going home… to Will.

He'd been amazing, she remembered. Calm, cool, so very in control. He'd thrown some clothes into an overnight bag for her, because she hadn't thought to pack anything, buckled her into her seat and, while he raced down the highway, held her hand as she'd called the airport to book a seat on the midnight flight to Cape Town. When she'd finally got through to the doctor who had been treating Daniel she'd been shaking so much that she'd hardly been able to talk, so he'd taken the phone and got all the relevant information. Daniel had had minor bleeding under his skull. They were keeping him sedated to give the swelling time to subside, he'd told her. He'd taken her credit card and swiped the automated ticket machine for her, holding onto her ticket and her until it had been time for her flight to be called.

When it had, he'd calmly boarded the plane with her—she hadn't realised that he'd purchased a ticket for himself as well—and he'd held her through the two-hour flight. She couldn't remember how they'd got to the hospital, just that Will had been there, solid and steadfast at the end of her hand. He'd bought her coffee, hired a car and taken a battered and dinged Nate back to his digs so that he could shower and rest. While Daniel lay statue-still, Will had held her while she wept.

He'd brought Nate back to the hospital and at around midday the next day, when Daniel had started showing signs of improving, Will had kissed her forehead and told her that he'd see her back at home.

She'd stayed in Cape Town for the week and she'd missed him. Ferociously. He'd called often, and while she'd been speaking to him her world had made sense. Her stomach had stopped churning, her breath had evened out and she'd relaxed. For those five, ten, fifteen minutes she'd felt settled, calm, relaxed.

Lu banged her head against the back of her headrest and mentally slapped herself.

She'd tried so hard to keep her emotional distance but she was falling for him. Even worse, was coming to rely on him. She wanted to have the right to call him, wanted to feel that he was the man she could lean on, rely on, love. And how stupid was that? She wanted him for everything: for companionship, friendship, sex, support...and worst of all for love.

When had this happened? *How* had it happened? She'd been so aware, so on guard, so determined not to allow herself to feel more.

She was *such* a moron.

'*Love, commitment, wasn't part of the deal.*'

Lu heard Will's voice in her head and closed her eyes. *Stupid, stupid girl.*

Anyway, she couldn't afford to rely on him—on anybody—for emotional support because when she did she fell apart.

If she hadn't had Will in her life she would have managed to keep calm, would have called on all that strength she'd learnt in coping with her parents' death, and just put one foot in front of the other and got the job done. But because Will *was* around, so strong and capable, she'd collapsed and allowed him to take over.

What if—God forbid—this happened again when Will was halfway across the world? How would she cope? She wouldn't have a strong shoulder to lean on. Mak was her friend, but he had his own crosses to bear. No, she couldn't allow herself to become weak, to rely on anyone else. To rely on Will.

She had to pull back. She had to put some distance between them. She had to be tough, be a survivor…

After all, she did it so well.

Will's shin slammed into the bag, followed by a fast fist, and he bounced away from the punch bag. Since he'd returned from his very brief visit to Cape Town he'd spent a ridiculous amount of time in this corner, muttering to himself.

He hated, *loathed*, the idea of Lu being on her own in Cape Town, even though Daniel was well on the road to recovery. He'd had to have surgery to pin a broken wrist later in the week and Will had wanted to be with Lu, even though it was just minor surgery. She worried, and he worried about her while she was worrying about them.

Was she eating? Sleeping? Had he done enough for her? Should he have stayed longer? Called more often? Offered to take a couple of days off work to be with her?

Will stepped away from the bag and put his fists on his thighs. He missed her, and speaking on the phone just didn't cut it. He missed her morning smile, waking up in the middle of the night to find her snuggled into his back, her arm around his waist. Damn it, he even missed her house—missed being in it with Lu. He could relax there, could kick back and just think. He could sit on the veranda and watch the ocean, work at her dining table or in her very messy study, lie on her leather couch and watch the sports channels.

Lu gave him space to move, to think, to *be*. Space to be alone but not to be lonely… She didn't prod or pry or make demands for him to give her anything more than what he was currently giving her.

It was fabulous. It was soul-deep petrifying. The fire still raged.

Will knocked his fist against the bag. Was he allowing himself to be seduced by the fairytale? This wasn't like him—wasn't the person who kept an iron grip on his control, his emotions—and he barely recognised himself.

She turned him upside down and inside out with her ability to decimate his control in and out of the bedroom. When he was making love to her he was outside himself, his mind switched off and his body taking over, taking control. With any other woman he would have sprinted away weeks ago, and although he'd thought about it he still hadn't managed to do it. He had decisions to make—career decisions about other franchises who wanted to work with him—and he wished he could talk to Lu about it. But he couldn't, because talking just strengthened the bond between them. He should be trying to break those bonds, not make them stronger. He had to dig deep and end this. The longer he delayed, the more difficult it would be.

He was leaving Durban—leaving her. That was non-negotiable. The fire was at full strength now and he knew that some time in the not too distant future it would start to burn out.

It would end. Soon. Something would happen to douse the flames or he'd leave. And the sooner he got used to that idea, the better.

* * *

The next morning Will placed a cup of coffee on the bed-side table next to Lu and sighed when she refused to meet his eyes. For most of the previous evening he'd tried to engage her in conversation, but that had been like pulling walrus teeth and he was thoroughly sick of it. For the first time ever they hadn't made love, and Lu had lain in his arms stiff and unresponsive.

'What's going on, Lu?'

Lu didn't meet his eyes. 'Nothing.'

'Bull! You're terse, quiet and irritable.'

'Sorry. I've got a lot on my mind. In case you hadn't no-ticed, it's been a tough week.'

Ooh, sarcasm. Just what he needed.

'Want to talk about it?' Will asked, knowing what her answer would be. But despite the massive lectures he kept giving himself about stepping back he needed to know what she was thinking, where she was at.

He wanted to stop caring about her—he did. He just hadn't the faintest idea how to do it!

'No, I don't want to talk.'

'Has there been more news from Daniel?' Another ques-tion. He was obviously a glutton for punishment.

'No, he's fine. Well, still headachy, but OK.' Lu sat up in bed, picked up her coffee cup and sipped.

'Well, if you're not going to talk to me I might as well just go.'

'I'm just dealing with some stuff, Will.'

'If you're going to deal with it in moody silence I'm not going to watch,' Will snapped.

Something flashed in Lu's eyes that he couldn't iden-tify. Fear? Relief?

'If you don't want to be here, Will, nobody is holding a gun to your head.'

'OK, *that* was bitchy, ' Will shot back. 'Stop shutting me out, Lu.'

'Oh, what? Like you do to me? All the time?'

'What does *that* mean?' he demanded.

Lu climbed out of bed and angled her chin. 'You seem to want to climb inside my head but you won't let me into yours!'

'What do you want to know?' Will asked.

Lu shoved her hands into her hair. 'You *know* what I want to know! I want to know what happened with your marriage. Why you are so anti-relationships! Are you still in love with her?' Lu asked.

'Jo? Hell no!' Will swore under his breath. 'You want to know? Fine—I'll tell you.' He sat down on the edge of the windowsill. 'It was anything but a fairytale. We got married when we were both twenty-two, and during the two years we were hitched I think we just entertained each other.' He raked a hand through his hair. 'We also played hard—far too hard. We had too much money and we thought we were very special. We married in a flurry of sex-fuelled adrenalin and over time the chemistry fizzled. I think if we'd spent more time together it would've fizzled a lot quicker.'

Now came the hard part.

'There were many reasons why it was on a downward slide, but I gave it the killing blow.' *Just spit it out.* 'She caught me cheating. It wasn't the first or the only time I did it, but it was the first time she caught me at it.'

Lu's expression remained neutral but he knew she was good at not reacting. Her eyes gave her away. Was that disappointment he saw? Yep, there it was. Just what he'd expected.

'OK. Carry on.'

'You want more? We allowed, even encouraged each other to walk on the wild side, but that was her line: infidelity. I crossed it. All the time. Probably hoping that she'd catch me at it. She eventually did.'

'Why didn't you just leave her?'

'Because I *liked* being able to say that I was married to one of the world's sexiest women. I was that shallow—that superficial,' Will retorted. 'I wasn't a nice guy, Lu. I'm still not.'

Lu didn't disagree with him and he felt disappointed. Then he got annoyed at himself for feeling disappointed.

'OK, I understand that you had a bad marriage, but why have you avoided relationships?' she asked.

Were they *really* going to discuss this now? Lu had her stubborn face on. Yep, they were. 'Jo was wild and exciting and the sex was crazy. Sex—attraction—fuels love, and when it burns out you are left with a pile of ashes.'

'I disagree with you. I think love fuels sex.'

'Yeah, that's what the fairytales want us to believe. It doesn't work like that. Not for me, anyway. I don't want to be trapped when attraction dies off—having to stay in a relationship because I'm obligated to. I don't trust the spark to last, Lu.'

'That's such a lousy excuse for not being brave enough to take a chance,' Lu stated.

'And you? Are *you* so brave?' Will shot back, needing to launch some arrows of his own. 'Isn't this ice princess act a way to distance yourself from me?'

He knew that he'd hit the target when temper shot into her eyes. 'No, it's you crowding me! Hovering! Will, I've been alone for a long time, and sometimes I'm not sure what to do with you! I just want some time on my own... some time to think!'

'You've had a whole week away from me to think!' He gripped the bridge of his nose and tried to find some control. 'I just wanted to help, Lu.'

He didn't know that those last few words would put a match to the powder keg of her temper.

'I don't *need* your help!' Lu cried. 'I didn't need it when I buried my parents, or when I lay in this bed, with two little boys sobbing their hearts out, one on either side of me. I didn't need it when they had measles, or when Nate got his heart broken. Where were you when I had to turn down every career opportunity I ever received because I had supper to put on the table? I don't *need* your help. I don't need *anyone*!'

Whoa! Will stepped back as her words whipped his soul. 'So why did you call me last week? Why didn't you just cope, Lu?'

'Because I was weak! You're leaving and I can't— *won't*—rely on you or anybody else!' Lu turned away to stare out of the window.

Will slapped his coffee cup onto the bedside table and glared at her stiff back. In his mind a video of a helicopter dumping a scoop of water on a bushfire played. Yet the fire still raged.

'Well, you can have as much time to yourself as you need.'

He was leaving soon anyway. What did he care?

Too much, he thought as he headed down the stairs to her front door. He stopped, leaned his forehead on the wood and told himself to walk through the door.

He cared. *Damn.*

The idea of leading the Rays onto the field was, in theory, a great idea for little Deon, but now that he could hear the forty thousand plus crowd roaring and see the craziness of the tunnel, with officials, medics and members of the press rushing in and out, he was thoroughly overwhelmed.

There was no chance that he'd run out onto the field by himself, Lu realised after trying to talk to him again.

He buried his head in Mak's stomach and refused to let his dad go. Kelby, standing to her left with a representative of the Rays' biggest corporate sponsor, sent her an enquiring look and she drew her hand across her throat.

Mak bent down to speak to Deon again. 'Bud, listen—the Rays are coming up from the dressing room. Look—there's Jabu.'

Deon shook his head and placed his hands over his face. Lu glanced at her watch and winced. In five minutes the opposition would storm onto the field, Deon or not. Both she and Mak knew that he wanted to do it, but he was swamped with fear.

Poor kid. Lu placed her hand on Mak's shoulder and as she did so felt the brief touch of a masculine hand on her back.

'Problem?' Will asked.

Lu looked around and couldn't help the flutter of her heart, the catch in her throat. She hadn't spoken to him since he'd left her house, and avoiding him had been easy this week as he had taken the squad for a team-building session up-country.

She'd felt lost and miserable all week.

Could she have been more horrible, mean, spiteful? She'd asked Will for help and he hadn't asked any questions. He'd jumped into the situation—spent his Saturday night travelling across the country so that she didn't have to be alone—and she'd repaid him by lashing out at him because she was scared of becoming reliant on him.

That was her problem, not his. He'd been honest with her. He hadn't offered anything more than friendship and by helping her, supporting her, he'd given exactly that. She'd repaid that generosity by goading him into telling her about his past, by verbally punching him when he'd offered help.

If the twins had acted like that she would have had more than a couple of words with them.

She had to apologise, and she had to apologise in a way that he'd know meant something. Sometimes words were too easy, but she had to try.

'Will, I—'

Will looked at her and she sighed at his poker face.

'What's the problem?' he asked, nodding at Deon.

'Stage fright,' Lu whispered over Deon's head.

'He can't do this, Will.' Mak looked at Will with agonised eyes.

'Sure he can; he can do anything he wants to do,' Will replied.

The match director lifted his finger to indicate that Deon should get into position and Lu noticed that both teams were lined up behind them in the tunnel—thirty big, burly, determined men.

Will dropped to his haunches and pulled Deon away from Mak, lifted up his face to make eye contact. 'Pretty scary, huh?'

Deon nodded furiously.

'Would you do it if someone went with you?' Will asked gently.

Deon nodded. 'Jabu.'

'Jabu can't do it, sport. He's got to lead the Rays on. That's an important captain's job.' Will smiled reassuringly. 'What about me? I've led a couple of teams onto the field and I kind of know what to do.'

Deon gave him an assessing stare and Lu had to bite her lip to keep from smiling. The kid was actually taking his time to decide whether Will was worthy of the honour. It seemed like an eternity before Deon nodded his head, stepped away from Mak and Lu and slid his small hand into Will's enormous one.

'Can you do this?' Lu hissed her question at him. 'Shouldn't you be somewhere?'

He should be on his way to the coach's box, from where he'd issue instructions to his people on the ground.

Will shrugged as he stood up. 'It's his dream. I can take five minutes to make it come true.'

Lu's eyes softened and she briefly touched his other hand with hers. 'You're a good man, Will Scott.'

Will sent her a small smile, tugged Deon into position, and the next moment they were walking onto the field. Lu's heart tumbled as her huge, sexy lover slowed his long stride so that Deon, holding the game ball, could keep up with him. When the crowd noticed who was on the field they let out a roar of approval and the sound ricocheted around the stadium.

'And it seems like Will Scott is accompanying Deon Sibaya onto the field today.' The commentator's voice skimmed over the crowd noise. 'Deon is the Rays' biggest and most special fan. He's a student at St Clare's in their special needs programme. And, ladies and gentlemen, following them onto the field, please welcome, from Melbourne, the defending champions!'

Oh, good grief. She was inches away from toppling off the I-love-you cliff, from throwing her heart at his feet. He was smart and strong. How could she *not* fall in love with him? He was an exceptional leader, great with kids. A wonderful inspiration to young men who, through him, could realise that life could be turned around, respect could be re-earned.

He was funny and flawed, hot but tender.

And she thought she might be in love with him. It didn't matter that he was leaving shortly, that he might not want to hear the words, she owed it to herself to tell him, to let him know. She also, at the very least, owed him an apology for acting like a brat.

It would mean opening herself up, laying her heart on the line, being vulnerable—but she had to do it. He might not want her love, might not do anything with it, but she didn't want to live with the regret of not telling him how she felt—how special this time had been with him, what an impact he'd had on her life.

Will and Deon had reached a quarter way across the field and Will kept a hand on Deon's shoulder as the opposition milled a few metres from them, bouncing on their toes, some doing hamstring stretches. Deon's eyes were as wide as flying saucers, Lu thought. Leaving Mak, who'd dropped his sunglasses onto his face to hide his tears, she moved to the side of the field and took her camera off her shoulder to shoot the Rays players as they hurtled past her.

'And, ladies and gentlemen, your team—the Stingrays!'

Lu held her finger on the button and hoped that she'd got some decent shots as the team stormed past her. Immediately she swung her camera around to the field, where Jabu ran directly up to Deon and Will and put out his fist for Deon to bump.

Will slapped Jabu on the shoulder and Lu swallowed.

She captured the image and kept shooting as Jabu repeated the gesture with his coach and Will and Deon turned to walk back towards her. When Deon spotted her on the sidelines he broke into a bumbling run, and she dropped her camera to catch him as he jumped into her arms.

'Did'ja see me, Lu? Did'ja?' he demanded.

'You are *such* a superstar,' she told him, and held out her hand as Will walked past her. He captured her fingers in his and squeezed. Lu, oblivious to the massive crowd, the important match that was about to start and the various photographers and officials milling about, looked up at him with star-shiny eyes. 'As for you, Will Scott…'

Will's slow, sexy smile dimpled his cheek. 'As for me what, Mermaid?'

'*You* are simply magnificent,' Lu said simply.

Will stepped closer and, ignoring the bouncing Deon

at their feet, caught her chin in his hand and tipped her face up. 'Funny, I was thinking the same thing about you.'

Will brushed his lips across hers in a kiss that was brief but still sent tingles down to her toes. 'Good luck,' she murmured against his mouth.

Will tapped her nose. 'Thanks. Good job, kid.' He ran a hand over Deon's hair. 'I've got a corporate function tonight, but I'll call you later, OK?'

'I'll be waiting.'

CHAPTER ELEVEN

HE DIDN'T CALL. Not that night. And on Sunday morning Lu looked at the Sacher torte she'd made the previous night and decided to deliver it in person. She needed to talk to Will, and the longer she delayed this conversation the easier it was to talk herself out of it.

I'm sorry I was so bitchy. I think that I might be in love with you. I thought that you might like to know.

Lu practised the simple words until she had them word-perfect but she suspected that they would fly away, never to be recaptured, when she actually had to say them to Will, face to face.

Shortly after nine Lu banged on the door to his apartment again and wished he'd hurry and open up. The triple-layer, meticulously crafted Sacher torte she'd made him was rather heavy. Lu knocked again and gnawed the inside of her lip. Maybe he'd changed his mind and was hiding behind the door, hoping she'd go away.

After waiting another couple of minutes with no response, she turned away and walked back to the lift.

Damn, she thought, blinking back tears. She'd thought they'd turned a corner yesterday at the match. She'd seen something in his face that had given her hope.

The doors to the lift were sliding open when he finally yanked open his door. 'Where the hell are you going with that cake?' he demanded.

Lu turned around slowly and sucked in her breath at Will, who was leaning against the frame of the door, a towel around those lean hips. She licked her lips as she walked back towards him. 'I'm holding the cake hostage. Where the cake goes, I go.'

'You drive a hard bargain.' Will stood back and jerked his head for her to come inside. He slammed the door closed behind her. 'Give me a minute to get dressed and I'll make some coffee to go with that cake.'

'I'll make the coffee,' Lu said as she walked into the galley kitchen and deposited the cake on the counter.

Flicking on the kettle, she looked at the empty boxes of Chinese takeaway on the counter. Behind the dustbin was an empty pizza box.

When Will returned to the kitchen, dressed in old jeans and a rugby jersey, she flicked the takeaway boxes with her finger. 'Don't you ever cook for yourself?'

'Nope,' Will replied as he joined her in the small space of the kitchen.

She could smell the soap he'd just used in the shower and peppermint toothpaste. Lu nodded to the stack of papers she'd placed on the narrow counter. 'I brought the papers.'

'Thanks. Sorry I didn't call. The function finished late and I was knackered.'

'No problem.'

She was here, with him, finally. There definitely was a God, Will thought, amazed at how happy he was to see her. They needed to talk today. He needed to tell her of the decisions he had to make, get her input, see what she thought. Lu was an integral part of his life now. He didn't know where they were going, but he owed it to her to talk it through.

He'd have to say things he didn't know how to say—try to explain feelings that he wasn't sure he'd identified yet—

find a path he couldn't see yet. Frankly, he'd rather drip hot wax in his eye, but he needed to talk to her.

Because he was so tempted to delay the conversation by taking her to bed, Will stepped backwards. The stack of newspapers fell to the floor and all the sections skidded across the tiles.

Lu looked down at the papers beneath the chair and frowned at the distinctive colours of a Rays shirt on the front page of the society section. 'Ha-ha, some Rays player is front page of the Lifestyle Section. I bet it's Matt again; he has a talent for hooking up with women who are newsworthy.'

Lu's blood ran cold as she realised that *she* was the person dressed in a Rays shirt, and it hit freezing when she read the words of the headline that swam in front of her face: *Is it love?*

Lu forced herself to focus on the picture of her and Will that took up the entire top half of the page. His thumb was on her chin and his eyes were blazing with attraction and passion and...love? It really looked like love.

Lu's heart wanted to thump out of her chest.

'Hey, what are you looking at?' Will demanded, and twisted to see what had captured her attention.

She felt his body tense.

'You have got to be freakin' kidding me!'

Lu looked at Will who, she could see, was enraged. He'd made the headlines again—and for all the wrong reasons. Woman-related, not rugby-related.

So the journos were commenting on their relationship? OK, take a breath. It couldn't be that bad, could it?

Lu snatched the paper from his hand and read snippets from the article as she paced the area in front of him. *'"Lu Sheppard has been employed by the Stingrays as the official photographer for the last four months... An inside source is quoted as saying that the couple seem very happy together."'*

Will stood up, slapped his hands on his hips and muttered a string of luminous blue swear words. 'What else does it say?' he demanded, his lips compressed in a thin line.

Lu glanced down at the paper again and her voice was tight when she answered him. 'They've never seen you look at anyone like that…have you fallen in love…who am I…?'

Will walked around to the other side of the counter, gripped it with white hands and stared at the floor. 'Hell.'

'There's more.' Lu's hands trembled. *"'Sheppard was absolutely unknown in photography circles before she was appointed as official photographer— introduced, I am told, to the publicity and PR department by Will himself. Was this a little nepotism on Scott's part? However it happened, hanging off Will's coat tails has been a very smart move by Sheppard…her career has been boosted by her association with the Rays and Will Scott. Bravo, Ms Sheppard. Though it can't be the world's toughest job being the sexy head coach's main squeeze."'*

Lu heard a freight train roaring through her head. 'I thought I was establishing myself, showing people who and what I can do, but it meant nothing. Everybody will now think that I only got the job because of you…'

Will made a move towards her but she held up her hand to ward him off. 'Please don't.'

Will jammed his hands in the pockets of his jeans. 'Lu, it's one opinion—and, crappy as it sounds, it doesn't actually matter. '

'It doesn't matter to *you*! You've established your career. You are respected for what *you've* done, what *you've* achieved. Every job I get from now on people will wonder whether I'm good or just good at sleeping with *you*!'

'You're overreacting, Lu.'

'Don't you dare say that to me!' Lu shouted, fury staining each word. 'You try working your ass off to build something special and then finding out that you're only in the
position because you're someone's roll in the hay!'

'You are not just a roll in the hay!' Will protested.

'Funny—that's what I thought I was. Isn't that what you
said I was? Or does a no-strings affair just sound classier?'

'You're upset and you're overreacting.'

Lu bent over, picked up the newspaper and scowled.
'This continues on page two.' Lu turned the page. 'Let's
see what else she has to say. *"Aside from Will's love-life, we
are all interested to see where he is headed career-wise.
My sources tell me that yesterday's match was his last as
caretaker coach, that John Carter will be back at the helm
on Monday. Will has been headhunted by an Auckland
franchise and, as it's the team where he started his professional career, it is expected that he will take their offer
of consultant coach. We understand that Will has booked
a flight to Auckland tomorrow night."'* Lu closed her eyes
against the pain before her head whipped up and her eyes
nailed him to the spot. 'You're going home? And you didn't
think this was worth mentioning to me?'

'I was going to tell you. Today. I just…'

'You've known about this for a while, haven't you?'

'Yeah. But—'

Her heart cracked. 'You didn't tell me, Will. You didn't
tell me about the job offers or that the coach was coming
back or that you were going home.' Tears rolled down her
cheeks. 'This is what I meant when I said that you don't
talk to me!'

'I haven't seen you. I've been away—'

'Don't!' Lu's words whipped around the room. 'Don't
make excuses. I've been at the end of my mobile every
minute since our last fight. You could've called—told me
this. You owed me that.'

Will rubbed his jaw. 'You're right. I just didn't know what to say.'

'*I'm going home on Monday*—that would've been a good start.' Lu scrunched the paper in her hand. 'Don't you think I've had enough surprises in my life? How can you feel so little for me, even if we are just friends, to do this to me? To brush me aside like this? I never expected love from you, Will, but I did expect some measure of respect!'

'I *do* respect you!'

'The hell you do.' Lu wiped her eyes with her free hand. 'You know what? Maybe it *is* just better if you stick to one night stands and walk away. I thought you had changed, but you're still the same selfish, arrogant guy that you were when you were twenty-four. You haven't grown up at all!' Lu slapped the newspaper against his chest. 'I'm done. Thanks for the fun, but we're over. I'm not prepared to bask in your reflected glory, for your popularity and fame to be credited for my hard work. It's too high a price to pay for hot sex and some laughs. And as for not talking to me—take your shriveled-up heart and your issues of control and shove them so far up your backside that they hit your tonsils!'

With those scorching words blistering the room, Lu walked out of his life.

Will sat on the edge of his bed in his Auckland house and looked around the exquisitely decorated room. He absentmindedly played with the cowry shell Lu had given him on the beach which he was now never without.

It looked like a hotel room, he thought. Not a place where someone lived. Where were the photographs? Lu's messy dressing table? The rows of hooks that held her beads and bangles? It smelled sterile and unused, cold and hard. Of dust and loneliness.

Will looked at the contract lying on the bed and picked

it up, not needing to read it again to understand the terms. He hadn't accepted anything, he was still considering all his options, and… Yes, what he was going to do about Lu was a huge part of that. The offer was pretty much the same offer as Kelby had given him—a consultant coach position until an opening for head coach came up.

He didn't want to play second string. He wanted to be in charge. Second string would mean giving up control, working under someone else's vision, under his rules. Not his style. But with the Rays it would only be for six months… Carter would retire at the end of the year.

And, most importantly, Durban held Lu, whom he now realised held his heart. When she'd woken up in his bed six weeks ago he hadn't realised that while he'd been rescuing her she'd been about to save him as well.

Save him from a life of bed-hopping and vacuous women, of brief encounters where bodies touched but souls didn't. From a life devoid of crazy outings—he *would* get her to skydive one day!—and arguments and tender moments and love-fuelled sex.

Her comment about him not changing at all had stung like a scorpion, and while he knew that he *had* changed, maybe he hadn't changed enough. Lu just made him want to be better. He wanted a life with his best friend. He wanted to dance with her on the veranda. He wanted to taste-test her baking and make her laugh. He wanted to be everything she needed, wanted her to be proud of him.

She made him believe in love, in hope, in fairytales.

He was absolutely, comprehensively in love with her. His heart and soul and body were lying at her feet.

The spark, he now realised, had to be nurtured in a fire, and the fire had to be fed. With quiet talks and shared experiences, with the giving and receiving of support.

With communication—which he was seriously crap at. But Lu—if he could ever talk her around—stubborn, brave and loyal, wouldn't allow the spark to die either; they were both fighters and if they could get past this they could not only keep the fire burning but they could also set the world on fire.

Will stood up and tossed the contract on the bed, reached for the small bag he'd yet to unpack. He was going back to Durban. He'd track Lu down and sort this train wreck of a relationship out. He knew it wouldn't be easy, but he'd give it everything he had.

She would be his.

Fuelled with hope and determination, he dialled for a cab to take him back to the airport. He was going home.

She was going to die. It was official.

Lu sat in the open door of the Cessna, facing out, and her feet dangled into open air. She reached out and gripped the knee of her partner in craziness and thought that along with getting involved with Will this was the stupidest she'd ever done and, she promised herself, would ever do.

Skydiving had been the last thing on her mind when she'd belted out of Durban. She'd originally planned to spend a couple of nights away, but she'd been so entranced with the quiet and the lack of contact with people in Himeville that it had been nearly two weeks before she drove out of the gates of the B&B and a hundred metres down the road saw a sign advertising tandem skydives.

What the hell? she had thought. What could be worse than having your heart shattered into a million pieces?

It was worse—or at the very least just as bad. Oh, dear God, was that a bird a million miles below them?

She didn't want to die... She wanted to go home and crawl into Will's arms and stay there for ever. She wanted to be woken up with his hard body pressed up against her, to hear his deep laugh, to be loved because she was com-

prehensively, staggeringly, mind-blowingly, fathoms-deep
in love with him.

She'd only fully accepted it as she'd walked away from
him, and every step that had increased the distance between them had been an effort to accomplish. It had been
as if her body recognised him as being the only one and
had been fighting to keep her in place.

But, as hard as leaving him had been, she knew that she
couldn't have stayed. He didn't value her as much as she
valued him, and sadly she couldn't make him. There was
nothing left of their relationship. He was gone, and she was
sitting in an aeroplane trying to prove a point to herself.

She could do anything she wanted to: she could try new
things, meet new people, fall in love. She could friggin'
skydive if she set her mind to it.

She had survived her parents' deaths, raising two boys,
was establishing a career. She could and *would* survive
losing Will.

It would hurt for a while, but then it would fade. Pain,
in whatever form it took, always did…she just had to get
through it.

She gritted her teeth. *Put one foot in front of the other
and keep on truckin'.* She could try pottery lessons again,
keep practising her surfing or learn to paint. There were
a million things she could try to pass the time while she
got used to not having Will in her life, her heart, her mind.

OK, lesson learnt, Lu thought. *Good talk to yourself.*

So, really, did she *actually* have to jump out of this plane
now? She was hovering near space, she was scared out of
her bracket, but since she'd got this far she knew she could
do it if she absolutely had to—she could do *anything* if she
absolutely had to—so she didn't really *have* to jump out of
the plane, did she?

She could just calmly tell the jump master that she'd
changed her mind. She was allowed to do that.

Lu made a slashing movement across her neck, but realised that he hadn't got her message when she and the plane parted company and they went tumbling through unsubstantial nothingness.

Oh, God, this was it…she was going to *diiiiiieeeee!*

CHAPTER TWELVE

LATER THAT AFTERNOON, Lu rolled her head on her neck, trying to work out the kinks as she parked her car in her garage. Her time in Himeville had turned out to be the break she'd needed to think her life through: cold days, freezing nights, a dead mobile battery and no internet connection. Except for a brief text to the twins as she left Durban, to explain that she was away for a couple of days, she hadn't spoken to anybody for ages.

She had needed not to speak to anyone for that long—needed to take the time to sort out her head and her life—and she was glad that she had. She felt settled, in control, calmer.

After greeting her dogs, who'd been fed by neighbours while she was away, Lu grabbed her bag and headed into her home. In the kitchen she swiped a clean dishcloth over her hair to soak up the raindrops and then wiped the freezing drops from her face.

She wanted a cup of tea, a hot bath and to climb into her huge bed. Himeville suddenly seemed a very long way away, so she deliberately recalled the conclusions she'd come to.

Lu held the back of a kitchen chair and looked out at the wild garden beyond the kitchen. There was no changing the past. It was what it was. Her parents had been irresponsible with money, but it would have been a million times worse if they'd died and left them with nothing… She wouldn't have been able to keep the twins and they would have had to go into the state system.

The thought of it made her shudder.

Her parents had sadly and tragically died, but they'd left them well provided for. She couldn't and wouldn't think about their financial situation before they'd passed…considering *what ifs* and *maybes* just did her head in. If they had lived they would have made a plan, and she knew that no matter what had happened their family would have remained together. They might have been irresponsible and flighty, but their loyalty to each other and their children had been absolute and unwavering.

Wasn't that what had driven her to keep the boys with her? Loyalty? Her parents, she finally realised, would be so proud of her for doing what she had, so maybe it was time to accept that. She hadn't done all the things that normal young adults did, but she could hold her head up high and say that she'd done what she needed to do.

Who cared if one bitchy reporter thought she'd used Will to boost her career? *She* knew she hadn't, Will knew she hadn't, and her bosses knew she hadn't. She had a career she loved and she was damned if she was giving it up!

As for Will… Well, there wasn't much she could do about him. He was back in Auckland and she was alone. She'd spent many long hours wondering what she'd do if he came back, if he offered her a long-distance relationship, if he wanted to resume their friends-with-benefits status. She wouldn't accept either, she'd decided. He had to step up or step away. Friends with benefits just wasn't her style. It was all or nothing. She deserved to have a real and solid connection with a man she knew would stand with her in rain and sunshine, and if he couldn't commit then that was his problem.

'The kettle's boiling dry.'

Lu looked around and blinked at Will, who was standing in the doorway to the hall. She gaped at him for a moment before snapping her mouth closed and sending him an uncertain look. 'Hi. I didn't hear you knock. Sorry.'

Will took two strides across the floor and lifted the kettle from the ring, shut off the gas. 'I didn't knock. I still have my key.'

Lu lifted her eyebrows at his terse tone. He was clearly annoyed, but she couldn't help but admire his broad shoulders in a bottle green sweater. His jeans were worn and faded, frayed at the bottoms where they touched the brown leather of his flat boots. His hair glistened with rain and his jaw was rough with evening stubble. He'd never looked more attractive.

Will found two glass tumblers and slammed them onto the counter. Another loud search produced a bottle of whisky that she hadn't even known was there. He poured a hefty measure in a glass, downed it in one quick swallow and then poured two fingers into both glasses.

'You've driven me to drink,' he muttered.

Taking the glass he held out, Lu looked at it and then looked over at Will, who leant against the kitchen counter, legs crossed in front of him, the light of battle in his eyes. He was more than annoyed—he was mad as hell. And she didn't need to be a rocket scientist to see that all his anger was directed at her.

In an effort to seem unperturbed Lu sat on the dining table and lifted her feet onto the seat of a chair. Will narrowed his eyes at her and she felt the full intensity of his laser stare. OK, this wasn't good. He was past mad and on his way to furious.

'Where the hell have you been?' he demanded through gritted teeth.

Lu ignored her drink and rested her forearms on her thighs. 'In Himeville.'

'I don't even know where that is! You disappear for two weeks and that's all I get? *In Himeville?*'

Lu cocked her head at his temper. She considered saying that the last time she'd checked she was a grown woman and she didn't have to explain to anybody where she was going or why. Something told her that would be placing a lighted match to a powder keg.

'Yes. In Himeville.'

'And you didn't think that I might wonder where you were?'

'I told Kelby that I'd be away for a couple of days,' Lu protested.

'I am not Kelby, and "a couple of days" is two or three—not ten!' Will snapped.

Lu's eyes widened, but Will wasn't finished yet.

'I didn't know where you were—whether you were OK—whether you'd had an accident. The twins didn't know where you were, and neither did your friends!'

'You weren't even here! You were in New Zealand!'

'I was in New Zealand for *ten hours*! If you'd given me a chance to explain I would've told you that it was a flying visit, a turnaround trip.'

'If you had called me and explained then I would've known that!' Lu ripped back.

'I tried to! Every hour for ten sodding days!'

'I needed some time away—to think,' Lu added, her tone hot with aggravation.

Will's roar escalated by thirty decibels. 'I've been going nuts worrying about you! I started calling hospitals, for God's sake.'

'Will you stop shouting at me? I think you're having a bit of an overreaction, here, Will.'

'Overreaction, my ass! Do you know where I should be right now? With my team, helping Carter prepare for a match in three hours, but instead I've been driving past your house praying that you would come home!' Will rubbed his hands down his face. 'You just don't get it, do you?'

Lu lifted her hands in confusion. 'Get what?'

Will stared at a point beyond her shoulder. His eyes were ringed with black, his face was drawn and his hair dishevelled. She saw him haul in a breath and open his mouth to speak, but the words didn't come out.

'Will, I'm sorry you were worried. Given our last conversation, I thought that you'd left town and that you would be grateful that I was out of your life. I'm fine and—'

'You *still* don't get it.' Will's voice was quiet now. It confused Lu more. 'Well, I'll just have to show you. Give me one minute.'

She watched, open-mouthed, as he whipped his slim mobile phone from his pocket and pushed some buttons. 'Mak—she's back.' He waited a few seconds before speaking again. 'Apparently she's been in Himeville—wherever that is.'

'I'm fine, Mak!' Lu protested, but Will sent her a look that suggested that she shut up.

His eyes never left hers.

He snapped his mobile closed, tossed it onto the counter. Lu echoed his movements and slid off the table, fisted her hands on her hips. 'I've said that I am sorry, but this really has nothing to do with you, and I—'

'Nothing to do with me?'

Lu was still trying to articulate her response when Will grabbed her, pulled her towards him and slanted his lips over hers, his mouth capturing the words she was still trying to say. Before she could think about objecting his tongue slid into her mouth and she lost the ability to think. Blood drained from her head and it was all she could do to keep on her feet as he kissed every objection away. His broad hands snaked up under her clothes and in one deft movement he unsnapped her bra. His warm hands were on her breasts, kneading her nipples to a pulsing ache that hovered just below pain.

Lu whimpered in his mouth, hooked her hands around his neck and boosted herself up. Her legs were anchored around his waist and the juncture of her thighs was riding his erection.

Will held her easily and just kissed her. And then he kissed her some more, open-mouthed and open-hearted. She could feel him vibrating, knew it was from emotion, and pushed her body into his, wanting to absorb every real emotion she could feel emanating from him.

Will sat her on the kitchen counter and held her face, his eyes tracing her features.

Lu bit her lip. 'Will? Why have you stopped?'

His fingers brushed her mouth, her cheek, caressed her ear.

'I needed to know that you were safe—physically, emotionally, mentally.'

Lu's concentration bounced between his words and his actions, her mind and heart trying to decode his words while her libido demanded that he kiss her some more.

She couldn't think.

'How do you think it felt to know that you were hurting and that there was nothing I could do to help you? That I wasn't there to get you out of your far too critical head? That I wasn't there to dry your tears?'

Lu bit her lip, unable to drop her eyes from his.

'There were lots of tears, weren't there, Mermaid?'

The mobile tucked into his back pocket beeped and Will yanked it out with his right hand. 'Kelby and Carter want to know where I am.'

Lu frowned as she jumped off the counter. 'I thought your contract with the Rays was over?'

'That's one of the many things I need to talk to you

about. I can't now…' He glanced at his watch. 'I have to get to the stadium. I am late as it is.'

'I agree that we need to talk,' Lu said, her hands twisting his shirt. 'But I'm not sure if you're going to like what I have to say.'

Will placed his hands under her elbows and easily lifted her so that he could look straight into her eyes. The muscles of his arms bunched as they held her up. His expression was pure determination and stubbornness. 'Well, then, you should know this before you say whatever you have to say. No matter where you run, I will find you. I am not letting you out of my life—ever. You are my world—all of my world. You are what I need. You are who I live for. Being with you is all I want.'

Lu felt the cords of tension around her heart snap. She was so stunned that she couldn't even smile. 'I—'

He lowered her to her feet. 'I've got to go, Lu, but take the next couple of hours to get used to the idea that you and I are *it*. That I love you and that neither of us is going anywhere.'

'But—'

Will dropped a kiss on her hair and his hand rubbed her shoulder. He looked worried and rueful, stressed and a little scared. Lu's heart swelled.

'Later—please? I'll be back after the game…around eleven. Wait up for me, OK?'

'Uh…OK.'

It was only long after she heard the front door close that the weight of his words truly sank in. Will loved her and wanted to be with her. She was going to have her own happily-ever-after.

Lu allowed the bubble of laughter she'd been holding in escape and twirled around, grinning like a loon.

Wait until he came home? She didn't think so.

* * *

The fact that the Rays had won and booked their place in the quarter-finals had nothing to do with him and everything to do with his team, Will decided ruefully as he waited to be called to do a post-match televised interview. He'd been less than useless for the entire eighty minutes. He normally had an impressive concentration span, but tonight he'd been ambushed by thoughts of Lu that he couldn't control.

Will looked out over the field, filled with fans of all ages celebrating their win, and wondered if Lu had watched the match. He was happy at the win—of course he was—but his thoughts were just filled with Lu. He'd messed up earlier by yelling at her and then confusing the situation further with that hot kiss. Then he'd added confusion to an already complicated situation by telling her that he was in love with her. Well, he was—but he could've found a more romantic way to tell her.

She was the sum total of what he wanted, needed and wished for.

But what if he wasn't what *she* wanted and needed? What had she meant when she'd stated that he might not like what she had to say? What could that mean? Why hadn't he just taken some more time and talked it through with her? At least he wouldn't be in this agony now.

Will looked at his watch. He'd have to be nice to the sponsors, congratulate his team, and then he could head home. *Damn*, this interviewer was dragging his feet. He shouldn't even be doing this interview, but Carter hated dealing with the press and had handed the responsibility over to him. He suspected that was what would happen for the next six months. Carter would get the glory and he'd do the work. He could live with that. In six months' time the team would be his again.

He wanted to get to Lu, but he also wanted to delay any

bad news as long as he could—he wanted to nurture the hope that they had a future. He'd been conscious of the fact that if she said that she didn't want him then he needed to be able to slink off and lick his wounds on his own. He doubted that he could have done any interviews if she'd given him the boot.

He saw the signal to step up and stand in front of the interviewer and hauled in a deep breath. *Be brief, be succinct, get it done and get to Lu.*

Lu, dressed in jeans, a bulky sweater and a cap pulled low over her eyes, watched as Will walked away from the cameras, ducked around a group of kids tackling each other and headed for the players' tunnel. He yanked down his tie and snapped open his collar button, ran his hand through his hair.

He shoved his suit jacket back to push his hands into his pants pockets. He looked tired and worried and near the limit of his patience. A teenage boy ran up to him and his smile wasn't as easy as it normally was as he dashed his signature across a rugby ball. She could see the tension in his shoulders, in the looks he frequently sent towards the exit.

Tucking her iPad under her arm, she jammed her hands into the pockets of her jacket and started to walk over to him.

'Will!' she called, and his head whipped around.

His eyes connected with hers and he angled his head, waiting at the edge of the field for her to reach him. When she was close enough to touch Will held out his hand to her and she saw some of his tension dissipate when her hand slid into his.

'You're here. Why?'

'I have something to show you. Will you come with me?'

'Sure. Where to?'

Lu nodded to the first row of seats in the almost empty stadium. 'Let's sit.'

Will looked around, unconvinced. 'It's rather chilly, and it's going to rain again. Don't you want to go inside?'

Lu shook her head as she led Will up the stairs and sat him down in one of the hard plastic chairs. She crossed her legs and sucked in her breath, looked at the field.

'When we fought I said that you haven't changed, that you are exactly the same as you were when you were twenty-four,' Lu said, her voice jerky. 'That was ugly and cruel and I'm sorry I said it.'

'Sometimes I wonder if it isn't the truth,' Will replied, putting his feet up on the chair in front of him.

'You know it's not, Will. I have the greatest respect for how you turned your life around and I'm so proud of you for doing it. I'm sorry that you still carry such guilt about that period in your life, but maybe you should forgive the young, stupid, dumb jock that you were.'

Lu pulled her iPad out from under her arm and turned it on.

'What's going on, Lu?'

Lu tapped the screen. 'You once asked me if photography was my passion…'

'It is—of course it is,' Will replied, his voice full of conviction as a series of her images flashed across the screen.

Will pointed at the screen as a photo appeared. 'Is this the image for the calendar shoot?'

Lu looked down at the photograph of the naked squad— boy bits hidden—and smiled. They were all laughing, all looking hot, all looking as if they were having the best time of their lives.

'Being in black and white, the image is stark—so why do I want to think it's in colour?' Will tipped his head, thinking. 'It's the emotion, the happiness…it gives an impression of colour.' Will looked at her, utterly amazed. 'It's a fantastic image…they look so happy. How did you do that, Lu? Suggest colour with emotion?'

'Tequila,' Lu quipped. 'Anyway, the reason I'm showing you these is because I've realised that while I adore my job, *you* are my biggest passion.'

More photographs followed, starting with the first one she'd taken of him, looking serious but capable. 'That night I thought I recognised your soul but now—' various shots of Will coaching followed '—I know I do.'

Lu sneaked a look at Will, who seemed to be fascinated at the images of him on the screen.

'Do you know that at least half of the thousands of images I've taken over the last month have been of you?' Lu asked him. 'I love this one,' she said, deliberately chatty, leaning back into his shoulder. Will was crouching on the field, surrounded by his squad, his expression serious but his eyes sparkling. 'It captures how you feel about rugby. *Your* passion.'

'Until you,' Will croaked.

Lu swallowed and blinked away her tears as she gestured to the screen again. 'The following photos capture what I love most about you…'

Will on her veranda eating cake, tossing a rugby ball to Deon on the beach, sharing a joke with Kelby, lying next to the pool in swim-trunks, sunlight glinting off his muscled frame.

Will laughed at some of the images.

Lu snuck her hand into his and tangled her fingers with his. 'This is what I do—what I am, Will. And it seems like you are my favourite subject.' Lu half turned in her seat to face him. 'Before you say anything I need to tell you that I took those huge canvases down from the hall and the living room and put them in the study.'

Will leaned forward and the emotion in his eyes made her blink.

'Why did you take them down, hon? You love those photographs.'

Lu pursed her lips. 'I do, but it's time to move on. I have so many photos of my parents and the twins scattered around. I don't want them to dominate my house and my thoughts any more. I want photos of us and you—family and new memories.'

Will's eyes smoked over. 'Lu…God…'

'My parents are gone, and I miss them, but it's time to let them go. The twins are leading their own lives and making their own decisions and I need to move on.'

'Move on to what, Lu?'

Lu smiled gently. 'You, me, *us*.'

Will's voice sounded uncharacteristically emotional when he finally answered. 'So there is an us?'

Lu stared at him, completely nonplussed. Judging by his the-axe-is-about-to-fall expression, Will still had doubts about her—doubts that she loved him. How could that be?

'Why wouldn't there be?'

'Because you said you had something to tell me that I wouldn't like…'

Lu had to smile. How could her smart man have got this so wrong?

'I was going to tell you that I want more from you than just being friends with benefits! You still look doubtful… *why?*'

'I just can't believe how lucky I am.' Will rubbed the back of his neck, his eyes filled with emotion. 'I just wish you could see yourself through my eyes—wish you could understand how extraordinary I think you are. You are a brilliant photographer and an amazingly unselfish, giving person. And I'm driven and ambitious and frequently selfish. I'm tough, and I'm scared that I will hurt you.'

'Will you cheat on me?' Lu asked, cocking her head.

'No.'

Will's answer was rock-fast and true. Lu hadn't even needed to ask the question. She'd already known the answer in her heart. But she'd thought that he needed to say it.

'Will you demand that I stop work?'

Denial, hot and fast, flashed in his eyes. 'No. You love your job—why would I do that?'

Lu looked down at their linked hands. 'Will, don't put me on a pedestal, because I *will* fall off. I did one good thing, and I'm proud I did it, but it's not all of who I am. I can be bitchy and moody, and I will have days when I want to bury myself in my studio and not come out. There will be days of tears and frustration, moments of madness, hours of irrationality. I will be occasionally insecure and will probably make some huge mistakes. So will you. But, to paraphrase that great blonde, Marilyn Monroe, if we can't handle each other at our worst then we don't deserve each other at our best. I'm not an angel, and neither are you, and I'd hate it if we were. I'm standing here, trying to tell you that I am just Lu...'

'And I think you are perfect—flaws and all.'

'And that I love you.' Lu's eyes filled with emotion.

Satisfaction flickered across his face as he rose to his feet. 'And I am *so* in love with you.'

Will lifted his hands to cradle her face, his eyes blazing with love for her. Lu sank into his kiss and joy bubbled up inside her as she leaned into his embrace, felt those strong arms envelop her.

She was where she belonged...finally. This man was her home.

She recognised a sound—the click and whirr of a camera going off...after all, along with Will's laughter it was her favourite sound in the world. Lu lifted her mouth from Will's and turned to see a dark-haired woman standing just below them.

'I'm Lin Reynolds. Can I ask you a couple of questions?' she demanded, looking up and into their faces.

Will's eyes blazed with fury. 'No. And isn't it a bit late for you to be asking questions? I thought you wrote articles first and checked your facts later.'

Lin Reynolds…the author of the article that had sent her running. Lu lifted her eyebrows as the woman tossed her head and scoffed at Will's statement.

'Like you would've answered any questions about *that* photograph!'

'Probably not.' Will wrapped his hand around the back of Lu's neck and his eyes softened as he looked at her. Happiness, satisfaction and relief blazed from his eyes.

'Go away,' he said, without taking his eyes off her face.

'What do you see in her, anyway?' the pushy reporter demanded.

Good grief, this woman was a pain in the ass.

Lu tipped up her head and sent him a naughty grin. 'Yeah, Will, what *do* you see in me, *anyway*?'

He looked straight into her eyes and he smiled softly. 'I think she's brave, loyal and loving. Sexy as hell, too.'

'Just because she was a glorified nanny?'

That was what she had thought—but she hadn't been. She had been the twins' link to their parents, their port in every storm, a solid and consistent loving presence in their lives.

She'd be the same for Will too.

And they'd share some very hot sex. *Whoo!*

'I know that look,' Will whispered, and grinned.

'You should,' Lu murmured, her eyes sliding to the right. 'She's still here…'

'She's persistent. I'll give her that,' Will said, and on a frustrated sigh he turned back to the irritating journalist. 'Having fun, butting in on a very private moment? And, by the way, what were *you* doing at nineteen? Sex, drugs and rock and roll? You just threw a very big rock through a very big glass house, Ms Reynolds.'

The woman folded her arms across her chest. 'I still think there's a lot more to this story than you are telling… just like there is a lot more to your divorce than you want everyone to know.'

'My divorce is now very old, very tedious news. The only thing you need to know is that I love Lu and—'

'I love him,' Lu chipped in, her grin widening at the thought.

'And…?' Lin leaned forward eagerly. 'Are you getting married? Making it legal?'

'We're not going to tell you that,' Will retorted.

'But…what else can I tell my readers?'

Lu, as she snuggled into Will's side, felt sorry for this sad woman who lived her life reporting on other people's lives. 'Really, Ms Reynolds, there isn't a story here. Will and I are together, we're crazy about each other, and we're going to be deliciously, boringly, brain-meltingly happy. Loyal, loving…monogamous. No fuss, no drama. He's going to keep coaching. I'm going to keep clicking.'

Will looked at her approvingly. 'That is it in a nutshell.' He looked at Lin and grinned. 'You can quote us on that.'

When the reporter was out of earshot Will wrapped his other arm around her waist and yanked her into him. 'Boringly, brain-meltingly happy, Mermaid?'

Lu grinned. 'It just tumbled out.'

'It sounds good to me. Let's go home.'

'Yours or mine?'

Will brushed his thumb across her lips. 'I'm really hoping that yours can become mine, too. At least for the next five years, since I've signed a contract with the Rays which will keep me here that long. I don't want to spend another night without you. You OK with that?'

'Very. I just want you…for always.'

Will's lips touched her in a love-soaked kiss that saturated every atom of her body, promising love and devotion and protection. Lu sighed into his mouth as she reached out and grabbed the shiny, star-spangled feeling of happiness.

She was, finally, Lu. And best of all she was monstrously in love with a man who loved her back. Life, she thought, as they walked with their arms around each other towards the exit, didn't get much more breathtakingly splendid than this.

EPILOGUE

SEVEN MONTHS LATER, on Lu's thirtieth birthday, her three men stood in front of the guests gathered on her big veranda to celebrate her birthday. Her breath caught in her throat. The twins were only just shy of Will's height—her two blond, brave, *nice* boys.

And Will, looking so very hot in black pants and a white cotton shirt that showed off his gorgeous body to perfection, stood between them, his hands jammed into his pockets, totally relaxed. Like Nate and Dan, he also wanted to make a speech, but unlike her brothers he didn't need key cards to remind him of what he wanted to say.

Will had a very clever mouth—in the bedroom and out.

Nate cleared his throat as Daniel tapped a spoon against the stem of his glass. The room quietened and Lu caught Will's eye and smiled at his wink.

'Thank you all for joining Daniel, Will and I at this occasion to celebrate Lu's thirtieth birthday. As most of you know, Lu raised us after our parents died when we were eight, and about a year ago we left her on her own to go off to university. We were terrified that she was going to hide out in this house and start talking to her cats.'

Laughter rumbled as Daniel took over the speech. 'Instead she met Will, and we're pretty chuffed because she chose someone who can organise tickets to any rugby game we want and who can invite us to practise with the Rays. Other than that, he's pretty useless.'

Will rolled his eyes as the boys slapped him on the shoulder. *Yeah, useless,* Lu thought. Except when they over-exceeded their allowance and tapped Will for a loan. Or when they needed advice on girls, or their studies, or just to chat. Will had slid into his role of advisor and older brother and the twins valued his presence in their lives. He was now so much more to them than Lu's live-in lover, and it made her heart jump into her throat just thinking about the bond they shared. If anything ever happened to her she knew they would never lose Will.

Daniel continued. 'But he does make Lu happy, and we cannot thank him enough for that.'

Tears brimmed in Lu's eyes and she saw Will's Adam's apple bob up and down as he swallowed his own emotion.

'So, Lu, we bought you another skydiving jump—not that you really did it the first time.'

Lu borrowed one of Will's favourite expressions. 'Hell, no!' she called out.

She'd told them that she'd skydived in Himeville but none of them had believed her, insisting that she was making it up to get out of really doing it. Lu insisted that she didn't care if they believed her or not, but the argument raged on.

'You are such a *girl*!' Nate said in mock disgust.

'And proud of it,' Lu retorted as the whole room laughed.

'Anyway,' Daniel continued, 'your real gift is a sort of combination gift…from Will, Nate and I.'

Lu tipped her head, curious.

Nate held her eyes. 'We'd like to give you the house, Lu. *This* house. We'd like to sign our shares in it over to you. Partly to say thank you for providing us with a safe place to be when our lives fell apart. Thank you for being so brave and loving us so much to do that.'

'And we'd really like you to live here with Will, but if he ever moves you to Auckland and coaches their team we will *not* be happy!' Nate added.

'Neither will I!' Kelby shouted from the back of the room.

Lu held her hand to her throat as tears streamed down her face. Will was a blurry mass of muscle as he stepped forward and took her hand. Lu blinked and he came into focus, a glinting ring between his thumb and forefinger.

Lu gaped at the aquamarine and diamond ring and then at him. 'Wha—?'

Will shook his head to silence her. 'My part of the gift is this, but unfortunately for you, it comes with me. I'd like to live here with you in this house, as your husband, your lover, your best friend. Marry me, Lu?'

'You want to get married again?' Lu managed to stutter.

'Not again…for the first time. Properly. Because I am utterly in love with you. Say yes, Lu.'

'I love you too. Yes. Of course!'

Will slipped the ring onto her finger as the room erupted into cheers.

'Say yes to skydiving, baby,' Will said as he bent to kiss her.

'Anything you want…' Lu replied, swept away by the emotional moment as she reached up to meet his mouth. Then her eyes narrowed and she slapped a hand on his chest. 'What? What did you just ask me? You sneaky skunk!'

Will just laughed, slid his arms around her and kissed her.

Lu sighed and sank into his embrace. She would argue with him about skydiving later…

Again.

* * * * *

HER LAST LINE OF DEFENCE

BY
MARIE DONOVAN

Marie Donovan is a Chicago-area native, who got her fill of tragedies and unhappy endings by majoring in opera/vocal performance and Spanish literature. As an antidote to all that gloom, she read romance novels voraciously throughout college and graduate school.

Donovan worked for a large suburban public library for ten years as both a cataloguer and a bilingual Spanish storytime presenter. She graduated magna cum laude with two bachelor's degrees from a Midwestern liberal arts university and speaks six languages. She enjoys reading, gardening and yoga. Please visit the author's website at www.mariedonovan.com and also her Sizzling Pens group blog at www.sizzlingpens.blogspot.com.m.

In memory of two humble men: my grandpa Oz, who merely "cleaned up in Europe"; and Great-Uncle Richard, who "watched the fireworks" while trapped under a bush on a hill in the Philippines.

And to my husband, who tells me you can indeed sleep on the back of an armoured tank if you get tired enough.

God bless all our soldiers.

1

"No, NO! HELL, NO! Not just hell no, fu—"

"At ease, Sergeant!" It wasn't a suggestion.

Luc Boudreaux clamped his mouth shut and wondered who in the hell he had pissed off badly enough to lead him to this. He thought he'd made it through his Afghan tour of duty without stepping on his crank. He'd stayed away from the local girls, avoided shooting anyone who didn't deserve it and brought some decent health care to several tribes whose only technology was Soviet-era weaponry.

He took a deep breath. "Sir, may I ask why I am being selected for this task?"

Captain Olson, his commanding officer snorted. "Can the 'sir' shit—you haven't called me 'sir' in years. Now pull the stick out of your ass and sit down."

Luc dropped into the beat-up office chair and stared at his boss across the equally beat-up desk. Special Forces spent their budget on gear, not furniture. "Okay, Olie, what the hell?" He spread his hands wide in frustration.

Magnus Olson, or "Olie" as he was known to his

men and half of Afghanistan, stroked the long blond beard that made him look like a recruiting poster for Viking pillagers. Luc guessed his own black beard made him a pirate poster boy. "Like I was trying to say before you ripped me a new one, here's the rest of the deal, and I have to admit it's a crappy one—you train Congressman Cook's daughter in jungle survival skills, and the fine congressman won't torpedo your career."

"What?" Luc leaped to his feet.

Olie let him blow off several choice remarks before lifting a meaty hand. "Okay, okay. Sit down, Rage, and I'll go over this again real slow with you."

For once, Luc was living up to his nickname of the Ragin' Cajun. Most of the time it was a team joke since he was usually a mellow guy. But now, no. The battle lines were drawn.

Olie reached behind him, pulled a beer out of the minifridge and tossed the bottle to Luc. "Drink up. We deserve it."

Luc popped the cap and took a long pull of the icy brew, suddenly weary. "Seriously, why me? Get a jungle survival school instructor. I have lots and lots of leave coming my way, and I need to get back to Louisiana." His parents and grandparents had had serious home damage from the last hurricane that blew through, and Luc was going to help them rebuild.

"'It has to be you, it has to be you-u-u-u,'" Olie crooned to the old show-tune melody. "You're the only guy I know who survived the jungles of San Lucas de la Selva alone for more than a month with only the clothes on his back and a machete."

"Oh, *mon Dieu.*" Luc sat up in horror. "His daughter is going to San Lucas de la Selva?"

Olie nodded, all traces of laughter gone from his face. "That she is. The lovely country San Lucas de la Selva, joke of the jungle, armpit of the Amazon."

Hellish nightmare here on earth was more like it. Luc was firmly convinced that his survival—and a close thing that had been—had rested entirely on his grandmother's daily rosary for his health and the fact that he shared a name with *le bon père* Saint Lucas of the Jungle, the rugged nineteenth century priest who had disappeared into the jungle to bring the natives to Christ. Three years later, explorers from the outpost had been stunned to find Saint Lucas alive and well, ministering to his local parishioners. Every stinking, nasty day in that jungle, Luc had prayed to Saint Lucas to, well, basically intercede for his sorry ass and get him the hell out of there. He'd prayed for other things, too, but they hadn't been granted.

And now it looked as if Saint Lucas was collecting on the promises Luc had made him. "This girl, she can't know what it's like down there, or else she wouldn't even think of going." Luc still got a chill down his spine when he saw a map of the Amazon.

"According to the congressman, his late wife grew up in a missionary settlement in San Lucas, where her parents were doctors."

"They lived there on purpose?" Luc couldn't even imagine. "And why can't the congressman talk his daughter out of it? Is she dumb or something? Has a death wish?"

"He's tried everything short of having the State Department pull her passport but she has apparently grown up on exotic tales of the jungle." Olie waggled his fingers in a fake-mystic way. "She's signed up to teach the locals in the same settlement—wants to follow in the family footsteps."

"And she's picking the jungle over politics."

Olie laughed. "Might be fewer snakes in the jungle."

Luc snorted. "So what the hell do I do, Olie? This jerk-off would really screw me over?"

"In a heartbeat." His CO looked away and drank some beer, flicking his forefinger against his thumb.

"What is it?" Olie only did that little thing with his hand when he was jittery.

"Nothing."

"Olie…" Luc cajoled him.

"Nothing. I said it was nothing, and I mean nothing, Boudreaux."

"No way." Luc shook his head in amazement. "He threatened you and the rest of the team, too, didn't he? And you didn't want to tell me 'cuz that would pressure me to agree."

"In case you haven't noticed, Sergeant Boudreaux, I am a big boy whose career doesn't depend on the good opinion of some shit-eating congressman—and yours doesn't, either."

"Shit," Luc said. He never figured on making general someday but didn't want to leave the army before he was good and ready. Or slink out with his tail between his legs as if he'd been dishonorably discharged. And to let Olie and the team get screwed over, too?

"I'll do it."

"You sure?" Olie gave him a steely glare.

"I'm sure." Luc managed to fake a laugh. "Maybe once Daddy's Little Princess sees what survival training is like, she'll go back to the snakes in Washington, D.C."

"YOU MADE ARRANGEMENTS for what?" Claire Cook dug her nails into her palms and winced at the pain.

"Jungle survival lessons." Her father gave her a wide smile and helped himself to a glass of sweet tea from the pitcher in the cherry-paneled, extra-large refrigerator. "Ah, delicious. Did you brew mint leaves into it, as well? Very refreshing."

Claire had been a politician's daughter long enough to know tap dancing when she saw it. "Survival lessons?" she prompted.

Her dad set down the glass and dropped his soothing tone. "Since you have decided this is your course of action, foolish as it may be, I am helping you to implement your choice in the safest way possible."

"Dad, really. The settlement at Río San Lucas is its

own little town—just like Cooksville." Their hometown was named after their ancestor, who helped settle
central Virginia before the Revolutionary War. The
redbrick house they were standing in had been com-
mandeered by the British as a barracks during that
war and barely escaped being burned by the Yankees
during what her grandfather Cook had always referred
to as the War of Northern Aggression.

But her dad was on a roll. "Cooksville isn't surrounded by deadly rain forest, killer snakes and venomous spiders."

Claire made a face. There he was harping on the
snakes and spiders again, just because she didn't even
like the supposedly harmless daddy longlegs spiders.
Maybe she should try killing them on her own rather
than yelling for their housekeeper, Louella. She
flinched at a tickle on her neck and realized it was a
stray dark hair falling out of her ponytail. She really had
to get over that.

"Not to mention jaguars, feral pigs and half-naked
tribesmen who would be more than happy to add an
exotically beautiful young girl to their harem, or
squad of wives, or concubine crew, or whatever they
call it down there."

Claire had to roll her eyes. Brown hair, brown eyes
and brown freckles scattered across a nose that hovered on the edge of snub was hardly exotic. And honestly, she'd had plenty of practice fighting off overly
amorous men among the suit-wearing tribes of the

Potomac River. A couple she hadn't fought at all, but her dad didn't need to know that.

"I will be fine," she enunciated carefully. "So thank you, but no thanks. Dr. Schmidt will show me the ropes once I get down there and I won't have any problems."

"Claire, Claire, Claire." Her father shook his carefully coiffed silver head in what she figured was mock ruefulness.

"Dad, Dad, Dad." She copied him right back.

He dropped the Mr. Nice Dad act and pulled on his congressman face—not the kindly, wise face the cameras saw, but the face his opponents saw when they tried to block his bills or basically thwart his not-inconsiderable will. "You will take this training, or you won't go to San Lucas. Not to teach, not to visit, not even to fly over it."

"And I told *you*, if you try to pull my passport, I will go to the media. I'm sure that TV reporter you accidentally called a 'slime-sucking son of a bitch' on live feed would be happy to interview me."

Her old man pulled his face into a half grin. "Ah, you wound me, Claire. To think that I of all people would be so obvious, and after all these years in politics, no less."

A knot tightened in her stomach. "If you're not going to be obvious, then what?"

"Dr. Schmidt is coming to the States on a fund-raising lecture tour in January, isn't he?"

"Yes." Claire eyed him narrowly.

"And the settlement gets most of its funding from American donations, doesn't it?"

"Yes," she muttered. Dammit, she knew what was coming.

"If the kind European Dr. Schmidt is found to have some problem that might prevent his American visa from being approved, perhaps the nasty rumor of association with the narcoterrorists in the south of San Lucas—"

"Dad!" Claire's chest tightened. "Dr. Schmidt has never associated with the drug runners—never!"

"Come on, Claire, we both know he doesn't ask many questions when some scumbag shows up with a mysterious gunshot wound he got while 'cleaning his automatic rifle.'" Her dad made air quotes with his fingers. "Your grandfather did the same thing when he ran the settlement, so don't try to tell me different."

Claire pursed her lips. "The settlement is neutral territory down there. That's why they need me as a teacher. The local villagers know it's safe to send their children for schooling so they can get an education, have a better life than what their parents had."

"And do what? Move to the city where they can live in slums and pick over the garbage dump for food?" Dad shook his head. "Your mother and I had this discussion a million times. What if they are better off in the jungle, doing what their ancestors have done for thousands of years?"

"And what did Mom say? She was the one who grew up in the settlement."

"Your mother was adopted into the tribe, knew the languages and cultures and was generally regarded as a world expert on San Lucas de la Selva, but even *she* didn't know the answers. How do you expect to?"

This was what was so infuriating about arguing with her father. He had the politician's trick of turning her argument back on her and twisting her words all around. She resorted to what *did* work: stubbornness. "I don't expect to fix everything. I expect to go."

"My God, you're pigheaded." He shook his head. "Just like your mother and grandfather. All right. You'll go—if you pass the survival training."

Claire protested but he held up his hand, his blue eyes blazing. "You are my only child, the only child of your mother, and I will be damned if I put you on a plane to the dangerous jungle when you can't even make yourself kill a harmless spider here in Virginia. I'm willing to let you go, but not as some lamb to the jungle slaughter."

"Fine." Claire gritted her teeth and relaxed. She'd been a Girl Scout, knew how to build a fire, find out which way was north. This would be similar, only designed for a more tropical climate than central Virginia. "How hard can it be?"

Her dad smiled, but it was his sharky smile that Claire had never seen directed at her before. "How hard can it be?" he mocked. "I guess you'll have to ask

Sergeant First Class Luc Boudreaux. He's the Green Beret soldier who will be training you."

"OH, WOW. YOUR dad said 'Green Beret Sergeant First Class Boudreaux'?" Claire's best friend Janey Merrick stopped midjog and bit her lip.

"Yes, why?" Claire sucked in some oxygen, glad for the break. Janey was in much better shape than she was, being an army first lieutenant at the Pentagon attached to some general's staff. She had gone through the Reserve Officers Training Corps at the University of Virginia, where she and Claire had met.

Janey pushed her light brown bangs off her forehead while Claire drank some water. "Green Berets are trained for anything and everything, but their specialty is working with and training indigenous forces. Back in the Vietnam War, they were the jungle warfare specialists—they called them the snake eaters."

"Snake eaters?" Claire's stomach pitched.

"They've branched out since, especially to desert and mountain warfare, but they are some of the toughest SOBs in the army." Janey eyed her. "Well, if you have a Green Beret sergeant first-class training you, I won't worry so much. Those guys know everything. You'll learn how to take care of yourself or die trying."

"Oh, Janey." Claire staggered to a park bench and collapsed. "Why did my dad do this to me? Am I going to have to eat snakes?"

Her friend laughed. "Because he doesn't want you

to go, and yes, probably. But they taste kind of like tough chicken—so I've been told. Hey, and here I was complaining about a desk job."

Claire sat up straight. When had she become a whiner? Whiners never won. "I'm still going to do it. I can eat snakes. I can survive in the jungle. I can do it." She jumped to her feet and jogged in place, ignoring the burn in her thigh muscles. "Let's go!"

Janey shook her head and smiled. "By the time you come back, you'll be able to kick my ass. Come on, soldier girl. I'll teach you some running cadences—they'll help you breathe better. Repeat after me—okay?" She broke into a jog and Claire followed. "I wanna be an Airborne Ranger."

"I wanna be an Airborne Ranger," Claire managed to gasp.

"Live the life of sex and danger."

"Live the life of—what?" Claire stopped again.

"Sex and danger, Claire, sex and danger. They go hand-in-hand for soldiers. The danger gets their adrenaline all revved up and they burn it off with sex." Janey grinned. "Remember that time we were supposed to go shopping and I told you I had to work all weekend? Well, last year I'd gone out a couple times with this one marine right before he shipped out."

"Yes?" Claire lifted an eyebrow.

Janey wiggled her eyebrows in return. "He shipped back in. In more than one way."

"Janey!" Claire scolded.

"I know, I know." Her friend didn't look abashed at all. "But, Claire, he was so tan and buff—and eager, after a year in the desert. Social opportunities there are mighty limited."

"So you took pity on a poor, lonely marine."

"Believe me, I got as much as I gave." Her friend got a quizzical look on her face. "I wonder if your Green Beret is fresh from the sandbox."

"Sandbox?"

"What the soldiers call their Middle East deployments."

Claire shrugged. "I don't know, and I don't care. Whoever he is, he's probably some suck-up who thinks he can advance his career by doing a favor for a congressman."

"If Sergeant First Class…you said Boudreaux, right? If SFC Boudreaux was an ambitious suck-up, he sure wouldn't be in the Green Berets. Used to be Special Forces was a dead end on the army career ladder. Not so much anymore, but these guys are not your loudmouth glory hounds who go overseas with their general on fact-finding missions and brag how they heard gunfire from five miles away." Janey frowned. "Man, I wanna go overseas. Riding a desk in D.C. is not what I had in mind when I joined the army."

"I wish Sergeant Boudreaux would go back." Claire knew she was probably pouting but didn't care.

"He's probably not any happier to do this than you

are." Janey did lunges to stretch her calf muscles. "He's either missing out on team training time or personal leave. Instead of hanging out in the woods, doing mock warfare with his buddies, or even better, getting laid and drunk, he's got to train some squeamish chick who once spent two hours looking for her convertible in the Tysons Galleria parking lot."

"So I'm directionally challenged—I came out the Macy's door instead of Neiman Marcus," Claire mumbled.

"Claire, your dad had dropped you off that day— you didn't even have your car."

"All right, Janey, all right." Claire's face flushed. "Maybe I do need to reinforce some outdoor skills."

Janey nodded and smiled encouragingly. "I'm sure you'll learn a lot of useful things from Sergeant First Class Boudreaux."

Claire knew her friend was worried about her being able to take care of herself, but at least Janey wasn't haranguing her like her dad. Once she got back from San Lucas, it was time to get her own place.

"We'd better move before we cramp up." Janey took off jogging backward, her face mischievous. "Here's a new cadence especially for you. 'I wanna be a Green Beret.'"

"I wanna…be a…Green Beret." Claire was starting to puff again.

"'Live the life of sex and foreplay….'"

"Janey!"

2

"READY TO GET UP AND at 'em?" Her father's falsely hearty voice boomed through the large conference room at Ft. Bragg, North Carolina. A gleaming wood table dominated the room with photos of base commanders and world maps framed on the walls. He gestured at one of his aides to set Claire's gear under a white dry-erase board. Claire was scheduled to start her training the next day, but her father had insisted on a meet-and-greet with her trainer before sending her off, and the commanding officer had wanted to inspect her gear. "Learn all about the great outdoors, eh, kitten?"

"Dad, please," Claire muttered. Bad enough she looked like some tricked-out Victorian explorer with seventeen pockets on her super-expensive, brand-new, quick-dry khaki vest and cargo pants. Bad enough she was like Jane about to meet her own personal ape-man. Bad enough she was twenty-four and was still called "kitten."

She tried to ignore her dad and her churning stomach, in that order, and focused on a large painted wooden logo on the wall. Black and silver, the words *De Oppresso Liber* were painted in a semicircle under a six-pronged star. She walked closer—the star was actually a pair of crossed arrows over a long, lethal-looking knife.

According to what Claire had found out searching online after her run with Janey, the Green Berets didn't need any arrows or knives. They could probably kill somebody with a paper clip and a plastic drinking straw—the bendy kind.

De Oppresso Liber. She guessed from her French and Spanish classes that the Latin motto meant From Oppression Freeing or something like that. Freedom from oppression. A noble goal.

In her own little way, that was Claire's goal, too. Not that anyone would consider her oppressed. After all, her father was one of the most powerful politicians in America, her family had plenty of money and she had never wondered if she would have enough to eat. Nothing to complain about, yet…

She wasn't truly free because she hadn't tried to be. No Declaration of Independence had flowed from her pen, no charge up San Juan Hill, no stand at the Alamo. Well, maybe not that last one—she had cried when she visited the mission-fort in San Antonio and seen where real heroes had given their lives for their beliefs.

But it had always been easier to go along with her dad's plans for her, especially after her mother died, when they had clung to each other in their grief.

Claire snuck a look at her father, who was giving a long list of instructions to his assistant. Her father had moved on, had even casually dated a few widows or divorcées. She was actually okay with that, knowing that he would always cherish the love he had for her mother. He had a good and full life, but Claire? Not so much.

Clinging time was over for Claire Cook, the Human Kudzu Vine. Her turning point had come six months ago on the second anniversary of her mother's death, when she had steeled herself to look through the family photo albums her father had shoved to the back of the library closet.

Her mother had been the antithesis of "cling," especially in the black-and-white photos of her as a young girl and then the faded color pictures of her as a teenager—always in the settlement or the jungle surrounding it. The only difference between her and the local girls was lighter skin and more clothing, on the insistence of her parents.

Claire moved along the wall to look at several photos of the base, as well as photos of men in green or tan uniforms. Each one's face was carefully turned away from the camera or otherwise indistinguishable on film. Men building shelters, carrying weapons, reading maps. Men who had no doubt about who they were and what they were meant to do.

Seeing her mother's joyful face and remembering the stories and struggles of their lives in San Lucas,

Claire had carefully closed the album and written her grandfather's successor, Dr. Schmidt.

Her father's droning voice had stopped, and a new electric current ran through the room. She turned away from the wall. Three men stood inside the doorway, the older one some kind of commanding officer and the younger two his subordinates.

Her father leaped to his feet and gave the officer a hearty handshake. "Ah, Colonel Spencer, we spoke on the phone. A pleasure to finally meet you in person."

"Congressman. Ma'am." The colonel gave her a curt nod. Claire nodded in return, noting he didn't verbalize his own delight. The colonel looked like a tougher twin of her father, his silver hair clipped close instead of styled, his green cammies neatly pressed.

If the colonel was spic-and-span army, his men looked like they belonged in the army jail. Were soldiers even allowed to wear beards? The taller, blond guy looked like he might be the cheerful type on a good day, but obviously today wasn't a good day. He, on the other hand, looked like Miss Susie Sunshine compared to his companion. Claire had a nasty feeling that the darker man more closely resembled a man named Luc Boudreaux than Blondie did.

Blackbeard in the flesh. His eyes were two pieces of black coal, cold and glittering. His hair waved well past his collar, his beard covering most of his tanned face. He looked as if he hadn't shaved in months.

Janey's words about being fresh from the sandbox popped into Claire's head. Fresh from the desert to the swamp. No wonder he looked ready to spit nails.

Colonel Spencer gestured to his men. "Congressman Cook, Miss Cook, I'd like you to meet Captain Magnus Olson and Sergeant First Class Luc Boudreaux. Captain Olson has kindly released Sergeant Boudreaux from his current duties to serve as your trainer."

Their lips tightened briefly under all the facial hair. How much pressure had her father exerted on them? They certainly didn't look like eager volunteers.

A knock sounded at the door. Claire gasped. "Janey, what are you doing here?" Her friend stood in her dress uniform, her hat under her arm.

Janey wouldn't meet her eyes and snapped a perfect salute to Colonel Spencer and Captain Olson. The colonel returned it and the captain waved his hand vaguely toward his eyebrow. "First Lieutenant Jane Merrick reporting for duty, sir."

"At ease, Lieutenant." He took the packet of papers Janey offered him and scanned through the sheets, a cynical smile spreading over his face.

"Duty?" Claire asked. As far as she knew, Janey's Pentagon stint was to last at least another six to eight months. Why would they send her to Ft. Bragg? "Are you here on account of me?"

"Sir, my commanding officer ordered me to report to Fort Bragg as a special liaison between his office and yours." Janey still refused to look at Claire, but the tips of her ears were turning red. Captain Olson and Sergeant Boudreaux didn't change expression but Claire sensed their disgust.

"Well, well." Colonel Spencer slapped her papers against his open palm. "An unexpected present from our brethren—and sisters—in arms at the Pentagon. My memory is a tad faulty—are we conducting some joint operation that requires a liaison?"

"Sir, I don't know. I am just following my orders." Janey looked miserable but didn't back down.

The colonel sighed. "Yes, I expect you are." He turned to Claire. "Miss Cook, I assume you know the lieutenant?"

"Yes, we were roommates at UVA—University of Virginia. Go Cavaliers," she finished weakly.

"I was a West Point man myself. Congressman Cook?" He turned to her father.

"Colonel," her father said brightly.

"I don't suppose you would know why First Lieutenant Merrick was plucked from her important desk job in our nation's military command center and sent down to pal around with us lowly Special Forces types, would you?"

"A chaperone." Claire jumped to hear the sergeant's clipped Cajun tones. "Congressman Cook got himself a chaperone for his li'l girl."

Her father's mouth twitched guiltily. Claire wanted to die a thousand deaths. "Oh, Janey, I am so sorry he dragged you into this. Dad, how could you? Janey doesn't deserve this."

"Yo' *papa* don't trust you're alone in the woods with a big, bad Green Beret?" For the first time, Sergeant Boudreaux met her shamed gaze with a mocking one of his own. "You must be quite the tiger."

"Shut your mouth, you!" Her father shot to his feet, his face mottled.

"No offense, sir, but you're not my commanding officer, and last I checked, Fort Bragg is still in the U.S. of A., where freedom of speech still applies."

"Zip it, Boudreaux," his captain said without heat.

"Zipping it, sir." He closed his mouth, his point made.

"No, you zip it, Dad!" Claire turned on her father. "That man is totally justified in his outrage."

"Outrage," Boudreaux mused. "Now that is a *fine* word for this situation."

"You zip it, too! I'm trying to defend you here," Claire cried in frustration.

He arched a black eyebrow at her. "*Bébé,* do I look like a man who needs defending?"

She huffed out a breath and turned back to her father. "You have constantly thrown up roadblocks to my plans, you have tampered with the workings of the U.S. Army, and meddled with the careers of Janey and at least three of her fellow soldiers. You've abused your authority and are a disgrace to your office."

"I don't know about that, *cher,*" Boudreaux interjected with a smirk. "Your daddy hasn't been indicted,

served prison time or accidentally killed someone—
he's an amateur in comparison to his fellow politicians."

Captain Olson unsuccessfully muffled a snort. Colonel Spencer intently studied the ceiling, his jaw twitching.

Claire clenched her trembling fists. "Dad, I have had
enough. I am going to San Lucas, Janey is going to
Washington and these nice men can go wherever they
had planned to go before you came along. Hopefully to
a barber," she added, ticked off at the sergeant's enjoy-
ment of her embarrassment. And who was he to call her
cher, anyway, in that mocking French-tinged accent?

She hurried from the conference room, ignoring her
father's shouts, wanting to escape. She dashed into the
humid Carolina afternoon, crossing the parking lot into
a small landscaped grove with a picnic bench. The scent
of pines didn't quite cover the smell of diesel and something else pungent—explosives? She wasn't sure. Claire
climbed onto the picnic table, her feet resting on the
bench.

A new scent came along, clean and masculine. She
turned and stifled a yelp. Good thing Sergeant
Boudreau was wearing cologne because she certainly
hadn't heard him approach. Of course, that would be
a plus in his line of work. He stood next to her and
stared across the parking lot, shoving his hands into
the back pockets of his jeans, tightening the thin fabric
across his zipper. Not that she noticed things like that.

"Don't worry—you're off the hook." Claire didn't want to meet his mocking glance again. "I'll be fine— the Río San Lucas settlement is like a small town, running water and everything so I can wash my hair." She gave a little laugh, trying to get him to leave her alone.

"Why you wanna go down to that jungle snake hole anyway, Mademoiselle Cook?" This time he wasn't mocking, just curious. "You got somethin' to prove to your *papa?*"

She tried to hide her flinch. "Maybe I have something to prove to myself."

"There are easier ways to do that. Go mountain climbing or white-water rafting if you want to see how tough you are. Walk across the country to raise money for cancer, but moving to the jungle doesn't make you tough—just foolish."

Claire saw red. "Shut up! You denigrate my mother, my grandmother and my grandfather." She slammed her fist into her palm as she named each of her family members. "They moved to San Lucas to serve people who had no one and had nothing. You talk to all the women who lived after my grandfather saved them during difficult childbirth—you talk to all their babies who lived because they had their mothers to breast-feed them. You ask them how foolish it is that they are alive and not buried in an unmarked jungle grave site!"

He stood in silence for a minute. "I apologize," he finally said.

Claire almost fell off the picnic table. "What?"

He ran a strong hand through his wavy hair. "I have been extremely rude and my *grand-mère* and *maman* would pass me a slap. My only defense is that I've been overseas away from civilization too long."

"How long?" she asked without thinking.

"Now that's classified information, ma'am."

His scornful attitude was back. "I'd say at least seven or eight months according to your facial hair," she retorted. "If you don't want people speculating, the least you could do is get a haircut and shave." He did look good as a pirate—maybe he was descended from Jean Lafitte, the famous Louisianan pirate.

"Maybe you should sign up as an intelligence agent instead. It was actually eight months and ten days." He rubbed his chin.

"Claire! Claire!" Her father's voice echoed out the main door of the office building.

She pressed her lips together. She was definitely getting her own place, San Lucas or no. Dad had gone too far.

"There you are, Claire." He hurried up to her, ignoring Boudreaux. "Now can you see how foolish this idea of yours is?" he asked, unknowingly echoing Boudreaux's earlier taunt.

Next to her, the Green Beret sucked in a breath, obviously waiting for her to lose her temper with her father like she had with him.

But her will had been tempered into steel. "Who's going to look like the bigger fool at the press conference I'll arrange—me, for wanting to go to San Lucas, or you, for throwing so many inappropriate roadblocks into my path? Now you're interfering with the U.S. Army."

"And during an election year, too," Boudreaux added helpfully. "Sir."

"You'd do that? To your own father?" He was practically stammering in indignation.

"You were always talking about retiring."

"Retiring! Retiring, not losing to that nobody state senator who's running against me."

"If your constituents don't like your little forays into meddling, they can vote their opinion. I may endorse your opponent myself," she added darkly.

Her father made a choking noise, but wasn't turning any funny colors or clutching his chest so Claire figured he was only pissed off.

She turned to the sergeant. "So you're off the hook with me. Again, I'm sorry for this mess, and I'll make sure it doesn't harm you or your career."

He stared silently at her, his dark eyes unreadable.

She fumbled slightly but finally shoved her hands into two of the pants' eight pockets.

Her father finally found his voice. "You ungrateful child!" He swung around and stomped off to where his aide stood back at the building practically wringing his hands.

"The man surely has a sense of the dramatic. I'm shocked he didn't quote *King Lear* at you."

"What?" Claire looked at him in surprise.

"I see you as more of a Cordelia type—the dutiful daughter who is the only one to stick with her cranky old dad."

Claire blinked. "Yes, I read *King Lear* in college. When did you read it?"

"The army sends Shakespeare comic books overseas for us to look at the pictures when we aren't blowing things up." He delivered his smarty-pants answer with a straight face.

"Oh, buzz off!" She jumped off the picnic table, intending to find Janey and beg her forgiveness.

Boudreaux blocked her way so quickly she didn't see him move. "I'll do it."

"Do what?" Claire turned to him.

"Train you. Get ready for San Lucas—as ready as you can be. As ready as anyone can be," he muttered to himself.

"You will?" Claire's heart beat faster.

"I'll tell you right now—you're nuts for wanting to go, and I fully plan on making you rethink your decision." Her stomach flipped at the first smile she'd seen from him, his teeth flashing white in his black beard. "In fact, I plan on making you *regret* your decision."

OLIE RUBBED HIS BARE chin, which was fish-belly pale in comparison to his sun-darkened cheekbones and forehead. He had dragged Luc off to the base's barber shop, as well, yesterday after the colonel had yelled at them a new one for looking scruffy, especially in front of so-called VIPs. "Rage, you said she spiked her old man's guns so he can't cause trouble for us. We're all off the hook—so why are you doing this?" He gestured to the bartender for a couple beers as they sat side-by-side in the Special Forces' local hangout.

Luc shook his head, his hair now too short to brush his collar. "I'm gonna try like hell to convince her to give up this dumb idea. But if I can't, the girl's gonna go, whether she knows jack-shit about the jungle or not. How will I feel four, five months from now if I hear she got snakebit, got herself sick eating something she shouldn't have, or worse, gets herself out in the jungle and doesn't come back?"

"Been known to happen." Olie nodded solemnly. The bartender set down their drinks.

"That it has." Luc nodded back. They had lost a team-mate in the same incident that had stranded Luc for five weeks. Luc knew it still ate up Olie, him being the commanding officer and all, even if it wasn't his fault. Luc lifted his mug in a silent toast to fallen brothers in arms. Olie lifted his in reply and they both drank solemnly.

After a few minutes, Olie broke the silence.

"As long as that's all you do with her."

"What's that supposed to mean?"

"Miss Cook is not exactly hard on the eyes, Rage. Pretty hair, bright smile and a sweet disposition all look mighty nice to a man who hasn't got laid for almost nine months. Maybe you should reconsider and take that cute lieutenant with you after all."

Luc straightened in outrage. "You saying she's not safe with me? That I need a chaperone to make sure I act as a gentleman and a soldier of the United States Army?"

"At ease." Olie waved a hand at him. "All I'm saying is that a ragin' Cajun, war hero-type like yourself might appeal to a girl who's finally away from her overprotective dad. Too much of that Frenchie accent and she may go crazy and throw herself at you."

"Right," Luc scoffed. "Princess Cook probably has some weenie boyfriend named Preston Shelby Blueblood the Nineteenth waiting for her back in ol' Virginia. He'll spend the next year screwing around on her while she's in San Lucas and ask her to marry him as soon as she gets off the plane. They'll have a couple kids while he keeps screwing around on her and dumps her for his secretary in ten years." He subsided into a funk, realizing he sounded like an idiot.

"O-kay." Olie raised his blond eyebrows. "Well, our immediate concern is not for her future marital happiness, so that's one burden we don't have to carry."

"Yes, sir," Luc muttered. What the hell was wrong with him? Her personal life was none of his damn business anyway.

Olie's cell phone rang and he flipped it open, answering with several "yes, sirs." He closed the phone and swiveled on the bar stool back to Luc. "Colonel Spencer says he made arrangements for you both with the marines at Parris Island. The swamp is about as close to jungle as you can get in the Southeast."

Luc wished he could take her back to Louisiana, but everything was still torn up from the hurricane last fall, and he didn't think he could stand being so close to home and not see his family. And he wasn't about to come home with a woman. His mother would never understand his unorthodox situation and would be calling Father Andre at the church to set a wedding date. He shuddered.

Olie continued, "She'll do her training during the day and sleep in the VIP quarters at night."

"Shit, they don't even want her to know how to make shelter at night? That's where you run in to trouble."

Olie grunted. "She probably gets her bed turned down and a mint on her pillow." He dug around in the nut dish and chose a big brown Brazil nut.

"Funny, I don't remember mints on my pillow when I was in the jungle—the only brown things under my head were bugs. And at one point, that bug *was* my bedtime snack." Luc ate a peanut. *Pistaches de terre,* they called them at home. Too salty—he liked plain boiled peanuts better.

Olie shook his head. "Not doing her any favors by letting her off easy at night."

Luc thought for several seconds. Nuts to the jarheads at Parris Island and their VIP quarters. Survival training without night training meant no survival at all. "This thing with Claire Cook is still an unofficial thing—I'm on leave as of now, right?"

"Yeah. Why?" Olie gave him a wary look, his fingers clamped around a cashew.

"Just want to make sure I'm not going AWOL if I take her on a side trip."

Olie dropped the cashew. "AWOL? Side trip?" He covered his ears with his beefy hands and shook his head. "As far as I'm concerned, the only side trip I need to know about is to the Parris Island ice cream stand."

Luc set down his empty mug. He knew just the place he would take her. One of his old buddies had bought a huge chunk of land abutting a national wildlife refuge and had invited Luc and the guys to use it whenever he wanted. It was really out in the middle of nowhere. The animals couldn't yet read the signs telling them they were leaving federal land, so plenty wound up at his friend's place. No marines, no babysitters, no chaperones. Him, her and the swamp.

People who weren't used to the swamp freaked out pretty easily at all the weird noises, smells and bugs. Maybe if they were lucky, he'd even take her out at night when the gators roared. "We'll be out in the swamp twenty-four, thirty-six hours tops before she starts crying to go home to Daddy."

"You think so, huh." His CO shook his head. "We'll see, Rage. We'll see."

3

A TAP SOUNDED ON CLAIRE'S hotel room door. She looked up from the San Lucas guidebook she had been reading and tucked a bookmark inside.

She hadn't ordered room service, and her father was still probably drinking bourbon and smoking illicit Cuban cigars at the hotel's private men's club with the esteemed senator for the state of North Carolina. She hopped out of bed and peeked through the peephole.

A black-haired stranger stood in front of her door, his face turned to the side. Wow, was he a looker with a strong, clean jaw and firm, full lips. His short haircut indicated that he was probably military despite the fact he wore jeans and a black T-shirt. What should she do? It was past midnight. "Yes?" she ventured, tugging her peach-colored cotton robe around her.

"Miss Cook?" He stopped scanning the hall and stared at the peephole.

She swallowed hard. "Sergeant Boudreaux?" she asked faintly. Good Lord, the man cleaned up well. Better than well, magnificently.

"You alone, ma'am?"

"Of course." She undid the chain and yanked open the door. "Who else would be here with me?" As if she'd brought a boyfriend when she had important preparation to do.

He gave her an amused smile. "Oh, I don't know— maybe your father or your friend the lieutenant."

"Oh." Her mind had immediately jumped to things of a sexual nature and she blamed *him*. Worst of all, he knew what she'd assumed.

"If you're not comfortable letting me into your room, we can meet downstairs in the bar."

"No, no, that's all right." She stopped clutching the door and opened it for him. "Come in."

"Thank you, ma'am." He stepped into her room and looked around. "Never been in this hotel before even though it's not too far from the base. Fancy."

Claire supposed it was, with its high ceilings designed for hot Southern nights, creamy warm yellow wallpaper and matching bedding. She snuck a glance at the dark wooden four-poster bed behind her, which seemed to have tripled in size since she'd answered the door.

His gaze followed hers. "Nice bed."

"Um, yes. Yes, it is, although I haven't really tried it out yet. Since we just got here today." She'd been too nervous to sleep, knowing she'd be out in the woods with him tomorrow, but that was nothing compared to having him in her bedroom. "You got a shave and a haircut." She couldn't think of anything else to say.

"You suggested it, didn't you?" He rubbed his chin. "Feels strange to have a smooth face after so many months."

Claire never guessed he was so handsome under all that hair. She couldn't stop watching his hand rub his tight, tanned skin. Her nipples tightened and she gathered her robe closer. "What brings you here, Sergeant?"

"You."

"What?"

"I need to make sure you're ready."

Oh, she was. But probably not for what he had in mind. "I'll be at the base at oh-seven-hundred hours like we planned." She thought her little foray into military time was pretty good, but he obviously disagreed.

"Real training should start at what we call 'oh-dark-thirty.'"

"What time is that?" It sounded terribly early.

"Whenever the CO hauls your ass out of bed— three, four o'clock in the morning."

"My goodness, that is early."

"The old army recruiting slogan had it right—'we do more before 9:00 a.m. than most people do all day.'"

"Shouldn't they have said 'oh-nine-hundred'?" He gave her a strange look. "I mean, using military time and all that…"

"Let me see your stuff." Without getting permission, Sergeant Boudreaux hefted one duffel bag. "Crap! Can you even lift this thing?" He easily tossed it to Claire, but its weight pitched her backward onto the bed and she found herself staring at the underside of the yellow canopy.

He muttered another curse and pulled the bag off her chest. "You okay?"

She nodded as she tried to catch her breath. Before she knew it, he was kneeling next to her on the bed and running his hands expertly over her shoulders and arms. He hesitated briefly as his fingers brushed the sides of her unbound breasts, but continued his check-up. "Take a deep breath."

Claire did, her robe falling open to reveal her sheer cotton nightgown. His gaze fell to the rise and fall of her breasts, and she realized the dark circles of her nipples were visible.

Boudreaux swallowed. "Does it hurt?" His voice was thick and sweet as cane syrup.

"Does *what* hurt?" Her nipples were starting to hurt from being so hard. Despite his rough exterior, his hands had been gentle.

"Your chest. I mean, when you breathe." His own breath was coming faster.

"You mean, here?" Some little devil made Claire massage the tops of her breasts and breastbone between.

His hands clearly gripped his jeans-clad knees. "Yeah. There. Do I need to call you an ambulance?"

She stopped, disappointed. "No. Are you trying to break my ribs so I don't go?"

He leaped off the bed so smoothly the only evidence he'd ever been there was his imprint on the duvet. "Back to the duffel." He crouched and unzipped it while she sat up. "Camping gear?" He lifted a sarcastic eyebrow. "What did you do, clean out the Bass Pro Shop?"

"No, of course not!" It had been the L.L. Bean catalog.

He pulled out each item, giving a running tally. "Sleeping bag, sleeping bag *pillow,* mess kit, ground sheet—okay, that might be useful…biodegradable dish soap?" He shook his head. "Planning on doing any dishes? A GPS unit—do you even know how to use this? Got any extra batteries? They go bad quickly in hot, damp climates. Oh, look, how useful. An unsharpened pocketknife. Got a whetstone?"

Claire shrugged. She wasn't sure.

Boudreaux continued, "No compass, no whetstone, no machete—"

"Machete? What's that for?"

"A machete, or ma-chay-tay, as our Spanish-speaking friends would call it, is *the* golden ticket to survival. You wanna make friends in the Amazon, you bring the natives high-quality machetes, and lots of them. If you've never seen the gardener on your family estate use one, they look like a really big knife curved on the sharp side."

Claire curled her lip at the crack about her "family estate." "Where do I get a machete?"

"I have several. You can borrow one for now."

She was already bringing medical supplies for the hospital and educational supplies for the school, but she'd have to talk to Dr. Schmidt about how to bring machetes. She didn't suppose she could throw several foot-long knives into her airline carry-on.

"And your other bag?" He lifted the smaller duffel bag. "Don't worry. Now that I know you have no upper-body strength I won't throw this at you."

"It's a bit late for developing upper-body strength, don't you think?"

He gave her an evil grin. "It's never too late for push-ups. And no girl push-ups, either, where your butt's sticking up in the air."

"You want me to drop and give you twenty? That way you can check how my butt is." She challenged him with her hands on her hips, knowing her loose nightgown would gape all the way down to her toes.

He noticed the same thing and backpedaled. "Maybe later." He crouched and unzipped the smaller bag. "Ah, clothes from the discount rank-amateur-survivalist collection."

"I did not shop discount," she informed him. He held up a khaki shirt.

"Not bad—quick drying. But four of them? And one's pink? No way I am going into the swamp with you wearing pink. Never hear the end of it." He dug around further. "Six t-shirts, three pairs shorts, three pairs hiking pants. A packable poncho—good for making shelter. What looks like seventeen pairs of socks."

"I blister easily."

He gave her an incredulous look. "You kidding me? Bad feet in the jungle? What, you wanna get jungle rot or blood poisoning from a bad blister?"

"They're special socks," she informed him.

"Mon Dieu." He shook his head. "Special socks. I'm beginning to sympathize with your father more and more, Claire."

It was the first time he'd used her first name, but she figured they'd moved past a certain formality when he'd run his hands near her breasts and stared at her nipples. She liked the way he said it in his French accent, the *R* at the end a little purring noise.

She was too busy mooning over that to notice he'd moved on to the deepest corner of her bag. "Hey!"

He had a fistful each of her bras and panties and was examining them with a clinical eye. Of course it wasn't any of her delicate, lacy things she had a secret weakness for—these were industrial-strength white or gray cotton sports bras and panties.

"Put those back, those are none of your business." She grabbed for them, but of course he was too quick.

"Everything about you is my business now, down to your underwear." He stuffed them into the bag. "Glad to see you brought one hundred percent cotton. Prickly heat and fungal infections are no joke."

Claire winced but he had moved on to the hiking boots she'd left next to the door. He examined the specially vented sides designed to drain water and sweat, tested the soles' flexibility and tugged on the laces. He stopped and examined one lace closely.

"Is it getting frayed?" She hoped not. She had gone online and researched her boots, knowing her feet would be her weak point. These were supposed to be the best jungle-trekking boots made.

Boudreaux unlaced one boot. She probably hadn't laced it up to Green Beret requirements. He straightened, his face serious, the boot dangling from his hand. "What do you know about the plans your father has made for your training?"

"Oh, um, he said we would all drive down to Parris Island tomorrow and get started. I'm not sure how far that is."

"It's about two hundred and fifty miles. Ever been there?"

She shook her head.

"It's the Marine Corps recruiting depot for the eastern United States. Big installation. The feds do their outdoor training there." He eyed her closely. "Your father made reservations for the two of you to stay in the VIP quarters at night after you train with me during the day."

"So we would go out into the woods for the day and come back every night?" It sounded cushy to Claire, but not particularly effective.

"You didn't know about your hotel arrangements?"

"I figured we'd pitch a couple of pup tents so I could learn how."

"Pup tents. Right." He held up her boot. "Did you realize you have a tracking device here?"

"A what?"

"Somebody planted what looks like a GPS tracking device on the tongue of your boot. See this black disc? Your other boot doesn't have it."

Claire stared at the plastic circle. "I barely noticed that—I thought it was an antitheft device from the store."

"It is. An antitheft device for *you*. Not your boot. Whoever planted this can log in to a GPS server and find exactly where your boot is, every minute of every day."

"Who would want to…" Claire's question trailed away. Of course she knew who wanted to track her— her father. Good grief, she'd seen ads for things like this, but to find lost children who'd wandered away at the playground, not keep tabs on a grown adult. Then a worse thought hit her. Had her father put trackers in her car, her purse?

She ran across the room and dumped her purse on the bed. "Check out my stuff. I need to know if I have any more electronic babysitters."

Boudreaux methodically examined every thing she normally carried with her. Claire blushed briefly when he found the little pouch that held her tampons and a couple condoms she'd forgotten about. His black gaze flicked to her face but he didn't change his expression.

He probed the lining of her purse and stopped. "Here." He pulled out a razor-sharp-looking pocket-knife and slit a seam before working something out with his fingers.

She leaned over his shoulder. "Another one," she said dully. It was a match to the one on her shoe.

"Want me to check your duffel bags?"

"No." She waved off his offer, slumping onto the bed, her shoulders hunching.

"You think it's your father?"

"Who else?"

"Disgruntled boyfriend? Someone who's unhappy you're leaving him for so long?" He looked down at her in concern.

She let out a decidedly unladylike snort. "Not hardly. I haven't even had sex in almost a year." She slapped a hand over her mouth. Great. Now she sounded like some sort of desperate weirdo.

He bit back a smile. "If it makes you feel better, neither have I."

Instead of clearing the air, their mutual admission of celibacy thickened it. The condoms on her bed beckoned. Condoms, bed and extended celibacy were a potent combination.

Who would need to know if she made a move on him? She was leaving for San Lucas in less than a month, where the sexual opportunities were probably slim. She'd never been so bold with a total stranger, but he had shown her flashes of gentleness under his tough exterior. "Luc." His name was strange and wonderful on her tongue as she ran her hand up his muscled forearm to where his bicep met his soft cotton T-shirt.

He stood frozen as a statue, the only movement in his body under his tight zipper. Emboldened, she brushed her palm over his rock-hard pec, his nipple responding instantly. He closed his eyes and shuddered.

"Luc, you feel—"

"Dammit!" His eyes flew open and he caught her wrist.

"What?"

"I feel *too* good, that's what. And you'd feel too good under me." He shoved her hand away from him. "And *this* is why women are not allowed in Special Forces. Your skin is too smooth, your body is too soft—hell, even that sweet peachy smell coming off your hair is a dangerous distraction."

"You think I'm a distraction?" Despite his rejection and backhanded compliments, she was pleased.

"I know so." He pointed a finger at her. "And you don't need any distractions, either. I will not be hanging around the jungles of San Lucas de la Selva ready to rescue you with my machete in my hand and my knife between my teeth. The only person you can depend on is *you*."

"How sad."

"What?"

"Don't you depend on your family? Your team?"

"Family will not get you out of a jam if you're far away, and your team, well…" He looked away for a second. "Sometimes your team is gone and it's just you."

"Oh."

He stared at her. "If you don't want to do this, back out. But if you want to have at least a fighting chance of taking care of yourself, come with me now."

"Now?" she squeaked. It was almost one in the morning.

"*Oui,* now. That Parris Island training is bullshit. You can't learn anything if you know you've got a hot shower and fluffy bed waiting for you at the end of the day. And don't forget, your *papa*'s going to hover over you with his little GPS tracker to make sure you don't get lost—a real eye in the sky."

Claire's lips tightened. In the heat of touching Luc, she'd almost forgotten about that sneaky trick. "What do I need to do?"

"Do everything I tell you." He pulled out a clean outfit for her and checked every item. "No tracking devices in the things. Get dressed."

"Okay." Some impish impulse made her shrug off her robe and stand before him in just her nightgown. He stared at her, his eyes dark and hungry. She started to push one strap off her shoulder when he snapped out of it.

"You, go in the bathroom, you. I'm going to my truck for a bag to pack your stuff." He hurried out, checking the hall before he left.

He wanted her, she could tell. But discipline was winning over desire.

LUC RUSHED TO HIS TRUCK, his muscles practically quivering from the effort to restrain himself from showing Miss Claire Cook how nice that big bed could be. He leaned his forehead against the frame of his red truck. He was totally crazy in the head, to think going out alone into the field with this woman was a good idea.

Hell, he was totally nuts to have turned her down. Sweet Mam'zelle Claire had practically thrown herself at him, condoms at the ready, and what had he done?

Turned her down. Turned down a sweet-smelling, shiny-haired, pretty lady with full, plump breasts and dark, shadowy nipples that had poked out like his cock when he touched her.

He cursed again. If only he'd had even a few days to go out, have a couple beers, meet some good-looking chicks who were interested in checking out his battle scars in close, personal detail. Maybe the top of his head wouldn't be about to blow off.

The guys on his team with girlfriends or wives didn't have this problem. They'd all disappeared into their bedrooms and didn't come up for air for at least a week.

But no girlfriend or wife for Luc. He'd seen too many relationships wrecked by Special Forces deployments, seen too many of his teammates dumped via e-mail or satellite phone. Green Berets weren't supposed to cry but he'd seen his teammates break down. Living in some cave ten thousand miles away from everyone you loved gave a "Dear John" knife in the back an extra-deep twist.

Luc wasn't so smug in his current situation, though. He rubbed his sweaty forehead with his sleeve. He needed to get himself under control or else he'd be making his way through the swamp with his pecker pointing the way.

"WHERE ARE WE GOING?" Claire was shouting since Luc had slipped in a CD of loud rock music. It was probably a good thing she couldn't understand more than a third of the lyrics. The green dashboard lights showed Luc's hard, set expression as he tapped his truck's steering wheel in time to the beat.

"South."

"Oh." They had left the main road several miles ago and were passing small towns, their lights darkened for the night. "I should call somebody to let them know our plans." She would need to use his phone, since hers had sported a tracking device, as well.

Luc lowered the stereo volume slightly. "You left two voice mails and a note for your father. I think he'll be okay. Pissed off, but okay."

"Yes, I know." Claire twisted her fingers as she looked around the truck's interior. She'd practically needed a ladder to climb into it, but the interior was almost as luxurious as her dad's Euro luxury car—soft leather seats, totally digital controls, a smooth ride. Only her father's German car didn't have a gun rack in the back window.

"Where are your guns?" she asked.

"Why you want to know? You gonna shoot me?"

"No, of course not." She was aghast.

"You might by the time we're done." He grinned. "I have a sidearm, a rifle and a shotgun in my bags. All properly unloaded and broken down, of course." He shot her a look. "You know how to use any of those?"

"Uh, some target shooting. Oh, and my dad took me skeet shooting once but I wasn't very good at it. The reporters kept distracting me."

"Election year, huh?"

"Every year is election year when you're a U.S. Representative." How many times had Claire and her mother been trotted out at a campaign event? "If it's not an actual voting year, it's a fund-raising year. My mother did most of the events until I got out of high school, and then she took a job teaching anthropology at the local college and I volunteered to do more."

"Wasn't your job to do his work for him, Claire."

"Public events always look better with family members." That was what her father had said.

"Especially if the family members are photogenic young women. Hope you didn't miss anything important."

"Not much. A couple sorority dances, an honor society induction, a semester in Paris that happened to be the fall term of an election year."

"A semester in Paris?" He gave a low whistle. "After all, how are you going to keep the girl on the Virginia farm, once she's seen Paris?"

"All right, that one still bothers me. I studied French for seven years and never even studied anywhere French-speaking. It was too late to even make arrangements to go to Montreal."

"You can practice your French on me anytime. Course, Cajun French is over three hundred years old, so you may sound a bit out-of-date."

"Really? I did read that in one of my French classes, but our teacher was Parisian and all she would say is that it sounds strange. Then she sneered a bit."

"Yeah, well, we Cajuns are the linguistic hillbillies of the Francophone world."

Claire burst out laughing. "Madame la Professeur always was a snob."

Luc grunted.

"Have you ever worked with French soldiers?"

He gave her an amused look. *"Peut-être."*

"Maybe? Oh, right, you can't say. Just like Janey. I'm sure she has lots of interesting stories to tell me but she can't because they're classified." The only story

Janey had told her recently was about her exploits with the sexually frustrated marine. If only Janey knew how close Claire had come to having an exploit of her own. But no, the darn man was determined to resist her. Rats.

"Loose lips still sink ships. Your friend is smart to keep her mouth closed."

"That's right, Janey will keep her mouth closed. Maybe I can call her really quickly to let her know what's going on." For some strange reason, Claire trusted Luc to keep her safe but she still wanted to talk to someone, anyone, before going into the deep, dark woods.

"Okay." Luc dug in the console and handed her a phone. "Use this one to call your friend, and then we have radio silence. No calls unless it's life or death." He turned down the rock music.

Claire dialed her friend's cell-phone number, hoping she wouldn't get mad that Claire woke her.

Janey answered. "Hello?" she shouted over a pulsing country music beat.

"Janey, it's Claire."

"Claire? Why aren't you asleep? Aren't you leaving at seven?"

"I'm too nervous to sleep." That part was true. "Where are you? I thought you were going to the Airborne Inn." Claire had invited Janey to stay with her but her friend had decided to check in to the base lodging.

"Captain Olson kindly offered to show me around Fayetteville and I took him up on it." Janey lowered her voice as much as she could, considering the loud music. "He went to the bar for some refills. Holy crap, Claire. He turned into some blond stud once all that hair was gone." Like any good army officer, Janey preferred clean-cut men. "I almost fainted dead away when I realized who he was. What about you? Why aren't you in bed getting ready for your big day tomorrow?"

"Well, 'my big day tomorrow' started tonight."

"What?"

"Sergeant Boudreaux came to my hotel room," Claire began.

"Claire!" Janey squealed. "Did he get a shave and haircut, too? I bet he's hot now."

Claire gave Luc a sidelong glance. *"Hot"* didn't even start to describe him. Tabasco-sauce hot was more like it.

"If he's in your hotel room, why are you bothering to call me? Can't you think of anything better to do? As soon as I can manage without looking slutty, I'm going to knock Olie down and lick him all over. Thank goodness he's not my commanding officer. I'd die from unrequited lust if he were."

"Janey…" Claire muttered. She did not need any more sexual images running through her brain. "We're getting an early start on the training. Sergeant Boudreaux is taking me to the training center tonight."

"Training center? You mean Parris Island?" Janey sounded confused.

Claire turned to Luc. "Um, not exactly."

"Oh, Olie's back. Olie, your boy Boudreaux picked up Claire tonight and they're heading to some training center that may or may not be Parris Island."

Claire heard a deep male voice rumble.

"Oh. Olie says he doesn't want to know a thing about what you and Boudreaux are up to. He says he wants plausible deniability."

"Plausible deniability?" Claire repeated.

Boudreaux guffawed. "Have your friend tell Olie we're eloping."

Claire covered the mouthpiece on the phone. "No, I will not have Janey tell him that!"

"Good psy ops, Claire. Psychological warfare. Your father will be so grateful we're not running off to get married that he won't care about his plans for Parris Island being ruined."

"No, Luc!"

Janey's voice sounded from the phone. "Claire, Claire, is he giving you trouble? Do you want me to come get you?"

For a second, Claire wanted to tell Janey yes, tell her to come rescue poor little Claire from the yucky bugs and slimy snakes and squishy things that were waiting to crawl up her leg and bite her. But she didn't. "No, Janey, I'll be fine. You and Olie have a good time, and please apologize on my behalf for everyone's inconvenience."

Janey grumbled. "You apologize too much. Now go kick some swamp butt and don't do anything I wouldn't do."

"Maybe I'll do exactly what you're going to do."

"What? Oh, Claire. In the swamp? You make sure to check your bedding before you crawl in, okay?"

"Okay." They said their goodbyes and Claire hung up. Janey was right to remind her. The only body Claire wanted to crawl into her bedding was Luc's.

4

"CLAIRE? WAKE UP, CLAIRE."

She bolted upright from the reclining truck seat. When had she fallen asleep? The sun peeped over the trees lining the bumpy country road. She wiped her mouth discreetly. No drool. Good. "Where are we?"

"Almost to our destination."

"Which is?" She levered the seat to an upright position and stared out the window. The terrain was flat, covered in tall pines common in sandy soil. They could have been almost anywhere in the Southeast.

He turned the truck into a nearly hidden driveway overgrown with thick shrubs. "My buddy's place. I made arrangements to use a corner of his land. He has so much, he'll never miss it."

"But where are we?" she persisted.

"Georgia or South Carolina, depending on what side of the Savannah River you cross."

"Oh." That wasn't really helpful. "Near the city of Savannah?" she asked hopefully. Savannah was a super-nice town, full of great restaurants and beautiful Southern antebellum mansions.

"No, not near Savannah, so don't get your hopes up." He obviously knew her line of thinking. "If you wanted comfort, you should have stayed home."

"Right." She forced a cheerful grin onto her face and grimaced as her stomach rumbled. "I'm going to eat breakfast real quick here." She reached into her bag for the box of granola bars she'd stashed away. "Want one?"

He looked at the box. "Honey s'mores with choco-chunks and minimarshmallows?" He sounded more astonished than appalled. "Is that supposed to be healthy?"

"No." She ripped open a wrapper and sunk her teeth into the gooey goodness, her speech muffled as she talked with her mouth full. Her father would be horrified. "Ish shupposed to be tashty."

"Ah, what the hell." He accepted one and grimaced as the bar stuck to his fingers. "It's the last snack you'll have until we're done."

The treat soured on her tongue. "Then I guess I better have another."

CLAIRE HAD ACTUALLY EATEN two more granola bars, and was beginning to heartily regret her decision as Luc gunned the small fishing boat's outboard motor. She didn't think it was possible to be seasick on a lake, but it *was* a rather large lake.

She concentrated on breathing deeply and focusing on the opposite shore, facing away from him. "It was nice of your friend to loan us his boat," she called.

"*Oui.*"

"Sorry he wasn't home so I could thank him. Is he on a hunting trip?"

Luc laughed. "No, he's in D.C. briefing the president today."

She turned to look at him and hastily swiveled away as her stomach jumped. "Aren't you the funny one. If you can't tell me things, say so. I'm used to security clearances, you know." His friend was probably at the local Piggly Wiggly stocking up on barbecue sauce and beer.

"No, Claire. He actually is in D.C. to brief the president. My friend is an expert on several Middle Eastern hotspots."

"Oh." Claire decided Luc was serious. "Maybe my father knows him."

"Maybe."

And that was the end of their conversation for several minutes. Claire slapped at several mosquitoes, glad she had put on plenty of organic citronella-based repellant. She probably smelled like the fuel in a tiki torch, but better than being bitten up. She also wore a packable sun hat with a floppy brim.

Behind her, Luc sat in silence, no humming under his breath, no whistling, not even a sigh now and again. If it wasn't for the fact the boat was still running smoothly and she hadn't heard a big splash, she might have thought he'd fallen overboard. Probably all his training. After all, it was a bad idea to go around whistling and sighing when you were trying to sneak up on people to kill them.

She shivered slightly. She'd thought about the proverbial "law of the jungle"—kill, or be killed. How many times had he been in that situation? She really hoped she never was. It was going to be bad enough that they would eat "off the land," as Luc had put it when he ripped the box of granola bars from her death grip and had tossed it into his truck.

Eating off the land conjured up all sorts of yucky images of her food sitting on the ground in the dirt. Kind of like when you dropped a really expensive piece of chocolate on the pool deck, but picked it up and ate it anyway…only much, much worse.

He slowed and turned the boat into a smaller creek off the main lake. The bugs were much thicker here, little gnats that buzzed around her eyes and mouth. The towering trees covered the waterway, big clumps of Spanish moss dangling from the long branches. "Hey, maybe we can use some Spanish moss for bedding."

"Not unless you like mites and bugs. Stuff's crawling with them."

"Never mind." Her thoughts churned as she and Luc cruised through the water, weaving their way up smaller and smaller rivers, farther and farther from the lake's relative civilization. Oh, dear, what was she in for? The VIP quarters at Parris Island were looking mighty nice about now. "What's our first step?"

"You're not going to have nearly enough time to

prepare, so I need to get you up to speed on the basics. Swamp is different than jungle, but the closest we can get for now. All sorts of tricks you can learn except one."

That didn't sound good. "What?"

"Toughness." He overrode her protests about how she had been getting in shape for this for months. "None of that matters like mental toughness. How tough are you?"

"Probably not very," she admitted.

He cut the engine and they drifted through the greeny-brown water. "Turn around, Claire. We're going slow enough that you won't get motion sick."

She thought she'd hid that pretty good. She frowned quickly before smoothing her face and turning around. "Yes?"

The early morning sun threw some dappled rays onto his face. Claire stifled a gasp. With a short coating of stubble, he was even more handsome than last night.

"You have to pay attention to me, Claire, or you won't learn." He gave her a narrow stare before continuing. "Your mind is your biggest asset. I've seen big, muscular men reduced to tears 'cause they weren't strong-minded. You know who survives best in crappy situations?"

"The ones who know the most about the jungle, or wherever they get stranded."

"Wrong. The ones who want to live the most. Mothers, who are trying to get home to their children.

Fathers, who walk fifty miles through snow for help for their families. The soldiers, who will be Goddamned if they let the jungle eat them up and spit them out." He broke eye contact and stared into the tangle of brush on the riverbank.

"Were you one of those soldiers?" Claire ventured timidly.

His bleak black gaze lasered into hers and for a second, she thought he wouldn't answer. "*Oui*. I have been in the jungle. It was not my friend."

She started to ask when, and where, but he guided the boat along the bank, stopping as gently as a kiss. Unfortunate comparison.

"From here, we walk."

"Walk? Where to?"

"Wherever I say."

Oh, goody. Sharing time was over—as if it had ever started—and now the work would begin.

"*Non, non, non! Merde!* Who taught you to sharpen a knife like that?"

Teaching her how to sharpen blades had been Luc's first task. Claire looked into Luc's sourpuss face from where she knelt over a wicked-looking knife and a whetstone. "The camp counselor." Citronella-scented sweat ran down her face, stinging her eyes even more than regular sweat. At least her salt provided valuable minerals for the cloud of buzzing bugs around her.

Luc made a uniquely French sound of disgust, a cross

between a huff and snort. "Your camp counselor was an idiot. Either that, or you weren't paying attention that day."

She wondered if the knife were sharp enough to stab him in the leg or something else nonvital. "Why don't you show me the right way?" She gave him the best kiss-my-ass smile a Virginia-bred young lady could muster.

Grumbling, he knelt behind her, fresh as a daisy. "Like so." He grasped her hand that held the hilt of her brand-new survival knife, and the one bracing the whetstone. Claire froze as his arms encircled her. How did the man smell so clean and sexy in the middle of a swamp?

He angled her thumb against the blunt edge and slowly helped her draw the blade back toward her in a smooth slicing motion. "Like that. Light pressure, gliding it smoothly. Stroke it across the stone." He flipped over the blade and stone and showed her how to hone the other side.

"That wasn't too bad." Claire fought the urge to fan herself, and not from the sticky heat or bugs.

He let go of her and stepped away. "Now repeat that a dozen times."

"Oh. It's not sharp enough now?"

He sighed. "'A dull knife is a dangerous knife,'" he recited in a singsong voice. "It will slide when you want to cut and it will cut when it stops sliding—probably when it reaches your hand. Now get moving. I have a couple machetes for you to sharpen."

Claire bent over the stone and dutifully sharpened the edges, finally holding it up for his inspection.

He gave a grunt and handed her a big, fat leaf. "Not bad. Cut through this."

It sliced the leaf cleanly. Geez. She hoped she wouldn't cut herself.

"Now the machetes." He pulled them out of a bag, and she recoiled a bit. My goodness, were they big and nasty-looking. He grabbed the hilt of one and slid it from its sheath, looking like a pirate pulling out his cutlass for a bit of pillaging.

And of course, there had to be a whole different way to sharpen machetes since the blade didn't need to be quite as sharp as her knife. After much eye-rolling on his part, he proclaimed her work "adequate, but nothing to be proud of," and she contemplated hitting him in the head with the hilt.

Fortunately, her good breeding prevented violence like that. That, and the fact she had no idea how to get back to his truck. Her stomach rumbled. "What time is it?"

He checked the sun from his cross-legged seated position. "Late morning. Why? You got somewhere you gotta be?"

She gritted her teeth. "No, I was wondering when you usually ate lunch out here. Off the land," she added, parroting his words.

"We eat after we purify water, and make shelter and a fire. Unless you plan to eat sushi or raw rabbit, you need a fire. Or we could go digging for grubs and worms. You don't need to cook those to eat them."

Claire grimaced. Her stomach had definitely stopped rumbling. Talk about eating off the land— more like eating stuff buried *in* the land.

Luc scowled at her. "Don't you make that prissy face at me no more, you. They are pure protein and will keep your body from cannibalizing your muscle tissue. Weak muscles won't get you far." He tossed her a canteen. "Drink. This is the last of the water we brought. We are on our own now."

And wasn't that the truth.

Luc had to give Claire some credit for not whining, but he wasn't about to praise her, not when she was greener than spring grass and rawer than the bluegills flopping around at their feet. She at least had been fishing before, even if she'd admitted her father had always cleaned the fish.

"Time to take that nice sharp knife of yours and let it do its job."

"Right." She stared down at the bluegills and took a deep breath. "Tell me what to do."

He walked her through scaling the first fish, which she managed okay. Several scales flew up and landed in her hair and on her cheeks as she scraped away, catching the midafternoon sun like those sparkles girls put on themselves before going to the bar.

She caught her plump lip between white teeth, turning the fish this way and that to clean the head and tail. He caught shadowy glimpses of her cleavage where she'd unbuttoned a couple buttons in the humid heat, especially when she leaned over to examine what she was doing. Sweat rolled down her neck and disappeared between her breasts.

He shifted uneasily, wanting to chase those droplets with his tongue. Who would have thought watching a woman scale a fish could be so sexy?

"All done!" She held up the glassy-eyed creature proudly—the fish, not Luc, who felt about as dazed. Well, the next step would be enough to cool any man's jets.

"Time to gut it."

Her face fell. "Right." She poked tentatively at the fish belly with her knife.

"No, not like that." Giving into a foolish impulse, he curved his arms around her like he had before with the knife sharpening. It hadn't been a good idea to touch her then and it certainly wasn't a better idea now.

"Okay. So show me." Her voice was a bit husky as he cradled her. She smelled of citronella, sweat and fish, and it aroused him more than the most expensive French perfume.

He'd show her, all right. Would he toss the damn fish away and roll around in the leaves and twigs with her, licking her until she was wet all over and eager for him? Or would he fight his trashy urges and keep his dick in his pants like he'd bragged to Olie he would?

Merde, merde, merde. It sure sucked—and not in a fun way—to keep a promise to his CO. And to Claire. Because if he gave in and screwed her silly like he'd been dying to, he'd never do anything else with her. She'd finish her survival training not knowing anything except how to sharpen a knife, how to scale a fish and how to sexually satisfy one extremely horny Green Beret. Not much help. Although that last part sounded very, very nice....

"Luc?" She licked her lips. "What now?"

He sighed again. "All right, insert the tip of the knife like so...."

THE FISH ACTUALLY DIDN'T taste too bad, smoky from its time over the fire she had built. Claire was glad she'd remembered another thing from her time at camp. Of course Luc had stomped all over her triumph by reminding her that the tinder and kindling was much drier here than in the jungle. Well, pooh to him!

She picked up another chunk of fish from the big green leaf she was using as a plate and popped it into her mouth, too hungry to care that she was the one who had cut its head off and ripped its insides out with her bare hands. That last bit had been a bit gross, but she guessed hunger was a powerful motivator. She never wanted to be hungry enough to eat grubs and other assorted larvae. She wondered if Luc had ever eaten larvae and decided that of course he had. Probably ate them by the handful, like popcorn.

He sat cross-legged about six feet from her, eating silently. When he wasn't ragging on her, he made absolutely no noise. And the swamp, or wetlands or whatever an ecologist might call it, was plenty noisy. Frogs clicked and croaked, birds whistled and honked, and the treetops rustled in the breeze.

Claire looked around. She didn't know if she'd ever been so isolated. Physically, at least. She was used to emotional isolation. Ever since her mother had died, she had been very alone, even among thousands of people in the midst of D.C.

She looked over at Luc, who stared into the fire. He was an enigma to her. Earlier, he'd had a larger-than-life charisma, drawing her attention like a honeybee to a flower. Now, it was as if he had sucked every last bit of his presence inside him and was no more there than the wisps of smoke climbing through the treetops.

Suddenly, she couldn't stand it—she had to get connected to someone, even if he wasn't interested in connecting to her. "Luc!"

He turned slowly to her, his thousand-yard stare sharpening as he focused on her.

She forced a smile. "What next?" He still didn't say anything, and Claire found herself babbling to fill the void. "I figure it's probably late afternoon, so we should probably decide where to pitch our tents before it gets dark, right? I've seen plenty of movies where they try to make camp late at night and it takes forever to pitch the tent and it always collapses anyway. And the mosquitoes—"

"Claire." His quiet tone cut in to her monologue. "You ever just sit and be?"

"Be what?"

He shook his head. "No, I suppose not."

"What does that mean?" She was starting to get angry now. Hadn't she done everything he'd asked today? Sharpened frightening blades, impaled worms on fishing hooks, even eviscerated some poor fish.

"Your mind runs a million miles an hour, Claire. I can practically see the brain waves buzzing off your head."

"Thanks, I guess. So what's the problem?"

"You spend too much time in your head, you're not gon' be a part of anything else." He gestured at the branches and the patches of bright blue sky above them. "You noticing any of this? Or are you trying to figure out what happens next, and what you're gon' have to do, and what I'm gon' do?"

"I don't think I'll have much luck figuring out that last one," she told him tartly.

She startled a quick smile out of him. He shook his head. "Close your eyes, Claire."

"Why?" She gave him a narrow stare. "Are you going to leave me here and sneak off and then I have to spend the night by myself?"

"Trust me, Claire. Close your eyes."

She gave him one last glare and squeezed her eyes shut. If he ditched her in the middle of freaking nowhere, he'd be sorry, although she wasn't sure how she'd do that. Maybe track him down and talk his ears off, since he didn't seem to like that.

"Claire." His deep, French-accented voice cut through her revenge fantasies and inspired some different ones. "Listen to the woods. Listen to the wind, the animals, the water."

Her eyes flew open. "Oh, are we doing guided meditation? I've done this before in hatha yoga class, except we imagined blue balls of light hovering over each chakra—"

He made a strangled sound. "Enough with the blue balls of light! Now close your damn eyes!"

"Fine." She arranged herself cross-legged with her hands in an obvious yoga mudra position before closing her eyes. "Okay, I'm listening. Wow, it's noisy out here."

"Shh. You can't talk and listen at the same time."

Since he wasn't going to let her out of this guided meditation, which it actually was, whether he wanted to admit it or not, she decided to give it a try. Like she had said before, it was a noisy place.

She concentrated on picking out different animal sounds—a small frog's chirp, a big frog's croak, so many different birds she couldn't tell them apart. Then the wind in the trees, swishing and brushing by the leaves.

It shifted and blew some smoke in her face and she fanned it away. Another good reason to keep her eyes closed.

Once the smoke cleared, Claire was surprised at how much she could smell with her eyes closed. She never really considered that sense too much, except when she was picking out body lotions or when she was hungry and everything smelled good.

She recognized Luc's scent right away. A bit of salty sweat, a bit of smoke and a more subtle masculine musk that she'd smelled as he had put his arms around her to instruct her.

What could she do to encourage him to take that further? He seemed impervious to their nearness, or else did a good job hiding it. If the dictionary had an entry for mental toughness, his picture would be next to it.

Maybe she would have to develop her own mental toughness and seduce *him*. She didn't think she'd ever really done that with a man. Sure, she'd smiled and put on sexy dresses, but it was to be expected that the man did the chasing. It was his nature, after all. Especially the nature of a man who chased people for a living.

"Stop thinking, Claire. Try *being*." His command cut through her planning, and she went back to "being," whatever that meant.

To her surprise, it was easier this time. She found herself swaying in time to her breathing, the ground solid and anchoring her. Luc's presence didn't distract her anymore, although she was aware of him. It really came down to Claire and what she had to learn to take care of herself. For the first time, the training didn't seem scary or impossible. Her mother would be proud of her. Maybe Claire could be proud of herself.

CLAIRE WIPED HER FOREHEAD as she swung her machete at a skinny little tree. Luc was showing her how to build a sleeping platform for a bed, and after he'd described in great detail the slimy, slithering and scaly creatures that roamed the jungle floor at night, Claire had agreed that was a very useful skill. She needed one more sturdy Y-shaped trunk for the fourth corner of the platform and was stripping away small branchlets.

Using the machete actually wasn't so bad, except for the fact she was having trouble keeping her balance and missed some branches. Whew, it was getting hot.

She wiped her forehead again, and this time, Luc noticed. "Hey, when was the last time you took a piss?"

"I beg your pardon." She drew herself up with hauteur worthy of her late Grandmother Cook.

"Excusez-moi, mademoiselle." He gave her a low, mocking bow. *"Quand est la dernière fois que vous avez pissé?"*

It didn't sound any better in French. "Before we left."

"Before we left my friend's house."

Well, technically yes. "Actually, at the hotel."

He swore in French. "Fifteen hours ago? And you didn't think that was a problem?"

She shrugged. "I've been busy." And she hadn't wanted to use the bathroom. Heck, there wasn't any bathroom *to* use.

"Drink." He shoved his canteen at her. The water had a somewhat chemical flavor from the purification tablets, but it was cool and soothing.

"You get a bladder infection or get severely dehydrated and I'll ship you back to your daddy before you can say 'Jack Robinson.'"

He was threatening her? "Shouldn't that be '*Jacques* Robinson?'" She glared at him and drank more water.

He glared back. "Now go into the bushes and do your business."

She looked away. "I don't know how."

She'd finally surprised him. "What?"

"Go outdoors."

He wiped a hand across his face and muttered several words under his breath. "I need to teach you that, too?"

She wanted to dig a hole in the larva-ridden ground and climb in. Mental toughness, mental toughness. She stuck out her chin at him. "Yes, you do."

"It's simple. Pick a tree, pull down your pants and do your business."

"But how do I wipe?"

"You don't."

"Oh, Luc." The idea of having to drip-dry was too much to stand right now.

"Okay." He blew out another French-sounding sigh and selected a leaf from a nearby tree. "Learn this leaf. Memorize it. Love it, because this is your new T.P. *Don't* use *anything* else."

She accepted the leaf and hastily did her business behind some ancient tree. She felt as if she were vandalizing it. Anyway, the next rainstorm would take care of it.

When she returned, he handed her another canteen and pointed her to a big log, where she sat. "Drink."

She tipped it to her mouth and grimaced. "What's that?"

"Treated water with ORS—oral rehydration salts. You'll need to drink all of this plus another. I want to see you running into the woods with another tree leaf within two hours."

"Fine." She forced herself to drink because she knew he'd meant it about sending her home. How humiliating that would be—not even managing twelve hours in the wilderness. Poor Claire, people would snicker, sent home because she couldn't pee in the woods.

She chugged the rest of the canteen and he handed her another. "Here's our next lesson—the jungle is full of fresh water. There's no reason to get dehydrated or overheated. One school of thought says to drink what you can find and get rid of the parasitic infections later.

But that's a last resort. So treat your water." He went on to describe several treatment methods, as well as how to drink from water vines and how to catch rain-water in a variety of containers. "San Lucas gets four hundred inches of rain per year—about ten times what Virginia gets, so that's plenty. You still have to treat it since you don't know what it carried down from the trees, but it's easy."

Claire was beginning to recover, with her second canteenful sloshing around in her stomach, and watching Luc's firm lips shape words and sentences was a lot of fun. His five-o'clock shadow only made him look more dashing and dangerous. Apparently the only danger he ran away from was the notion of having sex with her. She didn't know if that was a compliment or not.

"Claire! Claire!" He scowled at her. "Are you paying attention to me?"

"Of course." She'd been drinking in every detail of his rock-hard body under the black T-shirt and green camo pants. But he meant if she was paying attention to what he was saying. She repeated the last few para-graphs of his lecture, grateful for how she could re-member large chunks of information presented orally. Her brain had a digital audio recorder.

"Okay." He slitted his eyes, not quite believing her. "You need to finish your sleeping platform if you're better." He extended his hand to help her stand and she accepted.

He misjudged her weight and pulled a little too hard, dragging her chest-to-chest with him. She stared into his eyes. They weren't quite solid black but had some gold flecks in them. "Luc," she whispered, her breasts nestled against his solid torso.

"Claire," he whispered back. "I need you…."

"What?" Were his defenses crumbling faster than she'd hoped?

"I need you to…get off my foot and get busy!" His last words were almost a shout as he set her away from him. "Gon' go hunt for dinner now. Don't let the fire go out unless you'd prefer snake sushi."

She slumped in disappointment as he disappeared into the brush. Then she remembered his last words. Snake sushi? Her stomach churned. She fed the fire with some dry branches and chanted under her breath, "Tastes like chicken, tastes like chicken." And no chance for dessert tonight—granola bars *or* Luc. Both were off the menu.

THE SNAKE ACTUALLY HAD tasted like chicken, and Luc had showed her some wild plants that were so obviously onions that even she couldn't goof that part up and poison them both. The sun was setting beyond the trees and Claire slapped at several mosquitoes that had come out for blood.

Luc looked up from where he was poking at the fire. "Time to get ready for bed. Don't forget to brush your teeth with the treated water."

Claire nodded. She was beat after only getting a few hours of sleep last night in Luc's truck and working hard in the woods all day. She trudged off to her "pee tree" and gave herself a quick evening toilette. Not quite the spa tub and six-nozzled shower stall that she was used to. Heck, not even the toilet she was used to. Oh, well. There would be none of that at the settlement at Río San Lucas anyway. Pretty soon she would get used to it.

She walked back into the camp and stared at what was going to be her bed. Luc had checked the supports and leafy branches crossing them, and had pronounced the sleeping platform sturdy enough. He had rigged her mosquito netting to a branch above so it dangled over her bed like a princess canopy. To be on the safe side, she squirted on more insect repellent.

"Ready?" He straightened from the log and came to check on her.

"Ready." She hopped awkwardly onto the sleeping platform, trying not to wince as the branches she'd used for bedding poked her in several tender places.

He showed her how to tuck the netting around herself. "Make sure you always, always do this. Mosquitoes can carry four different kinds of malaria, dengue fever and even yellow fever. Malaria medicine and vaccinations are never one hundred percent effective for everybody."

Claire sighed. She was so tired that if a six-foot-long mosquito had swooped down on her like an eagle on a Chihuahua, she wouldn't have batted an eye. "You sure do tell sweet bedtime stories, Luc." She yawned. "Now unless you're going to kiss me good night, you probably should get some rest, too."

He backed away, his expression unreadable in the flickering firelight. "Good night, Claire. We're getting up at oh-dark-thirty tomorrow."

"Great." Claire snuggled into the branches, not even caring that one poked her in the butt. Tonight was no time to be the lead character in "The Princess and the Pea." The branches shifted ominously under her. Or more likely, she'd be the kid in the cradle after the bough broke.

5

LUC HAD HAD THE SAME crappy night's sleep as Claire
since he'd woken up every time she shifted position,
obviously uncomfortable in her bed of boughs. She
had finally drifted off to sleep around 4:00 a.m. as far
as he could tell, just when his internal clock was telling him to get up.

He rolled out of his shelter and took care of a few
early morning hygiene tasks. After starting the fire
again for some coffee, he strolled to Claire's bed and
stared down at her. Sleeping Beauty she was not, with
several mosquito welts on her neck where her net had
gaped and a red scratch on her cheek where a branch
had caught her. Her mouth hung open and she was
snoring slightly, as if the woods had activated some
hay fever.

So why did he have the urge to pull the netting
aside and kiss every single injury on her warm ivory
skin until they both felt a lot better?

He knew it was a bad idea—Claire Cook was a
pretty society girl who got a bee in her bonnet to go
out in the big, bad world to do some good. He shook

his head. And she couldn't find anything to do back home in Virginia?

Maybe she needed to get away from her father to do anything besides shop and have her cute peach toenails painted. He understood that well enough— he'd left home at eighteen to attend Tulane University, desperate to see something besides the backwoods of Louisiana. He'd messed around with odd jobs the summer after graduating from college and that fall had been the fall of 2001. After seeing the deaths of Americans at the hands of terrorists on live network TV, Luc had shown up at the army recruiting depot September 12.

The Army had taught him more than he could have imagined, and now it was his turn to pass his knowledge on. "Wake up, Claire." He reached through the gap in the netting and shook her shoulder.

"Go 'way," she muttered, slapping at his hand. He stared down at her. Civilians. Well, she was his "army of one," as the old recruiting ads used to say.

"On your *feet!*" he bellowed in his best drill sergeant imitation.

She jerked to a sitting position, her bloodshot eyes staring wildly. "What? What?" She focused on Luc. "Oh, you startled me half to death."

"Rise and shine, we're burning daylight." Without waiting to see if she was awake, he checked his map. "Today we work on map-reading and navigation. You got a good sense of direction?"

"Um. Sure."

Luc raised an eyebrow at her hesitant reply. "I take that as a 'no'."

"I could use some practice," she admitted, swinging her feet out of the shelter. She'd changed into shorts after going to bed and her legs were long, smooth and tanned. He gripped the metal compass case hard, rather than run his hand up her calf.

She started to stand and he stopped her. "Not in bare feet."

"Oh, right. You were telling me last night about all the icky ground parasites that can burrow into your skin." She reached for her boots and a fresh pair of socks that had been sitting in the tops of her boots.

He stopped her again. "Shake out your gear first."

She shook out the socks. "See? Nothing to worry about."

"Fine. Now the boots."

With an indulgent sigh, she dumped over one boot and fastened it onto her foot without incident. The second was another story.

Claire squealed, hopping around on one foot. "What—what the heck is that?"

Luc shook his head. "Brown recluse spider. Along with the black widow, one of two venomous spiders found in the U.S. Distinguished by its dark brown, sometimes yellow color with a black line pointing to the spider's rear. Venom occasionally causes tissue necrosis at the site of the bite."

"Venomous? Tissue necrosis at the site of the bite?"

"Yes, Claire. They crawl into close spaces to hide and bite people when they stick in their hands—or feet." The spider scuttled away toward the leaf litter and Luc stomped on it with his boot.

Wide-eyed, she stared at its mangled remains with disgust.

"Shake out your gear. In the jungle, you'll have spiders way bigger than this, lizards, centipedes, millipedes, ants—you name it." He handed her the boot.

"Yes, Luc." She gave it another vigorous shake and peeked into the inside for good measure before gingerly lacing her foot into it. She grabbed a T.P. leaf from her stash and ducked into the brush.

When she came back, she reached for her tiny bottle of hand sanitizer and squirted it over her hands.

He rolled his eyes. "That crap stinks to high heaven. What are you doing in the woods that you need that junk for?"

She wrinkled her nose at him. "Good bathroom hygiene is important for good health."

"O-kay." Once she got to San Lucas, she'd probably faint to see people washing, babies pooping and animal carcasses being cleaned in the local drinking water.

"Do you have any more purified water? I'm kind of thirsty." And probably hungry, too, judging by the way she looked around hopefully.

"What are our options for potable water?" He wanted to see if she remembered.

"Since we are at low altitude—any lower and we'd be underground—we bring the water to a boil and continue to boil for a minute."

Very good, but he wasn't going to tell her that. Soldiers didn't get trained by touchy-feely stuff. And she wouldn't get trained at all if he kept combining Claire and touchy-feely in the same thought. "And option two?"

"If you have no fire, drop an iodine-based water-purifying tablet in one liter of water, let sit for about a half hour and enjoy the chemical-flavored goodness."

"Better than parasite-flavored goodness. And if the water is particularly nasty, drop in a second tablet and filter out the scum with your teeth."

"Gross, Luc." She made to sit down on a log but he stopped her.

"Grab your groundsheet. Never sit on bare wood or ground."

"Why, more parasites?"

"Exactly." He himself was squatting at the fire's edge. He was used to it, not being around chairs for weeks at a time. He had poured her a cup of coffee and offered it to her when she returned with her ground-sheet.

She looked into the metal mug in surprise. "I thought we were living off the land. Did you pick, roast and grind some coffee beans while I was asleep?"

"No talking back to your commanding officer." He drank his scalding brew with a happy sigh. God, had he missed French roast in Afghanistan.

"Got any non-dairy creamer?" Her lips pursed gently as she blew into the mug. Her soft, pampered hands wrapped around the mug while she moved her mouth into the perfect kissing position before drinking a dainty sip. "Luc? Luc?"

"What? No, no creamer, and no coffee filter, either. We drink our coffee black in Special Forces—puts hair on your chest."

She stared at his chest where he'd tossed on another black T-shirt after a quick wash in the river. "You must have a lot of hair on your chest."

His nipples tightened at her sultry tone.

"Well?" She pursed her lips and blew again, her dark gaze never leaving his.

"I've never had any complaints." He gulped at his coffee. The little minx, was she trying to seduce him again? She might think she wanted a bit of fun before she shipped out, but not at the expense of her safety. He wanted to stand up and get away from her, but his compass wasn't the only thing pointing north. "Drink and let's get going. Breakfast isn't going to jump out of the water and onto the fire." He rubbed his stubbly jaw. "Unless I teach you how to gig frogs. Mmm, mmm, mmm, *les andouilles.*" He made some lip-smacking sounds and her expression turned from sultry to disgusted. "What, a fancy girl like you never ate frogs' legs at one of those fine French restaurants in our nation's capital?"

She shook her head.

"Too bad. Maybe we can find some wild onions or garlic to flavor them."

"Do I really have to eat frogs?" Her voice was almost a whisper.

He raised an eyebrow. "What did I tell you about insects?"

"They're pure protein and keep your body from cannibalizing your muscles." Her mouth pulled down. Whatever her squeamishness, she was definitely no dummy, quoting almost word-for-word what he told her.

"Frogs are the same, except with bones. And you gotta be fast to catch them. You got fast hands, Claire?" He cursed silently as she smiled at his Freudian slip.

"I've never had any complaints."

Word-for-word again. Too bad he couldn't tell her the words he longed to tell her.

CLAIRE STARED AT THE stick holding the fishing line that would hopefully catch their dinner. After two days of fish, she was about to grow gills.

If she weren't so exhausted, she'd be bored out of her skull. Instead, creeping mental numbness dulled her so much, she hardly noticed the blisters popping up on her little toes, the cramps in her calves and the throbbing ache in her lower back. Sitting on the hard ground did that to a person. Not that she was complaining or anything, at least not out loud.

She sighed again and unbuttoned her shirt. The

breeze cooled her bare stomach so well that she took the shirt off altogether. Her gray sports bra covered more than enough compared to the lacy lingerie she preferred but didn't have with her. She could have used another weapon to break down Luc's resolve.

She looked around idly, still self-conscious about sitting in the open wearing only her bra, but she was alone. Luc was off communing with nature, or conquering it and stomping all over it, more likely. He had said something about checking the traps they had set in the morning. She had no idea there were so many ways to lure small animals to their doom. She half hoped none of them would take the bait, but her growling stomach was overcoming more and more of her squeamishness.

Geez, if she was this savage after two days and nights in the wilderness, what would she do after a week? Probably eat raw bugs and cheerfully club alligators and hand-tan their skin. Claire snickered. What every stylish Virginia girl wanted: a purse from the alligator she killed herself.

The fishing line jerked, stirring Claire out of her hunger-induced fashionista fantasy of matching alligator hiking boots. She leaped up from the ground and grabbed the pole. "Easy, easy," she muttered, not wanting to lose this fish. Lifting gently, she pulled a good-size silver fish from the water. "Yay!" She grasped the fish behind the gills and unhooked it, wiping her slimy hand off on her shorts. The poor thing flopped around on the groundsheet. "Sorry, Charlie," she said, parroting the old canned-tuna ad, and laughed.

She reached for another worm and baited the hook. Janey should see her now. A girl who hadn't even done dishes without gloves was manhandling, or woman-handling, invertebrates with ease. Heck, someday she might even eat one! Or not, as something oozed from the worm. She grimaced and threw the line in.

Not much breeze was passing by, but enough to keep the bugs off anyway. Who would have thought the swamp would be somewhat scenic?

"Nice little bluegill you caught."

Claire leaped about four feet into the air. She hadn't heard Luc come up behind her at all. "Geez, Luc, you scared the tar out of me!"

He squatted beside her, his black gaze taking in her bare shoulders and tummy. "I made extra noise to see if you'd notice me. You can't afford to daydream out here."

"Yes, Luc." He was right with that one. "Did *you* catch anything?" She angled her shoulders so her breasts squished together for some cleavage. Obvious, but hey, it was the best she could do with a gray cotton bra.

He gestured at a stick leaning against a big oak tree. Several furry blobs hung from it.

"Oh. Rabbits." She'd eaten those from her dad's hunting trips, but they'd been cleaned and cooked for her. "They look so…sad."

He raised an eyebrow. "They're dead. They're not sad anymore. Not sad like you'd be without any dinner tonight."

Her fishing line jerked again. "Um, do you mind if I stay here and fish?" To underline her request, she pulled out another medium-sized fish and set it next to the other.

He opened his mouth in protest but she touched his arm. He was hot and hard under her touch, little black springy hairs tickling her fingertips. "Please? I know I need to learn how to…what's the phrase for processing animals?"

"Skin and gut?"

She grimaced. "Clean and dress was what I was trying to say. I promise, I'll do it the next time."

He stared into her eyes, his dark gaze unreadable, and then he stared down at her hand on his arm. She jerked it away. "I'm sorry, I'm covered in fish slime again. I really need a bath."

"I expect I'll need one, too, after cleaning all those rabbits by myself."

She smiled at him in relief. "Thank you, Luc."

He shook his head. "I'm not doing you any favors this way. Being squeamish is a good way to be hungry. You can clean those fish by yourself 'cuz you're working your way up to mammals soon." He straightened and walked away.

"Let's trap something that's not cute, okay?"

He stopped, an amazed look on his face. "How's lizard or rat sound?"

She made a sound of distress and he grinned. "Gotcha, *cher.*" Silently and with quick steps, he reached the string of rabbits and picked them up. It wasn't until he'd disappeared into the woods that she realized he'd called her *cher* and not Claire.

Cher meant *honey* or *sweetie* and was quite the slip of his normally guarded tongue, she mused as she baited the hook again and tossed it back. Maybe her gray bra was more powerful than she expected.

LUC STARED INTO THE fire that night, mentally begging Claire to get tired and go to bed. By herself. He was finding it harder and harder to resist her. No pun intended. He flicked a glance at her, the flames lighting the curves and planes of her face. She had the most flawless skin and full, plump lips that she was always slicking with some lip balm, puckering and pouting to make sure they were protected.

He dug his fingers into his knees until his knuckles went white. He had rough, hard hands, too rough for her delicate skin and soft body. His self-control around her was like a knife edge that had been honed too fine— sharp enough to cut but liable to snap at the slightest pressure.

She yawned and stretched, her breasts moving up and down under the fabric. At least she'd put her shirt on when the sun went down.

"Ready for bed?" He hoped his voice didn't sound too eager.

She shrugged. "I really wanted to wash before I go to sleep."

He grunted, immediately disturbed by the images that conjured. "Why bother? You'll need fresh bug spray after you finish."

"I know, but it's been so hot and sticky." She rubbed the nape of her neck. "I think I'm getting prickly heat."

Luc was, too, but not the rash kind.

"You want to check?" She lifted her ponytail of thick, dark hair and bared her nape to him.

"No, no," he said, backpedaling. "You'll need some water to wash with." He brought out the larger container of purified water. "You'll want some privacy, so I'll leave."

"You mean, wash right here?" She looked around nervously.

"Claire, we're in the middle of nowhere. The only other person for miles is me." He figured she was probably imagining local backwoodsmen spying on her through the foliage. "The fire is dying down to limit visibility and I'll reconnoiter the perimeter."

Her face cleared. "If that means keeping an eye out for any Peeping Toms, that sounds good." She went to her duffel bag and collected clean clothes, a washcloth and small bottle of biodegradable soap.

Luc faded away and slipped through the trees. The insects and birds were as noisy as before, not startled by any other human presence. He sniffed the air for any other scent of bug spray or fire. As he expected, nobody was around. Still, he circled their camp slowly and stealthily to keep in practice. He hadn't trained in swampy woodlands for a long time, being stationed in either the urban Middle East or its rocky, mountainous outposts.

His senses heightened as he went, his night vision sharpening as he smelled individual plants and picked out insect and birdsong. The vibrating rumbles of faraway gators bellowing made him smile. Just like home. His anger about being forced away from home on his leave had subsided, but something even more dangerous had replaced it: pure lust.

Why couldn't the congressman's daughter be married, or snooty or less attractive? Instead, Claire was single, available, sweet-natured and sexy enough to make him forget his name.

A hideous noise startled the normal sound-makers into frightened silence. Luc pulled his knife and ran toward the camp, his only thought to get to Claire. He cleared fallen logs and lurking branches with ease and made it to the darkened clearing within seconds. He dropped into a crouch at the edge to assess the situation.

Claire was standing alone, illuminated by the bluish light of the full moon. He relaxed briefly and sheathed his knife when he realized the noise was her off-key singing, but then she turned around and he saw everything he'd wanted and everything he shouldn't.

Her hair was piled on her head as she leisurely soaped the nape of her neck, running the washcloth over her shoulders and arms. Sudsy water trickled around her plump, round breasts and down to her dark nipples. He held his breath as one soapy blob clung to the peak of her breast before plummeting to the ground below.

"Au clair de la lune," he murmured to himself. "By the Light of the Moon" was an ancient French folksong, and *Claire* meant *light* or *bright*.

Her skin gleamed silver in the moonlight as if it held light of its own. Her belly curved into full, rounded hips guarding the dark treasure between them. He could only look at her as if she were Diana, the moon goddess come down to the woods to tempt him.

He muffled a groan as she washed her stomach and back, finally reaching between her legs. His own groin throbbed painfully in response. Without thinking, he eased open the first couple of buttons on his camo pants. He was stroking his cock when he realized what he was doing—becoming the Peeping Tom he'd promised to protect her against.

He groaned, cupping himself for a second before buttoning up with some difficulty. He'd promised Olie his word as a Green Beret that he could be trusted around Claire. Hell, he'd promised Claire she could trust him. Watching on her while he crouched in the woods playing with himself was *not* trustworthy, to say the least.

He gave her one last, longing glance and reluctantly turned his back. She continued her out-of-tune serenade as he sat in the darkness, wondering how the hell he would hold out against her charms.

6

CLAIRE FIGURED LUC wasn't interested in her anymore, despite the flash of heat they'd generated in her hotel room. Despite wearing her sports bra as a top all day, Luc wasn't biting at the bait, either avoiding looking at her or else keeping his gaze from her neck upward. She swiped her hand over her face, glad for the light clothing as she finished gutting yet another fish. It had become less revolting, if not less messy.

"Claire?" Luc had come up behind her again, but at least this time she'd heard him.

"All done with the fish. We can eat them for a late lunch if you want." She rinsed off her hands and wiped them dry on her poor abused pants. They practically stood on their own by now.

"In a few minutes. Right now I want to show you a survival kit I always carry." He sat cross-legged on her groundsheet and pulled out a small round tin about the size of a hockey puck. "You need to make one, too, and always, always carry it on your body. In a buttoned pocket, not a purse or backpack."

"I guess I could always stick it in my bra if I need to."

His gaze fell to her breasts before looking away. "Whatever you need to do." He undid the sticky tape around the circumference. "The tape keeps the container waterproof."

"In case I fall out of a boat or something?"

He froze midgesture and slowly opened the can the rest of the way. "Yes. Boating down the main river in Río San Lucas can be dangerous." He pulled out more things than she thought would fit in the tiny container, including waterproof matches and cotton balls soaked in petroleum jelly. She wouldn't have thought of other items, like fishing line and hooks, needles and thread, and even a flexible saw that coiled like a thick jagged wire.

"What is that at the bottom?" She spied a square plastic packet among the wound bandages and antibiotic and painkiller pill tubes.

"Water storage device." He made to repack the tin but she stopped him.

"It's so tiny, how can it hold water?"

He sighed and pulled it out.

"Wait, that's not a water storage device, that's a condom." She wrinkled her nose at him. "Honestly, Luc, I would think under the dire circumstances when you'd need this kit that a condom would be low on the priority list."

Darned if he wasn't blushing a bit under his sun-darkened skin. "Claire, we use prophylactic devices for plenty of things beside their original intent. We cover the rifle barrels with them to keep water from rusting them and we do use them for water storage. They store about a quart of water."

"Really? I had no idea they stretched so far." Claire grabbed the condom out of his hand. "Extra large, ribbed. Is it easier to grip the ribbed ones with wet hands?"

Ha ha, she was making him blush like a tomato. "It was the only kind they had."

"Is that the brand you usually use? I mean for carrying water and covering the tip of your...rifle?"

"Never mind," he growled, stuffing the packet into the tin and repacking the other items. "I figured you wouldn't take this seriously."

She frowned back at him. "Hey, no fair. Haven't I done everything you asked? Haven't I done everything you wanted?"

Luc clenched his fists. "Everything I asked, *oui*. Everything I wanted, *non*." He dragged her into his arms and kissed her. Claire barely had enough time to give a mental cheer before being swamped by the anger, frustration and lust that rolled off him in a passionate wave.

She eagerly opened her mouth under his, his tongue immediately rubbing along hers. He nibbled on her lips as if they were the sweetest candy, biting and sucking on her as if he were starving.

Claire was starving, too, starving for the body she'd been watching surreptitiously for days. She shoved her hands under his T-shirt and moaned at his slick, hot skin. Under her caresses, he was pure muscle and bone with not an ounce of fat. She suddenly felt self-conscious about her not-so-hard body and stopped touching him.

Luc made a sound of protest and pulled her even closer, crushing her breasts against him. She took this as the go-ahead she needed and indulged herself, tracing the indentations of his ribs, the heavy muscle of his back. Her fingers found a thick ridge of skin that marred his smooth perfection.

She pulled away. "What's that?"

"That feels very good."

She pressed into the scar. "That."

"Oh. Shrapnel."

"Shrapnel?" She was about to ask him for details when he pressed kisses from her jaw down to her neck, licking and sucking at her earlobe. His hot mouth sent sensual jolts down to her nipples and even farther south. She moaned his name and wiggled against him.

He broke their kiss. "*Non,* Claire, I shouldn't be doing this. I swore I'd be a gentleman around you, swore I'd keep my hands off you."

So that was why he'd been so standoffish. "I'm releasing you from your promise." She dragged his head down to hers and sucked hard on his bottom lip. He inhaled sharply but pulled away again.

"It doesn't work that way, Claire. A man's word is his honor."

Time for drastic measures. "I know you're an honorable man and you would never do anything to hurt me. That's why I choose you for this." She reached behind her and unsnapped her bra, dropping it on the ground. "I want you, Luc. Life is difficult. There is no dishonor in taking a bit of pleasure where we can."

He swallowed hard at the sight of her bare breasts. "I'm so hard I could hammer in tent pegs. I can't be leisurely or gentle, whispering sweet nothings in your ear."

Her nipples tightened, sending jolts down between her legs. "Will you make me feel good?" She couldn't believe she was seducing a sexy man like Luc in the middle of the day, outdoors, but she'd never wanted anything more.

"Better than you've ever felt before." He wasn't bragging, merely stating a fact.

"Then *oui,*" she whispered, eliciting a wolfish grin from him.

"I like hearing that word on your lips. You gon' say it a lot more times before I'm done with you." Luc stripped off his shirt, revealing what she'd only touched before. His chest was lightly covered in black hair, his coppery nipples pulled into tight disks. Several paler scars marred his skin. "Take off your pants."

She hurriedly unlaced her boots and shoved the rest of her clothing off. An unexpected rush of shyness came over her, and she hunched, curling her arms around her bent knees. He frowned in concern, and she realized he was having second thoughts.

Before he changed his mind, she forced herself to lean on her elbows, the breeze cool on her totally bare-naked body. Outdoors, in the middle of the day, no less.

His eyes darkened with lust, and he quickly made himself as naked as she was. Oh, my. His erection was as powerful as the rest of his body. The sunlight high-lighted its thick head and corded veins running its impressive length. Claire stared at him with a little bit of apprehension and a whole lot of awe.

"*Bébé*, don't keep lookin' at me like that." He acknowledged her gaze by growing even further, a silver drop appearing on his tip.

"Like what?" She rubbed her thighs together to try to ease her matching lust.

"Like you're the sexiest thing ever and you can't wait for me to fuck you."

Heat crept up her face. "I do want you to…" She just couldn't say it. "Do that."

"*Bon.*" He dropped to his knees beside her and cupped her cheek briefly, tracing his hand down her neck, over one breast and the curve of her hip. She dropped her knees apart and he immediately found her hidden nub.

She cried out and tipped her head back. He pushed her shoulder until she rested on the groundsheet. He stared eagerly down at her. "*Très, très belle, toi.*"

She blushed at being called beautiful. Then he stroked her and she forgot all about being embarrassed. His hands were rough but gentle as they brushed her skin. He circled one nipple and the other as they peaked and grew.

His expression was rapt. "Let me taste you, sweet Claire."

He lowered his mouth to one breast, delicately flicking it with his tongue. His fingers made similar motions on her—her…clitoris. If she was brave enough to do this, she could call her body parts what they were. She wrapped her arms around his neck, running her fingers through his thick black hair.

"*Oui,* that is good." He sucked hard on her breast and slipped a finger inside her, making her cry out. His erection jerked where it rested against her hip. "Claire, Claire, I need you so bad." He inserted a second finger, spreading them apart to stroke deep inside her. She cried out again. "You're so hot, *cher,* wet and ready. I know you can take me now."

"Yes, now, now." She couldn't believe this amount of foreplay had aroused her to such a fever pitch.

He took the condom from his kit and quickly covered himself. Kneeling between her legs, he stared down at her, pure lust and concern battling on his face.

She reached up to him. "Come to me, Luc."

He surrendered with a groan and stretched out on top of her. His erection prodded at her, the tip finally going in. She tensed for a second and relaxed as she realized it didn't hurt. He sensed that and quickly entered to the hilt. She gasped and he stopped. "Did I hurt you?"

She quickly shook her head. Filled her and stretched her more than she'd ever been, yes. Hurt, no. She experimentally tightened around him and he jerked inside her.

Sweat beaded on his lip. "Can't hold still, *bébé*, gotta move." He glided in and out of her. "You are paradise. Wrap your long legs around me."

She did, locking her ankles in the small of his back. He groaned again and took her on a wild ride as he pistoned in and out. All Claire could do was clutch his shoulders and hold on. He felt wonderful inside her, and maybe he'd touch her more once he was done.

But to her surprise, the delicious friction of his hard member was more than wonderful. He was rubbing all the right spots, her hips moving to match his. He noticed the difference and grinned down at her. "You're a real hot one, *cher*." He dropped to his elbows and bit her earlobe. "I bet you can come with just my thrusting."

She protested how impossible that was but he sucked hard on her neck. She clutched his shoulders. "Oh, Luc." Darned if her passage didn't tighten around him even more, and they both groaned.

"Can't last much longer, *bébé. Baise-moi, baise-moi.*"

His raw French excited her. She shook as her

tension built, her head whipping back and forth. He grunted and jolted into her, pushing her halfway off the groundsheet.

Soft cries came from her throat as her heels dug into his rock-hard behind. She arched her back to take all of him as deep as he could go. Their bodies slapped wetly together, their skin sticking and releasing with every motion. She was bound more deeply to him than she'd ever been to a man.

Not wanting to miss a single second, she opened her eyes and stared at him. His face was twisted in agony. He met her gaze. "Come with me, Claire. Right now, with my cock inside you. Jus' think of all the sex juice I got saved for you." He angled himself so he bumped her clitoris over and over.

She gave a brief scream as he swelled inside her even more.

"That's it—scream for me. Now I know how good your pussy feels around me, I'm not gon' let you go." He moved frantically. "Come, dammit, now. Now!"

She wrapped her arms around his shoulders and squeezed down hard on his cock. Amazingly, tremors blossomed, spreading to her sensitive nub and up her belly to her breasts, neck and face. She shook around him as he blasted her self-control to shreds. Her moans crescendoed into a scream.

Luc gave a shout of pure triumph and exploded inside her. He rocked into her supersensitized clitoris, causing a second matching explosion. His mouth fell open as he pounded into her for what felt like an eternity, his face contorted into mindless pleasure. She could only hold on through his marathon climax, marveling at his pent-up desire.

He finally came back to earth. "Ah…" He rested his forehead against her, his black hair soaked with sweat. "That was…that was…"

"Intense?" she suggested.

"Nuclear." He gasped for air and slid partway from her. "Ah, I want to stay here all day."

"Then do." Claire had the delicious feeling she had only seen the tip of the iceberg when it came to Luc's sexual prowess. "I want you to show me everything I've been missing."

He eased from her, his erection still impressive despite his release. They were lucky he hadn't broken the "water storage device." He disposed of it into the fire. "What have you been missing, honey?"

"Sex." The word was strange on her tongue but liberating. "I want more sex and lots of it. I never did it like this before."

"What, outdoors?" He looked puzzled.

"No." She blushed but continued on. "Never, um, climaxed with a man before."

"What?" His shocked expression would have been comical if she hadn't been serious.

She rolled on her side to face him. "It's true. I never met anyone who made me feel like this and I want you to teach me everything you know."

"Everything?" He ran his tongue over his lips. "I lost my virginity when I was fifteen and haven't looked back. I've done things you've never heard of. Things that would scare a sheltered lady like you."

"If you don't show me, I'll go back to Virginia and find someone who will." She was bluffing, but he didn't need to know that.

His eyes narrowed. "You don't mean that."

"I do, Luc. I've been living a protected life, and I mean to change that in the most intimate way possible. I want you to be my teacher."

"Claire, you make it so hard for a man to say no. A gorgeous, naked woman begs me for sex lessons, what do I say?"

"Part of you says yes." She ran her hand down his chest and took his cock in her hand, still slippery from his climax. "What does the rest of you say?"

He closed his eyes as she traced his length. "*Oui.* I can't help myself around you."

She grinned in triumph. He leaped to life under her touch. Several days in the woods, just the two of them as he taught her all sorts of amazing sexual experiences. "Do you have more condoms?"

He nodded. "A whole box. But you're not gonna need one now."

"Why not?"

"You want me to teach you everything?" He folded his hand around hers and moved them up and down his shaft.

"Yes, everything." Claire's breath came faster.

"Then you need to know how to touch me with your hand. Take my edge off." Their hands moved faster. "Make sure I can fuck you for hours after."

She gave a gasp and he grinned. "Why, Mademoiselle Claire, I noticed before but didn't want to embarrass you—it seems that you like dirty talk."

"I…I…"

"Don't worry your sweet li'l self about it." He rolled onto his back, never letting go of her hand. "I won't tell anyone as long as you please me."

"How do I do that?"

"Like this." He dragged her hand to his tip and down to the base in a slow, thorough pattern. Once she had that down, he had her kneel next to him. "Lean over my face."

"What?"

He pillowed his head on his arms. "I want to suck on you. First your sweet titties, and then…" He gave a very male shrug. "Wherever else I want."

A thrill coursed through her. "Yes, Luc." She angled her body so her nipples brushed his stubbled cheeks. She knew it felt good and leisurely rubbed his face back and forth before he pulled one tip hard into his mouth.

She bit back a moan. He hadn't played with her breasts much during their fast and hard coupling. It was difficult to keep a steady pace with her hand.

"I see I'm gon' have to take the edge off you, too."

She shook again as he unerringly found her clitoris. With hard, deft strokes, he had her climaxing and collapsing on top of him. She barely had time to catch her breath before he urged her upright again. "You shouldn't have come before I did. Touch me the right way."

Claire tried to do it the way he wanted, but he kept pinching and sucking her nipples, making her arch and cry his name. He stopped tormenting her with his mouth. "You need to come again, don't you?" He found where her juices had run down her inner thigh and rubbed them into her tender skin.

"Yes, Luc."

"Say, 'yes, please.'"

"Yes, please, Luc."

"What?"

"I need to come again," she whispered. He was spread out on his back like some Middle Eastern pasha, all muscle and slick bronzed skin. Her hand was pale and fragile-looking against his thick, blood-engorged erection. She couldn't believe how he had ensnared her so quickly into such raw sensuality. Cool, quiet Claire, kneeling naked in the woods, begging for a third climax.

"I didn't hear you."

She took a deep breath. "I need to come again."

He gave her a cat-that-swallowed-the-canary smile of triumph. "Damn right you do. You're the hottest piece of ass I've ever seen." His crude words heated her even further. "Spread your legs and ride my fingers."

He slipped two fingers inside her and added a third. She raised and lowered herself on the makeshift shaft and screamed as his thumb pressed her hidden nub. She was wetter than she'd ever been before and he took advantage of it, sliding and spreading his thick fingers. "*Oui,* there." He pressed inside her and she gushed over his hand, crying his name, crying for release that mercifully broke over her.

She collapsed on him, his one hand still buried inside her. With her cheek resting on his damp chest, she saw him reach around her and cup his cock. Half a dozen quick strokes and he finished what she'd started, his seed arcing high into the air as his heart pounded under her ear. She stared at the raw power of his second orgasm coming only minutes after the first.

She stretched out next to him as they both gasped for air. "You do have a lot stored up, don't you?"

"I wasn't lying when I told you I hadn't had sex in a long time. I was able to keep going without it until you broke the dam, *cher.* Now I don't know how I'm gon' get you trained in survival when all I want to do is train you in sex."

"Sex won't interfere, I promise." She crossed her heart, tracing her finger over her bare breast.

He raised an eyebrow. "Oh, yeah? How will we go on hikes when all I want is to pull down your pants and take you against a tree? How will I sit on that log and explain important things to you when all I want is you to kneel between my legs and suck on my cock?"

Claire shivered. "I've never done that to a man before," she confessed.

His grip tightened on her. "You keep telling me things like that, you gon' make me hard again," he rasped.

Claire smiled. She'd never been complimented like that.

"But, Claire, I need to confess something, too."

"What is it?" Had he changed his mind already?

He looked guilty for the first time since they'd met. "I have a tent and sleeping bags in the boat."

"You what?" Her nervousness vanished. "I've been sleeping on a bed of branches with sticks poking me in the butt with nothing but a foil blanket and mosquito netting for cover and you had a tent and sleeping bags?" She twisted her fingers into his chest hair and tugged hard.

"Ow!" He grabbed her hand.

She leaned over him. "What's the matter? The big, tough, Green Beret never had anyone pull on his chest hair before? Better not let the enemy know that or you and your men might wind up as bare-chested as an underwear model."

"At ease, *mam'zelle.*" He cupped her neck and pulled her down for a kiss. "You needed to learn to make a bed platform and sleep on it. But if you don't want me to pitch the tent, we could always try doin' it on your platform. Sure hope you built it well...."

She giggled and kissed him again. "Not that well, Luc. Even a sleeping bag on the ground would be a welcome change."

"Don't worry, *bébé*. You and I won't be doing a whole lotta sleepin'."

7

CLAIRE PLODDED THROUGH the woods after Luc. He had decided to find a new spot for their campsite and pitch the tent. The terrain was slightly different, more wooded than swampy and even more secluded. She had enjoyed the boat ride more the second time, but now they were making up for it on foot. It gave her plenty of time to think and plenty of time for second thoughts. How much did she actually know about this man? She had never in her life been so sexually impulsive and was starting to regret it.

Maybe if she got to know him better, it would ease her doubts. She took a deep breath. "So, where are you from, Luc?"

He replied after a pause. "Louisiana."

She wasn't an idiot—he was a Cajun, after all. "Yes, I know that, but which part? North, south, east—"

"South central Louisiana. Near the Atchafalaya Basin."

"What's it like?"

"Hot, muggy."

"Oh, like this?" Claire looked around.

"Some."

She pressed her lips together. "There's this interesting concept you may have heard of. It may not be part of Green Beret training, but it's called 'conversation.' I say something, and you say more than two words back to me."

"How about three?"

She shot daggers at his broad shoulders. He didn't want to talk? She'd fully compensate for it. "My full name is Claire Adeline Cook. My middle name is after my maternal grandmother, who was German, so no jokes about it. I'm an only child but I have a few cousins on my dad's side. I grew up in Virginia and I majored in humanities with concentrations in English and French literature." She thought for a second. "My favorite colors are peach and warm coral, which is actually an orangey kind of red, but that looks better in winter, whereas peach is a pastel better suited for summer. I have a horse named Pumpkin at home, and I won some riding competitions when I was a kid." She paused to drink from her canteen.

He still didn't reply, so she continued doggedly. "My best friend is Janey, whom you met. She's very busy with her army career, so I don't see her often. I enjoy yoga, French cooking and tutoring kids in an after-school reading program." She wound down, suddenly tired of trying to get a response from him.

They walked in silence for a few minutes.

"My full name is Luc Edouard Boudreaux. My middle name is after my father."

Claire stared at his back in amazement. It was the most he'd said about himself, ever. But he continued, "I have six older sisters."

Her eyes bugged out, but she didn't dare say anything to interrupt the flow.

"I have about thirty cousins last I counted, and I majored in English and drama at Tulane. My favorite color is army green, and I had a pet alligator when I was a kid. My best friend is Olie, who's also very busy with his army career, but I see a lot of him."

Claire smiled at his wry sense of humor.

"What else did I miss?"

"Hobbies."

"Running and weightlifting." He fell silent.

"Six sisters?"

"Yeah, I blame them for getting me into the drama thing. They were always dressing me up as the male lead in their plays."

"So that's how you know about Shakespeare."

"I was in a couple productions."

She quoted a few lines from Romeo and Juliet in a girlish English accent.

He slid effortlessly into a flawless accent and quoted the next lines right back to her.

"Very good." She applauded and he turned around to give her a sweeping bow, his machete dipping like an old-fashioned rapier.

"Better now?"

"What?"

He grinned at her. "Now that you know something about me."

Busted. "Yes, I do feel better. You may not believe this, but I don't normally jump into bed with strangers."

"We haven't made it to a bed, yet, *béb.*"

That must be short for *baby* in Cajun, kind of like being called "babe." Her face heated. "That's not what I meant."

"I promise not to think less of you, Claire. I'm honored you would break your own rules to be with me."

He had broken his rules, as well, but Claire worried he'd get all noble and self-sacrificing and refuse to come near her again if she mentioned it. She gestured at the wilderness around them. "Out here, rules were meant to be broken, right?"

"You're only allowed to break the ones that don't get you hurt."

She wanted to ask if he meant emotionally hurt, as well, but figured that topic was best left for another time, or perhaps left alone altogether. "So, six sisters—I can't even imagine! What are their names?"

He set off along the trail again. "Let's see—Evangeline is the oldest, then Jolie, Nicolette, Gabrielle, Acadia and finally Adeline right before me."

He said his sister's name with a French accent, but she recognized it. "That's my middle name!"

"So, you see why I wouldn't make fun of your name. Don't want two angry women comin' after me."

"Oh, I think you can handle yourself."

"Claire, you never met Adeline."

CLAIRE WAS STILL SMILING as she helped Luc pitch a tent barely enough for the two of them. That was okay. Like he'd said earlier, who was planning to sleep? She walked to where they'd set their packs. Her feet were sore and her socks soaked.

She pulled out a fresh pair and sat on yet another log to pull off her boots. "Oh, my gosh." Her sock was splotched in blood.

Luc whipped around from where he was checking their coordinates on his map. "What the hell?" He was at her side before she could blink. "Did you step on something, you?"

She peeled off her sock gingerly. The reddened areas she had so carefully cushioned in the morning were raw and bleeding blisters.

"Ah, boo, your poor feet." He tsked like an old lady as he knelt and examined her other foot, which was just as bad. He returned with some water and his first-aid kit before gently lifting one foot to rest on his thigh.

"Boo?" She tried not to wince as he doused her wounds with water before carefully disinfecting and bandaging them.

"What?" He didn't look up, intent on his task.

"What does 'boo' mean?"

He met her glance sheepishly. "It's an old Cajun term of endearment—like 'dear' or 'honey.'"

She smiled despite the pain. So he'd called her the equivalent of "honey" and had answered to it when she'd asked about it. "How on earth did they ever come up with 'boo'?"

"No idea. Cajun French is full of Spanish, African and Indian words. The university linguists adore comin' round with their digital recorders to talk to the *papères* and *mamères*—grandpas and grandmas. My own *mamère* is interviewed every Christmas, Easter and summer break."

"You're exaggerating."

"Not much. She informed us the last academic told her she was a national cultural treasure, so we'd better behave ourselves or she'd pass us a slap." He grinned. "A slap from a national cultural treasure still stings pretty good."

So did her feet. "I don't think I'll be able to hike very much tomorrow. Is there something we can work on close to camp?"

He frowned and finished doctoring her. "You think I make you hike on those feet, you?" She knew he was getting irritated when he added French-style reflexive pronouns. "What kind of man do you think I am?"

"A good one." She leaned forward and kissed his forehead.

He looked up, startled. "I don't know 'bout that, Claire."

"Well, I do."

He grunted and packed away his supplies before

pulling out her canvas sneakers she wore in camp at night to let her boots dry.

"I don't think my feet will fit in those anymore."

"Sure they will." He pulled out his razor-sharp knife and made several slits in the shoes to allow for her bandages. When he was done they looked more like sandals.

She eased her feet into them. "Thanks for taking such good care of me, Luc."

"*De rien,* it was nothin'." He shook his head. "Just because I broke my word about certain things doesn't mean I won't look after you." He picked up the water purifier and busied himself refilling the canteen.

He was still feeling guilty for giving in to her sexually. She smiled. "Luc?"

"Yes?"

She stood, wobbling slightly in her jerry-rigged shoes. He was at her side immediately. "Can you help me to the tent? I want to get off my feet."

He swept her into his arms and carried her to the tent flap, setting her gently down on the sleeping bags. After three nights of tree branches, they were heavenly soft.

"Better?" He knelt next to her.

She stroked his knee, daring to glide her hand up his thigh when he offered her no resistance. "I could be a lot better if you helped distract me."

His black eyes glittered in the dim light. "What kind of distraction did you have in mind, boo?"

"This." She moved her hand a few inches over and found his growing erection.

"You want this?" He undid his gear belt and unbuttoned his fly. She freed him from his briefs, cradling him with trembling hands as he swelled under her touch. "You want all of it?" He grabbed her wrist and made her cup his heavy sac. His weight and power sent a wet gush between her legs.

She nodded.

"Then lick me."

To call her unskilled in that area was an understatement. Still, she bent her head and licked him as if he were a big purple ice cream cone.

He jerked under her tongue, leaving an unfamiliar taste of salt and musk. *"C'est bon, ça."*

Good, that meant he liked it. She licked a few more times but he cradled the back of her head and urged her deeper. She struggled a bit, and he looked at her in alarm.

She paused and took a deep breath, then tentatively opened her mouth wider. He stopped her.

"I'm sorry if I wasn't any good at that." She blinked hard. So much for being a wild woman.

"I didn't stop you 'cause it made me feel bad—I stopped you because it didn't make *you* feel good." He nuzzled her neck until she tipped back her head. "I only want to make you feel good." He pressed kisses down her neck to her collarbone and rapidly undressed her, being extra careful of her feet. When he was done, she lay naked on the sleeping bags. "Claire, don't you look pretty enough to eat."

"Eat?" Did that mean what she thought?

"You ever had a man eat you up before?" He pressed his fingers between her thighs. "Take you into his mouth right here?"

She shook her head, wincing. She'd been in the woods for days without a proper shower, for goodness' sake. How could he want to do…that?

"Okay, *cher.*" His tone was gentle. "Someday soon, though. You'll love it, I promise."

Yeah, right. But her embarrassment was quickly forgotten as he stroked her clitoris. "The tongue, it's not so different from the finger. Hot, wet and slick, it slides over this little jewel back and forth, back and forth."

Her hips rotated as his hypnotic voice filled the tent.

"Your body, it tells me what you like. The finger, it touch, but the tongue, oh, the tongue, it taste what you like." He withdrew his hand and licked his fingers.

Her eyes flew wide with shock. "Luc!"

"Mmm, you taste go-ood." He grinned down at her with no signs of disgust. "Can't hardly wait to get my face snuggled up there." He put his fingers back. "Now if I was eatin' you up, I'd use both hands to spread your legs wide like so. And I'd take my thumbs to pull back the hood from your little jewel, like so. Then I real gentle tease you, an' tease you with flicks of my tongue—like this." As he played with her innermost flesh, Claire swelled and grew under his slow, instructive touch. How did he know the secrets of her body when she'd never discovered them for herself?

"Well, would you look at that? My fingers are telling me you like showing me your sweetness. Your little *chatte* is getting all pink and plump."

"*Chatte?*"

He gave her a sly smile. "*Chatte* is a female cat."

Cat, kitten—oh. "I never learned that slang word in French class."

"I should hope not." He gave her a look of mock outrage. "If all you fancy prep school girls went around petting your *chattes*, you never get any homework done."

She blushed. "I never did."

"Did your homework? You naughty girl."

"Not that! The other."

"No time like the present." He caught her hand and brought it down to her, um, well, *chatte*. She tried to pull away but he wouldn't let her. "I told you I would teach you everything you needed to know. You need to know this."

He moved her fingers across her clitoris. "Learn what you like. Fast and hard?"

She choked back a moan as he strummed her like she was a guitar.

"Or slower, in circles?"

"I…like it…all," she gasped.

"*Bon.* Now you gon' play with yourself while I fuck you."

She stared at him. "Aren't you, um, going to take off your clothes?"

"No, don't think so." He bent down to kiss her nipple. "I think you might like my soft T-shirt rubbing your titties." He pressed his chest against her bare breasts and she groaned. It did feel good.

"And I think you'd like my rough pants slapping your sweet li'l ass." He stroked himself a few times, his big hand working up and down his erection. "That's real good. Maybe I touch myself, then you touch yourself, we see who comes first?"

"No, Luc, I can't wait." The sight of him pleasuring himself was extremely arousing. He stared raptly at her naked breasts, hard nipples and wide-open thighs as if she were his most secret fantasy.

And he was hers. She took a deep breath and touched her clitoris. He groaned, and she took that for encouragement, stroking herself with more boldness than she ever had. She really did swell under her fingers, her juices easily slicking the way. Juicy enough for Luc to slide right in and mix his with hers. She wanted his bare skin inside her, his clothing rubbing her. "Come inside me," she whispered. The pressure was driving her crazy.

"Where, *cher?*"

"My *chatte.* Please," she added.

He stroked himself a few more times. "Since you asked so nice…" He sheathed himself in a condom and moved between her thighs. "Take me, *béb.*"

This time, he slid right in, locking them together.

"Ah, Claire, so fuckin' tight and hot. I never want to leave you." He kissed her, his tongue deep in her mouth. She sucked on it hard like she'd wanted to suck on his other body part and he groaned.

Claire instinctively raised her hips as he slid in and out of her. He broke their kiss to gasp for air. "Ride me, Claire. You ever get turned on bouncing up and down on that saddle of yours?"

She nodded. Not that she'd known what it meant at the time. Before she could say anything, he'd scooped her up and rolled onto his back so she was sitting on his cock, totally naked and exposed, her hair a mess and her breasts bouncing all over. "Ride me hard, Claire. I want to see your *chatte* coming up and down my cock, your ass rubbing my balls. Do it."

Claire hesitated for a second but he wrapped his big hands around her hips and lifted her up and down for a few seconds until she got the rhythm. After that, her body knew what to do.

She rose and fell on him, her hands braced on his taut chest. He tipped his head back and matched her rhythm. She decided for a little variety and swiveled her hips, leaning forward and back. She swore his eyes crossed as he swelled inside her even more.

Luc let go of her hips and squeezed her breasts, her nipples rubbing his rough palms. He found her rock-hard nipples and pinched them both at the same time. She cried out as the sensation shot straight down to her clitoris.

"Touch yourself again," he groaned. "Can't last much longer with you riding me like a stallion."

She slipped her finger over her clitoris, her nail brushing the base of his shaft. They groaned in unison. "Oh, Luc." She was shaking almost too hard to keep moving, but the pressure inside her was so delicious she never wanted it to end.

"Hurry, hurry," he urged her. His hands mapped her breasts, belly, bottom, blurring the boundaries between his body and hers. She contracted around him and he looked at her with glassy eyes. "Now?"

"Now!"

His fierce thrusts made her melt all over him, her *chatte* throbbing as he pounded deep inside her. She moaned his name, begged and pleaded with him, but he was merciless, dragging her into a second orgasm before letting go himself.

"Claire, oh, Claire…" He broke off into a shout of sexual triumph, bucking and pulsing as he emptied himself in a long, powerful climax.

THIGHS TREMBLING, SHE collapsed onto his cotton-clad chest. "Oh, Luc, that was wonderful." She tried to catch her breath as he rubbed her bare back.

"Wonderful," Luc echoed in a daze, floored by how wild she had been after her first tentative attempts. If he wasn't mistaken, that was the only time she'd ridden a man to completion. He helped her ease off him and tucked her into his side.

She rested her head on his shoulder as he stroked her silky hair. "Tell me, how does such a sexy woman make it to your age without certain experiences?"

"I assume you mean sexually?"

He nodded. "Not that I'm complaining. It gives me great pleasure to be your teacher." That was an understatement. One of his romance-reading previous girlfriends had called him an "alpha male," kind of like the alpha wolf that dominated the pack and earned his pick of the females.

And Claire was the best he'd ever picked. But he still wasn't sure why'd she'd picked him.

"It's kind of a boring story."

"We have all night." He kissed the top of her head.

"Well, I was almost engaged once. He was the president of his fraternity at UVA."

Luc hated him already.

"He was blond and handsome, played on the university tennis team and was premed."

Hmmph. Luc was his team's medic and wasn't impressed by any pretty-boy doctor wannabe.

"We even got pinned."

"Pinned?" What was that? He thought he knew pretty much every slang word for sex out there.

She blushed, her face heating against his arm. "Yeah, he gave me his fraternity pin to wear. It's regarded as a precursor to an engagement ring."

"Oh." Like giving a girl your varsity jacket before heading out to the sock hop. A whole world still existed that hadn't moved much past the nineteen-fifties.

"Have you ever pinned a girl, Luc?" she asked innocently.

Only if that was a slang term for sex. "No, I wasn't in a fraternity. So what happened to him?" Hopefully a slow and painful death involving invertebrates in bodily orifices.

The corners of her mouth turned down. "He was a cheater," she admitted. "With at least one of my sorority sisters, maybe two. Janey learned about it and told me. I didn't want to believe her, but she never lies. He admitted it when I confronted him." She gave Luc a small smile. "He was the human equivalent of a foil-wrapped chocolate Easter bunny—bright and fancy on the outside, but hollow and waxy on the inside. Too much will make you sick."

Poor Claire was still going through sugar withdrawal. Luc wondered what kind of chocolate he would be. "You're well rid of someone like that," he said dismissively, but she had turned her face away. "What else?"

"He said he had needs, and I hadn't satisfied them."

"That's garbage, Claire!"

She looked up, startled. "What?"

"You heard me. He was looking for an excuse to cheat."

"Yes, I know, but I didn't have any experience and—"

"And it was his job to show you how to please

him—his job to please you." He ran his hand down her arm. "Did he ever please *you,* Claire? Ever make you scream his name in pure ecstasy? Ever take you so high you thought you'd never come down?"

"No, never." She was trembling against him now.

"Then he wasn't a man at all. And you please me plenty." He pulled her under him and proceeded to show her how much she pleased him—several times.

When they lay together, sweaty and satisfied again, he asked the question that had popped into his head earlier. "So what kind of chocolate am I, Claire?" he asked lazily.

"Chocolate? Hmm, let's see. You'd be dark, strong chocolate that melted on my tongue and made me crave more."

"And you would be a *petite* bonbon. Delicate, sweet, with a creamy soft center." As he was saying the words, they were sounding sentimental even to him, as if he were developing feelings for this woman. True, he did have feelings for her: respect and admiration for her tenacity, her kind nature, how the sun picked up caramel highlights in her hair and how her lips curved to show-case her white teeth…*non.* Respect and admiration on a purely professional level was best. That was all.

THE NEXT DAY, LUC handed her his satellite phone. "We've been out here four days. You should call some-one to check in."

She accepted it reluctantly. Here in the woods was

their own little world, free from fathers and friends and family obligations. On the other hand, her father was quite capable of having one of his governor buddies call out the local National Guard to search for her.

Luc showed her how to work the phone. "Can they tell where I am?"

"No. One of our tech guys arranged it so the signal relays through several foreign countries. Unless they have access to Green Beret technology at the exact moment you call, they don't have a prayer of tracing us."

"Good." That made her feel marginally better. "Still, I think I'll call Janey." She dialed and had to smile when she heard Janey's cautious hello. Goodness only knew what was showing on her phone's caller ID.

"Janey, it's me, Claire."

After the relative peace of the woods, her friend's shriek jabbed through her head like a jackhammer. "Claire, oh, my God, where the hell are you? We're all going nuts here. I can't believe you went off in the woods with that guy. Are you okay? Your dad's about to call in bloodhounds and the FBI to find you even though he got your notes and voice mails."

"Janey, I'm fine," she answered, cutting through her friend's chatter. "I've had several days of survival training. Luc taught me how to clean and cook fish, rabbits and even snakes." She made a face.

"Wow," Janey said cautiously. "But, Claire, this isn't like you. I thought for sure you'd be back by now. You didn't even take three-quarters of your gear."

Claire fought down her anger. "Janey, my dad put GPS tracking devices in my stuff—my boots, my purse, my bags."

"Oh. That's a bit much, even for him."

"And he made all those arrangements for training me at Parris Island, having me sleep in the VIP hotel every night. Do you know what I've done out here? I built a sleeping platform out of real live trees with a real machete that I sharpened myself. I slept on it for two nights. And those were two long nights, Janey."

"Where have you slept the other nights, Claire?" her friend asked quietly.

"Once I proved I could do it, Luc let me off the hook and put up the tent he'd stashed."

"You know that's not what I'm asking."

"I know what you're asking and I'm not answering." She and Janey had always shared everything, but this thing with Luc was too raw and untested to giggle over with her friend. Not that Janey sounded in the mood to giggle.

"Roger that, Claire. What I don't know, I can't tell your father."

"Exactly. You can tell him I found his spies in the sky, and you can tell him that my survival training is on *my* terms." Luc raised his eyebrows at her emphatic conversation.

"Don't you think you should call him yourself to tell him? He is worried sick about you being alone in the woods with some stranger."

"He's not a stranger anymore."

"That's what I thought." Janey sighed. "When will you be back? *Where* will you be back? At least let me tell your dad that."

Claire considered that and nodded. "Let me check with Luc." She turned to him. "When are we coming back?"

He studied her for a second. "You want to go now?"

"No." She still had plenty to learn, about survival, as well as about Luc.

"Three days from now. We'll meet your father at the Special Forces compound at Bragg, where we first met."

She relayed the information to Janey.

"Okay, that will be the eleventh and plenty of time for you to pack for your flight."

"Oh, right." In the whole crucible of her experience, she had almost forgotten about leaving for the settlement at Río San Lucas.

"You are still going to South America, aren't you?" Janey's tone was dry. "That *is* the reason you're out in the woods eating snakes with a snake-eater."

"Honestly, Janey, 'snake-eater' isn't the nicest way to refer to Green Berets. Didn't Olie tell you that?"

"You don't even want to know what Olie told me." Her voice went from dry to pissed-off.

"Really? Well, you'll have to fill me in later. I don't want to run down the battery."

"I imagine not. According to my caller ID, you're calling from Uzbekistan. Quite the survival trip, that."

Claire finally had to laugh. "We're a bit closer than Uzbekistan, if my dad asks."

"Oh, he will, Claire. He will." With that foreboding prediction, they said their goodbyes.

Luc studied her face, his own unreadable. "She's worried about you?"

"Yeah," Claire admitted. "This is all pretty out of character for me."

"Me, too." He stared off into the woods. "Maybe I should have kept you at Parris Island. You still could have learned the basics."

She frowned at him. "How was I supposed to learn how to survive at night? How was I supposed to gut all those fish if I knew I had a hamburger and fries waiting for me for dinner? Hunger is a powerful motivator."

"I was hungry, too—hungry for you."

"Well, don't look so thrilled about it."

He wore a sourpuss expression. "I'm not happy. I'm letting my…need for you cloud my judgment. And clouded judgment gets people hurt."

"I won't get hurt."

"There's so much you need to know." He paced the clearing. "A proper course would take weeks, if not months."

She jumped in front of him. "But there are all those stories of people who survive terrible things without much or any formal training."

He crossed his arms in front of his chest. "And there are plenty of well-trained men who die anyway."

"So what's the point?" She made a sweeping gesture at the fire she had started with a flint and steel, the fish and game she had painstakingly cleaned, the water she had purified. "If none of this means a damn, why bother? If those big, tough men can't make it even with all their knowledge, I should curl into a ball and die if I ever get dumped in the middle of nowhere."

"Stop it!" He reached out and grabbed her arms, shaking her. "If you ever get into trouble, you will remember every damn thing I tell you and you will get your ass to safety. You are not going to die."

"Okay, Luc." She shook off his grip.

He stared at her and slumped onto a log, a stunned look on his face. "I'm so sorry. I shouldn't have touched you like that."

"No, you shouldn't have. Why did you?"

"'Cuz I can't stand the idea of you dying lost and alone—you dying, period." He rubbed his eyes. "I...well, I've lost teammates who seemed invincible."

She sat next to him. "Nobody is invincible. My mother lived in the jungle for over twenty years without any problems but then died from cancer." She slugged him in the biceps, definitely causing more damage to herself than him. "Oh, why am I lecturing you on danger, anyway? You jump out of planes, sneak around in enemy territory and probably go shark-hunting for fun in flippers with a knife clenched between your teeth. You are the last person to bitch at me about risk. Didn't you tell me you had a pet alligator when you were a kid?"

"Yeah." He finally grinned, showing her a couple round white scars on his forearm. "Li'l bastard got me good before I smartened up."

"Got rid of him?"

"No, got fast enough to avoid being bit. Once he got big enough to take an arm off, I let him loose in the swamp."

Claire sighed. "And you think I'm crazy for wanting to go teach some kids? Believe me, I'll stay away from the alligators."

"Okay, *béb*." He put his arm around her shoulders. "You're gettin' to be one tough chick. Maybe the gators'll swim away when they see you coming."

She laughed and leaned into his side. "You bet. They know I need a new alligator purse."

He laughed. "Since you're stickin' 'round for the end of training, I need to figure out what to cover next."

"What, you thought I'd quit before now?"

"That was before I knew you," he replied diplomatically.

"Since I've made it almost to the end, what comes toward the end of the training for a real Green Beret?"

"SERE training—survival, evasion, resistance and escape. SERE training is heavy duty and only a few soldiers can hack it. The rest wash out to their regular units."

"Oh. Are you going to teach me some SERE skills?"

"No way. You need months of training before you'd be even half-ready for that. I'm happy you know how to use a compass now."

Claire pursed her lips. She thought she'd done slightly better than that. "I bet you I can hide from you—at least for a while."

"*Cher,* you couldn't win a game of hide-and-seek with a two-year-old."

"Hey! You too chicken to try?"

He gave her an amused smile bordering on the edge of smirkiness. She hated when people smirked at her.

"I mean it. A big, bad Green Beret like you can't find a civilian out here? What kind of bayou boy are you?"

"Listen, I could track a mosquito through the air if I wanted. But I don't."

"What do you want?"

"You." He gave her a blatant stare that made her quiver, but not enough to back down.

"Well, you're not going to get me like that." She snapped her fingers. "You think I need more training— well, train me in this evasion stuff."

He rubbed his chin. "All right. You wanna do some evasion training, we'll do it. Gear up."

She quickly gathered her knife, compass, flashlight and canteen, strapping the machete in its scabbard to her waist. Its weight was comforting now rather than scary.

He examined her from head-to-toe, shaking his

head. "Damn, who'd have thought a woman could look so sexy wearing a machete."

"I'm full of surprises."

He gave her some last-minute instructions about avoiding snakes and gators. "Now the part that comes after evasion is resistance. When I catch you—"

"You mean 'if,'" she interrupted, trying for bravado.

"No, I don't. *When* I catch you, you are my captive and totally within my power. Under my absolute control."

"So what does that mean?"

"You have to do anything I want. Unless you want to resist me—you know, just for practice. That's the R in SERE. Resistance."

The part of being under his control sounded a bit menacing. Luc would never hurt her, but she wasn't tough enough to resist much.

He watched her closely. "You up for this?"

"Absolutely."

"I find you, you're mine. Every last inch of you. For as long as I say so."

She swallowed hard.

"I'll give you a half hour's head start. Enough time to get yourself away, but not too far lost. Ready?"

She nodded.

"Go."

She scurried out of camp, noting with irritation how he leaned against the log and tipped his hat over his eyes to take a catnap.

She'd show him. Her ancestors had hidden from the British and the Yankees both. Surely some of their abilities had been passed along. She stepped into the nearby stream, careful to not disturb any rocks to give away her moves.

Walking upstream was actually kind of pleasant, her poor, battered feet cooling after several minutes in the brackish water. The birds sang overhead and even that fat stick floating toward her was interesting.

Oh, no, that was a snake swimming downstream, not a stick. Well, that would be a real bite in the butt if she got snakebit. Claire stepped purposely to one side of the stream, trying not to scream and sprint from the water like she desperately wanted to. According to Luc, most snake species around here were non-venomous, except for two: rattlesnakes didn't swim and the other… The snake sensed the changing current and opened its white-lined mouth wide, its fangs a-popping.

This was the other venomous snake in the area—the cottonmouth. She gasped and froze, trying to gauge which way the snake would swim. *Away from me, away from me.*

Luc stared at Claire's retreating back through slitted eyes until she was out of sight. He jumped to his feet. A thirty minute head start? What was he, nuts? There were a thousand bad things that could happen to someone inexperienced in the woods.

He paced in the clearing for several seconds and grabbed his own canteen to go after her. No, wait. He stopped. He'd made a bet with her and he wasn't a cheater.

He started walking again. What was cheating compared to Claire's safety? He stopped again. But everyone was trying to keep her safe—that was the problem. Too safe for her own good. A baby bird who never dove from the nest had weak wings, easy prey for any chickenhawk that came after it. And much as he hated it, he wouldn't do her any favors by coddling her.

He checked his watch. Twenty-five minutes to wait. He had the feeling it might be the longest twenty-five minutes of his life.

THE CURRENT WAS SHOVING that snake right at her—she wouldn't escape the water in time and the snake could, of course, follow her up the bank. She looked around wildly for a stick or rock to chuck at its head, but no luck. A branch brushed her hair and she glanced up.

Was it thick enough to support her weight? Only one way to find out. She wrapped her hands around the rough bark and yanked. It didn't crack, so she swung her one leg up and then the other, struggling to lock her ankles together.

"Whoa!" Her backpack swung from her shoulders in a crazy arc and threatened to unbalance her. She glanced down and nearly fell into the water as the snake oscillated under her, gaping and hissing.

"No, no!" She dug what were left of her fingernails into the bark. His ghost-white mouth was even scarier close up, its fangs as long as her pinky finger. Why had she made that stupid bet with Luc? If he were here, he'd have probably killed it and cooked it by now. Instead she was going to be the snake's lunch.

After what seemed like an hour, the snake veered off and continued its reptilian way downstream.

And just in time because her arms and legs were about to give out. No more snakes in sight. She carefully lowered her feet into the stream and released the branch. Wincing, she examined the hunks of dirt and crud embedded in her skin and rinsed her hands. At least she wasn't bleeding too much. Once she found a stopping place, she'd disinfect the open cuts with her liquid hand sanitizer.

She walked upstream, her legs wobbling slightly from the adrenaline aftershock. Wow, she'd done it. She had saved herself from a nasty-looking snake. And all by herself. Maybe this survival stuff wasn't so bad.

But that didn't mean she'd won the bet. She glanced at her watch. Only five minutes before Luc started after her. She checked the riverbank for a place to step out of the water. She found a relatively flat grassy area that might not show her bootprints and hopped onto it.

Okay, now what? She saw a deeply wooded copse just past the grass and headed into the brushy part, careful not to break any branches. Luc had taught her the fresh green insides of broken wood were an obvious giveaway. She was really glad she'd worn long pants or else Luc would have been able to track the blood from her scratched legs. She didn't need any more injuries.

Geez, it was nice and cool in here, at least ten degrees cooler than in the open. Claire took the time to suck in a refreshing breath. But not too much time. Luc would move much faster than she did, especially with her snake delay.

Oh, a big tree with a hollow at its base was inside the grove. Claire picked up a stick and poked the leaf litter. Nothing came leaping out at her, so she decided to give that a try. The entrance was fairly overgrown but she still needed some camouflage.

Luckily there was a big pile of freshly fallen tree branches whose leaves had started to wilt. She shoved them in front of the hollow, climbed in and pulled her wooden screen closed.

Claire looked up. She'd never been inside a tree before. She had about eight inches of clearance above her head. She'd never been claustrophobic, so it was more cozy than enclosed. Her hidey-hole had kind of a musty, dry smell but wasn't unpleasant. She tried not to think of what kind of crud was lurking below the dry leaves underneath her.

Maybe she should clean her hands before they got infected. She manually picked out the last bark bits and pulled out her pocket hand sanitizer. She bit back a gasp as the rubbing alcohol hit raw flesh. Wow, that hurt. Waving her hands in the enclosed space, she wondered how long she would need to stay to prove her point. It wasn't as if Luc would stand in the middle of the woods and yell, "Ollie, Ollie, oxen-free" or "Come out, come out, wherever you are." She might need to spend the night in the tree. She hadn't considered that when she made the bet. But if she lost, she was his captive. Under his total control. For as long as he wanted.

So why wasn't Claire jumping out and calling his name?

Because this wasn't some sexy hide-and-seek game she was playing—this was a test of her skills and endurance.

It sure was quiet and cool inside here. She yawned. Between hard physical work during the day and heavy duty sex with Luc at night, she hadn't gotten much sleep all week. She rested her head on her bent knees. Maybe she'd close her eyes for just a minute.

8

LUC GAZED DOWN AT Claire sleeping soundly in her tree. She'd given it a good try, but he'd found overturned rocks and some bent blades of grass where she'd entered and exited the stream. Once he'd hit the clearing, he'd smelled the rubbing alcohol in her hand sanitizer, and that was it for her.

He wavered for a minute. Maybe he should let her off the hook, pretend she'd tricked him.

But if she didn't learn from her mistakes, why the hell was he training her? Would an enemy let her off the hook? No.

He bent down and clamped a heavy hand on her ankle. She let out a scream.

"Gotcha." Luc purposely hardened his expression, became a stranger.

"Yeah, you got me. How did you find me?" She wiggled out of the hollow and screamed again as he tossed her over his shoulder.

He ignored her question. "You gonna come easy or do I have to tie you up?"

"Tie me up?" she squeaked, his shoulder probably

pressing into her diaphragm. "Oh, no, you don't." She struggled against him, kicking her boots into his thighs and almost landing one where it counted.

He set her on her feet, careful to keep a mean look on his face. "I hunted you, I found you, and you're my captive now."

"What? No, that was a joke, right?" He pulled out a length of rope and tied her wrists together. "Luc!" She finally tried resisting and swung her hands at his head, which he easily ducked, tying her ankles together, as well.

He swung her onto his shoulder again and headed for camp. "You wanted SERE training, you got it. You survived for an hour, but your evasion and resistance leave something to be desired. As for escape, we'll see about that." Once he had her in the tent, she wouldn't be out of his sight.

"Hey, I did more than survive, I won that part." Her breath was choppy due to his quick pace. "Did you see that gigantic cottonmouth swimming downstream?"

"Yeah, why?" It had been a big son of a bitch. Used to them, Luc hadn't thought twice about it.

"It came straight at me. Fangs and all."

"What?" He slowed for a second. She hadn't been bit, had she? He picked up the pace to carry her to camp and his snakebite kit.

"But I escaped it." She gasped for air again. "Grabbed a branch…swung my legs up. Went right under me." She slammed his ass with her hands. "So there."

Good for her. He shivered for a second. What if she'd been bitten and he hadn't found her? She could have gotten seriously ill.

He forced himself not to soften. But she hadn't been bitten, and maybe some of her success was due to his training. Her wings were getting stronger.

"What…gave me away?"

Good, she wanted to know so she didn't make the same mistake. "You overturned a couple rocks, crushed some grass, but that stinky hand sanitizer was a dead giveaway."

"Crap," she muttered.

Luc allowed himself a grin since she couldn't see his face. To tell the truth, he was enjoying this walk with her curvy butt next to his cheek, her breasts rubbing his back. He ran his hand up her thighs and she let out a yelp.

"What are you doing?"

"Checking my prisoner for weapons."

"Don't have any there…you ass."

He wasn't sure. To him, her body was one deadly weapon as far as he was concerned. "You gonna honor our bet? Or weasel out?"

"What'd you have…in mind?" She sounded nervous but a bit excited, as well.

"*Oui ou non,* Claire?" Shoot, he shouldn't have used her first name. That made him seem like an easy mark.

"Yes, all right!"

Good. She was all his to do what he wanted to do. He'd make sure she enjoyed herself, as well, since watching her come was so fuckin' sexy.

A few minutes later, Luc approached their camp. "Ah, we're home." He dumped her onto the sleeping bag and she glared up at him.

"I suppose that little caveman stunt of yours made you all hot and bothered?" Her tone was frosty but he sensed the same excitement building in her.

"Sure did, *cher.*" Her breasts were bobbing up and down against her shirt. "I think I'm gon' make you all hot and bothered, too."

"Untie me." She held out her wrists imperiously for him to loosen her.

"Fine. But there'll be no escape for you." He cut her hands free, but quickly pushed her onto the bedding.

"Luc, what are you doing?" she all but squealed.

He'd been aggressive with plenty of bad guys and even a couple bad ladies, but they'd never brought out this almost animalistic lust that Claire was inspiring in him.

"You ever let a man do whatever he wanted with you, sweet Claire?" She shook her head. He hadn't thought so. "You never trusted any of them enough for that, did you?" She looked away but he read the truth in her eyes. "You trust me?"

She looked at him with her big brown eyes and nodded. His heart gave an extra beat. Her trust was beginning to mean the world to him. "I want to do all sorts of wicked, naughty things to you while you're like this, Claire."

Her pupils dilated and she gasped. Bingo.

He licked the shell of her ear and sucked on the lobe, sending shivers through her. "You want this, *oui ou non?*" he murmured. "You tell me *'oui,'* then no stopping." To seal the deal, he nuzzled her neck, where her pulse beat furiously.

She nodded slowly. *"Oui."*

"Now you belong to me." His blood pounded through his veins at the idea of making her totally his. "Say it."

"I belong to you," she whispered.

Damn right. His cock immediately hardened at her capitulation. He sat on his haunches and ran his hands leisurely over her clothed body. Breasts, belly, bottom. Down the outside of her legs and up the inside. He wiggled his hand between her thighs and pressed it to the searing heat between. Oh, yes, here was the proof that sweet Mademoiselle Claire was totally turned on by his game.

She gasped as he leisurely pressed the heel of his hand on her center. "Oh, Luc, there."

He immediately withdrew his touch. "You don't have any say, remember? You are only here to give me pleasure." That wasn't true, but it sounded good.

"Yes, Luc." She bit her lip with her white teeth and he nearly groaned himself.

He straddled her thighs, his erection resting right below her belly button. He unbuttoned her shirt, revealing her white cotton bra, two points pushing eagerly at the fabric. She lay quietly but watchfully, waiting to see what he would do next. Next was the front clasp of her bra, easily flicked open. He spread the cups apart and she was bare to the waist.

He would never get tired of seeing her plump breasts topped with sweet milk-chocolate nipples. They tightened even further under his hungry gaze. She instinctively tried to cover herself, but he wouldn't let her.

Instead she met his gaze defiantly. Good. He didn't want to break her spirit. He deliberately covered her breasts with his hands, thumbing her nipples. She tried to stifle a little moan, but that small sound sent a wave of triumph over him.

"You have pretty tits. Too soft and sweet for a rough man like me." He bent down and gently rubbed his cheek over her soft, soft skin, his stubble grazing her nipples. Her heartbeat strummed in his ear, a near match to his.

Despite his desire, he took his time, sucking on one peak as he toyed with the other. They swelled under his fingers and tongue as Claire's whimpers spurred him on. "Ah, you love this?" He didn't need any answer to know she did like what he was doing—the bucking of her hips giving her away.

He dragged his tongue lazily around her left breast,

looking into her hazy brown eyes before blowing a stream of cold air across her wet flesh.

"Luc!" She wiggled against him.

"Quiet!" he commanded. "Or else I'm gon' roll you onto your belly and give you a good spanking."

Damned if her hips didn't buck again, the idea arousing her and him, as well, as he imagined his hand on her bare ass, hearing her yelps of mixed pleasure and pain. He wiped his damp forehead. She was turning him into a real pervert.

He swung off her body and undid her pants, pulling them and her panties down to her ankles. She let her knees fall open, showing him everything. His nostrils flared at her scent. He'd been dying to taste for himself, but she'd been too shy.

Not anymore. He was in charge, right? Right. He stripped off her boots and clothing. Was she ever sexy, her breasts thrusting into the air, her slim waist curving into round, full hips and tapering into strong, sexy legs. Even her peach-painted toenails made him hard. *"Je vais te lécher le clito, toi."*

"You're going to lick my what?" She lifted her head, only to drop it as he put action to words and licked her hard clit for all he was worth. Now the hip bucking really began, forcing him to clamp his arms around her thighs to keep his face in her burning-hot *chatte*.

He was as hungry as if he'd come out of a six-week training exercise and she was a lavish buffet. He couldn't get enough of her salty-sweet taste, her musky smell, her silky thighs locking around his head. She was probably screaming but he couldn't hear so well. Her body told him plenty, though, her juices slicking his face. He darted his tongue over her clit, her pussy, even plunging deep inside her like a little cock.

Luc moaned into her body, imagining his big cock doing the same. Who was being tormented here, anyway? She shuddered under him, and he slipped two fingers inside her pussy and found a swollen nub on the wall. He pressed gently and she went wild, thrusting and arching until she came, shouting his name.

Claire finally calmed and Luc let her go, kneeling over her naked body again. "You never did that before, did you, *cher?*"

She shook her head, her face flushed and sweaty.

"Good." A primal satisfaction rushed through his veins, his adrenaline pumping as if he'd completed a successful mission. He had been the first. He stood and eagerly stripped off his T-shirt, pants and boots. His underwear was the last and most welcome to go.

Standing naked and erect over her sated form, he was a conqueror about to plunder her body. He'd introduced her to the joys of a thorough orgasm, made her scream in delight, and now it was his turn.

"What are you going to do now, Luc?"

"It's your turn to pleasure me now."

CLAIRE STARED AT HIM, still limp and sweaty from Luc's demanding mouth. She knew her face was red, and she hoped he thought it was from her climax instead of embarrassment. She'd always declined that particular act, and her boyfriends had probably been grateful, eager to get onto the main act.

But everything with Luc was the main act. She'd never imagined any sensations like the ones he'd demanded with that mouth, those lips, that tongue—even his teeth. He even might have bit her gently at one point.

That had been the best climax ever, and now it was his turn. She spread her legs wide, waiting for him to sheathe himself inside her. Maybe she could come again if he played with her.

Instead, he straddled her waist, careful to keep his weight off her, his powerful thighs bunching with the effort. His heavy penis rested on her stomach, his male sac tickling her skin. Instead of moving down her body, though, he moved up.

Leaning forward to rest his hands on either side of her head, he began thrusting, deliberately rubbing himself all over her breasts. His skin was soft and silky and hot—so very hot. He left a trail of slippery fluid on her skin, marking her as his. She never knew anything like this was possible as he drew circles around her nipples with his penis, making her hips wiggle under him again.

The pressure between her legs built, but Luc didn't show any inclination to hurry, no tendency to push inside her and relieve his own desire.

"Luc?" she asked. His eyes were closed, his breath coming quickly.

He opened his eyes. "What are you willing to do to please me, my captive?"

Her answer was immediate. "Anything."

"Bien. Léche-moi." He delicately brushed her lips with the tip of his erection, commanding her to lick him. Claire stared at him, her eyes wide. She knew if she'd refused, Luc would not force her, but she was deep in their fantasy and didn't want to leave it. She'd never done this before, either, but tonight was a night for firsts.

She opened her mouth hesitantly and he glided in, hot and salty inside her. He moved slowly in and out as she got used to the taste and feel of him. She flicked her tongue over his tip to taste him better and he groaned. He was burning hot, slick and salty.

Encouraged by his response, she relaxed her lips and let him sink deeper, her mouth learning his swells and contours, from the juicy, plump head topping his long, thick shaft. She was amazed she had managed to fit all of him before. Of course, coming three or four times tended to make that part easier.

His muscles were straining, and he was fighting the urge to take her roughly. She decided to play with him and sucked gently on him. He shivered, and she allowed herself a smile around him.

"Oui, bébé, oui, oui." He picked up the pace, her mouth caressing and sucking his swollen flesh.

Claire couldn't believe how exciting it was to have his powerful body moving over her. She felt powerful, too, his face contorting with his effort at restraint.

She had no such restraint. He had started this game of sex, and she was going to finish it. Now that she knew her power over this man, he was toast. She remembered a little bit of sexual trivia from Janey and hummed as she firmly sucked down on him.

He yelped, a burst of fluid coating her tongue. "No, Claire. Let me go, or I'll…I'll…" His words were interspersed with groans.

Shaking her head slightly, she ignored his pleas and licked him some more. He tried to pull out, but she sucked hard on him until he moaned. "Ah, my sweet…Claire… I'm gonna…come."

Claire gave a hidden smile of satisfaction and daringly scraped her teeth over his supersensitive shaft. Luc shouted his release, calling her name as he exploded into her throat. Claire inhaled deeply and swallowed his hot juices. It was amazing how sex with this man was so different than any other.

He finally stopped shuddering and withdrew, his arms and legs shaking as he dropped into a seated position on the sleeping bags, his back to her.

Claire stared at his bowed spine. Why wouldn't he look at her? Had she done it wrong? He'd definitely enjoyed himself. Maybe she'd hurt him, using her teeth like that. Or maybe he thought less of her for forcing him to finish like that. Maybe only bimbos let men do *that* to them. She blinked hard. Enough of this kinky stuff. She was obviously bad at it. "Luc? Did I do something wrong?"

LUC STARTED AT HER tentative voice. Of course—she wasn't used to this kind of sex game. He turned around. *Mon Dieu,* she was fighting back tears. Calling himself all sorts of bad names, he pulled her into his arms.

She stretched a bit, her breasts and hips wiggling in unconscious sensuality. Holy crap, he was fifteen kinds of horn-dog to even want to take her all over again right now. "You okay?" He hoped she'd think his erection was left over and not brand-new.

"Fine." She struggled into a seated position, her dark hair swinging in front of her face so he couldn't read her expression.

"Um, Claire, was that too much for you?"

"Of course not." He wasn't sure, but her laugh sounded fake. "It's just, I've never done…" She trailed off.

"Oh, of course not." Awkward, anyone? "Um, me neither." But he wanted to do it again. "Did you enjoy yourself?"

The visible curve of her cheek flushed. "Yes," she whispered.

Growing bolder, he cupped her chin and tipped her face to his. She avoided his gaze. "I enjoyed myself, too—you know that, don't you?"

"You did?" She looked at him in surprise. "I thought I hurt you."

"You? How could you hurt me?"

"With, um, my teeth." Her last two words were an embarrassed whisper.

Luc swallowed hard and got even harder. Her teeth scraping along his cock had thrown him bodily over the edge. "No. That was really sexy. Did I hurt you, kneeling over you, pushing into your mouth?"

She shook her head. "No. It made me feel... powerful." She finally met his glance. "Like I was the one in charge despite the circumstances." Her nipples were tightening again.

He stroked her cheek, running his hand down her slim neck to her fine collarbone. "You were in charge, *ma belle. Totalement* in charge of me. And I know you liked it when I licked your little *clito.*"

He helped her gently lay back down on the sleeping bags. He lay next to her, caressing her breasts.

"Yes." She breathed faster. "I loved it." She buried her face in his shoulder.

"Next time, though, you need to ask me for it. I'll teach you some French you never learned in class. Ready?"

She nodded.

"*'Léche-moi le clito, mon cher.'*" Her face heated against his skin. "Come on, it makes me hot to hear you say what you want."

"*Baise-moi, mon cher.*" Her words were muffled but

perfectly understandable. His eyebrows flew up. He doubted she had ever invited a man to fuck her before, but he was more than willing to be the first invitee.

"You got it, sweetheart." Without another word, he reached into his bag for protection and positioned himself between her thighs.

She wrapped her arms around his neck and he slid inside her. They both sighed, her eyes closing. She was tight and still wet from before and he fought to keep from coming again. He'd never been like this before, so eager with a woman that he lost control almost immediately.

She began moving under him, and he fell into a steady rhythm, dipping deep into her and pulling out until only his head stayed inside. She clutched at his shoulders, her breath singeing his skin. Mindful of their walk on the wild side, he kept it slow but she wouldn't stand for it, wrapping her legs around his hips and grinding into him, her hot, sweet pussy surrounding his cock in a luxurious prison. Ah, who was the captive now?

"Baise-moi plus, mon cher," she repeated, urging him to fuck her more. He gave up and slammed into her, plucking at her diamond-hard clit.

After that, she didn't say anything except his name, called over and over again. She spasmed around him, an orgasmic flush climbing her glistening breasts to her beautiful face. Her mouth fell open as she gasped. He didn't let up on the finger pressure and she moaned, coming a second time.

She dug her fingers into his ass, and he dropped to his elbows, twisting and writhing on top of her, around her, in her, telling her all sorts of nasty, naughty things he planned to do to her the next time. Tie her up, tie her down, spank her, lick her, spank her while he licked her, spank her while he fucked her…

To his more-than-pleasant surprise, Claire shook and squeezed around him a third time, her head tipped back and her mouth open in a wordless scream.

He threw his own head back in a yell of pure triumph and pistoned into her pulsing heat. His yell turned into a groan as he emptied himself into her welcoming body again. Coming again after such a short time threatened to blow the top of his head off, and he was so wild he barely stayed inside her. She clung limply to him until he pulled out of her with a groan.

"Luc, Luc." Her voice was hoarse by now. "I never knew…"

He had never known anything like that, either. "I know, I know." He cleaned himself quickly and pulled her into his arms, his mind whirling. His emotions had run the gamut today, from worry to triumph to this odd mix of lust and tenderness.

And soon the woman of his dreams would fly south to the place of his nightmares.

"HOW ARE YOUR FEET DOING, Claire?" Luc looked up from the gear he was packing.

She wiggled them experimentally. The raw patches had healed and she'd double-padded them today. "Pretty good, why?"

"I want to work on your map-reading skills." He pulled out a paper rectangle and spread out a topographical map.

Claire looked at the squiggles cautiously. It was very different from a forest or highway map, showing what Luc called "contour lines" to delineate the ups and downs of the land. There were also roads, bridges and electrical transmission lines, handy info for men like Luc who probably blew those up overseas. "What do I do?"

"We're here." His finger landed squarely on a spot next to a river.

"Really? Are you sure?"

He grinned. "I've known exactly where we've been the whole time. Why? You thought we were wandering around lost?"

She bit her lip. "Well…"

"Trust me—we're here. I want you to get us there." He pointed to a second tiny dot.

"What's there?" She peered at the dot. "Broomsburg? Is that a town?"

"More like a wide spot in the road—the only populated settlement in this area." He handed her a compass. "Which way do we go?"

Taking a deep breath, she watched the needle spin and settle facing north. She turned the map so that pointed north, as well, and peered at its layout. Taking a deep breath, she pointed to her right. "We go east."

He raised an eyebrow. "You sure?"

She looked at the map and the compass again. "We're here?"

"Oui."

"And we want to go here?"

"Oui."

"It's east. Let's go."

"Yes, ma'am." He snapped a salute. She bet he looked hotter than hot in his uniform. Well, it was unlikely she'd ever see that, wasn't it?

She folded the map so she could see the pertinent area and made sure she had enough water for a hike. It was fun to be in charge for once. Goodbye to the girl who had wandered the mall parking lot for almost two hours.

They walked steadily for about an hour, Claire making minor course corrections according to the map. She stopped and bit her lip when they came to a river that wasn't on the map. Had she taken them the wrong way? She double-checked their route but everything looked right.

"What is it?"

"The river—it doesn't belong here."

"Somebody forgot to tell it that." Luc stared at the sluggish brown water.

What should she do? She looked where they'd come from and hesitated.

"Make a decision, Claire. Forward or backward?"

Enough backtracking. She knew she was right and the river was wrong. Or the map was wrong. It was created by people, after all, and people made mistakes sometimes. "Forward. But we should cross at the narrowest point since we don't know how deep it is in the middle."

"Lay on, Macduff," he quoted in a perfect Scottish accent.

"Don't tell me you performed in *Macbeth,* too. And I thought it was 'Lead on, Macduff.'"

"Bad luck to say that play's name, *béb.* Better calling it the Scottish play. And no, that's the correct phrase."

"What part did you have?"

"The title role."

Claire shook her head. Luc Boudreaux would never be second fiddle to anyone. "Let's go. And while we walk, you can tell me if your Lady Macbeth was scary in real life." She picked her way down the riverbank.

"Hoo-wee, was she ever. That actress dabbled in hoodoo and claimed she called up dark spirits during her mad scene. All I know was she made the hairs stand up on the back of my neck. What can I say? There are plenty of strange things in the world."

"Like me running around in the woods?"

"You're doing a great job, Claire. I should have told you before, but I'm not used to giving compliments to the men I train. You've done better than some of them."

She smiled to herself. "Thank you." It was a great compliment, considering how little she'd known before setting off on their adventure together. She stopped and grabbed his hand.

"What?" He immediately scanned the woods for danger. "Did you see something?"

"Nope, just you." Impulsively, she stood on her tiptoes and pressed a kiss on his firm lips.

"Me, huh?" He returned her kiss, drawing her tight against him. The river rushed next to them, but not hard enough to drown out the roaring in her ears. His mouth was warm and wet, and he kissed her leisurely, as if they were sitting on a park bench with all the time in the world. She stroked the rugged line of his jaw with her free hand, and he turned his face to kiss her palm.

Her eyes flew open. His display of tenderness had surprised him, too, judging from how his black eyes widened before his customary cool mask dropped into place.

Claire turned back to her map, confused. She thought she was the only one who was fighting off feelings of affection, but if Luc started returning her feelings, she was sunk. Once in San Lucas, she could manage a wistful memory of the "one who got away," but if he *did* want to chase her, she was pretty sure she'd let herself be caught.

But that couldn't be her focus right now. She had to laugh. Here they were in some swampy woods that looked like a t-rex habitat, and her hard-as-nails Special Forces trainer was quoting Shakespeare to her. "So, you're a Shakespearean actor. Now you have to perform your favorite Shakespeare speech for me."

He hesitated for a second. "I've never performed this role before."

"Do I look like a drama critic?" She was carefully placing one foot after another to avoid slipping in the mud along the river. "Which one?"

"Okay. It's King Henry the Fifth of England rallying his outnumbered men before the Battle of Agincourt in 1415." He took a deep breath and started the monologue about how the valor of his soldiers would cause the entire kingdom to remember the battle and curse the fact they had not fought for England.

By the time he had reached the end, tears ran down Claire's cheeks and the path was a brown blur in front of her eyes. She swallowed hard several times before speaking. "'We few, we happy few, we band of brothers...'" she quoted, surreptitiously wiping her eyes. "I never knew where that quote came from."

"The St. Crispin's Day Speech. Really shows what it meant to lead men—Henry led by the strength of his conviction and the force of his personality."

"Is that how you feel? That you and your team are a band of brothers?"

"Absolutely." Not a trace of doubt entered his tone. "'For he to-day who sheds his blood with me shall be my brother.' I am their brother and they are mine. I would die for them and they would die for me. Some have, matter of fact."

No wonder there was little room for her—little room for any woman in his life. She needed to remember that before she did something stupid like fall in love with the man. It would be so easy to do—the way his rare smiles grew more frequent, the way his hand lingered on her as he helped her to her feet, the way he looked at her when he thought she wouldn't notice.

They would both return to their separate duties once the week was over. She would fly to South America and he would fly somewhere secret in another desperate region of the world.

She didn't know what to say, so she focused on the river now that her eyes were clear. It had narrowed to a point where she could see the rocky bottom. "Maybe we should cross here." She fiddled with the compass, unsure where the heck she even was.

Luc was silent behind her, not moving or giving her any hints. She remembered how old King Henry had led and summoned some hidden force of personality. "We cross here." Not waiting for Luc to agree or confirm her decision, she stepped into the cool water.

He followed her across without comment. She checked the map to reorient herself from the slight detour they'd taken and started walking again.

It wasn't until about ten minutes later that he

spoke. "Hurricane Inez came through several years ago. The flooding cut several new river channels. That was one of 'em."

"Oh." She spun to face him and whacked him in the chest with the map. "You gave me an old map? No fair! What kind of trick is that?"

"Did you check the date on the map?" He pointed to the corner.

She peered at the copyright. "1992. Oh."

"Never trust anyone else's gear. If you have to borrow, check it out first."

"Is Broomsburg still there? Or were its inhabitants driven away by the eruption of a long-dormant volcano that doesn't show up on this map, either?" She shook the paper at him.

He laughed and laughed. "Claire, you say the funniest things. Yeah, Broomsburg is still there and we need to get there. Take the point."

"Point of what?"

"Take the lead. 'Take the point' is army lingo for 'Lead the way.'"

"Fine." She looked at the map that was old enough to earn its driver's license and set off again. Still irritated, she was likely stomping through the woods slightly harder than necessary.

"Claire?" Luc's voice called.

"What?"

"You did fine. Thought on your feet like a real survivor. You can be my point man anytime."

"Thanks." A warm glow spread over her that had little to do with the sweltering heat.

"SO THIS IS BROOMSBURG?" Claire viewed the ramshackle collection of trailers and shacks with dismay.

"Congratulations, *cher.* You passed."

Not that visiting here was much of a prize. "It looks abandoned to me."

"People do live here." Luc pointed out several clues. "Satellite dishes on the roof, fat chickens running around and that pickup."

The monster red pickup truck was almost as nice as Luc's and probably cost more than ten of the dwellings—she couldn't bring herself to call them houses. "Do they even have indoor plumbing?"

He pointed to a hut tucked into the clearing's edge. "Easier to do your business outside than bother with a septic tank and all."

An outhouse. Ugh. And she thought peeing under a tree was bad. What the smell from that building must be…at least they were upwind.

A screen door smacked open on a pea-green metal trailer next to the red pickup. "What y'all doin' here?"

Luc smoothly swiveled her behind him. The speaker was a small woman, elderly, with slightly hunched shoulders.

"Hey. We just hikin' by on the way to the state park." He had purposely broadened his accent into deep Cajun.

"Y'all ain't from around here, that's fo' sho'." She eyed Luc suspiciously.

"From de bayou, *cher.* On a li'l honeymoon."

The woman raised an eyebrow. "What kinda crazy honeymoon is that?" She peered at Claire. "You sho' 'bout marryin' a man who take you to Broomsburg for a honeymoon?"

"We ran away from my daddy and don't want him to find us."

She cackled. "Don't worry none 'bout that. He never find you here. Nobody can."

And that was starting to worry Claire.

She clutched Luc's arm in what she hoped looked like newlywed affection. Just as she was about to drag him away, a little figure peered out the door. "Is it Momma?"

"No, Callie."

"What a pretty name." Claire looked closer at the young girl with pink cheeks and mop of dusty blond hair. "How old is she?"

"Five."

"Almost old enough for school." Claire smiled at the child.

"We'll see. School cain't keep teachers long 'nuff to stay open. Maybe jus' teach her at home."

Claire didn't know what to say to that. She had nothing against homeschooling, but it was obvious that educational resources were sorely lacking here. "Well, good luck."

A loud snore came from the trailer and the woman started.

Luc caught Claire's elbow and steered her away. "You take care, ma'am."

Callie and the woman disappeared into the trailer and Luc and Claire disappeared into the woods. Luc took the point this time and set a blistering pace.

It wasn't until about forty-five minutes later that he finally called a halt to the forced march. Claire dropped onto a log and sucked down most of her canteen. "Want to tell me what happened?"

Luc's face was set in harsh lines. "I didn't want to stick around to meet the man of the house, *béb.* Could be he was bad news."

"Like what, a criminal?"

"Who knows?"

Claire cast an anxious glance over her shoulder. "What kind of crime?"

"Maybe drugs—pot or meth, likely. Could even be he's an orchid poacher. Collectors pay crazy amounts for illegally harvested, wild-grown plants."

"Really? Orchids? That sounds bizarre."

He urged her to her feet again. "Same here as in San Lucas de la Selva. Poor people, uneducated people don't have the same choices, some turn to crime."

"Yeah, and some don't." Claire glared at him. "Were you poor growing up?"

"Family of nine, living in the middle of nowhere? Hell, yeah, we was poor. Never went hungry 'cuz Papa knew how to hunt and fish, but poor."

"And you had the same choice. Did you turn to crime?"

He shook his head. "My papa never hesitated to pass me a slap if I needed it. After all those girls, he wasn't 'bout to let his only son go bad, disgrace the Boudreaux name. Now let's go. We're breaking camp and moving soon as we get back." He took off walking again.

"Don't you want the map?"

"That ol' thing?" He grinned at her. "I curved our path around so we should hit camp in another hour or so."

"Oh." Claire sagged briefly before following him. Another hour. Well, better that than being tracked by insane rural drug pushers. On the other hand, Luc didn't seem worried, just cautious. He probably wouldn't be worried if a hundred guys were tracking him in the woods, instead of one woman limping after him.

Claire desperately wished she had someone to talk to about her growing feelings for Luc. Until now, she'd always had Janey or one of her sorority sisters to pore over every detail of her relationships. She supposed it was a bit junior-high, but then again, her previous relationships had been juvenile, as well—unlike the unnerving sensations Luc provoked in her.

Janey would tell her to enjoy Luc without giving herself up to him, but Claire had a sneaking suspicion Janey had never been with a man like Luc.

9

CLAIRE SCANNED THEIR new camp the next afternoon. Luc had moved them upriver and well away from Broomsburg, telling her better safe than sorry.

She actually preferred this setup. The river had carved out a natural swimming hole, away from the main current, where the water was relatively clear. They'd had an extremely fun skinny dip last night with the stars and moon shining above.

Then up came the sun. Her tender lover left and her hard-driving instructor returned. Today had been easier than their massive hike yesterday due to her feet giving her trouble, so he'd lectured her in depth on safe plants versus poisonous ones. Claire remembered every word with apprehension. Plants with milky sap were bad, wild mushrooms were bad, white berries were bad— heck, even the plant that made the deadly poison ricin grew wild in the jungle. He'd carried along a field identification guide to show her and after a while, all the plants started to look the same—green and deadly. Larva and frogs were looking mighty tasty after that lesson.

Once she'd bathed, Claire stretched out on a towel on the wide rocks surrounding the watering hole. She didn't want to do any more survival training. Not because she was tired, or lazy, but because she wanted to spend the rest of their time making love.

Unfortunately, Luc had other ideas. He was pushing her training harder and harder, trying to cram every bit of knowledge he had into her head as their time together drew to a close. All of a sudden, it was four days before she was to leave for San Lucas, and he'd promised to return her to Ft. Bragg tomorrow, three days before her plane took off.

Only one day left with Luc. At the moment, she was having a hard time remembering why she wanted to go live in Snakeland, South America, when she could stay in the States with Luc. Then she remembered: he'd never asked her to stay in the first place.

What did she have to do, beg the man? She stifled a giggle. She had certainly enjoyed it. What else did he have to show her? He had an almost unlimited repertoire of sexual tricks up his sleeve, but the one that was making her really hot thinking about it was the one he had mentioned but not tried.

Quickly, before he came along, she stripped off her clean clothing and rearranged herself to lie naked on her stomach. She'd never sunbathed naked before, but that was small potatoes compared to her other new experiences.

Her head was cradled on her arms as if she were resting, but she knew the instant he saw her. Mostly because he shouted her name.

"What the hell are you doing lying there naked?"

She rolled onto her side nonchalantly, pleased to see his agog expression. "Sunbathing, what else?" She ran a hand down her hip. "No swimsuit lines this way."

"Swimsuit lines? I never heard anything so asinine. If you were a soldier under my command, I'd—"

Claire interrupted his rant with a yawn. "I thought I was under your command. Your *every* command," she said significantly, eying the growing bulge under his zipper. "It's your job to make sure I learn my lessons, but I don't see that happening," she said with a sniff.

He stood there in shock until comprehension dawned. "Claire, do you want me to punish you?" His voice became silky and menacing.

She was starting to feel aroused. She shrugged. "What? Make me do push-ups?"

"Nothing so ordinary as that. Lie on your stomach."

Oh, boy, what had she started now? But she did as he told her, hearing the clinks and thuds of his clothing and gear drop to the ground. She was practically quivering in happy anticipation by the time he knelt behind her and shoved a makeshift pillow of their clothing under her cheek.

She folded her arms out in front of her and rested her chin on them.

"Don't move. A bad girl like you needs to learn how to listen."

Ooh, she wiggled a bit but stopped when his big hand slapped her bottom.

"Ouch!"

"Quiet." But he massaged the stinging spot all the same.

"But what did I do wrong?"

He spanked her other cheek, just like she'd hoped when she asked the question. The sting jolted her a bit, but felt surprisingly good. "You knew I'd come here and find you naked, didn't you?"

"Yes," she whispered. Another smack.

"And you knew I couldn't resist the sweet curves of your ripe ass sticking up in the air."

"Yes." This time it was a bit harder, but still good.

"In fact, you've been flaunting your sexy little body to me ever since I came to your hotel room. You wanted me to rip off that nightgown and show you who was boss." *Smack.* "Do you know how close you came to bending over that big soft bed with my dick rammed inside you?"

She shook her head, her cheeks brushing her upper arms. "How close?"

"This close." His erection brushed her stinging bottom. "I could have done anything I wanted to you, and you would have begged me for more."

"Yes, Luc." She would have eagerly slept with him that night, even though he'd been a stranger.

"And I saw you bathing in the moonlight and saw you naked for the first time—your high, tight tits, your sweet, creamy pussy."

He'd spied on her in the woods? She'd been thinking about him as she slowly washed herself with the cloth, almost giving in to the impulse to touch herself.

"Did you know I started touching myself? Your little peep show almost made me shoot my load. But I held off until you begged me to fuck you."

And it was the best decision she'd ever made. But in the spirit of the game… "I'm sorry, Luc."

"Are you?" Three quick taps. "I think you're getting off on your punishment, Claire." She gasped as he delved between her thighs. "Oh, you are. Your pussy is dripping wet without me touching you." He withdrew his hand.

"More, more." She wiggled her hips against the towels, but he clamped down with both big hands.

"You'll get more when I let you." He pressed a column of moist openmouthed kisses from the nape of her neck, between her shoulder blades, down the small of her back. She gasped as he nuzzled her stinging bottom. "Only bad girls let men do all sorts of nasty things to them. Are you a bad girl, Claire?"

"I'll do anything you want right now." An eager, greedy tone had crept into her voice.

"Good." He prodded her with his erection and she instinctively widened her legs. "Take me, Claire." Without waiting for her reply, he filled her completely.

They moaned in unison, locked together. "Take me, Luc," she echoed.

He slid in and out of her, nudging the deepest parts of her. She arched her hips, daring him to speed up. "That's it, *cher.*" He curved over her as his hard abs rubbed her bottom.

Luc reached under her belly and found her swollen pleasure point. Claire cried out as he plucked at her. With half-groaned words of encouragement, he stroked her to the edge of her release. She writhed against the towel.

"Come on, *béb,* scream for me. I wan' hear you call my name." He nipped at her neck just like the stallion he'd called himself the other day. His big body dominated hers, riding her hard like she craved. She shook underneath him and squeezed down around him. She took a quick breath only to spend it screaming his name.

He coaxed a long climax out of her before submitting to his own, calling her name, too.

They both finished and he rolled onto his back, dragging her with him. "Claire, you turn me into an animal."

"You do it to me, too, Luc. Me, too." She was becoming someone stronger and tougher, but she wasn't sure if she was strong or tough enough to deal with their inevitable separation.

10

"I WISH WE HAD SOME marshmallows." Claire snuggled against Luc as they sat next to the fire later that night.

"I can get some grubs if you want to cook something white and squishy on a stick," he offered, only grunting slightly when she elbowed him.

"Ugh. That is so gross."

"Take the plunge. You know you'll have to eat them sooner or later. May as well get it over now where you won't embarrass yourself."

She made a face at him.

"Eh, you'll be happy to eat them if need be. I was, once. All part of surviving in the jungle."

"Would you ever return to San Lucas?"

"San Lucas." He wrinkled his face. "Not my first choice. But I would if it were my duty, and only then. And primarily my duty would be to my teammates to make sure they didn't get killed."

Claire wondered if she was part of his duty, as well. "I do realize it's not all lying around and picking bananas and coconuts off the tree. My mother did mention some rough times, like when they all caught some intestinal parasite and were, um, sick to their stomachs for several days."

Luc didn't seem impressed. "Whoopee. If you haven't gotten some stomach bug, you haven't lived in the jungle."

"And she said two tribes didn't get along and her father had to patch up several men."

He rolled his eyes. "You ever think your mother might have cleaned up her stories for your benefit? You being a kid an' all. You learned about the nice parts of their lives—like those prairie pioneer girl books my sisters read when we were young. Only for your mother it was 'Little House in the Jungle'."

Claire smiled. She had loved those pioneer girl books—still had her original copies from childhood.

He continued, "She probably didn't want to tell you about the disease, the violence, the unpretty parts of it. That was the *only* part I saw."

"Why do you hate San Lucas so much? You get a funny look on your face whenever we talk about it."

He shook his head. "Claire, *cher,* I've been in the army long enough to go to some real shitholes, but San Lucas is the worst of the worst."

"But why?" she persisted. "Surely lots of those other places had warring tribes, parasites and dangerous animals. Why does San Lucas bother you?"

"Your father ever tell you why they chose me to train you? Over all the experienced jungle survival instructors and experts in the whole U.S. Army, why did they pick me?"

She shrugged. "They said you traveled there for several weeks and you knew the country well."

He snorted. "Too damn well. Look, I can't tell you why my team and I were there, but we were deep inside the borders, cruising in a small boat down the Río de la Selva—"

"Near the settlement?" she asked eagerly.

"South." He fingered the hilt of his machete, which was lying in its sheath on the ground next to him. "We came under attack. An RPG was fired into the boat."

"RPG?"

"Rocket-propelled grenade," he explained. "Low-tech but makes a hell of an explosion."

"Oh, my gosh. Were you hurt?" He had so many different scars she couldn't tell which were which.

"Some. Olie and I were farthest away from the impact, so we got dumped into the water. He made it to the other riverbank but I got swept downstream."

"Was it just you two? What happened to the rest of the team?"

His face froze. "More guerillas jumped out and emptied their AK-47s into the river. Missed some of the team who were already cut up by shrapnel, a couple others got shot in the shoulders or legs, and T-Bone, well, they got him."

"Got him?" She tightened her fingers around his.

"Right in the chest." He thumped his own. "I saw him get hit. He sank like a stone—nothing I could do."

"Oh, Luc, that's terrible." She had held her mother while she died, but her death was grindingly inevitable, a relief after weeks of suffering.

"I swam hard, but the blast stunned me and it was all I could do to keep from drowning. It was high-water season and the rapids took me away. Wound up going downstream in the wrong fork—through a long, deep gorge where I couldn't get out of the water."

"How far did you go in the river?"

"Afterward, we figured it was about twenty miles as the crow flies. As the Green Beret walks, it was a bit more."

"And you walked all the way back?"

"I couldn't go back, exactly. That's where they shot at us, after all." His dry tone didn't quite disguise his anger at what had happened. "I had to track back to the fork and down the correct branch to the local military installation that had been our rendezvous point."

"How far was it anyway?"

"A hundred miles. I was trekking for three weeks."

Her mouth fell open. "All that way by yourself? Without anyone else?"

He started to speak and hesitated.

"Did you have any company on your way? A local tribe or something?"

He sighed. "I did have company for a few days. Her name was Angélique."

"Figures you'd find a woman even in the jungle," she muttered.

His laugh was short. "Angélique was a baby."

"A baby?" She sat upright and stared down into his face, even though she couldn't see him well in the dark. "What in the world was a baby doing in the jungle?"

"Her family left her there."

11

LUC KNEW CLAIRE HAD no idea what he was talking about. Guess her mother had never filled her in on the less-savory local customs. "She probably hadn't ever been named, but I called her Angélique. She was a newborn with a bilateral cleft lip and cleft palate, as well, as far as I could tell. We didn't cover a whole lot of pediatrics in my medical training."

"That's where the lip doesn't grow together before birth, right? And a hole in the roof of the mouth?"

"Right."

"But I saw a commercial on TV for a charity that helps fix babies like that." Her smooth brow furrowed in confusion. "Why didn't her family bring her to the mission? Dr. Schmidt would have made arrangements for her to be treated."

Luc shook his head. "I don't know. She was all alone when I found her. I even thought that maybe because of her condition she'd been left to die. Some tribes believe disabled children are unfit to live."

She gasped. "And you took her with you." She knew him well.

"What else could I do?" He'd woven a sling of vines and leaves to carry the black-haired girl against his chest. She had stared at him with dark, hazy eyes, amazingly accepting of the total stranger who was carrying her through thick jungle. "I purified water for her and crushed some berries, but…" He shrugged helplessly. He'd even boiled some snake meat, but snake broth and berry juice were no food for a newborn.

"And she died." Claire's voice was full of sorrow.

"Oui." His throat caught. "She had newborn jaundice—comes from not having enough mother's milk. In her case, not any. She got more and more yellow until, well…" He was horrified to hear a sob tear loose. From him. What the hell? Green Berets weren't supposed to cry.

Claire gathered him into her arms, rocking him as if he were the baby. She kissed his forehead and hugged him. "You did your best, Luc. No wonder you hate San Lucas de la Selva—you saw the absolute worst of it."

He sat up and hastily wiped his cheeks, grateful for the dim light. "Life is cheap there. Maybe a tribe could have kept that baby alive long enough to get her to the mission or the military base, but luck was not on her side. *C'est tout.* That's all."

CLAIRE AWOKE SUDDENLY from a messy, disturbing dream where she was lost in a green maze. No surprise where that one had come from. Luc was still asleep, his breathing deep and even. He'd tried to hide his emotions, but she had felt the tears on his face and heard the heartbreak in his voice. Of all the reasons he hated and mistrusted the jungle, she never would have guessed his sad story of baby Angélique. She sniffled back tears, as well.

What good had anyone done for the people of San Lucas if such a thing were still possible? Common, even, to echo Luc's statement. Where, or how, could respect for an ancient culture supercede an innocent life?

She rolled to her side, empathizing with her mother, who must have run into similar disturbing situations. Naively, Claire thought people would come to the mission in a situation like that. After fifty years of co-existence, the tribes surely knew the mission offered medical care.

She also grudgingly admitted to herself that she owed her father an apology. He had tried to talk to her about the realities of life and death in the Amazon, but she had thought he exaggerated in order to discourage her.

But Luc's experience was a cold wake-up. If she went, she would need that same wake-up. If? She bit her lip. Was she chickening out? Fear of leaving her comfy existence, or the realization that being with Luc was becoming more and more important every hour they spent together?

It seemed impossible they had only know each other for a week. She'd dated her couple previous boy-friends for months and never felt this way about any of them. Of course, few men could measure up to Luc.

She let her mind wander to what might happen if she did cancel her plans. Would Luc even want to further their relationship? He'd never indicated that their rustic interlude was anything more than temporary. They hadn't even exchanged phone number or e-mail ad-dresses.

His sleepy drawl surprised her. "I can practically hear the wheels turnin' in your head." He rolled to his side and draped his arm over her. "Sorry I told you that sad tale—ain't never told no one but Olie and my team. Don't you worry about it."

But she did worry. She closed her eyes as he unex-pectedly kissed the top of her head. *"Fais do-do, cher."*

Claire's lips pulled into a small smile. Maybe she would *"fais do-do,"* or "go nighty-night." If there was one thing Luc's training had taught her, it was to sleep when she could.

CLAIRE MAY AS WELL have stayed awake all night for all the good it did her. Luc had hiked her for miles and miles the next day. Despite her special socks and pad-ding, her feet had broken open again and she wouldn't have been surprised to see blood oozing out of her boots. She staggered into their camp behind Luc. She supposed he might have stopped if he'd heard her collapse, but then again, maybe not. He had woken silent and pulled into himself again, obviously regretting he'd ever mentioned his hideous jungle journey.

She almost regretted it, too. Of all the things he could have opened up to her about—his childhood, his family, his training…but no. He had to break open his heart and show her the absolute rawest thing anyone ever experienced.

It broke her heart, too. All day, she'd had nothing but time to think about cheap life and easy death in the Amazon. What a fool she had been to think she could do anything. She wasn't even strong enough to listen to his story, much less live it.

She dropped her gear next to the tent. It could shatter for all she cared.

"Drink some water, Claire."

She ignored Luc. What did he care if she drank water or not? He was the one trying to run her into the ground. She crawled onto the bedding, not bothering to check it for bugs or animals.

"Get up." He stood over her, his arms crossed his chest.

"Buzz off." Why wasn't he even sweating?

"Get up, Claire." His black brows drew into a deep vee.

"No, Luc, this is too hard."

"What?" His eyebrows slammed together.

"I've had enough."

"Enough what?"

"Enough training. I'll never need to do any of this. I promise I'll never go off on my own. I'll always have somebody around to help me." She flopped onto her back and rested her forearm across her eyes. She squeaked as he tossed her over his shoulder. "Hey, put me down!"

"You ever gon' take a boat ride in San Lucas? Take a plane ride? Boats sink and planes crash. Then what you gon' do?" He stalked toward the watering hole.

Oh, no, he wouldn't. He did. "Luc!" Her scream was cut off as she hit the cold spring water and sank.

She sputtered to the surface. "You bully! You creep! You—you bastard!"

He squatted at the bank, unimpressed with her insults. "Who are you, Claire Cook? You some put-upon Southern Belle on your faintin' couch? You some Blanche Dubois? Well, this ain't no cheap dinner theatre production of *A Streetcar Named Desire*. This is goddamn real life and death here."

"Luc!" She wiped water out of her face, treading water in her boots.

He made no attempt to help her, his jaw tight and black eyes cold. "I've told you this before but it's not sinking in—you cannot depend on strangers. You cannot depend on anyone but yourself. Not me, not yo' papa, not some native dude wandering by who needs a new girlfriend. There is no such thing as the kindness of strangers in the jungle. You save yourself, or you die."

"Why are you being so mean? I tried to learn everything you taught me." She hauled herself out of the spring and sat on a log, water running off her in streams. She hoped it disguised the tears starting to run down her face.

Luc stood, looming over her. "Nobody can teach you mental toughness. You have to learn that for yourself. You have to dig deep, not think or hope, but know that you can survive. The jungle either accepts you or spits you out. It spits out the weak-minded ones."

She glared at him. "I am strong-minded! I'm leaving the country, I'm even leaving the continent. Would a weak-minded person do that?"

"You're going to your mother's hometown. Running to everyone who knew her and will take care of you to honor her memory. Not much of a gamble, is it?"

"Shut up!" Claire leaped to her feet. "At least I'm doing something, learning new things, risking myself. What do you do? You have your job and your teammates, and that's it. I bet they have somebody to go home to at night, but not you. Nobody to care for you, nobody you have to care about. I bet the last person you cared for was that poor little baby, wasn't it?"

Throughout her tirade he had kept a blank expression except for a minute flinch at her last question. "That's right, Claire. I am a weak, damaged man who can't let anyone into his life. Now can we finish your training, or do you want to die in the jungle?"

She stared at him. It was impossible to dent his iron will. Well, it was about time she grew an iron will of her own. "I will not die in the jungle. I will learn all you can teach me, and I will go out and live a true life instead of chasing after death." With that parting shot, she turned her back to him and walked into the woods.

LUC WINCED AS CLAIRE limped away. He'd heard her struggling through the last part of their march, but she needed to be able to walk at least fifteen kilometers without stopping. He'd go to her when she calmed down and examine her poor feet.

He sighed. Maybe he needed to examine himself, as well, remembering her words. Did he really chase after death?

He sat down at the water's edge and stared into its green depths. Yes, he did. He brought death to the enemies of the United States of America, thereby bringing life to the regular soldiers and civilians who would not become their victims. It was a difficult balance, especially considering his extensive medical training—to shoot with one hand and heal with the other.

But the only deaths he regretted were baby Angélique and T-Bone. During T-Bone's memorial service, the unit chaplain had quoted Psalm 121, the soldier's Psalm. "'The sun shall not smite thee by day, nor the moon by night,'" he murmured.

He opened his canteen and splashed some water on his face. It was still his job to make sure nothing smote Claire.

LATER THAT NIGHT, he slipped into the tent and lay down when he was sure she would be asleep. She wasn't. "Luc?" she murmured sleepily.

"Oui."

She rolled over and put her arm over him. "Sorry I said all that awful stuff today."

"S'okay, *cher.*" He tucked her hand into his and kissed her fingers. "I wasn't real kind, either."

"Can't even imagine that. First your friend, then a baby. My mother died peacefully in my arms—that was a blessing at the end." She yawned. "After the funeral was the first time in months we'd been able to take a breath. And of course we felt guilty about that."

Luc blinked. T-Bone had died in his arms, too, but not peacefully. By the time Luc struggled back to so-called civilization, he'd needed several weeks to recover from various parasitic and bacterial infections and regain his weight and strength. Then he'd rejoined his team. Had he ever been able to take a breath? No, but he'd sure felt the guilt.

"Did your friend leave a family behind?"

"Yeah. A wife and three little kids."

Claire was silent for so long he thought she'd fallen asleep. "Love is a risk no matter who you love."

"Your mama must have been a real special lady to have raised you so well."

"Thank you, Luc." She kissed his shoulder. "You would have liked her. She would have understood what you went through in the jungle."

"*Cher,* I don't even understand what I went through in the jungle." It was the first time he'd admitted that to anyone, even himself.

She rested her cheek on his shoulder blade. "Tell me, sweetheart."

He didn't know if it was her calm, sweet voice or the fact she'd called him "sweetheart," but something broke inside him. "Being in Special Forces, you train to be part of your A-team, part of your group, part of something bigger. You always ask yourself what you can do to help the team. When we were attacked, the worst thing was that I wound up alone. I'm not used to that with six sisters." He tried to joke.

"Yes, I know."

"And the baby was company, but then she wasn't." He didn't trust himself to say anything more. "So I was alone again. We talk about it, you know. What it would be like to be taken captive, put in isolation. I was free to move, free to find food and water, but I started to wonder if I'd ever get out."

"What did you do about that?"

He grimaced, glad she couldn't see his face. "I

talked to myself the whole damn time. Carried on long conversations with myself. Not out loud, in my head."

"So you hate being alone but you don't want anyone close to you, either."

"Sounds almost as crazy as my talking to myself, doesn't it?"

"I talk to myself all the time. 'What should I do today? What should I wear?' Heck, I even pretend my mom is there sometimes and I ask her what I should do."

"Nothing wrong with that." Her breath was warm and soft on his cheek, just like the woman herself. He was a man who faced problems head on, but he couldn't face the idea of leaving her.

"I get lonely, too, Luc. Even when I'm around hundreds of people at a party or at the mall, I look at everybody and wonder how I can be so alone. But with you, Luc, I never feel alone," she whispered. "Even if you're off in the woods doing whatever you need to do, I know you're there for me, and all I have to do is call your name."

Luc swallowed hard. "I know what you mean, Claire." It was as close as he could get to admitting how she affected him. "It is kind of nice coming back to camp and having you kiss me hello."

"Would that be so terrible to have when you finished your assignments? Having someone meet your plane and kiss you hello?"

It didn't sound terrible, it sounded wonderful. But

only if it was Claire. Disembarking and seeing her beautiful face light up as she spotted him, laughing out loud as they ran toward each other and kissing as if they could never stop. Then speeding home to jump into bed, not coming up for air for days. It was a deeper and more secret fantasy than any sexual ones he dared admit. "Some of the guys have that." They had sweet chubby babies and kids who waved American flags and screamed when they spotted their papas.

"But not you."

The image of black-haired, brown-eyed *bébés* in Claire's arms popped like a soap bubble. "No, Claire, not me." Silence grew between them, not the comfortable silence they enjoyed together. "If it makes any difference, I've never had that. If I ever could, it would be with you."

Hot tears leaked into his T-shirt. Oh, no, she was crying. He rolled over and scooped her into his arms. "Don't cry, Claire. I'm a bastard who doesn't deserve even one drop of your tears."

"Oh, Luc, don't say that. You're good, honest, decent. A real hero for people to look up to."

His hand froze as he stroked her hair. A hero for people to look up to? He had just swept this girl away from her well-meaning father, brought her out to the woods to push her through harsh conditions, and now she was talking about him as if he were some kind of hero? He'd been accused of arrogance before, but this took the cake.

His own throat clogged and he could only press her face against him as she sobbed. What the hell was wrong with him? Thank God he was taking her back tomorrow before he wrecked her even more.

She quieted after several minutes, worn out from her emotional and physical exhaustion.

"Go to sleep, Claire." He kissed the top of her sweet-smelling head.

She gave a shuddering sigh. "Okay, Luc." She yawned. "Love you."

His eyes flew wide in shock as she subsided into sleep. Love? Love? She didn't say that…she couldn't believe that—it was impossible. She didn't really know him. He was a beat-up, worn-out soldier who didn't deserve a woman like her.

He'd deliver her back to her father, back to her quiet, peaceful life. Back to the life where she could forget Luc Boudreaux and find a man who was worthy of the jewel that was Claire Cook.

12

CLAIRE'S STOMACH HAD been in knots the whole drive to Ft. Bragg. She was awake for the trip this time and got to see the South Carolina Low Country scenery before turning into the piney woods of North Carolina. It was pretty but not enough to take her mind off their upcoming arrival in civilization.

He stopped at the gates leading into Ft. Bragg and showed his military ID. They drove through the base for several minutes before reaching the Special Forces installation. The guards greeted Luc by name and waved them through. He pulled over in the parking lot next to the headquarters and jumped out of the truck without saying anything to her.

Claire sat for a second. That wasn't a good sign. She didn't expect a giant make-out session in the parking lot but she thought he'd at least say something to her.

She jumped down from the truck and circled to the tailgate, where he was unlocking her gear. "So, here we are."

"Yeah."

"Need some help with the luggage?"

A glimmer of humor peeked out. "No, I think I can manage. Ready to go see your father?"

She pursed her lips. Her daddy was sure to have plenty to say about her disappearing for a week, but she had plenty to say about her "spy in the sky" supplies. "He'll be pleased with how much I've learned." She winked at Luc, hoping he'd smile back.

He didn't, hefting her duffel bag. Maybe he was unsure of what to say, but she'd been thinking. "Luc, I was thinking about that girl in the trailer out in the middle of nowhere."

"Yeah?"

"What if I stayed here and took a job working with families like that…" She trailed off at the look of alarm on his face.

"Stay here, where? The U.S. or Fayetteville? Give up your plans for San Lucas?"

Stung, she snapped, "I'd thought you'd be happy. You're always telling me what a hellhole it is."

"That part hasn't changed. But I think you got tough enough to manage for the kind of work you'd be doing. And your *maman*'s friends will look after you."

"I can look after myself now. But I thought after what we—that time we spent together…" His face turned blank and hard, and she hated how her voice trailed away. He looked as if he were about to undergo a particularly unpleasant mission. Maybe breaking up with her was. "Oh. I see." She lifted her chin.

"Good luck, Claire." He cupped her jaw and

brushed a thumb across her cheek. Then he walked away.

"Kiss my ass, Luc!" she shouted after him. He wanted to be the Noble Soldier and walk off into the sunset, confident he was doing her a favor by leaving her first.

"What?" He turned back in shock.

"You heard me. You're running away."

His jaw clenched. "You should know, Claire. You're running off to the jungle because you can't stand up to your father if you stay in Virginia."

"I offered to stay with *you* since I love you, you dope."

The *L* word fell between them like an unexploded grenade. "I never asked you to love me."

This wasn't going at all how she'd planned. "Then you shouldn't have been so wonderful."

He looked like he sucked on a lemon. "You got the wrong man, Claire. You want wonderful, you keep looking. I'm not. I'm broken, no good for you, *cher*."

She shook her head. "I would rather spend a minute with you than a lifetime with another man."

"You don't have that choice—sacrificing yourself for me."

He still didn't understand that he was worth any sacrifice. "I don't have that choice since you're taking it away. You and my father have more in common than you think—you both know what's best for me. At least he does it out of love for me. You're only doing it to protect yourself."

"I'm trying to protect you, Claire."

"Well, don't. I don't want your protection. I have developed your fabled mental toughness. I love you enough to let you go." Tears stung her eyes and she knew she had to get away before he saw them. "Goodbye, Luc." This time, she was the one to turn her back on him and walk away.

And he didn't stop her.

AFTER HER FATHER HAD finished hugging her and lecturing her, after Janey had stopped giving her surreptitious stares of concern, after settling herself in her original hotel room with the clean, soft, empty bed, Claire locked herself in the bathroom and turned on the fan. The face that stared back was different. Tanned, more freckled, and thinner, but another less-definable change shadowed her eyes and hollowed her cheeks. Was it heartbreak?

It had to be, since her image suddenly blurred and crumbled, her tears running down the drain—just like her dreams of a life with Luc.

"WELL, LOOK WHAT THE cat dragged in—can it be? Why, it's my long-lost sergeant." Olie folded his arms across his chest and glared at Luc. "We thought a gator'd finally gotten you."

"Sergeant First Class Luc Boudreaux, reporting for duty." Luc snapped him a salute.

Olie pursed his lips. "You're lucky you're not reporting for a court martial, boy. Or a public flogging in the town square, if the good congressman had his druthers. Oh, at ease." He shook his head in annoyance.

Luc dropped into Olie's visitor chair.

"What do you have to say for yourself, Rage?"

Luc shook himself a bit. It had been a week since anyone had called him that, and the funny thing was, the rage he'd been carrying around since T-Bone and Angélique died had lifted. "I trained Miss Cook in basic survival skills as best as I could, considering the differences in terrain and climate compared to San Lucas. She is now somewhat proficient in food-gathering, fire-starting and map-reading. We even conducted a mini-SERE exercise." He forced himself not to think of how he had captured her and she had shown him who was really in charge.

Olie's eyes narrowed. Some of Luc's memories must have shown up on his face. "Is that all you trained her in, Sergeant? Because I distinctly recalling you giving me your word as a soldier and gentleman that Miss Cook was safe in your company. That you would not lay a single finger on her pretty self."

Luc couldn't meet Olie's glare. He had sworn, and he had broken his word.

"Dammit all, Rage." Olie thunked his fist down on the desk. "I specifically warned you she was too pretty and you were too horny to take her out in the woods alone, but do you listen to me? No, you don't."

"It wasn't like that," he growled.

"It wasn't?" Olie drummed his fingers. "I get it now—it was her idea, right? Maybe she's one of those party girls who wanted to get laid by a real American fighting man before leaving the country. I can understand that—you were horny, she was slutty—"

Luc was on his feet grabbing Olie by the lapels and giving him a good shake. "Don't you ever talk about Claire like that!"

Olie stared coolly at him. "So that's how it is."

Luc shoved him into his seat and spun away, shaking. He'd never lost his cool like that, much less laid hands on a superior officer. Olie could have him up on charges and Luc would deserve every one of them.

"Luc. Sit." Olie's tone was gentle.

Luc rubbed his face in an effort to regain his composure before turning around. "What do you mean, 'So that's how it is'?"

"You ever been in love before?"

"What?" Luc's eyes bugged out. "Hell no, and I ain't in love now."

"You say so." Olie steepled his fingers together, scrutinizing him head to toe. Luc hated that gesture.

"Yeah, I do say so. We did get, um, close, but I was upfront with her about how it never worked out with me getting close to one particular woman."

"You mean, fall in love?" Olie asked dryly.

He shrugged, not even wanting to say the word. "Claire tried to tell me it was okay if I ever had to leave, that she would be waiting for me when I came back."

"She was willing to give up her dream of doing good in the jungle to hang around Fayetteville, North Carolina, in that dingy bachelor pad of yours? Willing to stay here for the chance of being with you when you came home from your deployment? Away from her friends, her family, her job?"

Luc shifted. "We never discussed any details. I told her she'd always have regrets if she didn't follow her dreams. So…" He raised his palms. "I guess she's gonna follow them."

Throughout his explanation, Olie's ruddy face grew darker and darker until he looked like a tomato with blond eyebrows. It had been a long time since Luc had seen him that angry. "What? You think I should go along with this? It'll bring her nothing but heartache. You, of all people, should know that."

"We're not talking about me, you stupid jackass! You utter and complete moron." Olie called him another couple of profane names. "You dare call yourself a Green Beret? Wah, wah, wah." Olie leaped to his feet and came around his desk. "'I found this girl who loves my ugly ass and I don't have the balls to do anything about it.' You make me sick, Rage."

"Hey!" Luc jumped up, too, going toe-to-toe with his CO.

"Chickenshit." Olie shoved him in the chest. "Life

is handing you a gift and you're throwing it down and stomping your boots all over it."

"A gift?" Luc clenched his fists. "You think Claire will call it a gift when I go overseas for months or years at a time? When I don't come home for Christmas? Or if I *do* come home in a box and they hand her a folded flag? More like a mistake."

Olie stabbed his finger at T-Bone's photo on the wall. "Go ask Mariel," Olie thundered. Mariel was T-Bone's widow. "Go ask their kids. Was marrying him a mistake? Were their three kids a mistake?"

"No, of course not," he muttered.

"I know you went to visit Mariel once you got patched up. What did she tell you?"

Luc swallowed hard.

"Come on, what did she say?"

"She thanked me for trying to save him. That it wasn't my fault Tom died."

"Damn right. It was the fault of that SOB who sent an RPG into our boat and shot us up. What else?"

Luc wiped his stinging eyes. "She said she would have rather spent five minutes with Tom than fifty years with another man. But…" He stopped in shock. Claire had told him the same thing, almost word for word.

"And she meant it." Olie wiped his own eyes. "What woman is willing to put up with that? What woman would cry for us if we died, Rage? Only a woman who truly loves her Green Beret, that's who."

"Claire would." He looked at Olie, his heart pounding. "She said she loved me enough to let me go."

Olie crashed his palm down on the table. "Well, hallelujah, you're not as dumb as you look."

"But I let her go."

"I take that back—you're even dumber."

LUC OPENED THE FRONT DOOR to his apartment and tossed the fistful of mail onto his coffee table. His place wasn't much, but it was better than living on base. It was even clean for now, since his buddy's wife ran a cleaning company and had gone through the one bedroom, bath, kitchen and living room with her mop and vacuum since he'd returned from the sandbox.

At least here he could have some privacy, which had been seriously in short supply while he and his team were out in the field. Here he could sit and drink a beer reclining in his black leather sectional while he watched the huge flat-screen TV.

He pulled out a beer and flipped up the recliner while he surfed through the channels. Local news, nothing good on sports, some weepy chick flick, national news with talking heads yapping about Afghanistan and Iraq as if they could even find the places on a map. As if they could even find their asses with two hands and a map. He told them all where to go using several rude French verbs and was about to turn off the TV when Claire's father, of all people, popped up on C-SPAN. The man looked good on TV, Luc had to admit, a wise elder statesman-type. Luc shook his head. Bad enough he had to get that woman out of his system without seeing reminders of her on TV.

He shut off the TV and rubbed his eyes. Maybe he should try to get some sleep. He was planning to leave for Louisiana in a couple days and wouldn't get much rest sleeping on his parents' couch.

No more tents or swamps, at least not for now. Tonight Luc would sleep on a bed for the first time in a week.

Sleep alone for the first time since he and Claire had started making love.

And love was what it was.

He loved Claire. He should have known that back in the woods, should have known that when he'd dropped her off to her father, when he'd shoved her out of his life.

What was he supposed to do now? He stared blankly at the dark TV screen, as blank as his mind except for the overwhelming loss. For a man who made life-and-death decisions on a frequent basis, he was sure screwing up. He had used up more of his lives than a cat, and chances were he might not live to be an old man. Claire was only twenty-four. T-Bone's widow was only a couple years older.

He sighed and set down his beer. It was making him too sentimental, anyway. He reached for his mail, automatically flipping aside the junk into one pile, bills into another. There was no personal mail. Never was.

Finally, the catalogs on the bottom. He shook his head. What the hell kind of mailing list had he gotten on? Sure, he understood the knife and gun catalogs, but home decoration and fluffy gift catalogs? He was about to toss one aside when the model on the cover caught his eye.

No, it wasn't Claire, although her peachy skin and dark hair was a close match. Calling himself ten thousand kinds of a fool, he opened the pages to look for any more pictures of the model. He didn't have any photos of Claire.

After several pages of clever T-shirts, puppy statues and hand-painted wineglasses, he was about ready to close it when he spotted a ring. A simple gold band, it was engraved with the French script *"Vous et nul autre." You, and no other.*

Luc felt like the time Olie had sucker-punched him in the gut during hand-to-hand combat training. He read the catalog description—a reproduction of a medieval ring given by one lover to another.

You, and no other. That was who Claire was. Only Claire—no other woman would ever do for him. He flipped the recliner lever and leaped up. He knew what he had to do, and it didn't look like he'd sleep in a bed tonight, either.

"HERE. BLOW." JANEY STUFFED yet another tissue into Claire's hand. She'd been crying so much, it was hard to see the box. She wiped her eyes and her nose, but the tears didn't stop.

"Claire, you've been crying for three hours straight. If you don't stop, I'm gonna slip a sleeping pill into your milk shake to knock you out."

Her eyes widened. "You wouldn't."

Janey gave her a baleful glance. "Try me. You're making yourself sick with weeping over this guy? And you've only known him a week."

She dabbed her nose. "I told Luc I loved him. He was the first man I ever said that to, did you know that?"

Janey nodded.

"I told him I loved him and he said, 'Oh.'"

"'Oh'?" Janey's face mirrored Claire's own dismay. "Oh. Anything else?"

"He said he couldn't love me. He said he knew we'd become close over the past week or so, but he didn't want it to interfere with my plans. In other words, don't let the tent flap hit you on the way out." She sniffled again. "It only took that bastard one week to make me fall in love with him, and he told me to go ahead with my plans."

"You should go ahead with your plans. You know he will."

"That's right, he will. And to think I was thinking about canceling my trip to San Lucas to be with him."

"Geez, Claire, did you tell him that?" Janey grimaced.

"Well, not just to be with him. I thought I could call the social services office near Norfolk to see if they had any assignments nearby."

"Nearby to home, or nearby to Fayetteville?"

She shrugged. "I did mention Fayetteville."

Janey shook her head. "No wonder he bailed on you. You probably turned his life upside down, too."

"Oh, I did not. He probably does this all the time. Takes a woman out into the woods, trains her in survival skills, makes her fall in love with him, dumps her back in civilization literally and figuratively…" She balled up her tissue and threw it away, like Luc had thrown her away.

"Sounds like a lot of work for a guy who's hot enough to go into a bar and get a dozen invitations for sex within the first ten minutes."

Claire needed to stop thinking about Luc having sex with other women or else she was going to cry again. "Speaking of sexy guys in bars, whatever happened between you and that blond guy Olie?"

Janey's face hardened. "Never you mind that. Let's just say he's off my Christmas card list." She tapped her fingers on the table. "So Luc said he didn't love you?"

"No, he said he couldn't love me. Big difference, huh?"

"Actually, yes. Maybe he does love you, but he thinks it's impossible."

"He's worried about impossible?" Claire jumped to her feet and paced like a madwoman. "Janey, this guy has done more impossible things in his life than a million other guys. He survived being exploded out of a boat, shot at and nearly drowned before trekking one hundred miles alone through some of the worst jungle in the world and—let's face it—he trained me to not get lost in the woods and to skin and gut small animals without throwing up. If he can do that, he can practically leap tall buildings with a single bound."

"Luc's a real hero, Claire. Olie said he's being awarded for a Silver Star for the enemy reconnaissance he conducted in Afghanistan. That's classified, though."

"Well, he's not earning any medals for valor from me. He's a chicken when it comes to important stuff like love and happiness."

"You can't make him into somebody he's not, and you can't be someone you're not. If he wants to love you, that has to come from within him. Remember Felicia?"

"From college?"

"The very one. She picked out a boyfriend who liked blondes, so she went blond. He liked tall girls, so she wore heels all the time and wound up needing the foot doctor. He liked dumb girls so she flunked most of her classes. And what happened to her after the university asked her to leave for bad grades?"

Claire winced at the memory. "Her boyfriend dumped her for a short, brunette Rhodes scholar. He said his new girlfriend was 'genuine.' And Felicia got arrested for breaking all the windows in his car."

"Bad hair, bad feet, bad grades and a criminal record. The moral of this story is to be yourself. What do you want to do? Not what do you want to do if Luc does this, or if Luc does that. What does Claire Adeline Cook want for herself?"

"I don't know. I'm a chicken."

"Don't tell me that! You were the one who bathed and fed her mother as she was dying. You were the one who took care of her dad when he was so sad he wanted to die. You dummy, you've been brave all along. Eating snakes and sleeping in trees has nothing to do with bravery."

Claire stopped midstep. "You know what, Janey? You're right. I've had mental toughness the whole time, and Luc hasn't. Just because he's a hard-ass soldier doesn't mean he knows doodley-squat about anything—especially this love stuff. He was all gung-ho when we were having sex four or five times a day, but he started kissing my hair and telling me things he'd never told anyone else before. It was too much for him to manage."

"Sex four or five times a day?" Janey whispered faintly. She blinked several times and fanned herself.

"Yes, and it was great," she said. "He showed me things I never even dreamed of doing."

Janey hesitated briefly and gave in to her curiosity. "Like what?"

Luc didn't love her, so why would he care if she bragged a bit? Claire smugly gave her the general out-line, enjoying being the sexpert for once. But when she described how they'd acted out several fantasies, Janey interrupted her with a groan.

"Enough, enough! A week ago you were practically a virgin. Now you're into roleplaying?"

"When the right man comes along, Janey my girl, anything is possible."

"Keep it up and you'll make me sorry Olie and I didn't hook up that night."

"I expect you to tell me what happened with that."

"Not now. One crisis is enough. Focus, Claire. Get your mind off Luc's poor overworked ding-dong and figure out what you want to do about the rest of him."

"Nothing." She shook her head. "He knows where I am. He can come to me."

"What if he doesn't?"

Claire sighed. "I leave for Virginia tomorrow, and I leave for San Lucas three days after that. If I don't see him before then, I'll know he wasn't brave enough to fight for me, decorated hero or no."

"CLAIRE, HONEY? CAN I come in?" Her dad stood in her bedroom doorway at home in Virginia.

She looked up from where she was sitting on the window seat in her old comfy robe and pajamas. "I thought you were asleep, Dad." She'd found it impossible to sleep, as well, and had been staring out the darkened window, trying not to think of Luc. He hadn't called her hotel in Fayetteville, hadn't called her house in Virginia. She guessed she knew his answer.

"No, I had some paperwork to read and well…" He shoved a hand through his silver hair. "I don't want you flying off to San Lucas before we have a chance to talk."

"Talk about what?"

"Anything you want, Claire. Your trip, your time in the woods, your…" He trailed off again.

"My mother?" she guessed.

"Her, too." He sat facing her on the seat.

She didn't want to talk about her mother, so she picked option one. "I leave the day after tomorrow, and I'm really excited." But she sounded about as excited as someone looking forward to cutting the grass.

"I'm glad." Dad looked away. "I'm sorry about how I handled everything, including those stupid electronic trackers. I shouldn't have tried to talk you out of going to San Lucas and I shouldn't have pressured you into last-minute survival training." He finally smiled at her. "You finally ran away from home—most kids do that when they're teenagers."

"I guess I'm a late bloomer."

"Dads never like to see their daughters grow up into beautiful women, but…" He lifted his hands in a helpless gesture. "You've become a beautiful woman and I'm very proud of you."

Claire stared at him. "Really?"

"Of course. Don't I always introduce you as 'my beautiful, talented daughter, Claire'?"

"Oh, that." She leaned against the wall. "At political rallies? I could look like a plow horse in a skirt and everyone would still clap."

Dad frowned. "Just because I'm a politician doesn't make me a liar about you. My constituents can see for themselves, you know. And if you want to use your talents to help those unfortunate souls in San Lucas, you have my blessing and support." He rested his loafer on his opposite knee. "Hmm. I may need to organize a congressional fact-finding mission to San Lucas. After you get settled in, of course," he added hastily as she narrowed her eyes at him.

"I will be fine. I actually did learn a lot about jungle survival from Luc—Sergeant First Class Boudreaux."

"Did you?" Dad tapped a finger on his ankle.

She took a deep breath, surprised at the pain that hit her middle when she thought of Luc. "Yes, how to find clean water and food, map-reading, avoiding poisonous snakes—did I tell you how I swung myself into a tree branch with an angry cottonmouth swimming at me?"

"Yes." He closed his eyes and shuddered. "I'd prefer to forget that horrible image. But you did well. I knew Sergeant Boudreaux was the right man for the job."

Claire tried to keep a neutral expression on her face, glad for the dark room.

"Of course, I never expected you to disappear into the rural Low Country alone with the man," her dad mused. "If I'd known that, I would have picked someone who wasn't quite so handsome and dashing."

"Don't forget heroic." She couldn't keep a tinge of bitterness from her voice. "Janey says he's up for a Silver Star for action in Afghanistan." Too bad he was a coward when it came to her.

"Indeed." He nodded. "I hope he enjoys the medal because if he's hurt you, they'll present it to him along with his discharge papers."

"What?"

"I may be an old widowed dad, but I can still recognize certain manly emotions, shall we say. And that young Cajun had a boatload of them crossing his face when you left."

"Like what?"

"Regret, sorrow, affection…maybe even love?" He lifted a bushy eyebrow.

She was already shaking her head. "No, Dad. Luc may have been fond of me after working together so closely, but his love is for the army and his band of brothers. That's how he thinks of his team. No women allowed." She gave him a weak smile.

Dad grunted, obviously not convinced. "If you won't let me abuse my congressional powers and ruin his military career, can I at least punch him in the nose?"

That shocked a giggle out of her. Punching seemed so low-class for a man like her patrician father. "We're Virginians, Dad. How about you horsewhip him?" They had several whips in the stable.

"Excellent." He brightened immediately and declaimed in a theatrically hammy Southern accent, "'Suh, you have offended the Cook family honuh. Prepay-uh for your trouncin'.'"

She was laughing hard enough to hurt her sides. "Oh, Dad, you should have been a professional actor."

He grinned at her. "My dear, I already am. Some days the Capitol dome is the best-looking theater in America."

"It will be strange to be so far from it," Claire mused.

"Your mother threatened to go back to San Lucas at least once every election cycle. But she loved me more than I deserved and hung around anyway."

"I miss her."

"I do, too." Dad pulled her into a hug. "I wasn't much help when she was so sick, I'm sorry to say. But you were the brave one. You always have been." He kissed her forehead.

She choked back a laugh. "Everybody has been telling me that—that I was brave all along but didn't realize it."

"It's true. You are a wonderful young woman, and woe to anyone who doesn't know it." He wrinkled his nose as if he'd smelled something bad. "Even that doltish young sergeant."

"Dad, forget about him."

"Can't I lie in wait for him outside his barracks late one night and jump him?"

She laughed. Her dad, a silver-haired, Mr. Rogers

look-alike, leaping onto the back of a Special Forces soldier. "No."

"How about I key his monster truck?"

"No."

"Puncture those huge tires?"

"No."

"Sprinkle itching powder into his army-issue boxers?"

Claire decided not to tell her dad Luc wore briefs. "No." She was laughing too hard to speak clearly by then.

"Curses, foiled again." He twisted an imaginary mustache. "Then he'll just have to live with his own regrets like the rest of us."

"Did Mom have any regrets?"

"Only that she couldn't stay with us longer. None about how she lived her life, and especially none about you."

"That's a good way to live."

Her dad kissed her cheek. "Amen."

13

CLAIRE WAS DEEP IN her closet, pulling out the big suitcase she planned to pack medical supplies in for her trip to San Lucas. It was customary to bring a tiny suitcase of clothing and personal items and your approximate body weight in bandages, antibiotics and antimalarial medications.

The doorbell rang and she called downstairs for Louella to answer it. When the bell rang again, she remembered Louella was running errands in Cooksville, so she jogged downstairs in her denim cutoffs and lime-green tank top.

She pulled open the front door. "Yes?" Her voice trailed away. Luc stood on the wide front porch in a button-down black shirt and matching pants. He looked lean, dark and heartbreakingly handsome. "Luc. What are you doing here?"

"I came to see you."

"Oh, come in." Her stomach quivered as he followed her into the high-ceilinged entryway. "Would you like some lemonade? Louella made it fresh this morning with real lemons and mint simple syrup. She loves making everything from scratch," she called over her shoulder as she scurried into the kitchen.

Over the past few days, she'd imagined a hundred different scenarios if Luc actually did show up. He'd drop to his knees to beg her forgiveness; she'd chew him out and point a haughty finger toward the door. But she hadn't imagined she'd run away from him and offer him a cold beverage.

She pulled the pitcher from the fridge before he stopped her. "Claire, I don't want any lemonade."

"You don't?" She stood there stupidly as her hands sweated more than the pitcher.

"No." He took it from her and set it in the fridge. "I've been thinking about what happened between us and I realized it shouldn't have ended that way."

"Oh. So you came to end it another way." Talk about twisting the knife.

He grabbed her clammy hand. "I..." He blew out his breath in a nervous puff. "I don't want it to end at all."

"You don't?" Her fingers tightened on his. "What about all your talk about how you didn't want to have anyone waiting for you because of the danger involved?"

He shook his head. "The only danger is not being with you."

Claire couldn't believe he was saying the things she longed to hear. "Two days ago, you were telling me about all your buddies who got dumped overseas. What if you have regrets the second I fly away? Do I have to dread opening my mail for fear of a 'Dear Jane' letter?"

He caressed her cheek. "Like a very wise and beautiful woman once told me, sometimes a man has to stop chasing death and live a true life. And I want to live that true life with you." He pulled a gray velvet pouch from his pocket and tipped a gold circle into his palm. "Read it."

She picked it up from his warm hand. "'*Vous et nul autre.*' '*You and no other.*'" The ancient words of love were engraved in a medieval script on the ring. It was beautiful and she could hardly believe he was offering it to her. "Oh, Luc. Where did you get this?" She pressed her hand against her mouth.

"The operator was a bit worried when I asked where the warehouse was, but when I told her I was a soldier and needed it for my girlfriend, she gave me their address in Atlanta."

"You drove to Atlanta for this?" That was a five-hour drive from Fayetteville and another seven-hour drive to Cooksville.

He nodded, his expression nonchalant but his eyes gleaming. "I drove all night and bought it when they opened at oh-eight-hundred. Then I stopped at home, took a shower and drove here."

Her eyes widened. "When was the last time you slept?" He was probably hallucinating from sleep deprivation by now. She hoped he remembered giving her the ring when he woke up tomorrow.

"A while ago. But that's not important, Claire. You are. We are."

Her eyes filled. "Oh, Luc. I thought you didn't care." His face blurred and he pulled her into his arms.

"Don't cry, *cher* Claire. *Je t'aime toujours, ma douce.*"

She cried even harder. It was the first time he had told her he loved her, would love her forever. "I love you, too, always."

He gave a big sigh of relief. "We love each other, right?" She nodded. "Give me a kiss, then, sweetheart."

She tipped her mouth up to his, her wet cheeks sliding over his as he kissed her gently.

"But I'm leaving for San Lucas the day after tomorrow!" she wailed. "I can't let them down—I have fifty pounds of medication that they're counting on."

"They're counting on more than that, Claire. They're counting on *you.*" He kissed her again. "Go to San Lucas, *cher.* I'll be waiting for you when you come home."

"But what if you get deployed before I return?"

"Then you'll be waiting for me when I come off that plane, waving that American flag and running to kiss me hello. We got a deal?"

"Deal." She threw his arms around her neck.

He pulled away, his black eyes serious but full of love. "And if something happens to me, Claire, always know that I tried my damnedest to come back to you. You have my heart, my love."

She had to swallow hard. "You have my heart, too, my love."

"Good." He had a catch in his voice, as well. "Very, very good."

Epilogue

CLAIRE FELT THE ENGINES downshift even before the captain made her announcement that they were landing at Ronald Reagan International Airport in Washington, D.C. The sight of the huge metropolitan area was quite a shock after a year of seeing nothing but dense green vegetation and occasional brown soil or muddy water from the air.

The sparkling white marble dome of the Capitol building beckoned her home. Her workaholic dad wouldn't be in his office this afternoon, anyway, since he was meeting her plane.

Luc, though. Luc was another story. According to his last e-mail, his team was conducting a major training exercise in the national forest near Ft. Bragg, so she'd have to wait to see him until he had finished.

Despite their physical separation, they had grown closer over the past year, thanks to e-mails and occasional phone calls. He always ended their communications telling her that she had his heart, his special way of telling her he loved her.

Claire grabbed her bags and disembarked. Her

father and their housekeeper Louella held a banner. *Welcome home, Claire.* She ran to her father, holding him tight. "Oh, Dad." She kissed his smoothly shaved cheek and noticed a little more white in his hair. She hoped she hadn't caused it with her year away.

Louella was next in line for a cushiony embrace, exclaiming how tanned and skinny Claire was, promising to cook her favorite foods to plump her up.

Claire smiled. "I'm so glad to see you both. I can't wait to get home."

"We're glad to see you, too." Her dad wrapped his arm around her shoulder. "Now, before we go, we have a surprise for you."

"Really? A welcome-home gift?"

"You could call it that." Dad spun her in a half circle and Luc stepped out from behind a pillar.

Claire covered her mouth in shock and screamed. He wore his dress green uniform, his brand-new Silver Star gleaming above several rows of decoration.

"Welcome back, *cher.*" He opened his arms wide and she sprinted into them, laughing and crying. She dragged his mouth down to hers, the loving touch of his lips like cool, fresh water after a year of thirsting for him. He threaded his fingers into her hair and drank her in, as well.

She could have remained entwined with him forever, but her father's discreet throat-clearing and Louella's sentimental sniffs reminded her they stood on the airport concourse. "What are you doing here? I thought you were out in the field."

"The exercise got canceled last minute and I came to Virginia."

"You should have called me." She grabbed his chin and kissed him again.

He pulled away from her. "I had some business to take care of before I could come meet you." He looked over her shoulder at her father and Louella. "Your papa and I got off on the wrong foot last year, so I wanted to meet him again—and tell him of my intentions."

"Intentions?"

Then she was the only one standing as he dropped to one knee, still holding tight to her hand. "Claire, your father has given his permission to ask for your hand." He reached into his uniform jacket and pulled out a small black box. "Claire, will you marry me?" He pulled out a sparkling white diamond solitaire set in gold.

She covered her mouth again, this time to press back tears of happiness. Instead of putting it on her hand, he tipped up the band so she could read the engraving inside. "*'Vous et nul autre.'*" She pulled the gold chain out from under her shirt that held the matching ring he'd given her a year earlier. "You and no other, Luc."

"*Oui ou non, béb?*" His eyes twinkled at her. "Will you take this rough Cajun soldier for your husband?"

"*Oui.*" He slipped the ring on her fourth finger and she dragged him to his feet for more kisses. "A million times, *oui.*"

HER HARD TO RESIST
HUSBAND

BY
TINA BECKETT

Born to a family that was always on the move, **Tina Beckett** learned to pack a suitcase almost before she knew how to tie her shoes. Fortunately she met a man who also loved to travel, and she snapped him right up. Married for over twenty years, Tina has three wonderful children and has lived in gorgeous places such as Portugal and Brazil.

Living where English reading material is difficult to find has its drawbacks, however. Tina had to come up with creative ways to satisfy her love for romance novels, so she picked up her pen and tried writing one. After her tenth book she realised she was hooked. She was officially a writer.

A three-times Golden Heart finalist, and fluent in Portuguese, Tina now divides her time between the United States and Brazil. She loves to use exotic locales as the backdrop for many of her stories. When she's not writing you can find her either on horseback or soldering stained glass panels for her home.

Tina loves to hear from readers. You can contact her through her website or 'friend' her on Facebook.

To my husband, who stands beside me
through thick and thin.

And to my editor, Suzy,
for making me dig deeper than I ever thought I could

CHAPTER ONE

Tracy Hinton didn't faint.

Her stomach squirmed and threatened to give way as the scent of death flooded her nostrils, but she somehow held it together. Calming herself with slow, controlled breaths was out of the question, because breathing was the last thing she wanted to do right now.

"How many are there?" She fitted the protective mask over her nose and mouth.

"Six deaths so far, but most of the town is affected." Pedro, one of her mobile clinic workers, nodded towards the simple clay-brick house to his left, where an eerily still figure was curled in a fetal position on the porch. Another body lay a few yards away on the ground. "They've been dead for a few days. Whatever it was, it hit fast. They didn't even try to make it to a hospital."

"They were probably too sick. Besides, the nearest hospital is twenty miles away."

Piauí, one of the poorest of the Brazilian states, was more vulnerable to catastrophic infections than the wealthier regions, and many of these outlying townships relied on bicycles or their own two feet for transportation. It was hard enough to make a twenty-mile trek even when one was young and healthy, which these poor souls had not been. And cars were a luxury most couldn't afford.

She wouldn't know for sure what had caused the deaths until she examined the bodies and gathered some specimens. The nearest diagnostic hospital was a good hundred miles from here. In any case, she'd have to report the possibility of an epidemic to the proper authorities.

Which meant she'd have to deal with Ben.

Pedro shook his head. "Dengue, you think?"

"Not this time. There's some blood on the front of the man's shirt, but nothing else that I can see from this distance." She stared at the crude corral where several pigs squealed out a protest at the lack of food. "I'm thinking lepto."

Pedro frowned. "Leptospirosis? Rainy season's already over."

The area around the house consisted of a few desiccated twigs and hard-packed clay, confirming her colleague's words. The sweltering heat sucked any remaining moisture from the air and squeezed around her, making her nausea that much worse. Situated close to the equator, the temperature of this part of Brazil rarely dipped below the hundred-degree mark during the dry season. The deadly heat would only grow worse, until the rains finally returned.

"They have pigs." She used her forearm to push sticky tendrils of hair from her forehead.

"I saw that, but lepto doesn't normally cause hemorrhaging."

"It did in *Bahia*."

Pedro's brows went up. "You think it's the pulmonary version?"

"I don't know. Maybe."

"Do you want to take samples? Or head for one of the other houses?"

Reaching into the back pocket of her jeans, she eased out her cellphone and glanced hopefully at the display. No bars. What worked in São Paulo obviously didn't work here. "Is your phone working?"

"Nope."

She sighed, trying to figure out what to do. "The tissue samples will have to wait until we come back, I don't want to risk contaminating any live patients. And maybe we'll come within range of a cellphone tower once we hit higher ground."

Benjamin Almeida pressed his eye to the lens of the microscope and twisted the fine focus until the image sharpened, making the pink stain clearly visible. Gram negative bacteria. Removing the slide, he ran it through the digital microscope and recorded the results.

"Um, Ben?" His assistant's hesitant voice came from the doorway.

He held up a finger as he waited for the computer to signal it had sent his report to the attending physician at the tropical disease institute of *Piauí*. The man's office was fifteen steps away in the main hospital building, but Ben couldn't take the time to walk over there right now. Dragging the latex gloves from his hands and flicking them into the garbage can to his right, he reached for the hand sanitizer and squirted a generous amount onto his palm.

"Yep, what is it?" He glanced up, his twelve-hour shift beginning to catch up with him. There were two more slides he needed to process before he could call it a day.

"Someone's here to see you." Mandy shifted out of the doorway, the apology in her cultured Portuguese tones unmistakable.

"If it's Dr. Mendosa, tell him I just emailed the report. It's a bacterial infection, not a parasite."

A woman appeared next to Mandy, and Ben couldn't stop his quick intake of breath. Shock wheeled through him, and he forced himself to remain seated on his stool, thankful his legs weren't in charge of supporting his weight at that moment.

Inky-dark hair, pulled back in its usual clip, exposed high cheekbones and a long slender neck. Green eyes—right now filled with worry—met his without hesitation, her chin tilting slightly higher as they stared at each other.

What the hell was *she* doing here?

The newcomer adjusted the strap of a blue insulated bag on her shoulder and took a small step closer. "Ben, I need your help."

His jaw tensed. Those were almost the exact words she'd used four years ago. Right before she'd walked out of his life. He gave a quick swallow, hoping his voice wouldn't betray his thoughts. "With what?"

"Something's happening in São João dos Rios." She patted the bag at her side, words tumbling out at breakneck speed. "I brought samples I need you to analyze. The sooner the better, because I have to know why people are suddenly—"

"Slow down. I have no idea what you're talking about."

She bit her lip, and he watched her try to collect her thoughts. "There's an outbreak in São João dos Rios. Six people are dead so far. The military police are already on their way to lock down the town." She held her hand out. "I wouldn't have come if this wasn't important. Really important."

That much he knew was true. The last time he'd seen her, she had been heading out the door of their house, never to return.

He shouldn't be surprised she was still roving the country, stamping out infectious fires wherever she went. Nothing had been able to stop her. Not him. Not the thought of a home and family. Not the life she'd carried inside her.

Against his better judgement, he yanked on a fresh pair of gloves. "Do I need a respirator?"

"I don't think so. We used surgical masks to collect the samples."

He nodded, pulling one on and handing another to her, grateful that its presence would hide those soft pink lips he'd never tired of kissing. Ben's attention swiveled back to her eyes, and he cursed the fact that the vivid green still had the power to make his pulse pound in his chest even after all this time.

He cleared his throat. "Symptoms?"

"The commonality seems to be pulmonary hemorrhage, maybe from some type of pneumonia." She passed him the bag. "The bodies have already been cremated, unfortunately."

"Without autopsies?" Something in his stomach twisted in warning.

"The military let me collect a few samples before they carted the bodies away, and the government took another set to do its own studies. I have to document that I've destroyed everything once you're done." She lowered her voice. "There's a guard in your reception area whose job it is to make sure that order is carried out. Help me out here. You're the best epidemiologist around these parts."

He glanced at the doorway, noting for the first time the armed member of the *Polícia Militar* leaning against the wall in the other room. "That wasn't one of my most endearing features, once upon a time."

He remembered all too well the heated arguments they'd had over which was more important: individual rights or the public good.

Biting her lip, she hesitated. "Because you went behind my back and used your job as a weapon against me."

Yes, he had. And not even that had stopped her.

His assistant, who'd been watching from the doorway, pulled on a mask and moved to stand beside him, her head tilting as she glanced nervously at the guard. Her English wasn't the best, and Ben wasn't sure how much of their conversation she'd grasped. "Is he going to let us leave?" she asked in Portuguese.

Tracy switched to the native language. "If it turns out the illness is just a common strain of pneumonia, it won't be a problem."

"And if it isn't?"

Ben's lips compressed as he contemplated spending an unknown amount of time confined to his tiny office.

With Tracy.

He had a foldable cot in a back closet, but it was narrow. Certainly not large enough for…

"If it isn't, then it looks like we might be here for a while." He went to the door and addressed the official. "We haven't opened the tissue samples yet. My assistant has a family. I'd like her to go home before we begin."

Ben had insisted his office be housed in a separate build-ing from the main hospital for just this reason. It was small enough that the whole thing could be sealed off in the event of an airborne epidemic. And just like the microbial test he'd completed for a colleague moments earlier, any results could be sent off via computer.

Safety was his number-one priority. Mandy knew the risks of working for him, but she'd been exposed to noth-ing, as far as he could tell. Not like when Tracy had rushed headlong into a yellow fever epidemic four years ago that had forced him to call in the military authorities.

The guard in the doorway tapped his foot for a second, as if considering Ben's request. He then turned away and spoke to someone through his walkie-talkie. When he was done, he faced them. "We'll have someone escort her home, but she'll have to remain there until we know what the illness is. As for you two…" he motioned to Ben and Tracy "…once the samples are uncapped you'll have to stay in this building until we determine the risks."

Mandy sent Ben a panicked look. "Are you sure it's safe for me to leave? My baby…" She shut her eyes. "I need to call my husband."

"Have Sergio take the baby to your mother's house, where she'll be safe. just in case. I'll call you as soon as I know something, okay?"

His assistant nodded and left to make her call.

"I'm sorry." Tracy's face softened. "I thought you'd be alone in the lab. I didn't realize you'd gotten an assistant."

"It's not your fault. She's worried about the risks to her baby." His eyes came up to meet hers, and he couldn't resist the dig. "Just as any woman with children would be."

He mentally kicked himself when the compassion in Tracy's eyes dissolved, and anger took its place.

"I *was* concerned. But it was never enough for you, was it?" Her chest rose as she took a deep breath. "I'm heading back to São João dos Rios as soon as you give me some answers. If I'm going to be quarantined, I'm going to do it where I can make a difference. That doesn't include sitting in a lab, staring at rows of test tubes."

He knew he'd struck a nerve, but it didn't stop an old hurt from creeping up his spine. "Says the woman who came to *my* lab, asking for help," he said quietly.

"I didn't mean it like that."

"Sure you did."

They stared at each other then the corners of her eyes crinkled. She pulled down her mask, letting it dangle around her neck. "Okay, maybe I did…a little. But at least I admitted that I need you. That has to count for something."

It did. But that kind of need was a far cry from what

they'd once had together. Those days were long gone, and no matter how hard Ben had tried to hold onto her back then, she'd drifted further and further away, until the gulf between them had been too huge to span.

Bellyaching about the past won't get you anywhere.

Ben shook off the thoughts and set the insulated bag on an empty metal table. He nodded towards the aluminum glove dispenser hanging on the far wall. "Suit up and don't touch anything in the lab, just in case."

She dug into her handbag instead and pulled out her own box of gloves. "I came prepared."

Of course she had. It was part of who she was. This was a woman who was always on the move—who never took a weekend off. Tracy had thrown herself into her work without restraint...until there had been nothing left for herself. Or for him.

He'd thought she'd stop once the pregnancy tests went from blue to pink. She hadn't. And Ben hadn't been able to face any child of his going through what he had as a kid.

Gritting his teeth in frustration, he glanced around the lab, eyeing the centrifuges and other equipment. They'd have to work in the tiny glassed-off cubicle in the corner that he'd set up for occasions like this.

Keeping his day-to-day work space absolutely separate from Tracy's samples was not only smart, it was non-negotiable. If they weren't careful, the government could end up quarantining his whole lab, meaning years of work would be tossed into the incinerator. He tensed. Although if their findings turned up a microbe that was airborne, he'd willingly burn everything himself. He wouldn't risk setting loose an epidemic.

Not even for Tracy. She should know that by now.

"I have a clean room set up over there. Once we get things squared away with Mandy, we can start."

Tracy peered towards the door where the phone conversation between his assistant and her husband was growing more heated by the second. "I was really careful about keeping everything as sterile as I could. I don't think she's been exposed to anything."

"I'm sure it'll be fine. I'm going to take your bagged samples into the other area. Can you wipe down the table where they were with disinfectant?"

As soon as Ben picked up the insulated bag, the guard appeared, his hand resting on the butt of his gun. "Where are you going with that?"

Ben motioned towards the clean room. "The samples can't infect anyone else if they're kept enclosed. You can see everything we do from the reception doorway. It'll be safer if you keep your distance once we've started testing, though."

The guard backed up a couple of paces. "How long will it take? I have no wish to stay here any longer than I have to."

"I have no idea. It depends on what we're dealing with."

Putting the bag in the cubicle, he gathered the equipment he'd need and arranged it on the set of metal shelves perched above a stainless-steel table. He blew out a breath. The eight-by-eight-foot area was going to be cramped once he and Tracy were both inside.

An air handler filtered any particles floating in and out of the clean room, but there was no safe way to pump air-conditioning into the space. They'd have to rely on the wheezy window unit in the main lab and hope it kept them from baking. He could offer to send Tracy on her way before he got the results—but he was pretty sure he knew how that suggestion would be met, despite her waspish words earlier.

You couldn't coax—or force—Tracy to do anything she didn't want to do. He knew that from experience.

Mandy appeared in the doorway to the reception area just as Ben turned on the air filter and closed the door on the samples.

"It's all arranged. Sergio called my mom and asked if she'd care for the baby overnight. He's not happy about staying home from work, but he doesn't want me to stay here either."

"I don't blame him. But look on the bright side. At least you can go home." He smiled. "Tell Sergio he should count his lucky stars I haven't stolen you away from him."

Mandy laughed. "You've already told him that yourself. Many times."

Tracy spun away from them and stalked over to the metal table she'd previously sanitized and began scrubbing it all over again. She kept her head down, not looking at either of them.

"Is the guard going to take you home?" He forced the words to remain cheerful.

"They're sending another policeman. He should be here soon."

"Good." He had Mandy go back and wait in the reception area, so there'd be no question of her being anywhere near those samples. Returning to the sealed cubicle, he slid the insulated bag into a small refrigerator he kept for just this purpose. The air was already growing close inside the room, but he'd worked under worse conditions many times before. Both he and Tracy had.

He could still picture one such occasion—their very first meeting—Tracy had stepped off the *Projeto Vida* medical boat and stalked into the village he had been surveying, demanding to know what he was doing about the malaria outbreak twenty miles downriver. He'd been exhausted, and she'd looked like a gorgeous avenging angel, silky black hair flowing behind her in the breeze, ready to slay him if he said one wrong word.

They'd barely lasted two days before they'd fallen into bed together.

Something he'd rather not remember at the moment. Especially as he was trying to avoid any and all physical contact with her.

She might be immune, but he wasn't. Not judging from the way his heart had taken off at a sprint when he'd seen her standing in that doorway.

Tracy dumped her paper towel into the hazardous waste receptacle and crossed over to him. "I just want to say thank you for agreeing to help. You could have told me to get lost." She gave a hard laugh. "I wouldn't have blamed you if you had."

"I'm not always an ogre, you know."

Her teeth caught the right corner of her bottom lip in a way that made his chest tighten. "I know. And I'm sorry for dragging you into this, but I didn't know where else to go. The military didn't want me to take the samples out of São João dos Rios. They only agreed to let me come here because you've worked with them before…and even then they made me bring a guard. I honestly didn't think anyone else would be affected other than us."

"It's not your fault, Trace." He started to reach out to touch her cheek, but checked himself. "The government is probably right to keep this as contained as possible. If I thought there was any chance of contamination, I'd be the first one to say Mandy needs to stay here at the lab with us."

He smiled. "If I know you, though, not one microbe survived on that bag before you carried it out of that town."

"I hope not. There are still several ill people waiting on us for answers. I left a colleague behind to make sure the military didn't do anything rash, but he's not a doctor, and

I don't want to risk his health either." She blew out a breath. "Those people need help. But there's nothing I can do until I know what we're dealing with."

And then she'd be on her way to the next available crisis. Just like she always was.

His smile faded. "Let's get to work, then."

The guard stuck his head into the room. "They're sending someone for your friend. They'll keep her at home until the danger has passed."

Ben nodded. "I understand. Thank you."

When he went to the doorway to say goodbye to Mandy, she kissed his cheek, her arms circling his neck and hugging him close. When she finally let go, her eyes shimmered with unshed tears. "I'm so grateful. I can't imagine not being able to tuck my Jenny into bed tonight, but at least I'll be closer to her than I would be if I stayed here."

His heart clenched. Here was a woman whose baby meant the world to her—who didn't need to jet off to distant places to find fulfillment. Unlike his parents.

Unlike Tracy.

"We'll work as quickly as we can. Once things are clear, make sure you give her a kiss and a hug from her uncle Ben."

"I will." She wiped a spot of lipstick from his cheek with her thumb. "Be careful, okay? I've just gotten used to your crazy ways. I don't want to break someone else in."

Ben laughed and took off one of his latex gloves, laying his hand on her shoulder. "You're not getting rid of me any time soon, so go and enjoy your mini-vacation. You'll be back to the same old grind before you know it."

Mandy's escort arrived, and as soon as she exited the building, he turned back to find Tracy observing him with a puzzled frown.

"What?" he asked.

She shrugged. "Nothing. I'm just surprised you haven't found a woman who'd be thrilled to stick close to the house and give you all those kids you said you wanted."

"That would be impossible, given the circumstances."

"Oh?" Her brows arched. "And why is that?"

He laughed, the sound harsh in the quiet room. "Do you really have to ask?"

"I just did."

Grabbing her left hand, he held it up, forcing her eyes to the outline of the plain gold band visible beneath her latex glove. "For the same reason you're wearing this." He stared into her face. "Have you forgotten, *Mrs. Almeida*? You may not go by your married name any more, but in the eyes of the law…we're still husband and wife."

CHAPTER TWO

SHE'D FORGOTTEN NOTHING.

And she'd tried to see about getting a divorce, but being overseas made everything a hundred times more complicated. Both of the Brazilian lawyers she'd contacted had said that as an American citizen, she should return to the States and start the proceedings there, as she and Ben had been married in New York. But asking him to accompany her had been out of the question. Even if he'd been willing, she wasn't. She hadn't wanted to be anywhere near him, too raw from everything that had transpired in the month before she'd left *Teresina*—and him—for ever.

Staying married probably hadn't been the wisest move on her part but she'd thrown herself into her work afterwards, far too busy with *Projeto Vida*, her aid organization's floating clinic, to set the ugly wheels in motion. Besides, a wedding ring tended to scare away any man who ventured too close. Not that there'd been many. Her *caution-do-not-touch* vibes must be coming through loud and clear. She'd never get married again—to anyone—so keeping her wedding ring and her license made keeping that promise a whole lot easier.

Too bad she hadn't remembered to take the ring off before asking Ben for help.

She realized he was still waiting for a response so she

lifted her chin, praying he wouldn't notice the slight tremble. "We're not married any more. Not by any stretch of the imagination. You made sure of that."

"Right." Ben turned away and gathered a few more pieces of equipment.

Her thumb instinctively rubbed back and forth across the ring, a gesture she'd found oddly comforting during some of the tougher periods of her life—like now.

Strange how most of those times had found her wearing surgical gloves.

Studying Ben as he worked, Tracy was surprised by the slight dusting of grey in his thick brown hair. She gave herself a mental shake. The man was thirty-eight, and she hadn't set eyes on him in four years. Change was inevitable. What hadn't changed, however, were the electric blue eyes, compliments of his American mother, or how they provided the perfect counterpoint for tanned skin, high cheekbones and a straight, autocratic nose—all legacies from his Brazilian father. Neither had he lost any of that intense focus she'd once found so intimidating.

And irresistible.

Snap out of it, Tracy.

She donned the scrubs, booties and surgical gear Ben had left out for her and moved into the glassed-in cubicle where he was busy setting up.

"Close the door, please, so I can seal it off."

"Seal it off?" Swallowing hard, she hesitated then did as he asked.

"Just with this." He held up a roll of clear packing tape. "Is your claustrophobia going to be a problem?"

She hoped not, but feeling trapped had always set off a rolling sense of panic that could quickly snowball if she wasn't careful. It didn't matter whether the confinement was physical or emotional, the fear was the same. Glancing through the door to the reception area, she noted the exit to the outside world was plainly visible even from where she stood. "As long as I know there's a door right through there, I should be fine. The room being made of glass helps."

"Good."

Ben taped the edges of the door, before removing the insulated bag from the fridge and examining the labels on each tube inside. Selecting two of them, he put the rest back in cold storage.

"What do you want me to do?" Tracy asked.

"Set up some slides. We're going to work our way from simple to complex."

He turned one of the tubes to the side and read her label out loud. "Daniel, male, twelve years." He paused. "Living?"

"Yes." Her heart twisted when she thought of the pre-teen boy staring at her with terrified eyes. But at least he was alive. As was his younger sister Cleo. Their mother, however, hadn't been so lucky. Hers had been one of the first bodies they'd found in the village. "Febrile. No skin lesions visible."

"Signs of pneumonia?"

"Not yet, which is why this seemed so strange. Most of the dead had complained to relatives of coughs along with fever and malaise."

"Liver enlargement in the dead?"

She swallowed. "No autopsies, remember? The military destroyed everything." Her voice cracked.

Ben's gloved hand covered hers, and even through the layers of latex the familiar warmth of his touch comforted her in a way no one else ever could. "Why don't you get those slides ready, while I set up the centrifuge?"

Glad to have something to take her mind off the horrific scene she and Pedro had stumbled on in São João dos Rios, she pulled several clean slides from the box and spread them across the table. Then, carefully taking the cotton swab from Ben's outstretched hand, she smeared a thin layer of material on the smooth glass surface. "What are you looking for?"

"Anything. Everything." The tense muscle in his jaw made her wonder if he already had a theory. "You'll need to heat-set the slides as you smear them."

He lit a small burner and showed her how to pass the slide across the flame to dry it and affix the specimen to the glass.

The sound of a throat clearing in the outer doorway made them both look up. Their guard cupped his hands over his mouth and said in a loud voice, "Your assistant has arrived safely at her home."

Ben flashed a thumbs-up sign. "Thanks for letting me know."

Tracy's fingers tensed on the slide at the mention of Ben's assistant, which was ridiculous. Yes, the woman had kissed him, but Brazilians kissed everyone—it was a kind of unspoken rule in these parts. Besides, the woman had a family. A new baby.

Her throat tightened, a sense of loss sweeping over her. Ben had wanted children so badly. So had she. When she'd fallen pregnant, they'd both been elated. Until she'd had a devastating piece of news that had set her back on her heels. She'd thrown herself into her work, angering Ben, even as she'd tried to figure out a way to tell him.

That had all changed when he'd sent the military in to force her out of a stricken village during a yellow fever outbreak. She knew he'd been trying to protect her and the baby—not from the disease itself, as she'd already been vaccinated the previous year, but from anything that had taken her out of his sight. She hadn't need protecting, though. She'd needed to work. It had been her lifeline in a time of turmoil and confusion, and his interference had damaged her trust. She'd miscarried a week later, and the rift that had opened between them during their disagreement over the military had grown deeper, with accusations flying fast and furious on both sides.

In the end she'd opted to keep her secret to herself. Telling him would have changed nothing, not when she'd already decided to leave.

Work was still her number-one priority. Still her lifeline. And she needed to get her mind back on what she was doing.

Tracy took the long cotton swab and dipped it into another of her sample jars, laying a thin coating of the material on a second glass slide, heat-setting it, like she'd done with the first. "Do you need me to apply a stain?"

"Let's see what we've got on these first."

"There were pigs in a corral at one of the victims' homes. Could it be leptospirosis?"

"Possibly." He switched on the microscope's light. "If I can't find anything on the slides, we'll need to do some cultures. Lepto will show up there."

He didn't say it, but they both knew cultures would take several days, if not longer, to grow.

Tracy sent a nervous glance towards the reception area, where the guard lounged in a white plastic chair in full view. He twirled what looked like a toothpick between his thumb and forefinger. For the moment his attention wasn't focused on them. And he was far enough away that he shouldn't be able to hear soft voices through the glass partition.

"That could be a problem."

Ben turned toward her, watchful eyes moving over her face. "How so?"

"I told the military police you'd have an answer for them today."

"You did *what*?" His hand clenched on the edge of the table. "Of all the irresponsible—"

"I know, I know. I didn't have a choice. It was either that or leave São João dos Rios empty-handed."

He closed his eyes for a few seconds before looking at her again. "You're still hauling around that savior complex, aren't you, Tracy? Don't you get tired of being the one who swoops in to save the day?"

"I thought that was *your* role. Taking charge even when it's not your decision to make." She tossed her head. "Maybe if you'd stopped thinking about yourself for once…" As soon as the ugly words spurted out she gritted her teeth, staunching the flow. "I'm sorry. That was uncalled for."

"Yes. It was." He took the slide from her and set it down with an audible *crack*.

The guard was on his feet in an instant, his casual manner gone. *"O que foi?"*

Ben held up the slide. "Sorry. Just dropped it." Although he said the words loudly enough for the guard to hear them, he kept his tone calm and even. Even so, the tension in his white-knuckled grip was unmistakable.

The guard rolled his eyes, his face relaxing. "I'm going to the cafeteria. Do you want something?"

How exactly did the man expect to get the food past the sealed doorway? Besides, she wouldn't be able to eat if her life depended on it. "I'm good. Thanks."

"Same here," said Ben.

The guard shrugged and then checked the front door. He palmed the old-fashioned key he found in the lock before reinserting it again, this time on the outside of the door.

He meant to lock them in!

"No, wait!" Tracy stood, not exactly sure how she could stop him.

"Sorry, but I have my orders. Neither of you leaves until those samples are destroyed."

She started to argue further, but Ben touched her shoulder. "Don't," he said in a low voice.

Holding her tongue, she watched helplessly as the door swung shut, a menacing snick of the lock telling her the guard had indeed imprisoned them inside the room. A familiar sting of panic went up her spine. "What if he doesn't come back? What if we're trapped?"

Stripping off one of his gloves, he reached into his pocket. "I have a spare. I know you don't like being confined."

Sagging in relief, she managed a shaky laugh. "You learned that the hard way, didn't you?"

The vivid image of Ben playfully pinning her hands above her head while they'd tussled on the bed sprang to her mind. The love play had been fun. At first. Then a wave of terror had washed over her unexpectedly, and though she'd known her panic had been illogical, she'd begun to struggle in earnest.

A frightened plea had caught in her throat, and as hard as she'd tried to say something, her voice had seemed as frozen as her senses. Ben had only realized she was no longer playing when she succeeded in freeing one of her hands and raked her nails down his face. He'd reeled backwards, while she'd lain there, her chest heaving, tears of relief spilling from her eyes. Understanding had dawned on his face and he'd gathered her into his arms, murmuring how sorry he was. From that moment forward he'd been careful to avoid anything that might make her feel trapped.

A little too careful.

His lovemaking had become less intense and more controlled. Only it had been a different kind of control than what they'd previously enjoyed, when Ben's take-charge demeanor in the bedroom had been a huge turn-on. That had all changed. Tracy had mourned the loss of passion, even as she'd appreciated his reasons for keeping a little more space between them. Her inability to explain where the line between confinement and intimacy lay had driven the first wedge between them.

That wedge had widened later, when he'd tried to limit her movements during her pregnancy, giving rise to the same sensation of being suffocated. She'd clawed at him just as hard then, the marks invisible but causing just as much damage to their marriage.

The Ben of the present fingered the side of his face and gave her a smile. "No permanent damage done."

Yeah, there had been. And it seemed that one patch of bad luck had spiraled into another.

"I always felt terrible about that," she said.

"I should have realized you were scared."

"You couldn't have known."

Even her father hadn't realized their play sessions could change without warning. There'd always been laughter, but the sound of hers had often turned shrill with overtones of panic. A gentle soul, her father would have never hurt her in a million years. It didn't help that her older sister had been a tough-as-nails tomboy who'd feared nothing and had given as good as she'd got. Then Tracy had come along—always fearful, always more cautious. Her father had never quite known what to do with her.

She was still fearful. Still flinched away from situations that made her feel trapped and out of control.

And now her mom and her sister were both gone. Her mom, the victim of a menacing villain who'd stalked its prey relentlessly—turning the delicate strands of a person's DNA into the enemy. Passed from mother to daughter. Tracy had been running from its specter ever since.

Ben donned a fresh glove and picked up the slide he'd smacked against the table, checking it for cracks. Without glancing up at her, he said, "You look tired. I put the folding cot in the corner in case we needed to sleep in shifts. If I know you, you didn't get much rest last night."

"I'm okay." He was right. She was exhausted, but no way would she let him know how easily he could still read her. Or how the touch of concern in his voice made her heart skip a beat. "It's just warm in here."

"I know. The air-conditioner in the lab is ancient, and the filter doesn't let much of it through, anyway."

Even as he said it, a tiny trickle of sweat coursed down her back. "It's fine."

He pushed the slide beneath the viewer of the microscope and focused on the smear. "How old are the samples?"

"Just a couple of hours."

He swore softly as he continued to peer through the lens, evidently seeing something he didn't like. He took the second slide and repeated the process, his right hand shifting a knob on the side of the instrument repeatedly. Sitting up, he dabbed at perspiration that had gathered around his eye with the sleeve of his lab coat then leaned back in for another look.

"What is it?" She felt her own blood rushing through her ears as she awaited the verdict.

It didn't take long. He lifted his head and fastened his eyes on hers. "If I'm not mistaken, it's pneumonic plague, Tracy." Shifting his attention to the test tube in her hand, he continued, "And if you're the one who took these samples, you've already been exposed."

CHAPTER THREE

TRACY SAGGED AND swallowed hard, trying to process what he'd said through her own fear. "Are you sure?"

"Here." He moved aside so she could look at the slide.

Putting her eye to the viewfinder, she squinted into the machine. "What am I looking for?"

"See the little dots grouped into chains?"

"Yes." There were several of them.

"That's what we're dealing with. I want to look at another sample and do a culture, just in case, but I'm sure. It's *Yersinia pestis*, the same bacterium that causes bubonic plague. I recognize the shape." He rolled his shoulders as if relieving an ache. "Bubonic plague normally spreads from infected rats through the bite of a flea, but if the bacteria migrate to a person's lungs, it becomes even more deadly, spreading rapidly from person to person by way of a cough or bodily fluids. When that happens, the disease no longer needs a flea. We'll want to put you on a strong dose of streptomycin immediately."

"What about you?"

"I'll start on them as well, but just as a precaution." Ben dripped a staining solution on another slide. "Most of the people who work in the lab are vaccinated against the plague, including Mandy. But I assume you haven't been."

"No, which means neither has... Oh, God." She rested

her head against Ben's shoulder for a second as a wave of nausea rolled over her. "That town. I have to get back there. They've all been exposed. So has Pedro."

"Pedro?"

"*My* assistant."

Just as he pushed the slide back under the microscope, the lock to the outer door clicked open before Tracy had a chance to figure out how to proceed.

The guard pushed his way inside, glancing from one to the other, his eyes narrowing in on her face. She sat up straighter.

"Problema?" he asked.

Instead of lunch, he only held a coffee cup in his hand.

A tug on the back of her shirt sent a warning Tracy read loud and clear, *Don't tell him anything until I've taken another look.* The gesture surprised her, as he'd always been buddy-buddy with the military, at least from what she'd seen over the course of their marriage.

Still holding one of the slides, he casually laid it on the table. "We need to run a few more tests before we know anything for sure."

"No need. Our doctors have isolated the infection and will take the appropriate containment measures."

Containment? What exactly did that mean?

Her brows lifted in challenge. "What is the illness, then?" Maybe he was bluffing.

"I'm not at liberty to say. But my commander would like to speak with Dr. Almeida over the phone." He gave Tracy a pointed stare. "Alone."

A shiver went over her. Alone. Why?

What if the government doctors had come to a different conclusion than Ben had? What if they were assuming it was something other than the plague? People could still die...still pass it on to neighboring towns. And São João dos Rios was poor. How many people would lose loved ones due to lack of information?

Just like she had. She knew the pain of that firsthand.

She'd lost her mother. Her grandmother. Her sister—although Vickie's illness hadn't been related to a genetic defect. The most devastating loss of all, however, had been her unborn child. Ben's baby.

All had died far too young. And Tracy had decided she wasn't going to waste a second of her time on earth waiting around for what-ifs. Movement, in her eyes, equaled life. So she'd lived that life with a ferocity that others couldn't begin to understand.

Including Ben.

Genetic code might not be written in stone, but its deadly possibility loomed in front of her, as did a decision she might someday choose to make. But until then she was determined to make a difference in the lives of those around her.

Or maybe you're simply running away.

Like she had with Ben? No, their break-up had been for entirely different reasons.

Had it?

She pushed the voice in her head aside. "Why does he want to talk to Dr. Almeida alone?"

"That's not for me to say." The guard nodded towards the bag. "Those samples must be destroyed."

"We'll take care of it." Her husband's voice was calm. Soothing. Just as Zen-like as ever. Just as she imagined it would have been had she told him about the life-changing decision she was wrestling with.

And his icy unflappability drove her just as crazy now as it had during their last fight.

How could he take everything in his stride?

Because it was part of who he was. He'd grown up in Brazil…was more Brazilian than American in a lot of ways.

As Ben stripped the tape from around the door and sanitized his hands before stepping into the hallway with the guard, Tracy sighed. She never knew what he was thinking. Even during their marriage he'd been tight-lipped about a lot of things. But as aloof as he'd been at times, she'd sensed something in him yearning for what he hadn't had when growing up: the closeness of a family.

It still hurt that she hadn't been able to give that to him. That even as she was driven to work harder and harder by the loss of her baby and by whatever time bomb might be ticking inside her, she was gradually becoming the very thing he despised in his parents.

Her sister had died never knowing whether or not she carried the defective gene. It hadn't been cancer that had claimed Vickie's life but dengue fever—a disease that was endemic in Brazil. She'd been pregnant at the time of her death. Her husband had been devastated at losing both of them. As had she. But at least Vickie had been spared the agonizing uncertainty over whether or not she'd passed a cancer gene down to her child.

As much as Tracy had feared doing just that during her pregnancy, she'd never in her weakest moments wished harm to come to her unborn child. And yet she'd lost the baby anyway, as if even the fates knew what a bad idea it was for her to reproduce.

Her vision suddenly went blurry, and she blinked in an effort to clear her head from those painful thoughts. As she did, she realized Ben and the guard had come back into the room and were now staring at her.

"What?" she asked, mentally daring him to say anything about her moist eyes.

Ben's gaze sharpened, but he said nothing. "I need to

leave for São João dos Rios. Do you want me to drop you off at the airport on my way out of town?"

"Excuse me?"

Why would she need to go to the airport? Unless…

No way!

Her hands went to her hips. "I'm going with you."

Both Ben and the guard spoke at once, their voices jumbled. She caught the gist of it, however. Evidently Ben had been invited to go but she hadn't been.

Outrage crowded her chest. "I'm the one who took the samples. I've already been out there."

"And exposed yourself to the plague in the process."

"Exactly." Her hands dropped back to her sides, palms out. "I've already been exposed. And I'm a doctor, Ben. I've spent my life fighting outbreaks like this one. I should be there."

His voice cooled. "It's not up to me this time."

"*This* time. Unlike the time you sent your goons into that village with orders to send me packing?" She almost spit the words at him. "My assistant is still in São João dos Rios. I am not leaving him out there alone."

Stepping around Ben, she focused on the guard. "I'd like to speak with your superior."

The man blinked several times, as if he couldn't believe she was daring to defy whatever orders he'd received. "I'm afraid that's not possible—"

Ben's fingers went around her upper arm and squeezed. "Let me talk to her for a minute."

Practically dragging her to the other side of the room, his stony gaze fastened on her face. "What are you doing?"

"I already told you. I'm doing my job."

"The military wants to handle this their way. They'll go in and treat those who aren't too far gone and make sure this doesn't spread beyond São João dos Rios."

"Those who aren't too far gone? My God, stop and listen to yourself for a minute. We're talking about human beings—about children like Daniel and Cleo, who are now orphans. They deserve someone there who will fight for them."

"You think I don't care about those children? I was the one who wanted you to slow down during your pregnancy, to..." He paused for several long seconds then lowered his voice. "I care just as much about those villagers as you do."

His surgeon's scalpel cut deep. She could guess what he'd been about to say before he'd checked himself. He still thought her actions had cost the life of their child. And the worst thing was that she couldn't say with any certainty that he was wrong. She'd worked herself harder than ever after she'd had the results back from the genetic testing—struggling to beat back the familiar sensation of being trapped. But that wasn't something she wanted to get into right now.

"Let me go with you." She twisted out of his grasp so she could turn and face him. "Please. You have pull with these guys, I know you do. Call the commander back, whoever he is, and tell him you need me."

He dragged a hand through his hair then shook his head. "I'm asking you to walk away, Tracy. Just this once. You don't know how bad things might get before it's over."

"I do know. That's why I need to be there. Those two kids have already lost their mother. I want to help make sure they don't lose their lives as well."

She was not going to let some government bureaucrat— or even Ben—decide they were a lost cause. "I'll take antibiotics while I'm there. I'll do whatever the government people tell me to do. Besides, like I said before, my assistant is still in the middle of it."

She couldn't explain to him that she really did need to be there. This was part of what being alive meant—fighting battles for others that she might not be able to fight for her-self. She took a deep breath. "Please, don't make me beg."

A brief flicker of something went across his face then was gone. "Listen, I know—" Before he could finish the guard appeared in front of them, tapping his hat against his thigh, clearly impatient to be gone. "We need to leave."

Tracy kept her pleading gaze focused on Ben. *He had to let her go. He just had to.*

Ben swore and then broke eye contact. "Call General Gutierrez and tell him we're on our way. Both of us."

The man didn't bat an eyelid. "I'll let him know."

Exactly how much influence did Ben have with these officials? She knew his salary came from the government, but to say something like that and expect it to be accepted without question…

She swallowed. "Thank you."

Jaw tight, Ben ignored her and addressed the guard again. "We'll follow you out to the village once I've de-stroyed the samples. We need to use my four-wheel drive to haul some equipment."

The guard swept his hat onto his head before relaying the message to his superiors. When he finished the call, he said, "My commander will have someone meet you at the town square and direct you to the triage area they've set up. But you must hurry."

Ben nodded. "Tell them we'll be there within three hours."

"Vai com Deus."

The common "Go with God" farewell had an ominous ring to it—as if the man had crossed himself in an attempt to ward off evil. And pneumonic plague was all that and more. Its cousin had killed off large swaths of the world's population in the past.

Despite her misgivings about working with Ben again,

a couple of muscles in her stomach relaxed. At least she wouldn't have to fight this particular battle on her own.

Ben would be there with her.

And if he found out the truth about the genetic testing she'd had done before their separation?

Then she would deal with it. Just as she'd dealt with the loss of her baby and her own uncertain prognosis.

Alone.

As they hurried to finish loading his vehicle, a streak of lightning darted across the sky, pausing to lick the trunk of a nearby tree before sliding back into the clouds. The smell of singed wood reached Ben a few seconds later, followed by an ominous rumble that made the ground tremble.

Tracy, who stood beside him, shuddered. "Only in *Teresina*."

He smiled. "Remember the city's nickname? *Chapada do corisco:* flash-lightning flatlands. If ever lightning was going to strike twice in the same spot, it would be here." He shut the back of the grey four-wheel-drive vehicle. "I'd rather not put that theory to the test, though, so, if you're ready to go, hop in."

She climbed into the SUV and buckled in, staring in the direction the jagged flash had come from. "That poor tree looks like it's lightning's favorite prom date, judging from the color."

Scarred from multiple strikes over the years, it stubbornly clung to life, clusters of green leaves scattered along its massive branches. Ben had no idea how it had survived so many direct hits.

Their marriage certainly hadn't been as lucky.

He got behind the wheel and started the car. "It'll eventually have to come down."

"Through no fault of its own," she murmured. "It's sad."

Was she thinking of what had happened between them? It had taken every ounce of strength he'd had after she'd left, but he'd forced himself to keep living. In reality, though, she had been gone long before she'd actually moved out of the house. He'd accepted it and moved forward.

Right.

That's why he was on his way to São João dos Rios right now, with Tracy in tow. He should have just shut her down and said no. General Gutierrez would have backed him in his decision. So why hadn't he?

"You sure you want to do this? The airport is on our way. We could still have you on a flight to São Paulo in a jiffy."

She jerked in her seat, gripping the webbing of the seat belt before shifting to look at him. "I can't just turn my back on the town. That's not how I operate."

Really? It had seemed all too easy for her to turn her back on him. But saying so wouldn't help anyone.

They reached the entrance to the highway, and Ben sighed when he saw metal barricades stretched across its width.

The four-lane road—long under construction—was still not finished.

He coasted down a steep incline to reach the so-called official detour, which consisted of a narrow dirt track running parallel to the road. It looked more like a gully from water run-off than an actual street. As far as the eye could see, where the highway should have been there was now a long stretch of hard-packed orange clay that was impassable. At the moment trucks seemed to be the only vehicles braving the washboard tract Ben and Tracy were forced to use. Then again, there was no other option. Most things, including food, were moved from city to city via semi-tractor-trailers. And with the current conditions of the highway it was no wonder things were so expensive in northeastern Brazil.

"How long have they been working on this?" Tracy asked.

"Do you really need to ask?"

"No. But it *was* paved the last time I was here."

They'd spent most of their marriage in *Teresina*, the capital of the state of *Piaui*. He'd rearranged his job so he could stay in one place. Ben thought Tracy had been willing to do the same. How wrong he'd been.

She *had* come off the medical boat and put someone else in her place, but that was about the only concession she'd made to their marriage. By the time he'd realized she was never going to slow down, he'd lost more than just his wife.

"Yes, it was paved, after a fashion." He grimaced. "I think the shoulder we're on is in better shape than the highway was back then."

Ben slowed to navigate a particularly bad stretch where torrential rains had worn a deep channel into the dirt. "Well, some parts of it, anyway."

"My car would never survive the trip."

He smiled. "Are you still driving that little tin can?"

"Rhonda gets great gas mileage."

His gut twisted. He could still remember the laughter they'd shared over Tracy's insistence on keeping her ragamuffin car when they'd got married, despite the hazardous stretches of road in Teresina. To his surprise, the little vehicle had been sturdier than it had appeared, bumping along the worst of the cobblestone streets with little more than an occasional hiccup. Like the bumper she'd lost on a visit to one of the neighboring *aldéias*. She'd come back with the thing strapped to the roof. He smiled. When he'd suggested it was time to trade the vehicle in, she'd refused, patting the bonnet and saying the car had seen her through some tough spots.

His smile faded. Funny how her loyalty to her car hadn't been mirrored in her marriage.

He cast around for a different subject, but Tracy got there first.

"How's Marcelo doing?"

Ben's brother was the new chief of neurosurgery over at Teresina's main hospital. "He's fine. Still as opinionated as ever."

She smiled. "Translated to mean he's still single."

"Always will be, if he has his way." He glanced over at her. "What about you? How's *Projeto Vida* going?" The medical-aid ship that had brought them together was still Tracy's pet project.

"Wonderfully. Matt is back on the team and has a baby girl now."

Tracy's sister had died years ago, leaving her husband, Matt, heartbroken. "He remarried?"

"Yep. Two years ago." She paused. "Stevie…Stephani, actually, is great. She loves the job and fits right into the team."

"I'm glad. Matt seemed like a nice guy." Ben had met him on several occasions when they'd traveled to *Coari* to deliver supplies or check on the medical boat.

"He is. It's good to see him happy again."

Which was more than he could say about Tracy. Maybe it was the stress of what she'd been dealing with in São João dos Rios, but the dark circles under her green eyes worried him. He glanced to the side for a quick peek. The rest of her looked exactly as he remembered, though. Long, silky black hair that hung just below her shoulders. The soft fringe of bangs that fluttered whenever the flow from the air-conditioning vent caught the strands. Lean, tanned legs encased in khaki shorts.

And as much as he wished otherwise, being near her again made him long for family and normalcy all over again. He'd always thought she would bring stability to his life, help to counteract his tumultuous upbringing. His parents had drifted here and there, always searching for a new adventure while leaving their two young sons in the care of their housekeeper. In many ways, Ben had felt closer to Rosa than to his own mother, so much so that he'd kept her on at his house long after his parents had moved to the States on a permanent basis.

He'd thought life with Tracy would be different. That their children would have the close-knit family he'd always longed for as a kid. But Tracy, once the first blush of their marriage had faded, had started traveling again, always finding some new medical crisis to deal with, whether with *Projeto Vida* or somewhere else.

He could understand being married to your career— after all, he was pretty attached to his—but he'd learned to do it from one central location. Surely Tracy could have done the same.

Instead, with every month that had passed, the same feelings of abandonment he'd had as a kid had taken root and grown, as had his resentment. And once she'd fallen pregnant, she'd seemed more obsessed about work than ever, spending longer and longer periods away from home.

When he'd learned she was dealing with a yellow fever outbreak in one of the villages he'd finally snapped and called his old friend General Gutierrez—despite the fact that he knew Tracy been vaccinated against the disease. His ploy had worked. Tracy had come home. But their marriage had been over, even before she'd lost the baby.

So why hadn't he just settled down with someone else,

like Tracy had suggested a few hours earlier? Marriage wasn't exactly a requirement these days. And why hadn't Tracy finally asked for a divorce and been done with it?

Questions he was better off not asking.

"What's the time frame for pneumonic plague?"

Her question jolted him back to the present. "From exposure to presentation of symptoms? Two days, on average. Although death can take anywhere from thirty-six hours after exposure to a week or more. It depends on whether or not other organ systems besides the lungs have been compromised."

"Oh, no."

"Speaking of which, I've brought packets of antibiotics in that black gym bag I threw in the back. Go ahead and dig through it and take a dose before we get there."

Tracy unhooked her seat belt and twisted until she could reach the backseat. She then pulled out one of the boxes of medicine and popped a pill from the protective foil. She downed it with a swig from her water bottle then shoved a couple of strands of hair back from her temple. "You have no idea how glad I am that you were able figure it out so quickly."

"I think I do." Surely she realized he was just as relieved as she was. "Not everyone has the equipment we do."

"Or the backing of the military."

He ignored the bitterness that colored her words. "Part of the reality of living in a developing country. We'll catch up with the rest of the world, eventually. Marcelo's hospital is a great example of that. It's completely funded by sources outside the government."

"So is *Projeto Vida*." She paused when they hit another rough patch of road, her hand scrabbling for the grip attached to the ceiling. "Speaking of funding, we'll need to check with the nearest pharmacist to make sure they have enough antibiotics on hand. I'll pay for more, if need be."

"I was already planning to help with the costs." He glanced over and their eyes caught for a second. When he turned his attention back to the road, her fingers slid over the hand he had resting on the emergency brake before retreating.

"Thank you, Ben," she said. "For letting me come. And for caring about what happens to those people."

He swallowed, her words and the warmth of her fingers penetrating the icy wall he'd built up over the last four years.

It wasn't exactly the thing that peace treaties were made of, but he got the feeling that Tracy had just initiated talks.

And had thrown the ball squarely into his court.

CHAPTER FOUR

MILITARY VEHICLES BLOCKED the road to São João dos Rios—uniformed personnel, guns at the ready, stood beside the vehicles.

"They're not taking any chances," Ben muttered as he slowed the car on the dirt track.

"In this case, caution is probably a good thing." As much as Tracy worried about the presence of the Brazilian army, she also knew the country's military had helped ease Brazil's transition from a Portuguese colony to an independent nation. Not a drop of blood had been shed on either side. The two countries were still on good terms, in fact.

There was no reason to fear their presence. Not really. At least, that's what she told herself.

Ben powered down his window and flashed his residence card, identifying both of them. "General Gutierrez is expecting us."

The soldier checked a handwritten list on his clipboard and nodded. "You've been told what you're dealing with?"

No. They'd been told nothing other than Ben being asked to come, but Tracy wasn't sure how much this particular soldier knew. She didn't want to start a mass panic.

Ben nodded. "We're aware. We brought masks and equipment."

She didn't contradict him or try to add to his words. She

knew he'd done quite a bit of work for the military and he'd probably identified many other pathogens for them in the past. They had also taken the time to track her down and challenge her work four years ago, when Ben had asked them to, something that still had the power to make her hackles rise.

The soldier nodded. "I'll need to search your vehicle. General Gutierrez said there were to be no exceptions. So if you'll both step out, please."

Ben glanced her way, before putting the car in neutral—leaving the engine running and nodding at her to get out. He handed her a mask and donned one himself as he climbed from the vehicle.

The soldier looked in the backseat. He then gave the dizzying array of equipment they were carrying a cursory glance but didn't open any of the boxes. He seemed to be looking for stowaways more than anything, which seemed crazy. Who would want to sneak into a plague-infested area? Then again, she'd heard of crazier things, and nobody wanted this disease to get out of the village and into one of the bigger cities. *Teresina* wasn't all that far away, when you thought about it.

Ben came to stand next to her, and she noticed he was careful not to touch her. She swallowed. Not that she wanted him to. She'd had no idea they'd be thrown together in a situation like the one they were currently facing. But despite the pain that seeing him again brought, she couldn't have asked for a better, or more qualified, work partner.

She heard her name being called and turned towards the sound. Pedro hurried toward them, only to be stopped by another soldier about fifty yards before he reached them. The man's point came across loud and clear. Once she and Ben crossed this particular line, there'd be no going back until it was all over. Who knew how long that could be?

"Ben, are you sure you want to do this? You can drop me off and go back to Teresina. There's no reason to risk yourself and all your work."

A muscle spasmed in his jaw, his eyes on Pedro. "*My* name was the one on the dance card, remember?" He shoved his hands in his pockets. "Besides, this is part of my job. It's why I work at the institute."

"Yes, well…" She didn't know how to finish the statement, since her reasons for wanting him to go back to the safe confines of his office was nothing more than a bid to keep her distance. She'd used his invitation as a way to regain access to the town, but she was also smart enough to know they might need his expertise before this was all over. So she held her tongue.

She glanced back at the soldier, who was currently peering beneath the car at its chassis.

Really? The guy had been watching way too many TV shows.

"Can I go in while you keep looking? My assistant is motioning to me, and I want to start checking on the patients." Daniel and Cleo were in there somewhere.

The soldier waved her through, even as he switched on a flashlight and continued looking.

"Tracy…" Ben, forced to wait for his vehicle to pass inspection, gave her a warning growl, but she shrugged him off.

"I'll meet you once you get through the checkpoint. Don't let them confiscate the antibiotics."

And with that, she made her escape. Securing her mask and feeling guilty, she stepped around the line of military vehicles and met Pedro, pulling him a safe distance away from the soldier who'd stopped him.

"It's pneumonic plague," she whispered, switching to Portuguese while noting he was already wearing a mask. "You'll need to start on antibiotics immediately."

"I thought so. They're staying pretty tight-lipped about the whole thing, but they've set up a quarantine area. Those who are ill have been kept separate from those who still appear healthy—which aren't many at this point."

"Any more deaths? How are Daniel and Cleo?"

"Who?"

"The two kids we found in the field."

Daniel, the boy she'd taken samples from, had been lying in a grassy area, too weak to stand and walk. His sister, showing signs of the illness as well, had refused to leave his side. They'd carried them back to an empty house, just as the military had shown up and taken over.

"No change in the boy, although there have been two more deaths."

"And Cleo?"

"She's definitely got it, but now that we know what we're dealing with, we can start them both on treatment." Pedro slung his arm around her and squeezed. "Can I say how glad I am to see you? These soldier boys are some scary dudes."

He said the last line in English, using his best American accent, which made Tracy smile. She glanced over at Ben, who was still glowering at her, and her smile died.

The soldiers weren't the only scary dudes.

Pedro continued, "The military docs have IVs going on some of the patients, but they wouldn't tell me what they injected into the lines."

"Strange." She glanced at one of the houses, which currently had a small contingent of guards at the doors and windows. "Did they say anything about antibiotics?"

"I think they're still trying to get a handle on things."

Ben joined them on foot, and she frowned at him. "Where's your car?"

"They're going to drive it in and park it in front of one

of the houses. They've evidently got a research area already set up."

He glanced at Pedro, whose arm was still around her, obviously waiting for an introduction. Okay, this was going to be fun. She noticed Pedro also seemed to be assessing Ben, trying to figure out what his place was in all this. He'd never asked about her ring, and she'd never volunteered any information. Several people had assumed she was widowed, and she'd just let it ride. Maybe she could simply omit Ben's relationship to her.

Well, that would be easy enough, because there was no relationship.

"Ben, this is Pedro, my assistant." She hesitated. "Pedro, this is Ben, head epidemiologist at the *Centro de Doenças Tropicais* in Teresina. He's the one I went to see." Maybe no one would notice that she'd conveniently left out his last name. Not that she went by it any more.

Ben held out his hand. "Ben Almeida. Nice to meet you." He slid Tracy a smile that said he knew exactly what she'd done and why. "I also happen to be Tracy's husband."

The look of shock in her assistant's eyes was unmistakable, and he quickly removed his arm from around her shoulders. He shot her a look but dutifully shook hands and muttered something appropriate. She, on the other hand, sent Ben a death stare meant to cut him in two. Instead, he seemed totally unfazed by her ire.

Ben nodded. "I've heard Tracy's account of what happened here. Why don't you tell me what you've observed?"

It was said as if she was clueless. Pressure began building in the back of her head.

Her assistant knew better. "Well, she's probably told you more than I could. We've got about fifteen cases of… Tracy said it's pneumonic plague?"

"Yes." Ben's eyes followed the progress of some men

in hazard gear as they went from one building to another. "And judging from the way they're treating it, they know what they're dealing with. Are they still burning the bodies?"

"Yes. Two more in the last couple of hours," Pedro said.

"The boy whose sample I brought in—Daniel—is still alive, but he's pretty sick. His sister is as well."

She didn't need to say what else she knew: antibiotics needed to be started within twenty-four hours of the appearance of symptoms to be effective. Ben would already know that. The treatment window was narrow, but she wouldn't give up, no matter how sick the patient.

Tracy ached for the two children, their mother ripped from them without so much as a funeral service or a chance to say goodbye. Just thrown onto a flaming pyre to destroy any pathogens. How many other kids would watch helplessly as the same thing happened to their relatives? As much as she knew it had to be done, it still didn't make it any easier. How would she feel if the body being burned was Ben's?

No. Not Ben. She wouldn't let her mind go there.

"Where are they putting you up for the night?" she asked Pedro.

"They've got medical civilians in one house and military personnel in another. They post guards out front of both of them, though."

Ben's four-wheel drive pulled up beside them and the soldier poked his head out of the open window. "I'm taking your vehicle to the research center we've set up. Do you want a ride?"

"We'll follow on foot," Ben said. Tracy got the idea, he wanted to continue their conversation in private. "And if you could put Dr. Hinton in the same house as me, I'd appreciate it. I haven't seen my wife in quite a while and would like some alone time with her if possible." He quirked an eyebrow at the man, while reaching over and taking her hand in his and giving it a warning squeeze. The presumption of his move made the rising pressure in her head grow to dangerous levels.

Her poor assistant squirmed visibly.

If Pedro hadn't been beside them, she'd have made it plain how little contact—of any sort—she wanted with him. But she knew Ben well enough to know he didn't say or do anything without a good reason.

The driver grinned and promised to see what he could do.

But, oh, she was going to let Ben know she was *not* happy with that arrangement. She hadn't wanted anyone to know what their relationship was, and now everyone in town would be snickering behind their backs.

"Nice work," she hissed.

Pedro shifted from foot to foot. "I'm sorry, I had no idea you were... I just assumed you were..."

"Single?" Ben supplied, an edge to his voice.

Wow, was he actually doing this? He'd never expressed any hint of jealousy when they'd been together. And she didn't appreciate it now.

"No, not exactly. I just knew she didn't have anyone living with her."

Ben's brows lifted. "You knew that for a fact, did you?"

"Well, yes. W-we had staff meetings at her house on a regular basis."

Tracy took a closer look at her assistant's face. There was discomfiture and something else lurking in his brown eyes. Oh God. Surely he wasn't interested in her. She'd never given him any reason to think she might be remotely attracted to him.

At least, she hoped she hadn't. And yet Ben had automatically assumed Pedro might have his eye on her. Why would he even care?

She touched Pedro's arm. "Ben and I…well, it's complicated."

Complicated. It was. At least for her. And Ben had probably never forgiven her for walking away from their marriage without a word. But what could she have said, really?

Not only do I not want to get pregnant again, I might choose to have my non-cancerous breasts removed.

She could still explain, if she wanted to. But after the way he'd run roughshod over her four years ago, going behind her back and manipulating her into coming home, he'd pretty much snuffed out any feelings of guilt on her part.

Ben had been part of the reason she'd struggled with making a final decision about what to do about her test results. But now that he and the baby were no longer part of the equation, she'd put things on hold, choosing to make a difference in the lives of others instead.

Dragging her attention back to Pedro, she tried her best to finish her earlier statement. Putting more emphasis on the words than was strictly necessary, she wanted to make sure she got her point across to both of them.

"Ben and I are separated. We have been for quite some time. So anything that happens between us will be strictly business."

Now, if she could just convince herself of that, she should be good to go.

CHAPTER FIVE

There was a reason it was called the Black Death.

There was nothing pretty or romantic about the plague. And the pneumonic form of the disease was the most dangerous, rapidly killing those it touched.

Ben stepped into the tiny house where the patients were being housed, and he fought a wave of pure desolation as he looked over the place. Tracy seemed just as shocked, standing motionless in the doorway beside her assistant.

Simple green cots were packed into what used to be a living room, laid out in two rows with barely enough space between beds for doctors to work.

Ben counted silently. Fourteen patients. And not all of them had IVs started. In fact, when he looked closer, he saw that the wall over some of the cots had a crude "X" penned in black ink.

A chill went over him. Deathbeds.

His gaze moved further and he spotted two men he assumed were doctors, still wearing that hazard gear he'd spotted earlier. The pair stood on either side of a bed, assessing a woman who was wailing, the sound coming in fits and starts that were interrupted by coughing spasms. One of the men leaned past the patient and slashed a mark over the bed.

Just like that. Bile pumped into his stomach in a flood.

Tracy's gaze met his, her eyes reflecting pure horror. She reached out and gripped Pedro's sleeve. "So many."

The man nodded. "I know."

None of the trio had on the protective clothing worn by the other doctors, other than masks and latex gloves, but as Tracy was on antibiotics and Pedro had just been given his first dose, there was no need. He assumed the heavy gear worn by the other men would be done away with pretty soon.

Besides, it was stifling in the room, the number of bodies cranking up the temperatures to unbearable levels. There wasn't even a fan to move the air around, probably out of fear of microbes being carried outside the room. But none of these patients—even the ones without the fatal mark on the wall—would last long if they couldn't cool it down.

Ben decided that one of his first orders of business would be to set up some kind of misting system.

Tracy moved towards him and touched his arm, pointing to the left at a nearby patient. It was a boy who Ben assumed was the one she'd been so worried about. There was a black squiggle over his bed but it was incomplete, as if someone had started to cross him off the list of the living and had then changed his mind.

"I'm going to check on Daniel and Cleo."

Pedro made a move to follow then noticed Ben's frown and evidently thought better of it, shifting his attention to a patient on the other side of the room instead.

Why did he care if the man had a thing for Tracy? Unlike him, the assistant seemed to have no problem with her job. He probably traveled with her every chance he got.

A steady pain thumped on either side of his head, and he squeezed the bridge of his nose in an effort to interrupt the nerve impulses.

While Tracy checked on the boy, he made his way to

the suited pair across the room. He identified himself and flashed his ID card, causing one of the men's brows to lift. "You're the *epidemiologista* General Gutierrez sent for?"

Ben nodded. "Are you marking these beds on his orders?"

"Well, no. He won't be here until tomorrow." They glanced quickly at each other. "But we can't take care of fourteen patients on our own, so we've been…" The words trailed away, but Ben understood. They were deciding who was worth their care and who was beyond saving.

"Well, Dr. Hinton and myself will be joining you, so let's set up a rotating schedule. Between all of us I'm sure we can make an effort to see *all* the patients." He let his emphasis hang in the air.

"But some of them won't last a day."

"And some of them might," he countered. "Why don't you explain to me who you've assessed, and we'll divide the room into critical care and non-critical, just like you would for field triage. It'll help us divide our efforts."

Neither man looked happy to be challenged, but they didn't contradict him either. If he knew General Gutierrez, the man had told them to follow his recommendations. The doctors gave him a quick rundown and Ben made a list, marking "TI"—for *tratamento intensivo*—next to those patients who were in critical condition and needed extra care. Not one "X" went next to anyone's name.

Ben moved over to the older woman who'd cried out as the men had marked her bed and found she was indeed critical, with red staining around her mouth that signaled she was producing bloody sputum. He laid a gloved hand on her forehead and spoke softly to her, her glassy eyes coming up to meet his, even as her breath rasped in and out, breathing labored. "We're going to take good care of you, okay?"

She blinked at him, not even making an effort to speak.

Ben called out to Tracy. "I want IVs started on all the patients who don't currently have one. We're going to push antibiotics into them. All of them." Then he turned to one of the men and nodded towards the radio on his hip. "Can you get me General Gutierrez? He and I need to have a little chat."

She didn't know what he'd done, but Ben had obviously spoken to someone in authority and asked for some changes. The cots—with the help of other soldiers—had been rearranged according to how ill each patient was. Daniel and Cleo had ended up on opposite sides of the room.

Heart aching, she moved from the boy to another patient, trying not to think about his prospects as she quickly filled a syringe from a vial of antibiotics and inserted it into the injection port of the IV line, marking the time and amounts in a small spiral-bound notebook they'd made up for each patient.

She caught Pedro's eye from across the room and smiled.

"You doing okay?" she mouthed, receiving a thumbs-up in return. Although not a doctor, Pedro had accompanied her on many of her forays into villages and had helped enough that she knew he could hold his own in an emergency. She also trusted him enough to know he'd ask for help if something was beyond his capabilities.

Her shirt was soaked with sweat and she'd gone through masks at an alarming rate. She hoped Ben had brought a big supply. He'd mentioned setting up a rudimentary misting system to help cool off the room.

Right now, though, he was seeing to the unloading of his car, and she refused to think about where they were going to sleep tonight. Ben had said the same "house"…not the same "room" when he'd made his request. But he'd also made it plain that they were married, so she had no doubt they'd be placed together. What was he thinking? Surely he had no more desire to be with her than she had to be with him?

Okay, maybe "desire" was the wrong word to use. Because put them in a room alone together and they tended to combust at frightening speed. She remembered her fury as she'd walked into that village to confront him on their first meeting. She'd heard there was an epidemiologist heading her way down the river but that he was taking his sweet time.

Unwilling to wait for him to stop at every village and sample the local cuisine, she'd powered back upriver and stomped her way to the heart of the village. He'd been standing in the middle of a group of men, a big smile on his face. She'd opened her mouth to throw a vile accusation his way, only to have the words stop in her throat the second their eyes had met.

He'd stared at her for several long seconds then one eyebrow had quirked upwards. "Are you here for me?"

"I…I…" Realizing she'd looked like a fool, she'd drawn herself up to her full height and let him have it.

She'd let him have it again two days later. In an entirely different way.

Oh, God. She could *not* be in a room alone with the man if she could help it. So what was she going to do?

Stay with her patients as much as possible, that's what. She'd already been here for almost eight hours. And it was now a few minutes past the end of her shift. If she knew Ben, he would make them all stick to the schedule he'd drawn up—whether they wanted to or not.

Even as she thought it, she reached Cleo's bed and leaned over her. The girl gave her a tremulous smile, which she returned.

"Hey, how are you doing?"

"Sleepy, and my head hurts." Cleo's voice was a thread of sound.

"I know." Headaches were one of the symptoms of the plague, but Cleo's episode didn't seem to be progressing as rapidly as Daniel's had. "You need to rest. I'm sure—"

Something cool and moist hit her left ankle and swept up the back of her leg until it reached the bottom of her shorts. Stifling a scream, she straightened and spun around to find empty air. She lowered her gaze and spied Ben, on his haunches, about a foot away, a spray bottle in his hand. Half-thought words bubbled on her tongue but didn't find an exit.

He got two more squirts in before she found her voice. "What do you think you're doing?"

Holding the pump bottle up, he said. "We have a room full of sick people. All we need is to have a dengue outbreak on top of everything."

Repellant. Ah. She got it.

But why was he the one spraying it on her? He could have just handed her the bottle and ordered her to put it on.

"You were busy," he said, as if reading her thoughts. "And sometimes with you it's easier to act than to argue."

Like their first kiss? When he'd dragged her to him and planted his lips on hers without so much as a "May I?"

She swallowed, hoping he couldn't read the direction of her thoughts. Or the fact that seeing him kneeling in front of her reminded her of other times when he'd done just that.

Before she could grab the bottle out of his hand he went back to work and sprayed the front of her legs. "Turn around."

"Are you going to personally spray Pedro and the other workers, too? Or just me?"

"They're not wearing shorts." His brows went up. "Didn't think it was as urgent."

She couldn't stop the smile or the roll of her eyes, but she obediently turned around. In reality the chill of the spray against her super-heated skin was heavenly as he slowly misted the back of her right leg. Looking down, she found Cleo looking up at her.

"He's bossy," the little girl said. Her voice was weak but there was a ghost of a smile on her face.

Tracy couldn't stop the laugh that bubbled out, her heart lightening at Cleo's ability to joke. "Oh, honey, you have no idea."

Ben's bossiness had a tendency to come out in all kinds of ways. Some of those she was better off not thinking about right now.

The spraying stopped and Tracy glanced behind her to find Ben staring up at her. Standing abruptly, he shoved the repellant bottle into her hands. "I'll let you finish up the rest. Give it to the other workers after you're done. And make sure you stay protected while you're here."

With that he walked away without a backward glance.

Stay protected? With him in the immediate vicinity?

She gave a huge sigh.

It would take a whole lot more than a bottle of repellent to do that.

CHAPTER SIX

HE WAS A masochist.

Ben stared at the figure sleeping in the hammock—her back to him—and wondered what on earth he'd been thinking by demanding they sleep in the same room. He obviously hadn't been thinking at all, but the sight of Tracy standing next to Pedro had sent a shaft of what could only be described as jealousy through him.

Why?

She could have been sleeping with twenty men a day after she'd left, and he'd have been none the wiser.

Yeah, but he hadn't had to stand there and witness it.

Even as he tried to convince himself that was the reason, he knew it went deeper than that. Deeper than the desire that churned to life as he stared at the sexy curve of hip flowing into a narrow waist. A waist that hadn't even had time to expand much before their baby had been lost.

She'd gotten off work two hours ahead of him, just as his schedule had dictated, which was a relief because she'd obviously come right back to the room and gone straight to sleep.

Which was exactly what he should be doing.

Tomorrow was going to be just as difficult as today.

Having Tracy here brought up all the tangled emotions he thought he'd already unraveled and put to bed. Sighing, he toed off his shoes, glad he'd donned a pair of athletic shorts to sleep in, because there was no way he was sleeping in just his boxers.

He slid into his hammock, trying to keep the creaking of the ropes to a minimum as he settled into place.

Someone like Pedro would have been ideal husband material for Tracy. He obviously didn't mind her vagabond spirit. In fact, he traveled with her on a regular basis, if appearances were anything to go by.

But then again, Pedro wasn't married to her. He hadn't had to sit at home wondering why she wanted to be anywhere else but with him. Wondering if, once their child was born, the baby would be dumped in the care of his housekeeper, just as he'd been when he'd been little.

Anger churned in his chest at the thought.

So why had seeing her bending over that little girl's bed, shapely bottom facing him, made the saliva pool in his mouth? And when she'd leaned further over, the long, lean muscles in her calves bunching as she'd gone on tiptoe to adjust the sheet on the far side of the cot, his body had roared to life. There hadn't been a drop of anger in sight.

He'd wanted her. Just as much as he always had.

He'd meant to hand her the bottle of repellent with a brusque order to put some on, but he'd been desperate to erase the images cascading through his mind. Squirting a healthy dose of cold liquid on her had seemed like the ideal way to shock her into moving—and shock his own body back to normal. Like a virtual defibrillator, halting a deadly spiral of electrical impulses before they'd overwhelmed his system.

His actions had backfired, though.

She'd turned around, just like he'd hoped, only his senses hadn't righted themselves, they'd gone berserk. And when he'd heard that low, throaty laugh at something her young patient had said, his stomach had turned inside out, drilling him with the reality of how stupid his move had been.

Besides, he'd had other things he needed to attend to.

Like going out and dunking his head in a bucket of water.

Which he'd done. Literally.

When he'd gone back inside, Tracy had already finished spraying herself down, the shine from the repellant glinting off the tip of her upturned nose, making his gut twist all over again.

He'd spent the rest of the day hanging mosquito netting around all of the patients' beds and caring for the ones who were the farthest away from his ex-wife.

Now, if he could just convince himself she really was his ex, he'd be just peachy.

Only two days into the outbreak and she was dog-tired. And hot.

So terribly hot. And now they were up to twenty patients, rather than fourteen.

The tiny house was still stifling, although Ben had figured out a way to combine fans with periodic jets of fine mist that reminded Tracy of the produce sections she'd seen at US supermarkets. It did help, but still…the place could never be deemed "cool."

Then again, it never really cooled off in this part of the world. Tracy had become soft, working in São Paulo for much of the year. The sticky heat that blanketed the equator—a place where seasons didn't exist—was unrelenting, reaching into every nook and cranny.

It had to be just as hard for Ben, who worked in an air-conditioned office nowadays, rather than doing fieldwork like he'd done when they'd met.

They'd administered a therapeutic dose of antibiotics

into all their patients, but they were already seeing the truth of that narrow window of treatment. The patients who'd been diagnosed after help arrived and given antibiotics immediately were doing better than those who had already been ill when they'd arrived.

The statistics held true, with the sickest of their patients continuing their downward spiral. Still, they had to keep trying, so they stayed their course, using either IV antibiotics, intramuscular injections or, for those who could tolerate it, oral doses. Two more had died since their arrival, but at least Ben had ordered those awful marks above the beds to be scrubbed clean.

Amazingly, Daniel—although gravely ill—was still hanging in there.

She glanced over at Ben, who was injecting his next patient, squeezing the woman's hand and offering her an encouraging smile that she couldn't actually see—because of his mask—but the crinkling at the corners of his eyes gave him away. Oh, how Tracy had loved seeing those happy little lines go to work.

He put the syringe into the medical waste container they'd set up, and Tracy reminded herself to check on the supply of disposable needles. He caught her looking at him from her place beside Daniel's bed and made his way over to her. She tensed, just as she'd done every time they'd had to interact.

"Why don't you take a quick nap?"

She shook her head. "I'm okay. Besides, I've had more sleep than you have."

Something she would know, as she'd heard him get up in the middle of the night and leave their room both nights they'd been in there. Maybe he was as restless as she was.

Well, whose fault was that? He'd been the one who'd insisted they stay together, which had made things incredibly awkward with Pedro.

And there were no real beds, so it wasn't a matter of her getting the bed while he slept on a pallet on the floor. No, all the workers had been assigned military hammocks, the residents' original hammocks having been confiscated, along with most of their fabric or upholstered possessions. Once some of the patients recovered, they'd have the added hardship of knowing many of their household clothes and belongings were long gone. Destroyed for the good of the village.

Tracy, for once, had agreed with the decision when Ben told her about it.

In addition to the bed situation, there wasn't much privacy to be had anywhere in the town. Showers had been set up in a clearing and the stinging smell of strong disinfectant soap had become an all-too-familiar fragrance around the compound. But even that couldn't totally vanquish the warm masculine scent that greeted her each night from the neighboring hammock where Ben lay.

Hanging side by side, the two hammocks were slung on three hooks, sharing one at the lower end, while the two upper ends branched apart onto two separate hooks, so that the hammocks formed a V. Knowing their feet were almost touching each and every night had been part of the reason for her sleeplessness.

So she'd lain awake for hours, despite her growing fatigue, until Ben—like he'd done the previous two nights—had slipped from his bed and out of the room. Only then had she finally been able to close her eyes and relax.

Ben looked like he was about to press his point about her taking a nap when the front door to the house banged open and a fierce argument carried through to where they were standing.

What in the name of...?

Both she and Ben moved quickly into the hallway, not wanting someone to be inadvertently exposed to the sickroom. They found one of the military police who'd been assigned to enforcing the quarantine arguing with a young girl who was around six years old. Tear tracks marked the dust on either side of the child's face, and her feet—clad only in flip-flops—were caked with dirt.

"What's going on?" Ben asked in Portuguese.

"She insists on speaking with a doctor, even though I've explained she can't go in there."

Tracy moved forward. "It's okay. I'll go outside with her."

"Tracy." Ben put a hand on her arm, stopping her.

She sent him a look that she hoped conveyed her irritation. "Someone has to talk to her. Better me than them." She aimed a thumb at the poor soldier.

"You need to at least take off your gear before you go out there."

"I will." She spoke softly to the child, telling her it was okay, that she'd be out in a minute. The girl nodded, the wobbling of her chin as she turned to go wrenching at Tracy's heart.

Ben caught the eye of one of the military doctors and told him they'd be back in a few minutes. They both stripped off their protective gear in the clean area and scrubbed with antibiotic soap. Tracy used her forearm to swipe at her damp forehead, frowning when Ben lifted a hand toward her. She took a quick step back.

"You have suds." He pointed to his own forehead.

She reached up and dabbed it away herself, avoiding his eyes, then pushed through the screen door at the back of the house. They made their way round to the front and the little girl rushed toward them. Ben stepped in front of

Tracy, causing her to give a sigh of exasperation. "Ben, please. She's not going to hurt anyone."

Moving around him, she knelt in front of the child. "What's your name?"

"Miriam."

Tracy wanted to gently wipe a smudge on the little girl's forehead, much as Ben had tried to do with her a second ago, but she was too afraid of spreading germs at this point to touch anyone outside the village. "Okay, Miriam. What did you want to tell us?"

"You are doctors?"

"Yes. We both are. It's okay. Is someone sick?"

The girl clasped her hands in front of her and nodded. "My *mami*. She has been ill for two days, but told me not to tell anyone. But now…" Her voice broke on a low sob. "But now she does not wake up, even when I try to feed her broth."

"Where is she?"

"At my house. But it is a long way from here."

The first twinge of alarm filtered up her back. "How far?"

"The next village."

Horrified, Tracy stood in a rush and grabbed Ben's hand, her wide eyes on his. "Could it have spread beyond São João dos Rios?"

No! They'd been so careful, no one had been allowed to leave the village once the military had arrived.

But before that?"

His fingers closed around hers, giving them a quick squeeze, then addressed the child, whose small forehead was now scrunched in distress. "Was your mother coughing?"

"Yes. She said it was just a cold, but I am afraid…" She motioned around the quarantine village. "We have heard what happened here. They say the military is shooting anyone who is sick. I had to sneak past them to find you."

Tracy's heart clenched. She knew how suspicious some of these towns were of government officials. But those fears only helped spread sickness and disease. Because people who were afraid tended to hide things from those who could help them.

Like Tracy had when she'd left Ben four years ago?

No, it wasn't the same thing at all. She forced a smile to her lips, knowing it probably looked anything but reassuring. "No one is shooting anyone."

"Will you come and help my mother, then?"

Tracy glanced at the house, where one of the military police watched them closely. Would they let her travel to the village or would they insist on sending someone else? It was a tough call. She didn't want to risk spreading anything, but the more people involved, the more places the disease could be carried. "Yes, honey, I will."

When she tried to move towards the guard, Ben clamped down on her hand. "What do you think you're doing, Tracy?" he murmured, sending a whisper of air across her cheek that made her shiver.

"You heard her. Her mother is sick."

"You could end up making things worse for everyone."

The shiver turned to ice in her veins. Those words were too close to the message he'd sent with the military four years ago. Her brows went up and she looked pointedly at the guard behind them. "I'm going, whether you approve or not. You could always send your little friends after me. You seem to be quite good at doing that."

"Come on, Tracy. You know why I sent them. You were carrying our child."

She did know—and maybe she'd been foolish to travel alone, but she'd been just six weeks along and she'd already had her yellow fever shot. She also knew her reason for taking off that week had had little to do with the village and everything to do with the results of her test. Even so, the blinding humiliation of seeing those uniformed officials set foot on that beach—and knowing her husband had been behind their presence—still stung.

They glared at each other. The last thing she needed to do right now was antagonize him further. She forced her voice to soften. "Please, try to understand. I *have* to check on her mother. My job is part of what keeps me going."

"Keeps you going?"

That last phrase had slipped out before she realized it. Leave it to Ben to catch it as it flew by.

"I mean, my job is important to me, that's all."

His gaze raked her face, and she held her breath, hoping the raw fear that slithered up her throat wasn't visible. Breaking eye contact, he glanced down at the girl, whose terror was much more on the surface. "Fine. We'll both go. But we need to take precautions. We're on antibiotics, so I'm not worried about us, but I also don't want us carrying anything back that way."

Was that why he'd been worried? Maybe she'd misjudged him.

"What about Miriam?" She kept her voice just as low, switching to English to make it harder for the little girl to understand what she was saying. "They may not let her leave São João dos Rios, now that she's been exposed."

"I know. I'll talk to the guard and get her started on antibiotics."

Poor girl, she had no idea that by trying to get help for her mother she might become a virtual prisoner. And if the worst came to the worst, and her mother had the deadly disease, she might never see her again.

A familiar pang went through Tracy's chest. Her mother

had died while Tracy had been here in Brazil. Six months after she and Ben had married, in fact. Her mother had had no idea she was sick during the wedding rehearsal or as they'd planned what should have been a happy occasion. But then she'd been diagnosed a few weeks after the ceremony. She'd died months later.

Squaring her shoulders, she went through the motions of going with Ben to talk to the guard, who in turn had to make a phone call up his chain of command. An hour later, she, Ben, and four military personnel were on their way to the next village. Ben had his arm around her in the backseat of the four-wheel drive to help steady her as they hit pothole after pothole, the scarred tract rarely seeing much in the way of motor vehicles.

Loaded to the gills with medical equipment, as well as Ben's lab stuff, she leaned against him, allowing him to pull her even closer as she prayed that whatever they found would not be as bad as she feared.

"Bronchitis," Ben declared.

Tracy almost laughed aloud as a giddy sense of relief swept over her. "Are you sure?"

Ben sat behind the house on a low three-legged stool, studying the last of the slides through his microscope.

"I don't see any sign of plague bacteria. And she's awake now. No fever or symptoms other than some thick congestion in her chest." He leaned back and looked at her. "She probably kept going until she was literally worn out, which was why Miriam couldn't wake her up. Regardless, we don't have a case of the plague here."

"Thank God." Her legs threatened to give out, and she had to put a hand on Ben's shoulder to brace herself.

He glanced up at her, concern in his eyes. "Hey, sit down

before you fall down." Before she realized what he was doing, he'd pulled her onto his left knee.

"Sorry," he murmured. "There's nowhere else to sit."

She nodded. "I'm sorry about what I said earlier. About you sending the military after me."

"Don't worry about it. You were upset."

She blinked. He'd just given her absolution. Whether it was for sins of the past or sins of the present was immaterial right now—not when the blood was thickening in her veins, the air around her turning crystal clear with secret knowledge.

The sudden sound of his breath being let out and the way his arm tightened around her back were her undoing. All she could think about was that she owed him a huge "thank you." Before she could stop herself, she looped her arms around his neck and leaned forward to kiss him.

CHAPTER SEVEN

HER LIPS GRAZED his cheek.

Ben wasn't at all sure how it happened. First she was apologizing then her mouth was on his skin. The instant it happened, something from the past surged inside him, and he brushed aside the gesture in favor of something a little more personal. If she was going to kiss him, he was going to make damned sure it counted. Using his free hand to cup her head, he eased her round until she faced him.

He stared at her for a long moment, taking in the parted lips, glittering eyes...an expression he knew all too well. He lowered his head, an inner shout of exultation going off in his skull when she didn't flinch away but met him halfway.

Their lips connected, and it was as if a match had been struck in the presence of gasoline fumes. They both went up in flames.

A low moan slid between them. One that most certainly hadn't come from him. Taking that as a signal to continue, his fingers lifted and tunneled deep into her hair, the damp moisture of her scalp feeling cool against his overheated skin.

Ignoring the microscope and slides, he shifted her legs sideways until they rested between his, without breaking contact with her mouth for even a second.

The change in position pressed her thigh against his

already tightening flesh, which was pure torture—made him want to push back to increase the contact. He forced himself to remain still instead, although it just about killed him. It had been four years since he'd held this woman in his arms, and he wasn't about to blow it by doing anything that would have her leaping from his lap in a panic. Realistically, he knew they weren't going to have sex behind the house of an ill woman, but he could take a minute or two to drink his fill of her.

Only, he'd never really get his fill. Would always want more than she was willing to give.

He licked along the seam of her mouth, asking for permission. She granted it without a word, opening to him. He went deep, his hand tightening in her hair as he tipped her head sideways seeking to find the best angle possible. She wiggled closer, taking him almost to the brink before he got himself back under control.

He gave a hard swallow. *Slow.*

Exploring the heat and warmth he found between her lips, he tried to rememorize everything and realized he didn't need to. Because he'd forgotten nothing. Not the taste of her, not the shivers he could wring from her by using his teeth in addition to his tongue.

And when he could no longer contain his low groan, her fingers came up and tangled in his hair. He could feel the battle going on within her and fought against his own need to control the situation, letting her lead instead.

Unfortunately, she took that as a signal to pull back, her breath coming in husky snatches of sound that he found erotic beyond belief.

She took a couple more quick gulps before attempting to talk.

"Ben," she whispered, her mouth still against his. "What are we doing here?"

In spite of himself, he smiled. "I thought that was fairly obvious."

"Mmm." The hum of sound drove him crazy, just like it always had. "This is a mistake. You know it is."

"I know." He bit her lower lip, sucking on the soft flesh before releasing it with a growl. "Doesn't mean I didn't enjoy it, though. Or that you didn't either."

"I know." No arguments, no denying that she felt the same. Just an acknowledgement of what was obvious to both of them.

It had been an incredibly long week, and all he wanted to do was wrap his arms around her, make slow, satisfying love and then go to sleep still trapped inside her. Just like they used to.

But he knew that was the exhaustion talking. Not to mention that thing wedged against her hip, which was busy shouting out commands he was doing his best to ignore.

Sorry, bud. You're out of luck.

Tracy leaned her forehead against his and gave a drawn-out sigh. "We need to get back to the other village if this one is in the clear."

She heaved one more sigh, before climbing to her feet, looking anywhere but at his lap, which was probably smart. "I'm sure we're both so tired we're not thinking straight. We'll regret this once we've had some sleep."

She might, but he wouldn't. Not even if he slept as long as Rip Van Winkle. He'd still wake up and want to kiss her all over again.

He closed his eyes for a long moment then started undoing his equipment without a word.

She laid a hand on his shoulder. "If it's any consolation, you're right. I enjoyed it too. You always were a great kisser."

Some of the tension in his spine seeped away. Questions from four years ago resurfaced and he couldn't keep himself from asking, "Then why were you always in such a hurry to leave?"

"Please, don't, Ben. Not right now."

And her response was exactly the same as it had been back then. She hadn't wanted to talk about it—had just wanted to head off on her next adventure.

There was nothing left to say, then. "I'll get some medicine out of the car and explain the dosage."

She nodded. "I'm sure they'll even let Miriam come home as there's no evidence of pneumonic plague here. We'll put her on the prophylactic dosage of antibiotics and she should be fine."

Stowing his equipment in a large box and carefully stacking his microscope on top, all he could do was wish for a prophylactic dose of something that would cut through his current jumble of emotions and put him back on the road to normalcy.

Normalcy. Wow. If he ever found a pill that would restore that, he'd end up a very rich man.

Tracy could have kicked herself. She'd let him kiss her. *On the mouth.* Worse, she'd kissed him back. Crazily. As if she couldn't get enough of him.

Her chaste little gesture of thanks had flared to inferno proportions in a nanosecond.

The chemistry between them was just as potent as ever. Something she never should've doubted. Something she should have been braced for and never allowed to happen.

And why on earth had she let herself be drawn into an argument about the past? Because she was trying to keep her distance emotionally? You sure couldn't tell it from where she stood. Because the only message she'd been sending while perched on his lap had been more along the lines of throw-me-on-my-back-and-take-me-hard.

To allow that to happen, though, would only make things more complicated. Especially now. She could admit that she still cared about him, but it didn't mean they could—or should—be together. If she thought there was a chance, she might try to explain what had happened all those years ago. But it wouldn't do any good at this point. And the last thing she needed was Ben's pity. Hanging onto the anger from the past might be best for both of them right now, because in another week or so they'd be heading in opposite directions.

Lying in her hammock, hours from the time they'd finally climbed into Ben's SUV and headed back to town, she still longed to reach across the space and take his hand. Touch his face. Kiss his lips.

Why? None of it made any sense.

There were less than two feet separating them. Less at the foot end of the hammocks. And she'd never been more keenly aware of that fact than she was now. The village was still and quiet. The military doctors had taken up the night shift, leaving Tracy and Ben to get five or six hours of sleep, which was what she should be doing right now, rather than lying here staring at the ceiling. Luckily, Ben was facing away from her and couldn't see her restless movements. He'd fallen asleep almost as soon as his body had hit the hammock, while she'd pretended to do the same. Was still pretending, in fact.

Just like she'd pretended that kiss today was the result of exhaustion and stress.

He turned unexpectedly, and Tracy clamped her eyelids shut, trying to breathe slowly and deeply, even though her heart was pounding out a crazy tattoo. The sound of a throat clearing, some more rustling and then a low, exasperated curse met her ears. She felt a rush of air against her and the movement of his hammock disturbing hers where they intersected at the bottom.

Soft footsteps. Another oath. Then the sound of a door quietly opening and closing. Just like the last three nights.

She waited for several seconds before she got up the courage to open her eyes again and peek.

Yep. He was gone. Where was he disappearing to each night? The restroom? If so, that meant he'd be back in a matter of minutes—which he never was. She pushed her fingers through the open-weave fabric of her hammock in irritation, squeezing the fibers tight. Instead of wondering where he was, she should be using this time to try to go to sleep.

Fat chance of that now.

She continued to lie very still, waiting, staring at the closed door on the other side of the tiny room.

But fifteen minutes later there was still no sign of him, just like on previous nights. Had he decided he couldn't sleep? Yes, it was hot in the room—the fan doing nothing more than fluffing the balmy air—but it would be just as hot no matter where he went.

Did this have something to do with their kiss, earlier? If that were the case, then what was his excuse on the other nights?

Crossing her arms over her chest, she closed her eyes again and tried for the umpteenth time to go to sleep. Morning was going to come, and with it a whole new day of struggles and trials as they tried to care for their remaining patients.

Seven more days. That's how long Ben figured it would take to get the epidemic under control.

And that's how long she had to kick this stupid attraction to the curb and keep herself out of Ben's bed.

Seven, very long days.

CHAPTER EIGHT

"CLEO'S RIGHT HERE, honey."

Gently placing a moist cloth across Daniel's feverish brow, Tracy nodded at the neighboring cot, where Ben was adjusting the IV pole.

The boy had finally regained consciousness, four days after being found in the field. His first words had been to ask about his sister. The plea had remained throughout the day, sometimes interrupted by bouts of coughing, sometimes gasped between harsh breaths, but he never relented. The question was there each time he rallied for a few moments. And it made Tracy's heart squeeze. It was as if, even in his precarious state, he refused to believe Cleo was alive unless he saw it for himself.

Ben had finally relented and offered to shuffle patients around so that the brother and sister could remain close to each other's sides, despite the fact that he'd wanted patients placed according to severity of illness. Daniel was still gravely ill, whereas Cleo's sickness had not ravaged her young body as much as those of some of their other patients. She said her head still ached, but she hadn't worsened.

Daniel's glassy eyes swiveled to the right. "Clee," he whispered, shaky fingers reaching across the space and then dropping before he succeeded in reaching the other bed.

"She's here, Daniel, but she's asleep right now. We have

to let her rest so she can be strong and healthy again." Her gloved fingers brushed back a moist lock of hair, a rush of emotion clogging her throat. "You need to do the same. She'll still be here when you wake up."

If you wake up.

She immediately dismissed the thought. Daniel's vitals had slowly grown weaker over the last couple of days, but he continued to fight harder than anyone she'd ever seen. And so would she. She'd come here to fight for these kids, against the military's wishes…against Ben's wishes. And she was going to damn well keep on fighting.

Maybe there was a message for her in there somewhere. But she was too tired to dig for it right now. Maybe later.

As if he sensed the direction of her thoughts, Ben came to stand beside her. "You need to get some rest as well. You look exhausted."

"We're all tired." She reached up to wipe a trickle of perspiration from her temple only to have Ben beat her to it, using one of the dry compresses to blot her forehead. She gave him a weak grin. "You'd think after almost a week I'd be used to the heat. I travel down the Amazon all the time."

They both froze, and Tracy wondered if he was remembering that last fateful trip.

Ben had accused her of neglecting their marriage, of being careless with their baby's health. Had she? Had her own plight so blinded her that she'd taken unnecessary chances?

She'd never know. And there was nothing she could do to go back and change things anyway.

Guilt gnawed at her, just as strong now as it had been back then.

"You're good with them, you know."

The change in subject made her blink. "With who?"

He nodded toward the kids. "These two."

"I care about all my patients."

"I wasn't accusing you of anything, Tracy. Just making a statement."

She considered that for a moment. The anger had been so strong at the end of their marriage that it was hard to hear anything he said without the filters of the past. Maybe she should start trying to take his words at face value. Maybe he could start doing the same.

She perched on the side of Cleo's bed, her fingers feathering through the girl's hair. A low sigh came from the child's throat, and she snuggled into her hand.

Tears pricked very close to the surface but she ignored them as best she could. "I can't imagine how they're going to feel when they wake up and realize their mother is gone. For ever."

Well, she took that back. She knew how that felt but she'd at least had her mom with her until she was a grown woman. These kids would never know how that felt. She wished there was some way she could take that pain from them.

"Sometimes a parent doesn't have to die to be gone," Ben murmured.

She glanced up at him, but he was staring through the dusty window across from them.

"Are you talking about your mom and dad?" Ben and Marcelo's parents hadn't been around much as they'd been growing up and both men carried some resentment about that. That resentment had carried over to Ben's marriage.

Her traveling had been a constant source of arguments almost from the moment they'd both said, "I do."

But Ben had been just as gung ho about his job when they'd met. She hadn't understood exactly why he'd wanted to give all that up. Well, that wasn't quite true either. When she'd found out she was pregnant, she'd been all set to let her office take over a lot of *Projeto Vida's* off-site calls. Then things had changed.

And Ben had reacted badly to her need for space…for time to think. In reality, she probably should have told him sooner, but she'd still been reeling from the news and grieving over her mother's and sisters' deaths.

Ben's eyes refocused on her. "No. Just talking in generalities."

He was lying. But it was easier to let this particular subject go. "I forgot to ask. How's Rosa?"

"Fine. Still at the house."

She wasn't surprised. The old housekeeper—who'd been widowed at a young age and had never remarried—had practically raised Ben and Marcelo. Of course Ben would keep her on. It was another thing they'd argued about.

Oh, not about Rosa still living there—Tracy loved her almost as much as Ben—but that he wouldn't hear of the housekeeper having any part in raising their child. The early elation of finding out she was pregnant hadn't lasted long.

When he'd asked about her plans for her job once the baby was born, she'd flippantly responded that Rosa would be thrilled to help during her absences—that she'd already asked her, in fact. Her words had been met with stony silence. Seconds later Ben had stalked from the room and slammed through the front door of the house.

Only afterwards had she realized how her comment might have sounded. She'd apologized and tried to explain once he'd come home, but she'd got the feeling Ben had heard little or nothing of what she'd said.

She sighed. "I miss Rosa."

"I'm sure she misses you as well."

Her heart aching, a silent question echoing inside her head: *And what about you, Ben? Do you ever miss me?*

* * *

"Don't move too quickly. You're still weak."

Tracy put her shoulder beneath Daniel's arm and, with Pedro on his other side, they helped him walk slowly around the clearing in front of the house in an effort to ward off the possibility of deep vein thromboses from all his time in bed. Day five, and the patient who'd set off the frantic race to save a village seemed to have turned a corner—against all odds. Just yesterday they'd wondered if he would even make it. Somehow the twelve-year-old's body was fighting off the disease when by most medical journals' estimations he should be dead.

"M-my sister?" His voice was thin and raspy.

"Cleo is at the cafeteria. You have some catching up to do, you know," she teased. "Do you think you can handle the thought of sipping some broth?"

"I'd rather have *beijú*."

The local flatbread made from cassava flour was typical up here in the northeastern part of the country. Tracy had missed the gummy bread in São Paulo, although she could still find it on occasion.

Pedro shook his head. "I think we'd better stick to broth for today, like Tracy said."

Daniel made a face. "Not even beans and rice?"

"Soon," Tracy said with a smile. "Maybe in another day or two, okay?"

His already thin shoulders slumped, but he didn't argue as they led him over to the temporary mess hall the military had set up. The tent was divided into sides. Medical personnel and healthy villagers on one side and those with active infections on the other. Donning her mask, she ducked beneath the canvas door flap to deliver her patient.

Four long tables with wooden benches were mostly empty. There weren't very many patients at the moment who were well enough to actually walk the short distance from their beds. Huge fans sucked heat from the inside and blew it out, keeping the place from turning into an inferno as the sun baked the canvas roof. In fact, more of the flaps were open today, a sign the military knew things were looking up for the stricken town.

A wave from across the space caught her eye.

Cleo, seated at a front table, smiled, her dark eyes lighting up as she saw them come in. "Daniel, you're awake!" She motioned him over.

Tracy delivered their charge to the table and brother and sister were reunited—outside the sickroom—for the first time in over a week. Cleo's smile wavered and then she wrapped her arms around Daniel's neck and sobbed quietly. Tracy was forced to separate them gently when she grew concerned about the boy's system being overloaded. Before she could ask the person in charge of meals for a cup of broth, one magically appeared on the table in front of them.

Cleo, who'd begun to recover more quickly than Daniel, had black beans and rice on her plate—and Tracy could swear that was a piece of fried banana as well. Her own mouth watered, so she could only imagine how Daniel felt. But he dutifully picked up his spoon and gave a tentative taste of the contents of his cup. Despite the liquid diet, he closed his eyes as if it were the finest caviar.

"Good?" she asked.

He nodded, taking another sip.

Pedro glanced at the serving area. "I'm going to head over and get in line before it closes. What do you want?"

"I already have Tracy's food."

The voice came from behind them just as a tray was plonked down in front of her. A creamy-white *beijú*, slathered in butter, was folded in half and propped up on a neat mound of rice and beans. And, oh! A *whole* fried banana.

"Not fair," muttered Daniel, who looked longingly at the plate and sucked down another spoonful of his broth.

She glanced to the side and saw Ben, his eyes on Pedro as he set down a second tray beside hers. She gave her assistant an apologetic shrug. "Get something before they run out. I'll see you later, okay?"

Ben waited for her to sit before joining her. Irritated, she realized she'd been looking for him all day.

"You're supposed to be on the doctors' side of the tent, you know," she said, cringing as the words left her mouth. Great. No "Thank you" for the food. No "How are you?" Just a veiled accusation.

"Hmm. Well, so should you. I saw you come in and thought you might like an update on our situation."

Our situation?

Oh, he meant here in town. He wasn't referring to that disastrous kiss.

"Is that where you've been? With the military?"

"The guys in charge wanted me to fill them in. General Gutierrez is here and heard most of the news from his own doctors, but he wanted to make sure it matched the civilian report. The military's reputation tends to be a touchy subject."

"Since when?" As soon as the words were out of her mouth she wished she could call them back. "Sorry. That hadn't come out right."

He ignored her and leaned around her back to lay a hand on Daniel's shoulder, smiling at the boy. "I'm surprised to see you out of bed."

Cleo blinked at him with huge brown eyes. "What about me? Are you surprised to see me, too?"

"Definitely. But very glad." He then ruffled Cleo's hair, which caused the seven-year-old to giggle. The happy sound made Tracy's heart contract. The man was a natural with children. He should have lots of them. All swarming around him like a litter of cute puppies.

"I haven't heard a peep about any so-called meetings. Why didn't someone call me?" She wasn't really peeved but needed to get her mind off Ben and his future children. Because it hurt too much to think about it. Not when she'd decided her previous pregnancy would probably be her last.

He glanced away. "I wanted to let you sleep in a little while longer. It's been a difficult week."

Come to think of it, no one *had* come to wake her up for her normal seven a.m. shift. Had that been Ben's doing as well? Her heart tightened further.

He was a good man. He'd deserved so much better than what she'd given him.

She cleared her throat, trying to get rid of the lump that clogged it. "Thank you. You weren't there when I woke up."

Turning to look at her, he lifted a shoulder. "I'm an early riser. Always have been."

Yes, he had been. But he hadn't normally left their bed in the middle of the night and not returned. A thought came to her. Maybe he'd found somewhere else to hole up. A streak of something white hot went through her. She had noticed a couple of female soldiers eyeing him. But surely…

Daniel lifted the last spoonful of broth and leaned back with a tired sigh.

She wanted to know what had been said during the meeting but she also needed to take care of her patients' needs. "Are you guys ready to go back to your room?"

Ben frowned down at her untouched tray, while Daniel shook his head. "Can I please stay here for a little while longer? I'm tired of lying in bed, and I want to talk to Cleo."

There was a sad note in the words, and Tracy had a feeling she knew what he wanted to talk to her about. What were these kids going to do when this was all over? A thought that had plagued her repeatedly over the past couple of days.

She nodded. "We'll move to another table and give you some time alone, okay? If you need me, just wave, and I'll see you."

She and Ben picked up their trays. She noticed he headed for a different table than Pedro's. Thankfully her assistant was busy talking to one of the military doctors. Maybe he wouldn't notice.

She realized she wasn't the only one who hadn't touched her plate. "Eat. Then I want to hear about what went on at the meeting."

He lifted his brows. "I'll eat if you will."

Her lips curled into a reluctant smile, and she realized how little of that she'd done over the last week. "Deal."

The next fifteen minutes were spent in relative silence as she enjoyed her first quiet meal since they'd arrived. When she bit into her *beijú* she couldn't stop a low groan of pleasure. Ben remembered exactly how much butter she liked on it. And even though the bread was no longer warm, it was still as good as she remembered. "I have to take some cassava flour back with me so I can make this at home."

Ben didn't respond, and she only realized how that sounded when she noticed a muscle working in his jaw. Surely he knew she'd have to go back to São Paulo soon. Their life together was over, no matter how much she might wish otherwise.

Shaking off her regrets, she forced her back to straighten. "So, how did things go this morning?"

Cutting a chunk of fried banana and popping it into her mouth, she waited for him to fill her in.

"Tell me something," he said instead.

Her whole body went on alert. Because it was he who was supposed to be telling *her* something, not the other way around. And if he asked her about her reasons for leaving, she had no idea what she was going to say. Because for all her raging about Ben's ridiculous actions in sending in the cavalry when she hadn't been in any real danger, she knew it was only a symptom of an underlying problem.

Yes, he'd betrayed her. Yes, he should have come himself, instead of pretending the military had other reasons for her not being in that village. But her reasons for leaving were way more complex than that. Because in the same way the townsfolk's coughs were only a symptom of a raging wildfire burning below the surface, so were her issues.

"I thought we were going to talk about your meeting."

If she thought she could change the subject that easily, she was wrong.

"Why haven't you filed for divorce? Surely you could meet someone who loves your job just as much as you do." His glance went to the table where Pedro sat.

"I—I told you. It's hard to get a divorce from inside Brazil."

"And you mean to tell me that after four years there's been no one you've wanted to spend your life with?"

"If you're talking about Pedro, we're just coworkers." After Ben, she'd wanted no one. "I just haven't had the time to file the paperwork. It would mean a trip to New York."

She tried to turn the conversation back to him. And realized she really did want to know. "What about you?"

"I have no desire to go down that road again."

A spike of guilt went through her heart. Had she done that to him? Been such an awful wife that he'd never consider marrying again? She'd just assumed he'd be happier once she was out of his life, that he'd find someone who could give him what she didn't seem able to. "I see. But surely someday…"

"I don't think so." He dropped his utensils onto his plate with a clatter.

Surely he couldn't kiss her like he'd done a few days ago and not want that with someone else.

"You'd have eventually hated me, Ben. We both know that. It was better that I left." Defective gene or no defective gene, she and Ben had never seen eye to eye on her job.

But would she have traveled as much without that fear prodding her from behind?

He turned to face her. "I never hated you, Tracy. But I deserved better than a letter left on my desk."

He was right. She'd left him an ugly, anger-filled missive detailing everything about their marriage she found unbearable, ending with the military invasion of the village that had ended in her expulsion. Part of that rage had been due to feelings of helplessness over her test results. Part of it had been caused by grief over the loss of her child. But the biggest part of it had been guilt at having failed him so terribly. She'd been too much of a coward to stick around and tell him to his face that it was over.

"You're right, Ben. It won't help, but I was dealing with something more than my pregnancy at that time."

"Something about your job?"

"No." It was on the tip of her tongue to tell him when Daniel waved from across the room. She realized this was neither the time nor the place to dredge up issues from the past. Not when there were lives in the balance and patients who needed her. "I have to go. I can't change the way things played out, Ben. All I can say is I'm sorry."

"Yeah, well, so am I." Before she could even get up from her place, Ben was already on his feet—had already picked up both their trays and was striding towards the front of the tent where the trashcans were located.

As she went over to Daniel's table, she realized Ben

had never told her what the meeting this morning had been about.

And right now she didn't care.

CHAPTER NINE

THEY'D LOST ANOTHER patient during the night, and now this.

A flash of anger went through Tracy's eyes. "We have to stay for a week *after* the last patient recovers? You've got to be kidding. I can't be gone from my job for that long."

Her job. That's what it always came down to.

Unless it was more than that. She'd talked about dealing with other issues during their marriage that had nothing to do with her job. Or her pregnancy. He'd racked his brains, thinking back over every last detail he could remember.

And had come up blank.

Except for a vivid image of that kiss in the neighboring town a few days ago. He couldn't seem to get it out of his head.

In fact, the memory haunted him night after night and infected his dreams. The dreams that drove him from his bed and into the narrow hallway just outside the door. His back was killing him, but it was better than the other part of his body that was also killing him.

"The army is worried about keeping the disease contained, so they're upping the quarantine time." He frowned. "And because we traveled to that neighboring village, they want to keep tabs on it as well and make sure no one starts exhibiting symptoms."

She glanced around the sickroom at the dwindling number of patients. "We'll be sitting here alone, twiddling our thumbs, by that time, and you know it."

More than half of the surviving patients had gone on to recover, and the ones who'd shown no symptoms at all were still on doses of antibiotics and would be for several more days. She was right, though. Once the remaining cases were under control, there'd be no more risk of person-to-person contamination. And they'd be stuck here for a week with nothing to do.

Tracy walked over to one of the patients and checked the IV bag, making sure it didn't need changing. "We wore masks while we were at the other village, Ben."

"Not the whole time."

He saw from the change in her expression that she knew exactly when they'd gone without wearing their protective masks. Right before—and during—that deadly kiss.

She lowered her voice, even though she was speaking in English and no one would understand her. "No one saw us."

"Someone did." He nodded when her eyes widened. "And they reported it to the general."

"I thought you guys were big buddies."

"We're friends. But he's also a stickler for the rules."

"I found that out the hard way." Her eyes narrowed. "Listen, I can't stay here for ever. I have no cellphone reception, and there's no way I can get word back to *Projeto Vida* that I'll be delayed even longer. They need to at least let Pedro head back to the office."

He sighed. They hadn't seen much of Tracy's assistant since lunch the other day, and he wondered if the other man was actively avoiding them. Then again, why would he? Ben's lack of sleep was obviously catching up with him.

"They're not letting anyone out, and I wouldn't try to press the issue, if I were you."

"Did you set this up?"

"Get over yourself, Trace. This has nothing to do with you. Or me, for that matter."

She closed her eyes for a second. "You're right. Sorry."

He thought she actually might be. "Maybe I can ask him to get in touch with your office. I'm sure they must have a satellite phone or something they're using for communication."

Moving over to stand beside her, he touched her hand. "Listen, I know this hasn't been easy. Maybe I shouldn't have let you come in the first place, I don't know. But I'm really not trying to manipulate the situation or make things more difficult than they have to be. It's just as inconvenient for me to be stuck here as it is for you. I have my lab—my own responsibilities. Mandy can't hold down the fort for ever."

Her gaze softened. "Don't think I don't appreciate being able to come, Ben. I do." She hesitated then wrapped her fingers around his. "It just feels…awkward. And I know this is just as hard for you as it is for me. I really am sorry."

When she started to withdraw, he tightened his fingers, holding her in place. "Whatever else happens, it's been good seeing you again." The words had come out before he could stop them, and he could tell by her sharp intake of breath they'd taken her by surprise.

"You too."

Then what were those other issues you mentioned?

He somehow succeeded in keeping the question confined inside his skull. Because he already knew he wouldn't get an answer. Not until she was good and ready to tell him—if she ever was.

The woman was hiding something. But he had no idea what it was.

The last thing he wanted to do, though, was to fall for her all over again, and then stand around cooling his heels, hoping each time she left that when she returned, she'd be back to stay. He might be a glutton for punishment, but he was no fool.

So what did he do?

For a start, he could act like the scientist he was—examine the evidence without her realizing what he was doing. Just like he found various ways to look at the same specimens in his lab—using dyes, centrifuges, and cultures, until they revealed all their secrets.

He was trained to study things from different angles. His fingers continued to grip hers as he glanced down into those deep green eyes. That's what he had to do. Probe, study, examine—kiss.

Whatever it took.

Until she gave up every last secret. And then he could put his crazy emotions to rest once and for all.

Pure heaven.

Tracy sank into the fragrant bubbles, finding the water cool and inviting. Anything warmer would have been unbearable with the sizzling temperatures outside today. She remembered they hadn't even needed a hot-water heater for their showers in Teresina—the water coming from the taps had been plenty warm enough for almost everything.

She sighed and leaned her head back against the rim of the tub. She had no idea how Ben had arranged to have one of the large blue water tanks brought in and set up behind the house, but he had. He'd also had folding screens erected all around it for privacy.

The tanks were normally installed on residential rooftops as a way to increase water pressure. She'd never heard of bathing in one, but as it was the size of a normal hot tub, it was the perfect depth, really. He'd even managed to rustle up some scented shampoo that had probably come from the local market—although the store hadn't been open since the outbreak had begun.

She hadn't dared strip completely naked, but even clad in her black bra and panties the experience still felt unbelievably decadent. Better yet, Ben had stationed himself outside the screened-off area, making sure no one came upon her unexpectedly—not that they could see much through the thick layer of bubbles.

Why had he done it? Yes, they'd both been exhausted and, yes, despite her tepid showers, her muscles ached with fatigue from turning patients and making sure she moved their arms and legs in an effort to keep blood clots from forming.

Where had he even gotten the tank? It looked new, not like it had been drained and taken off someone's house. Well, once she was done, she'd let him have a turn. Only the bubbles would be gone by then and he'd be getting used water—unless they took the time to refill the thing. And she knew Ben was concerned enough about the environment that he wouldn't want to double their water usage.

Or... She pushed up out of the water and stared down at her chest. Her bra was solid black, so nothing showed through. In fact, her underwear was less revealing than what you'd find on most Brazilian beaches. So maybe he could just join her.

A faint danger signal went off in her head, its low buzz making her blink as she sank back into the water.

What? She wasn't naked. Far from it.

Ben had already seen her with a lot fewer clothes. And it wasn't like anyone was going to venture behind the house. The property itself was walled off with an eight-foot-high concrete fence—which was typical in Brazil. The screens were merely an added layer of protection.

If *she'd* been hot and sweaty when he'd unveiled his

surprise, then he had to be positively baking. Especially as he was now standing guard in the sun just beyond the screens. And the water really did feel amazing.

"Ben?" His name came out a little softer than necessary. She figured if he didn't hear her, she could just pretend she hadn't said anything.

"Yep?"

Okay, so she was either going to have to suck it up and ask him if he wanted to join her or just make up some random question.

"Um…I was wondering if you wanted to— I mean the water isn't going to be as fresh once I get out, so do you want to…?" Her throat squeezed off the last of the words.

Ben's face appeared around the side of one of the screens. "Excuse me?"

"As long as we both have some clothes on, we can share the water." She couldn't stop a sigh as she curled a hand around the rim of the tank and peered over the top. "I know you won't pour a new bath for yourself."

"I'm okay." There was definite tension in his jaw, which should serve as an additional warning, but now he was making her feel guilty on top of everything else. Especially when she spied a rivulet of sweat running down the side of his neck, and he lifted a hand to dash it away.

"Come on. Stop being a martyr. You've earned a break. Besides, it'll help cool you off."

"That, I doubt." The words were so low she wasn't sure she'd heard them correctly but, still, he moved into the space, hands low on his hips.

He was soaked, his face red from the heat.

"Look at your shirt, Ben. You're practically steaming." She wouldn't mention the fact that seeing her husband layered in sweat had always been a huge turn-on. Maybe this *was* a mistake. But there was no way she was going to call back her words now. He'd think she was chicken.

So...should you stand up and cluck now...or wait until later?

He mumbled something under his breath that sounded weirdly like, "You're a scientist. Examine, probe..."

The rest of the sentence faded away to nothing.

"Come on, Ben. You're making me feel guilty."

His lips turned up at the edges. "And are you going to make *me* feel guilty if I refuse?"

"Yes." She realized once she'd answered him that his last phrase could have been taken more than one way. But then again she was hearing all kinds of strange stuff today.

When his hands went to the bottom of his shirt and hauled the thing up and over his head, her breath caught in her throat as glistening pecs and tight abs came into view—accompanied by a familiar narrow trail of hair that was every bit as bewitching as she remembered.

Okay, she had definitely not thought this through. For some reason, in her mind she'd pictured him clothed one second and in the tub the next. But then again, stripping outside the fenced area wouldn't help any, because he would still return *sans* most of his clothes.

His hands went to the button of his khaki cargo pants. "You sure about this?"

She gulped. "As long as you have something underneath that."

His smile widened. "It depends whether you're talking about clothing or something else."

Oh, man. She did remember he'd gone commando from time to time, just to drive her crazy. She'd never known when he'd peeled his jeans off at night what she'd find.

When his zip went down this time, however, she breathed

a sigh of relief, followed by a glimmer of disappointment, when dark boxers came into view.

As if reading her thoughts, he said, "No reason to any more."

That little ache in her chest grew larger. He no longer had anyone to play those games with.

As he shoved his slacks the rest of the way down his hips and stepped out of them, she tried to avoid looking at him as she thought about how unfair life was. This was a man who should be in a monogamous, loving relationship. He'd been a great husband. A fantastic lover. And he would have made a terrific father.

"You do have clothes on under those bubbles, right?"

"A little late to be asking that now, don't you think?" She wrinkled her nose and snapped the black strap on her shoulder as evidence. "Of course I do. That invitation wouldn't have gone out otherwise."

His smile this time was a bit tight, but he stepped into the huge tub and slid beneath the water in a single quick motion. Too quick to see if the thought of them in this tank together was affecting him as much as it was her.

Oh, lord, she was an idiot. But as the water licked the curve of his biceps with the slightest movement of their bodies, she couldn't bring herself to be sorry she'd given the invitation.

"Nice?" she asked, making sure her bra-covered breasts were well below the waterline. Since it was almost up to her neck, they were nowhere to be seen.

He responded by sinking down further until his head ducked beneath the surface then rose again. A stream of bubble-laden water sluiced down his face, his neck…that strong chest of his… She only realized her eyes were tracking its progress when his voice drew her attention back up.

"Wish I'd thought of doing this days ago."

"Huh?"

He shook his head with a smile. "Nothing. Yeah. It's nice." He stretched his arms out along either side of the tub and watched her. "So, how was your day?"

Maybe this wasn't going to be so weird after all. "Tiring. Yours?"

"Interesting."

"Did General Gutierrez call another meeting?" If Ben had left her out of the loop again, she was going to be seriously miffed. Those were her patients as well. And she'd been first on the scene when the distress call had gone out.

"No, still the same game plan in place, from what I understand." He lowered his hands into the tub and cupped them, carrying the water to his face and splashing it. If he'd been trying to rinse away the remaining bubbles he'd failed because now they'd gathered like a thin goatee on his chin.

"Um…" She motioned to her own chin to let him know.

He scrubbed the offending body part with his shoulder, transferring the bubbles, then took up his position again, arms spread along the curved blue rim. She tried to make herself as small as possible.

"So, you said your day has been interesting. How so?" She kept her hands braced on the bottom of the tub to keep from slipping even further down into the water. Besides, the less of herself she exposed, the less…well, *exposed* she felt.

He shrugged. "Just doing some research."

"On our cases?"

"Our cases. That's exactly it."

She narrowed her eyes. Why did she get the feeling that the word "cases" was being thrown around rather loosely—at least on his side.

"Did you come to any conclusions?"

"Not yet. But I'm hoping to soon."

The look in his eyes was intense, as if he was expecting to see something reflected back at him.

She cleared her throat. "Daniel is almost better. A few more days and he should be able to be released. Cleo is still complaining of a slight headache, though, and she isn't progressing as quickly as she was earlier."

"Hmm...I'll check her when I get back." His lips pursed. "I've been thinking about those two—Daniel and his sister, I mean. You're good with them."

Something in her stomach tightened. "Like I said earlier, I try to care for all my patients."

"I know you do."

"I feel terrible that their mother didn't..." The tightening spread to her throat, choking off the rest of her words.

"I know, Trace. I'm sorry." He shifted and one of his legs touched hers, his foot lying alongside her knee. She got the feeling the gesture was meant to comfort her because she was too far away for him to reach any other way. The tub was narrower at the bottom than it was at the top, and even though she knew why he'd done it, it still jolted her system to feel the heat of his skin against hers. She returned the pressure, though, to acknowledge what he'd done.

"Thanks," she said. "That means a lot to me."

She licked her lips, expecting him to move his leg away as soon as she said the words, but he didn't. Instead his gaze held hers. What he was expecting her to do, she wasn't quite sure. A shiver went over her when his foot slid along the side of her calf, as if he'd bent his knee beneath the water. Had he done that on purpose?

There was nothing in his expression to indicate he had.

Not only did he not move away, a second later she felt something slide against her other leg. She gulped. Now, that hadn't been an accident. Had it?

And the bubbles were starting to dissipate, popping at

an alarming rate. Soon she'd be able to see beneath the water's surface. And so would Ben. So she either needed to wash her hair and get out fast or she needed to stay in and…

That was the question. Just how brave was she?

And exactly how far was she willing to let him go?

CHAPTER TEN

SHE DIDN'T KNOW what to do.

Ben watched the quicksilver shift of expressions cross her face the second his other leg touched hers—puzzlement, realization, concern and finally uncertainty.

"Tracy." He leaned forward and held out his hand to her, keeping his voice low and coaxing. "I know it hasn't been easy coming here—working with me. And I wasn't even sure I wanted you here. But it was the right thing to do."

The right thing to do.

And what about what he was doing now?

He had no idea if it was the right thing or not. But the second she'd invited him into the tub he'd wondered if this was where she'd been heading the whole time. Especially when he'd started shucking his clothes and he'd seen the slightest glimmer of hunger flash through her eyes. She'd quickly doused it, but not before it had registered for what it was. He'd seen that look many a time back when they'd been a couple.

The question was, should he push the boundaries? She was vulnerable. Tired—she'd admitted it herself. Wasn't he taking advantage of that?

He started to pull his hand back when she startled him by reaching out and placing hers within it, saying, "I know it was. So is this."

Without a word she held on tight and tugged, a movement that sent her sliding across the tub towards him. Her feet went up and over his thighs, hitting the curved plastic on either side of his hips. Her forward momentum came to a halt, and his libido took up where momentum left off.

Raw need raced through his system, replacing any ethical questions he'd had a few seconds ago. With a single gesture she'd admitted she wanted him. At least, he hoped that's what it meant.

"When do you need to be back to work?" he asked.

"I'm off until tomorrow." Still two feet away from each other, her gaze swept down his face, lingering on his mouth.

Until tomorrow. That meant he had all night. He forced himself to take a long, slow breath.

He smiled. "You know, we should have thought of putting a tub like this in our back yard. It's almost as big as a pool. The only problem with it is you're still much too far away."

"Am I?" Her thumb swept across the back of his hand beneath the water. "I've come halfway. Maybe it's your turn now."

"Maybe it is." He pushed himself across the space until, instead of being separated by feet, they were now inches apart. "Better?"

She smiled. "Yes, definitely." She released his hand and propped her fingers on his shoulders, smoothing across them and sending fire licking through his gut in the process.

He curled his legs around her backside and reeled her in the rest of the way, until they were breast to chest and she had to tip her head back to look at him.

"So, here we are," he murmured. "What do we do now?"

"Do you have to ask?"

His lips curved in a slow smile. "No, but I thought I should check to make sure we were on the same page."

"Same page of the very same book."

That was all the confirmation he needed. He cupped the back of her head and stared into her eyes before doing as she'd asked: meeting her halfway. More than halfway.

He swore, even as he kissed her, that he was still working on his plan. Still analyzing every piece of information. But that lasted all of two seconds before his baser instincts kicked in and robbed him of any type of higher brain function. He'd hoped to get an inkling of whether or not the old attractions were still there.

They were.

And at the moment that attraction was groveling and begging him not to screw this up by thinking too hard.

So he didn't. The fingers in her hair tightened, the silky strands growing taut between them. A tiny sound exited her throat that Ben definitely recognized. Tracy had always been turned on by control.

His over her. Or at least that's what she let herself believe.

In reality, though, she'd always wanted to control every aspect of her life, whereas he was happy to take things as they came. But in the bedroom it was a different story. Handing him the reins got her motor running, and right now Ben was more than happy to oblige.

Using his grip on her hair to hold her in place, he kissed along one of her gorgeous cheekbones, taking his time as he headed towards her ear.

"Ben."

His eyes closed at the sound of his name on her lips. Oh, yeah. It had been four long years since he'd heard that husky whisper—half plea, half groan. And it drove him just as crazy today as it had back then.

His teeth closed over her earlobe, while his free hand trailed slowly down the curve of her neck, continuing down her spine in long feathery strokes, until the line of her bra interrupted him. He circled the clasp a time or two, his finger gliding over the lacy strap that transected her back. One snap and he had it undone.

A whimper escaped her throat, but she couldn't move, still held fast by his hand in her hair. He tugged her head back a bit further, exposing the line of her throat, and the vein beating madly beneath her ear. He licked it, pressed his tongue tight against that throbbing pulse point, glorying in the way those rhythmic waves traveled straight to his groin, making him harder than he ever remembered being. Unable to contain his need, he whispered, "I want you. Right here. Right now. Say yes."

She moistened her lips, but didn't keep him waiting long before responding. "Yes."

"Yes." He breathed in the word and released her hair, his hands going to the straps on her shoulders, peeling them down her arms and letting the piece of clothing sink to the bottom of the tank. He parted the bubbles on the surface of the water until her breasts came into full view.

"Beautiful." He cupped them. "Get up on your knees, honey."

She did as he asked, a water droplet clinging to the hard tip of her left nipple. Who could blame it? Certainly not him, because that was right where he wanted to be.

Lowering his head, he licked the drop off, her quick intake of breath telling him she liked the way he lingered, her fingers on the back of his head emphasizing her point.

He pulled away slightly, and looked up at her with hooded eyes. "Ask for it, Tracy."

Her lips parted, but she didn't utter a word, already knowing that wasn't what he was looking for. Instead, she kept her hands braced against his nape, and arched her back until the breast he'd been courting was back against his mouth. She slowly drew the erect nipple along his lower lip.

"That's it," he whispered against her skin. "I love it when you do that."

He opened his mouth, and she shifted closer. When his lips closed around her and sucked, her body went rigid, and she cried out softly. He gave her what she wanted, using his teeth, his tongue to give her the same pleasure she'd just given him. God, he loved knowing what she wanted and making her reach for it. His arms went around her back, his hands sliding beneath the band of her panties and cupping her butt. He slipped his fingers lower and encountered a slick moisture that had nothing to do with the water all around them. Raw need roared through him.

Knowing he was coming close to the edge of his own limits, he found her center and slid a finger deep inside her, then another, reveling in the way she lowered herself until they were fully embedded. He held her steady with one hand while his mouth and fingers swept her along re-membered paths, her breathing picking up in time with his movements.

Not long now.

And he was ready for her. More than ready. He ached to be where his fingers were.

He clamped down with his teeth and at the same time applied steady pressure in the depths of her body, and just like in days past, she moaned loudly, her body stiffening as she trembled on the precipice before exploding around his fingers in a series of spasms that rocked his world. Within seconds he'd freed himself and lifted her onto his erec-tion, sweeping aside the crotch of her panties as he thrust hard and deep.

Hell. His breath left his lungs as memories flooded back.

Except everything was even better than he remembered, her still pulsing body exquisitely tight, her head thrown back, dark, glossy hair tumbling free around her bare shoulders as she rode him. Over and over, squeezing and releasing, until he could hold back no longer and with a sharp groan he joined her, falling right over the edge into paradise.

CHAPTER ELEVEN

A DISASTER. THAT'S what yesterday's session in the water tank had been.

Tracy stood in front of the tiny mirror in the bathroom and examined her bare breasts. Really looked at them for the first time in a long time. She'd spent the last several years avoiding everything they represented.

And yet they'd brought her such pleasure yesterday.

It was a paradox. One she'd tried to blank out by pretending they didn't exist. Only Ben had forced an awareness that was as uncomfortable as it was real. How much longer was she going to keep running away?

I'm not!

Tracy continued to stare at her reflection, her lips giving a wry twist. She'd believed those two words once, even as she'd scurried from one place to another. Now…? Well, now she wasn't so sure.

She should tell him. Now that the anger was gone, he should know the truth of what she'd been facing back then.

Why? What good could possibly come of it now that they were no longer together? Did she want him to feel guilty for what he'd done? For touching her there?

No. She wanted him to remember it the same way she did—as a pleasurable interlude that shouldn't be repeated.

She raised her hands and cupped herself, remembering

the way Ben's fingers had done the same—the way he'd brought his mouth slowly down…

Shaking her head, she let her arms fall back to her sides.

As great as their time together had been, retracing her steps and venturing back into an unhappy past was not a wise move. Ben had been miserable with her by the end of their marriage.

But how much of that had been her doing? Had been because of what she'd become? A phantom, too scared to sit in any one spot for too long—who had felt the walls of their house closing in around her any time she'd spent more than a couple of weeks there.

So how could she have let yesterday happen?

She had no idea.

Even though she could freely admit it had been a mistake, could even recite each and every reason it had been the wrong thing to do, she couldn't force herself to be sorry for those stolen moments. She'd always known what she'd felt for Ben was powerful—that she'd never feel the same way about another man—and being with him again had just driven that point home.

Which meant she couldn't let it happen again.

Reaching for her clothes, she hurriedly pulled them on, turning her back to the mirror like she always did and feeling like a fraud. It was one thing to admit her reasons for doing something. It was another thing entirely to change her behavior. Especially when that behavior had served her perfectly well for the past four years.

At least…until now.

By the time she made it to the makeshift hospital, Daniel was sitting in a chair next to his bed, his chin on his chest. His eyes were dry, but his arms were wrapped around his waist as if he was in pain.

She squatted next to him. "Daniel, what's wrong? Does something hurt?"

He shook his head, but didn't move from his slumped position.

"Then what is it?"

Several seconds went by before he answered her. "Where will we go?"

The question was so soft she had to lean forward to hear it, and even then she wasn't sure she'd caught his words.

"I'm sorry?"

Lifting his head, he glanced around the space. She twisted to do the same and noted several of the beds were newly empty—fresh sheets neatly pulled up and tucked in as if ready for new patients. Only there probably wouldn't be any.

There'd been no deaths in the last day or so, and the people who'd become ill after the teams had arrived had ended up with much less severe versions of the illness. It definitely made a case for early intervention.

"This is…was our living room…before my mom—before she…" He stopped and took a deep breath. "Once Cleo and I are well enough to leave here, where will we stay?"

Tracy's heart broke all over again. She'd been worrying over her little tryst with Ben when Daniel and Cleo were now facing life without the only parent they'd ever known. And because the two had no relatives that anyone knew of, and as their home was now being used as a temporary hospital, there was literally nowhere for the siblings to go once they were cleared of infection. Oh, the military would probably take them to a state-run orphanage once the quarantine period was lifted. But until then? No one was allowed in or out of the village.

Surely they could stay here in what had once been their home. But where? Every room was being used, whether to house soldiers or medical personnel. It was full. More than full. Even Pedro—whom she'd barely had a chance to speak to in recent days—had moved from where he'd been staying and was now bunking with members of the military unit assigned to São João dos Rios.

She thought for a minute. Ben kept talking about how much he cared about these kids. Maybe it was time to put that to the test. "We can ask to have two more hammocks put up in the room where Dr. Almeida and I sleep. At least until we figure something else out."

Once she'd said it she wondered if that wouldn't make the whole thing feel a little too much like a family for comfort. And she didn't want to give Daniel and Cleo the idea that they could stay together permanently. Because that wasn't on the cards.

Besides, she wasn't sure Ben would be thrilled about sharing his room with a preteen and a child, especially after the slow smile he'd given her that morning. The one that had her face heating despite her best efforts. He'd even stayed and slept in his own hammock last night—a first since they'd arrived. Was it because of what they'd done?

She must have thought so because it was what had set off the self-examination in the bathroom. She hadn't touched herself like that in a long time.

"Will the soldiers let us go with you?" Daniel gave her a hopeful smile.

No backing out now.

"I don't see why they wouldn't, but you'll have to get well first, which means you'll need to get some rest." What else could she say? They couldn't just let Daniel and Cleo wander the streets or sleep in one of the unoccupied houses. The pair had had a home and a family not three weeks ago. And now it was all gone.

She'd been there, done that. She could at least try to

help these children as much as she could before she had to leave—be their temporary family, kind of like a foster-care situation. At least until they figured out something a little more permanent.

How was she supposed to do that before she headed back to São Paulo?

Something she didn't want to think about right now.

Just then, Ben walked into the room, his brow raised in question when he saw the two of them sitting together. She stood, glancing down at Daniel, and noted with horror he had a huge smile on his face.

Don't, Daniel. Not yet. Let me talk to him first.

But even as she thought it, the boy spoke up. "Tracy says Cleo and I can stay with you once we are well."

Ben's glance shot to her. "She did? When?"

"Just now. I explained we did not have any place to go, and she offered to let us stay with you. Cleo was scared." He blinked a couple of times as if that last statement had been hard for him to admit. "We both were…about what might happen. If they tried to take Cleo away from me…" He didn't finish the rest of his statement.

Ben's face grew stormy. "Tracy? Would you like to explain?"

"I, um… Well, I simply said we would figure something out…"

"Figure something out," he parroted.

Daniel's smile never wavered. He had no idea Ben's now icy glare was sucking the heat right out of the atmosphere.

Nodding, Daniel continued, "Yes, so Cleo and I wouldn't be alone—so we could stay together."

Oh, no! He'd obviously misunderstood her intentions—had thought she'd meant the living arrangements would continue even after they left the town. Ben was going to blow his top.

"Well, Daniel, I'm glad to hear she's making those kinds of plans." He moved toward her. "Can I borrow her for a minute?"

"Yes, I have to tell Cleo the good news, anyway. One of the doctors is helping her walk around the yard outside. She should be back in a minute."

Right on cue, Cleo and her companion came through the door and made their way slowly towards them.

"Tracy, do you mind?" Giving a sharp nod toward the door to indicate she should follow him, Ben stalked toward it.

Gulping back her own dismay, she forced a smile to her face. "I won't be long. Could you tell Cleo I'll be back to check on you both in a few minutes?"

As upset as Ben was, she couldn't help but feel a fierce sense of gratitude over the kids' steady improvement. From all indications, they were going to recover fully.

Two miracles in a sea of sorrows.

They'd lost fourteen patients in all. In such a tiny village it was a good percentage of the population. They'd have a hard time coming back from this without some type of government aid. Whether that meant sending them to another town and bulldozing these homes, or finding a way to get things up and running again, nothing would truly be the same again. They would not soon forget what had happened here.

Neither would she.

Pushing through the door, she saw that Ben was already striding down the hallway on his way out of the house. She hurried after him, knowing he must be furious. But once he heard her explanation, he'd understand that…

The second the bright noonday sun hit her retinas, a hand reached out and tugged her to the side, into the shadow of the house.

"Would you like to tell me what the hell that was all about? You expect those kids to stay with us once we leave here? Kind of hard, as we no longer live in the same house. Or even the same state."

"No. Of course not. He took my words the wrong way. I was only talking about here in the village. That they could stay in our room once they left the hospital." She reached out to squeeze his fingers then let go. "They have nowhere else to go. I didn't know what to say."

"So you said they could stay with us?" He swore softly. "Are you that worried about being alone with me, Tracy?"

She looked at him blankly for a second or two. "What are you talking about?"

"I'm talking about what happened between us yesterday." He propped his hands on his hips. "I think it's a little late to start worrying about your virtue—or reputation— or whatever you want to call it."

What a ridiculous thing for him to say. "You're wrong. This has nothing to do with what happened. Nothing."

"Then why?"

Was it her imagination, or was there a shadow of hurt behind his pale eyes?

"They have nowhere to go until the outbreak is over. This was their house, remember? Once they're released from care, they'll be expected to leave, just like our other patients have. They have no relatives here—or anywhere else, if what Daniel said was true."

Ben pivoted and leaned against the wall, dragging a hand through his hair, which was already damp from the heat of the day. "You're right. I thought…"

Since he didn't finish his sentence, she had no idea *what* he thought.

Maybe he was worried she was making a play for him. That she wanted to move back to their old house. No, that didn't make any sense. He'd given no hint he wanted to start things back up between them. For all she knew, he'd just needed to get laid, and she'd practically put up a neon sign saying she was ready, willing and able to take care of that need.

What had she been thinking, inviting him to get in the tub?

Well, it was over and done with. They were both adults. They *both* had needs—heaven knew, hers hadn't been met in quite some time. Four years, to be exact. She hadn't been with anyone since she'd left him.

To say that the experience yesterday had been cataclysmic was an understatement. A huge one.

"Maybe we can put up a curtain or something." She pressed her shoulder to the wall and looked up at him. "Can they stay with us? At least for a little while?"

"Of course they can." The words were soft, but he seemed distracted, almost as if his mind was already on something else entirely. "I'll check with General Gutierrez, and see what he can do about finding them a place to stay after the quarantine is lifted."

"Thank you." She leaned closer and stretched up to kiss his cheek, her hand going to his arm and lingering there. "And I'm sorry Daniel dropped it on you like that. He asked, and it was the only thing I could think of. I was hoping to talk to you alone before we made any decisions."

"What are you going to do about the other part? If he misunderstood, someone is going to have to talk to him."

"I know." She blew out a breath. "Let's give it a few days, though, okay? Until they're stronger and we see how things are going to play out here. Maybe someone in the town can take them in."

"That might pose a bit of a problem." He paused before

covering her hand with his own. "I came by to tell you something is getting ready to happen."

Her internal radar went on high alert. "With the military?"

"Yes. I sat in on another meeting today." His jaw tightened. "The news wasn't good. And despite what you think, my opinion doesn't always hold that much sway."

Her skin grew clammy at the way he said it. "What are they going to do?"

Tracy had heard tell of things going on behind the scenes where the military police were concerned. Although many were honest, hard-working, family men, there were others who wouldn't think twice about asking for a bribe.

She'd also heard stories about other branches of the police colluding with the drug cartels that worked out of the *favelas*. The shanty towns were notorious for narcotics and illegal dealings. Many of the slums actually had armed thugs guarding the roads leading to the rickety housing developments. It was not only dangerous for the police to enter such places, it was often deadly. Only the corrupt cops could enter and leave with impunity.

"Nothing's been decided for sure. They're still discussing options with the central government."

The hair on the back of her neck rose at the quiet way he said it. She thought again about Daniel's words and the way she'd found him sitting in that chair. He'd seemed almost hopeless. An unsettling thought occurred to her.

"When Daniel mentioned having nowhere to go, I assumed he was talking about for the next several days. But you and he both jumped to the same conclusion about my offer. You both thought the offer was something more permanent."

"Yes."

"Why is that?" Her voice dropped to a whisper. "What's going to happen here, Ben?"

When she tried to drop her hand from his arm, he held on, fingers tightening around hers. "Remember I told you they were going to lift the quarantine in another week? That we—along with the rest of the medical and military personnel—would be allowed to leave once there were no new cases of the plague?"

"I remember."

"Have you looked around you lately? At the survivors?"

She tried to think. One young mother said her husband was trying to pack all their belongings. She'd assumed it was because they wanted to leave for a while to try to forget the horrors of what had happened here. But what if that was not the reason at all? "I know one couple is preparing to leave. So the military must be planning on lifting the quarantine for everyone at the same time."

"Oh they're lifting it all right. The people you mentioned aren't the only ones getting ready for a big move. There are signs of packing going on all over town. Windows being boarded up. *Acerolas* being bulk-harvested from trees."

She had noticed the berries being picked and put into baskets.

"So everyone is going to leave when this is over? They're going to board up the entire town?" If so, what did that mean for Daniel and Cleo?

"No, they're not going to board it up."

"What, then?"

He drew a deep breath then released it on a sigh. "They're planning to destroy the town once this is all over."

Her eyes widened. "Destroy it? How?"

"The same way they're destroying the bodies. They're going to torch everything, until nothing is left of this place but ashes."

CHAPTER TWELVE

A FAMILY. HE'D always wanted one, but not this way. Not at someone else's expense. And certainly not at the expense of an entire village.

He could still hear the pained cry Tracy had given when he'd told her the news.

Ben leaned against the wall as she helped Daniel attach one end of the hammock to the protective iron grating that covered the window. She gave the rope a tug to make sure it would hold. He'd offered to help, only to have her wave him off, saying Daniel needed something to do.

Maybe she did as well.

He tried to read her body language and the furtive glances she periodically threw his way. They hadn't had much of a chance to talk since she'd had to go back to work at the hospital, but her horror when he'd shared the military's plans had been obvious. They both knew it happened in various countries. Not just in Brazil. It could even happen in the United States, if there were ever a deadly enough epidemic. The same heartbreaking choice might have to be made: contain it, for the good of the general population.

In this case, he wasn't sure it *was* the only option. But in a poor state like *Piauí*, it was the easiest one. São João dos Rios was pretty far off the beaten path. It would be expensive for the military to come in and check the village periodically to make sure the outbreak didn't erupt again, as they still hadn't isolated the initial source of the infection. And if it did recur and spread to a place like *Teresina*— the state capital—it could affect hundreds of thousands of people. If he thought fourteen deaths were far too many, how would he feel if that number was multiplied tenfold?

Hopefully Tracy realized he'd been upset for another reason entirely when she'd explained about Daniel and Cleo sharing their room. And the spark that had lit in his gut when Daniel had talked about them all living together had been hard to contain once it had started burning, although he'd better find a way to extinguish it quickly, because Tracy had no intention of letting this arrangement become permanent.

Well, neither did he.

But he *had* been hoping to have Tracy to himself a little while longer before they went their separate ways. Why he wanted that, he wasn't sure. Maybe just to understand her reasons for inviting him into that tub. To say it had been unexpected would be an understatement.

That was the least of his worries right now, however. The folks in charge were concerned about this getting out to the press. Yeah, hearing that your own military had sluiced cans of gasoline over an entire village and set it ablaze would not be the most popular story. Which was why they were trying to go about it quietly and peacefully. They'd spread the word that stipends would be awarded to anyone who agreed to leave town after the quarantine was lifted.

If they could relocate all the townsfolk before the match was struck, no one would be the wiser—except Ben and a few other key people—until long after the fact. Telling Tracy had probably been a mistake, in fact. But given their history—and her distrust of the military—what else could he have done? Keeping this to himself would have given her one more reason to hate him.

As far as Ben was concerned, as long as no one was hurt, these were just buildings. But he knew Tracy would feel differently. It was one point they'd argued about in the past. He tended to see things with a scientific bent, rather than an emotional one. But it was also one of the things he'd loved about her. She was the balance to his cold, analytical stance, forcing him to see another side to issues. Which made his actions in the past seem childish and petty. If he'd waited until she'd gotten home to talk to her calmly and explained his concerns, would things have turned out differently?

Possibly. There was no way to know.

But it was another of the reasons he'd talked about the military's plans this time. Nothing good could come from discovering the truth from someone else. If she realized he'd kept the information to himself, she'd be furious. And that's the last thing he wanted. Especially after their time in that home-made hot tub—or cooling tub, in this case.

Daniel secured the last of the knots and tried to hop onto the hammock to check it out, but ended up being flipped back onto the floor instead. He lay there panting as if he was exhausted, which he probably was. He was still weak from his illness. Ben pushed away from the wall and reached the boy before Tracy did, holding out a hand. "Easy. You need to regain some strength before trying stuff like that. Besides, you've been on a cot for the last week and a half. You'll have to get used to sleeping in a hammock again."

Daniel let Ben help him up and then rubbed his backside with a rueful grin. "I feel so much better than before, so I forget." He glanced around the space, already cramped from three hammocks. "Where will Cleo sleep?"

"We'll string another hammock above yours. Kind of like bunk beds. Only you're taller, so you'll sleep in the top one." Ben nodded at the bars on the windows. "They're strong enough to support both hammocks."

Tracy stood next to him. "Good idea. I was beginning to wonder how we were all going to fit."

He gave her a pained smile. "I could always put you up on top, but…" He let the words trail off, knowing she'd catch his implication.

True to form, pink stained both her cheeks, and she turned away to adjust the fan they'd brought in from one of the other rooms. "This will help keep the mosquitoes away, as most of nets are being used by the hospital."

"We never used them at home anyway," Daniel said.

Tracy's sister had died of dengue fever, so she was a little more paranoid about using the netting than many Brazilians. He couldn't blame her. He still remembered the day he'd come home to find the milky netting draped across their huge canopy bed. Despite the fact that her reasons for putting it up had had nothing to do with romance and everything to do with safety, he still found it incredibly intimate once they were both inside. And when he'd made love to her within the confines of the bed, there'd been a raw, primitive quality to Tracy that had shaken him to the core. She'd fallen pregnant that night.

A shaft of pain went through him.

Her eyes met his and she gave a rueful smile, her face growing even pinker. She was remembering those nights as well. He could at least be glad some of those memories made her smile, rather than filling her with bitterness.

And then there were these two kids. What was going to happen to them if the village really was burned down?

Something else he was better off not thinking about, because there wasn't a thing he could do about it.

Tracy says Cleo and I can stay with you once we are well.

If only it were that easy.

Wasn't it?

He swallowed, the words replaying in his head again and again. Evidently that "bath" had permanently messed something up in his skull. Was he actually thinking about taking on somebody else's kids?

He forced his mind back to the mosquito-net conversation between Tracy and Daniel, which was still going strong.

Interrupting her, he said, "We haven't been using nets either, Trace. It's not dengue season anyway."

"I know."

He sensed she wanted to say something further, maybe even about their current situation, but Daniel's presence made sharing any kind of confidences more complicated, if not impossible. And that went for any other kind of intimacies they might have shared in this room. Because with Daniel officially sprung from the infirmary, there was no possibility of that. But he would have liked to have talked to Tracy about…stuff.

Maybe even apologize for his actions four years ago.

"Will they still let me see Cleo?"

Surprisingly, Daniel had recovered faster than his sister, who would be in the infirmary for another day or so. And if he knew Tracy, she'd be sleeping in a chair next to the girl's bed, in case Daniel's absence made her jittery.

Tracy glanced at her watch. "I don't see why not. It's only seven o'clock. Curfew isn't for another three hours."

That was another thing. Yesterday, the military had suddenly instituted a curfew without warning. They'd said it was to prevent looting now that more people were recovering, but Ben had a feeling it had more to do with news being passed from person to person than anything else. Why prevent looting in a place they were planning to burn down?

No, it made no sense, other than the fact it was easier to keep an eye on folks during the daytime. If they imposed a curfew, they had more control over what went on after dark.

"Okay," Daniel said, then hesitated. "Do you need me to help with anything else?"

Tracy shook her head and smiled at him. "No, just be back by ten—tell Cleo I'll be there in a little while. And we'll try to rustle up a snack before bedtime, okay? We need to build up your strength."

The concern in her voice made Ben's heart ache. Tracy would have been a good mother had her job not consumed her every waking moment.

Job or no job, though, his own behavior back then wasn't something he was proud of.

It made him even more determined to set the record straight and see if they could make peace about the past. With Daniel sharing their room, he wasn't sure when he'd get the chance. But he intended to try. The sooner the better.

Tracy glanced at the door as it closed behind Daniel. She was still having trouble processing what Ben had told her. They were going to burn the town down? Without letting anyone have a say?

What would happen to Daniel and Cleo if that happened? She'd hoped maybe someone here would be willing to take on the kids since places like São João dos Rios tended to be close-knit communities. But if they all were forced to scatter in different directions, the kids might end up in a slum or an orphanage…or worse.

"What are those kids going to do now, Ben?" She pulled

her hair up into a loose ponytail and used the elastic she wore around her wrist to secure it in place. Her neck felt moist and sticky, despite the gusts of warm air the fan pushed their way from time to time.

"I don't know." He leaned down to the tiny refrigerator he'd brought from his lab and opened the door. Tossing her a cold bottle of water, he took one out for himself, twisting the top and taking a long pull.

Tracy paused to press her bottle against her overheated face, welcoming the shock of cold as it hit her skin. Closing her eyes, she rolled the plastic container along her cheek until she reached her hairline, before repeating the action on the other side. Then she uncapped the bottle and sipped at it. "There's something to be said about cold water. Thanks."

"No problem. How long do you think he'll be?"

"Daniel?" She turned to look at him, suspicion flaring within her. "He'll probably be a while. He and Cleo are close."

"They certainly seem to be."

Surely he wasn't thinking about trying something in the boy's absence. "Why did you ask?"

"What Daniel said made me think about their future, and I thought we could try to figure something out, especially if the military's plans become a reality."

"What can we do?"

"I'm not sure." He scrubbed a hand across the back of his neck. "Maybe one of the villagers could take the kids with them when they leave."

"I thought about that as well, but I don't see how. The whole town will be uprooted and scattered. Most of them will have to live with other people for a while, until they get back on their feet. Adding two more mouths to the equation...?" She took a quick drink.

"You know how these things work, Ben. The people here

are barely scraping by. To lose their homes, their livelihood? The last thing they'll be thinking about is two orphaned kids—no matter how well liked they are."

And how was she going to walk away from them when the time came? How could she bear to look those children in the eye with an apologetic shrug and then climb into Ben's car?

There was a long pause. Then Ben said in a low voice, "Ever since Daniel misunderstood what you meant, something's been rattling around in my head."

"Really? What?"

Before he could say anything, Daniel came skidding down the hallway, his face as white as the wall behind him. "Please, come. Cleo is sick. Really sick."

CHAPTER THIRTEEN

TRACY STROKED CLEO's head, while Ben glanced at the readout. "Almost three hundred. No wonder she's not feeling well."

Her blood-sugar levels were sky-high.

"She's mentioned having a headache on and off, but I thought it was because of the plague. I had no idea. Is she diabetic?"

"I don't know." He glanced at Pedro, who was standing near the head of the bed and had been the one to send Daniel to find them. "Did anyone notice her breath smelling off?"

A fruity smell was one sign of diabetes, and something one of them should have noticed.

Tracy bristled at his tone, however. "We've been fighting the plague for the last week and a half, Ben. We weren't looking for anything else."

"It wasn't a criticism. Just a question. Would you mind calling Daniel back into the room?"

Poor Daniel. He'd been banished as they'd tried to assess a thrashing Cleo, who not only had a headache but stomach cramps as well. It had seemed to take ages for Ben to get the finger-prick. They'd need to get a urine sample as well to make sure the child's body wasn't flooded with ketones. Without enough insulin to break down sugar, the body would begin converting fat into energy. That process resulted in ketones, which could quickly grow to toxic levels.

Cleo had quieted somewhat, but she was still restless on her cot, her head twisting back and forth on the pillow.

The second the boy came into the room, Ben asked him, "Does your sister have diabetes?"

"Diabetes?" A blank stare was all he received. "Is it from this sickness we had?"

Of course he wouldn't know anything about glucose levels or what too much sugar circulating in the bloodstream could lead to. Many of these people didn't get regular medical care. And what they did get was confined to emergencies or critical illnesses. Surely if the girl had type-one diabetes, though, someone would have figured it out. "Could her glucose levels have been affected by the plague?" Tracy asked.

"Possibly. Serious illnesses can wreak havoc on some of those balances. Or maybe her pancreas was affected. The plague isn't always confined the lungs. We'll pray the change is temporary, but in the meantime we need to get some insulin into her and monitor her blood-sugar levels."

"And if it's not temporary?"

"Let's take one thing at a time." Ben stripped off his gloves and tossed them, along with the test strip, into the wastebasket. "If the glucose doesn't stabilize on its own, we'll have to transport her somewhere so she can be diagnosed and treated."

"The hospital in *Teresina* is good."

Jotting something in a spiralbound notebook, he didn't even look up. "But she doesn't live in *Teresina*."

"She doesn't live anywhere. Not any more."

Unfortunately, she'd forgotten that Daniel was in the room. He immediately jumped on her statement. "But I thought we were going to live with you."

She threw Ben a panicked glance and was grateful when he stopped writing and came to the rescue.

"We're still hammering out the details."

Oh, Lord, how were they going to fix this? Hoping that one of the villagers would take the kids had already been a long shot. But if Cleo did have diabetes, it was doubtful if anyone from São João dos Rios would have the resources to take on her medical expenses.

She could offer to take the kids herself, but things in her life could change at any moment. Just that morning she'd faced that fact while staring in the mirror. She was going to have to do something about those test results—like sit down with a doctor and discuss her options. The more she thought about it, though, the more she was leaning toward a radical solution, a permanent one that would give her peace of mind once and for all. For the most part, anyway.

Maybe she could talk to Ben. Tell him what she was facing. And ask him if he would take the kids instead, at least on a temporary basis. Just until they figured out what was going on with Cleo.

And if he said no?

Then she had no idea what she was going to do. But one thing was for sure. She was not going to abandon Cleo. Not without doing everything in her power to make sure the girl was in good hands.

After they got a dose of insulin into her, they monitored her for the next two hours, until her blood-sugar levels began to decrease. An hour before curfew and knowing there would be little sleep to be had, Tracy asked Ben to walk with her to get a cup of coffee from the cafeteria, leaving Pedro and Daniel to stand watch. Several carafes were still on the buffet table, left over from the evening meal. Two of the pitchers even had some warm dregs left in them. Ben handed her a cup of the thick, black liquid and she spooned some sugar into hers to cut the bitter edge, while Ben drank his plain.

He made a face. "Not quite like I make at home."

Tracy smiled. "You always did make great coffee."

They wandered over to one of the tables at the back of the room. Ben waited for her to sit then joined her.

She nursed her cup for a moment before saying anything. "Do you think Cleo's blood sugar is going to drop back to normal once she's better?"

"I hope so."

"Ben...about what Daniel said..." She drew a deep breath and then blurted it out. "Maybe you could take them."

"Take them where? They don't have family that we know of."

Oh, boy. Something was about to hit that wheezy fan in the window behind her. But she had to ask. Had to try. "No, I mean maybe you could take them in for a while. Make sure Cleo gets the treatment she needs. It wouldn't have to be permanent."

Ben's brows drew together, and he stared at her for several long seconds. "What?"

Once the words were out, there was no retracting them, and they just seemed to keep tumbling from her mouth. "You always said you wanted kids. Well, this is the perfect solution—you won't even need a wife to birth them for you."

"I won't need a wife to...birth them?" His frown grew even stormier. "Is that how you felt about your pregnancy? That I was dooming you to be some type of brood mare? And our baby was just an inconvenience to be endured?"

"Oh, Ben, of course not. I wanted that baby as much as you did." She set her coffee down and wrapped her hands

around the cup. "There were just circumstances that…
Well, it doesn't matter now."

"What circumstances?"

"I don't want to talk about that. I want to figure out how
to help these kids."

"And your way of doing that is by asking someone else to
take them on?" He blew out an exasperated breath. "What
are they supposed to do while I'm at work? Cleo can't monitor her own blood sugar."

"Daniel is practically a teen. And he's already displayed
an enormous amount of responsibility. If she is diabetic,
he could help." She plowed ahead. "You've seen how well
behaved they are. They could—"

"I can't believe you're putting this all on me, Tracy." His
fingers made angry tracks through his hair. "If you feel so
strongly about it, why don't *you* take them?"

She knew it was an illogical thought, but if she ended
up having surgery, who would watch the kids while she
was recovering? It wasn't simply a matter of removing her
breasts and being done with it. She wanted reconstruction
afterwards. Each step of the process took time. Hospital
time. Recovery time.

Both physical and emotional.

She decided to be honest as much as she could. "I can't
take them, Ben. If I thought there was any way, believe
me, I'd be the first to step up to the plate. They beat the
odds and survived the outbreak—when none of us thought
they could—so it just doesn't seem fair to abandon them
to the system."

"Said as if it's a jail sentence."

"*Teresina* is poor. I've seen the orphanages, remember?
I was one of the physicians who helped care for those children when I lived there."

"Let's go for a walk." He stood, collecting both of their

half-empty cups. "I don't want Daniel to come in and find us arguing over his fate."

Fate. What a funny word to use. But it was true. What Ben decided right here, right now, would determine those kids' futures. He could make sure Cleo got the treatment she needed. Even if this was a temporary setback, getting her glucose levels under control could take time.

Ben tossed the cups in the wastebasket and headed out the door, leaving Tracy to hurry to catch up with him.

"Won't you at least consider it?" she asked, turning sideways as she walked next to one of several abandoned houses.

He blew out a rough breath. "I don't know what you want me to say here, Tracy. I'll have to think about it. It would help to know why you're so dead set against taking them yourself."

"I travel a lot. My career—"

"Don't." The angry throbbing of a vein in his temple showed how touchy a subject this was. "Don't even play the travel card—you already know how I feel about that. Besides, I have a career too. So do millions of parents everywhere. But most of them at least want to spend a little time with their husbands and kids."

Shock roiled through her. Was that how he'd seen her? She'd known he hadn't like her traveling. Known it was because of how his parents had treated him and his brother, but hearing him say it outright hurt on a level it never had before.

"I did want to spend time with you." Her voice was quiet when it came out.

She should have told him the truth, long ago. But when he'd sent the military after her as she'd been trying to figure out how to tell him about the test results, she'd felt hurt and betrayed. And terribly, terribly angry. Angry at him, angry about her mother's death and angry that her future might not be the one she'd envisioned.

Maybe she'd turned a large part of that anger on Ben, somehow rationalizing that he didn't deserve to know the truth after what he'd done to her. Convinced herself that she didn't care what he thought—or that he might view her behavior through the lens of his childhood.

Abandoned by his parents. Abandoned by his wife.

What did that make her?

She closed her eyes, trying to block out the thought of Ben sitting alone at home night after night, while she'd tried to outrun her demons. "It's okay. If you can't take them, I'll find someone else."

"Who?"

"Pedro, maybe."

The frown was back. "You'd really ask your assistant to take two kids that you're not willing to take yourself?"

Her eyes filled with tears. "It's not that I'm not willing to. There are times I think about what our child might have looked like and I... Maybe I can take them for a while and then figure something else out." She bit her lip, unable to control the wobble of her chin.

Ben took a step forward so she was forced to look up at him then brushed wisps of hair from her temples. His hands slid around to cradle the back of her head. "I didn't say I wouldn't take them. I just said I needed to think about it. So give me a day or two, okay?"

She nodded, her heart thumping in her chest as his touch chased away the regret and did strange things to her equilibrium. "Okay."

"How do you do it?" He leaned down and slid his cheek

across hers, the familiar coarseness of his stubble wrenching at her heart.

"Do what?"

"Talk me into doing crazy stuff."

"I—I don't."

"No?" His breath swept across her ear, sending a shiver over her. "How about talking me into getting in that tub?"

Oh. He was right. She had been the one who'd invited him in. "Maybe it's not me. Maybe it's this climate. The heat messes with your brain."

"Oh, no. This is all you. *You* mess with my brain."

She didn't know if he thought she messed with it in a bad way or a good way. She suddenly hoped it was good. That he remembered their life together with some fondness, despite the heartache she'd caused him.

His lips touched her cheek then grazed along it as he continued to murmur softly to her. "Tell you what. The kids can come live at the house—temporarily, until Cleo is better and we can find something else."

She wasn't sure she'd heard him correctly. She pulled away to look at him, although the last thing she wanted was for his mouth to stop what it was doing. "You'll take them?"

"I think you missed the pronoun. I said 'we.'"

"What do you mean?"

"I'm not going to do this by myself. If Cleo's condition doesn't stabilize and this turns into full-blown diabetes, she'll need to be transported back and forth to a specialist. Her insulin levels will need to be monitored closely at first."

"Daniel—"

"Daniel is responsible, yes, but he's still just a kid. He's grieving the loss of his mother. I don't think it's fair to expect him to take on the bulk of Cleo's care."

"I agree."

"So the 'we' part of the equation means we share the

load. You and me." His sly smile warned her of what was coming before his words had a chance to register. "Until *we* can arrange something else, you'll need to come back to Teresina. With me."

CHAPTER FOURTEEN

"WHAT?"

Ben had expected an angry outburst the second she realized what he was asking. What he didn't anticipate was the stricken pain that flooded her eyes instead.

Warning bells went off inside him.

"It won't be that hard. You can relocate for six months to a year—help the kids get through one school year. You'll be closer to the Amazon, anyway, if you're in *Teresina*, because *Projeto Vida's* medical boat operates out of *Manaus*."

She stopped walking and turned to face him. "Ben, I—I can't."

Something in her face took him aback. What was going on here?

"Why can't you? And if you mention the word 'travel,' the deal is off." He held his ground. "I want Cleo to get the best treatment available. In fact, I want that just as much as you do, but you've got to tell me why you can't sacrifice one year of your life to help make sure she does."

She turned away from him and crossed over to the trunk of a huge mango tree, fingering the bark.

Not about to let her off the hook, he followed her, putting his hands on her shoulders. She whirled round to face him.

"You want to know why I'm reluctant to commit to a

year in Teresina? Why I traveled so much while I was carrying our child?"

"Yes." He kept his eyes on hers, even as the first tears spilled over her lashes.

"Because I have the BRCA1 mutation. And I don't know when—or even if—that switch might suddenly flip on."

"BRCA…" His mind went blank for a second before his training kicked in. "One of the breast-cancer markers?"

A lot of information hit his system at once: Tracy's mother's early death from the disease, her grandmother's death. Next came shock. She'd been tested for the gene variation? There's no way she'd draw that kind of conclusion without some kind of definitive proof. "When did you find out?"

"A while ago." Her green eyes skipped away from his. "After my mother passed away."

An ugly suspicion went through his mind. Her mom had died not long after they'd married. A lot of things suddenly became clear. The frantic pace she'd kept. Her withdrawal a month or so before she'd finally walked out on him. "It was while you were pregnant, wasn't it?"

She nodded.

"You went through genetic testing and never said a word to me?"

"I didn't want to worry you. And then when the test came back positive…" She shook her head. "I was trying to think of a way to tell you. Before I could, you sent the military into that village. I was angry. Hurt. And then I lost the baby."

And then she'd lost the baby.

A streak of raw fury burst through his system closing off his throat and trapping all kinds of angry words inside as he remembered that time. She'd stood in his office a week and a half ago and accused him of going behind her back, and yet she'd traipsed around the country, carrying this huge secret.

Oh, no. That was where he drew the line.

"Yes, I did go behind your back, and I was wrong for doing that. But how is that any different than what you did? You went behind *my* back and had yourself tested for a gene that could impact your life…our future as a couple. How could you have kept that a secret?"

"You're right, Ben. I'm sorry." Her hands went to his, which had drawn up into tight fists as he'd talked. Her fingers curved around them. "At first I was just scared, wondering what it meant for our baby—and if it was a girl, if I would pass the gene to her. Then I worried about how this would affect us as a couple. I—I didn't want your pity."

"Believe me, pity is the last thing I'm feeling right now." At the top of the list was anger. Anger that she'd suffered in silence. Anger that she hadn't trusted him enough to say anything.

"I probably should have told you. I know that now."

"Probably? *Probably?* I cannot believe you just used that word."

She swallowed. "Okay, I *should* have told you."

"We were supposed to be a couple, Tracy. A team. I shared every part of my life with you. Didn't keep one thing from you."

"I know it doesn't seem right. But when you've had some time to think about it—"

"I don't need time to think."

When he started to pull away from her completely, she gripped his wrists, holding him in place. "Try to understand, Ben. My mom had died of cancer six months after we were married. We got pregnant sooner than we expected to, and I started to worry. Being tested was something I did on impulse, just to put my mind at ease. I didn't expect the results to come back the way they did."

"And yet you kept them to yourself. Even when they did."

"Yes."

The anger drained out of him, leaving him exhausted. "It explains everything."

And yet it explained nothing.

Not really. Millions of women faced these same kinds of decisions. And most of them didn't shut their loved ones out completely. Only Tracy had also been facing the loss of their child in addition to the test results. Not to mention what she'd viewed as a betrayal on his part.

He wrapped his arms around her and pulled her close, tucking her head against his shoulder.

"I'm sorry, Ben," she repeated. The low words were muffled by his shirt, but he heard them, sensed they were coming from her heart.

He didn't respond, just let the charged emotions crash over him until they were all spent.

Nothing could change what had happened back then. It was what it was. She'd made her decision, and now he had to make his. How he was going to handle this newfound knowledge?

"This is why you don't want to take Daniel and Cleo yourself."

"Yes."

Wow. He tried to find the right words but found himself at a loss. Maybe like she'd been when she'd found out?

He gripped her upper arms and edged her back a little so he could look at her face. Fresh tear tracks had appeared, although she hadn't let out any kind of sound.

"This isn't a death sentence, Tracy." He wiped the moisture from her cheeks and eyes with the pad of his thumb.

"Carrying the gene mutation doesn't mean you'll develop the disease."

"My mom and grandmother did."

"I know. But knowledge is power. You know to be vigilant."

"I know that I might have to take preventative measures."

Something she'd hinted at earlier. "Tamoxifen?" He'd heard that some of the chemo drugs were being used as a preventative measure nowadays, much like the antibiotics they'd used on those exposed to the plague in São João dos Rios. All in the hope of killing any cancer cells before they had a chance to develop and multiply.

"Some women choose to go that route, yes."

"But not you." It was a statement, because from her phrasing it was clear that she wasn't looking at that option. Or had looked at it and rejected it.

"No. Not me." She licked her lips. "I've been weighing the benefits of prophylactic surgery."

"Surgery…" He blinked as he realized exactly what she was saying. "You're thinking of having an elective mastectomy?" Against his will, his glance went to her chest and then back to her face.

"Yes. That's what I'm saying. I don't know the timing yet, but I realized not long ago that if I can head it off, that's what I'm going to do."

Shit.

He remembered their time in the tub and how he'd gently caressed her breasts. Kissed them. What had she been thinking as he'd brought her nipples to hard peaks? Even then, she hadn't said a word. Maybe she had been committing the sensations to memory.

Okay, now *his* vision was starting to go a little funny. He tightened his jaw. Tracy had said the last thing she wanted from him was pity. He needed to suck it up. Then again, she'd had a whole lot longer to process the information than he had. And ultimately she was right. It was her decision to make. He might disagree or object or even urge her to go ahead and do it, but he wasn't the one who'd have to live with the aftermath. Tracy was.

And he'd had no idea what she'd been facing all this time. He was surprised she hadn't chosen to have the surgery right after their break-up.

He decided not to say anything. Instead, he opted to go a completely different route.

But before he could, she spoke again. "So you see why I'm reluctant to say yes. I was planning to meet with a doctor when I got back to São Paulo."

"Give it some time, Tracy. Neither one of us should make any hard and fast decisions right on the heels of fighting this outbreak." He tucked a lock of hair behind one of her ears. "I'll be honest, though. I don't think I can commit to taking on Cleo's treatment on my own. And I'm not sure it would be fair to her or Daniel. I'm away a lot. Sometimes for days at a time."

"Kind of like I used to be." The words had a ring of challenge to them.

"The difference is I don't have a partner or children at home. Not any more."

She sighed. "And I did."

His thumb stroked her earlobe, watching as her pupils dilated at his touch. "Give me six months to a year of your time, Trace, and I'll take the kids on. I'm not asking you to renew our wedding vows or even get back together. We just have to…work as partners. For the sake of the kids, until Cleo is fully recovered and we can find a better place for them."

"I don't know. Give me a couple of days to make a decision, okay?"

"You've got it. But as for timeframes, we don't have that long, remember? São João dos Rios has less than a week. And then Cleo—and everyone else—will be escorted out."

CHAPTER FIFTEEN

INSULIN WAS A blessing and a curse.

A blessing because the change in Cleo had been almost immediate when they'd pushed the first dose into her. A curse, because this might be something she'd have to do for the rest of her life.

It explained why her body had taken so much longer to recuperate from the plague than that of her brother. She'd improve a little bit and then go back three steps for seemingly no reason. They'd assumed it was because she was one of the first victims. In reality it had been because the sugar had built up in her system like a toxin, infecting her tissue as surely as the plague had.

The insulin had worked. Today the little girl was well enough to walk the short distance from the village to a clearing to accompany Daniel, Ben and herself as they took care of some important business.

Just like a little family.

And that made her heart ache even more as they caught sight of the first of the cement markers on the other side of a small wooden fence.

"Will I see Mommy again?" Cleo's voice wobbled the tiniest bit.

"I think you will, honey. But only after you've had a long and healthy life."

Tracy wanted to do everything in her power to make sure that happened.

Even move back to *Teresina* for a while?

Ben stopped at an empty site beneath a tree, carrying a flat sandstone rock in one hand and a hammer and chisel he'd found in a neighbor's shed in the other. "How does this spot look?"

"Beautiful," Tracy said. "How about to you guys?"

Cleo nodded, but Daniel remained silent, his mouth set in a mutinous line, looking off to the left. He'd been silent since Cleo had asked if their mother would have a grave and a stone like their grandparents did. But when they'd given the boy a chance to remain behind, he'd trailed along at a distance, before steadily gaining ground until he'd been walking beside Ben.

"*O que foi?*" Cleo went over to Daniel and took his hand in hers, her concern obvious. "*Estás triste?*"

He shook his head. "*Vovô está por aí.*"

Ah, so that's why he was looking in that direction. His grandparents' graves were to the left. Cleo had assumed, like Tracy had, that Daniel was struggling with his grief. And maybe that was partially true. But he also wanted his mom's grave to be next to that of his grandparents.

"Can you show us where they are?" she asked.

Without a word, Daniel trudged to a spot about twenty yards to his left, where a weathered tombstone canted backwards.

Ben laid his tools on the ground and set to righting the stone as best he could, packing dirt into the furrow behind it. The names Louisa and Jorge were inscribed on the top, along with the surname Silva. Louisa had outlived Jorge by fifteen years.

Other than the leaning headstone, the graves were neat, with no weeds anywhere to be seen. They'd been well tended—probably by the mother of Cleo and Daniel. It made it all the more fitting that her grave be next to theirs.

"This is perfect," Tracy said.

Daniel gave a short nod, to which Cleo added her approval.

Kneeling on the packed ground next to her, Ben pulled out the sheet of paper that had the children's mother's full name on it and picked up his chisel and hammer. The first strike rang through the air like a shot, and Cleo flinched. Tracy put her arm around the girl and they stood quietly as the sound was repeated time and time again. A cadence of death…and hope.

Sweat poured down Ben's face and spots of moisture began to appear on his dark T-shirt, but still he continued, letter by letter, until the name of Maria Eugênia da Silva Costa appeared on the stone, along with the dates of her birth and death.

Cleo had stood quietly through the entire process, but when Ben glanced up at her with his brows raised, she knelt beside him. With tender fingers she traced the letters one by one while Daniel stayed where he was. He'd brushed his palm across his face as if chasing away sweat—but Tracy had a feeling a rogue tear or two might have been part of the mix.

Handing a bunch of wildflowers to the little girl, she watched as Cleo and Ben carefully placed the stone and cross, setting the tiny bouquet in front of the objects. Glancing at Ben, who'd slicked his hair back, she cleared her throat. "Would you mind saying a few words?"

Blotting a drizzle of perspiration with his shirt sleeve, he stood, lifting a brow. "It's been a while since I've gone to church."

"I'm sure you can think of something." Tracy knew she'd lose it if she tried to say anything.

Cleo rose as well and gripped her hand fiercely.

"Right." He put his hand on one of Cleo's shoulders and motioned Daniel over. The boy moved forward, his steps unsure as if he didn't want to face the reality of what was about to happen. Tracy knew just how he felt. Somehow seeing your mother's name carved into cold, hard stone made things seem unbearably permanent. Even more permanent than the granite itself.

As if aware of her thoughts, Ben started talking, his voice low and somber. "We want to remember Maria Eugênia and give thanks for her life. For the brave children she brought into this world and nurtured to be such fine, caring individuals." Ben's eyes met hers. "We leave this marker as a reminder of her time on this earth. A symbol that she was important. That she was loved. That she won't be forgotten. By any of us."

Cleo's hands went up to cover her face, her small shoulders shaking in silence, while Daniel stood unmoving. Ben knelt between them. One broad-shouldered man flanked by two grieving children.

Oh, God.

One of the tears she'd been blinking away for the last several minutes threatened to break free. But this was not the time. This wasn't about her. It was about these kids. About helping them through a terrible time in their lives. About helping Cleo get to the root of her medical problems.

She went over and gave Daniel a long hug. And then she knelt in front of Cleo, her eyes meeting Ben's as she brushed a strand of hair from the child's damp head and then dropped a kiss on top of it.

Suddenly she knew she wouldn't need a few days to decide. In the scheme of things, what was six months or a year when she could make a difference in these kids' lives for ever? Wasn't that what she'd come here to do? What she'd done even as she'd faced her test results? As impossibly hard as it might be to see Ben each and every day, she was going to *Teresina*. She was going to help make sure Daniel and Cleo were put in a situation where they could flourish and grow. And where Cleo—as Tracy had promised her—would have that chance at a long and healthy life.

Ben stood in the door of the sickroom and peered around one last time. Every bed was empty of patients, the IV poles disassembled and the military vehicles had headed out one by one, leaving only a small contingent to carry out General Gutierrez's final order. Ben had insisted on staying behind to make sure the last survivors had packed up and moved out of town, which they had.

Maybe it was the life-and-death struggle that had gone on here, maybe it was the unrelenting horror of what they'd seen, but most of the inhabitants had seemed only too happy to clear out. Most of them—except Cleo and Daniel—had relatives to turn to and those who didn't would have help from the government to start over, including jobs and subsidized housing, until they got back on their feet.

Several of the villagers, when they'd discovered what Ben had done for Daniel and Cleo's mother, had made similar monuments for their own loved ones and set them in various locations around the cemetery. Ben had wrung a promise from the general that the graveyard would remain untouched.

São João dos Rios was now a ghost town—already dead to all intents and purposes.

And soon his wife would be moving back into his house with a ready-made family in tow. He wasn't sure what had suddenly caused her to say yes. He only knew as the four of them had knelt in front of Maria Eugênia's grave, she'd met his eyes and given a single nod of her head.

He'd mouthed the words, "You'll go?"

Another slow nod.

There'd been no emotion on her face other than a mixture of grief and determination, and he'd wondered if he'd done the right thing in asking her to come. But he couldn't take on two kids by himself and do them justice. Daniel was a strong young man, a few years from adulthood, and Cleo a young girl whose body was still battling to adapt to diabetes, while her mind buckled under a load of grief and loss.

Right now, Tracy and the kids were going through Daniel and Cleo's house and collecting an assortment of sentimental items, and if he knew Tracy, she was making the case for each and every object with the soldier General Gutierrez had left in charge. His friend wasn't an unreasonable man, but he took his job seriously. He was not going to let this pathogen out of the city, if he could help it.

All clothing and linens had to be boiled before they were packed into crates and given a stamp of approval. The hours had run into days as people waited in line for their turn to sanitize their belongings.

A movement caught his eye and he frowned as he spotted Tracy's assistant heading over to the house. He hadn't realized the man was still here, although in the confusion of the last few hours he couldn't remember seeing him leave. Obviously, he wouldn't have without saying goodbye to his boss.

He turned, ready to follow, when Tracy came out of the house and met him. Pedro said something to her and she shrugged. But when the man laid his hands on her shoulders, a slow tide began to rise in Ben's head and he pushed off to see what was going on.

The first voice to reach his ears was Pedro's. "You can't be serious. *Projeto Vida* is your life. You can't just abandon it. What about the medical ship?"

Tracy shook her head and said something, but he couldn't quite make out her words. Ben moved a little faster.

"Why can't someone else deal with them?"

"Because there is no one else, Pedro. It's something I have to do. You and the rest of the crew can hold the fort until I get back."

Until she got back. Why did those four words make his gut churn?

Pedro evidently saw him coming and took his hands from her shoulders. It didn't stop him from continuing his tirade, though. "How long do you think that will that be?"

"Six months. Maybe a year." She glanced back at the door to the house. "Please, keep your voice down. We haven't talked to the kids about time frames."

"Why don't you just bring the kids down to São Paulo?"

"You know I can't do that. It wouldn't be fair to them or to you all. Our hours are all over the place and we're rarely in the office a week before we're off again."

The turning and shifting in Ben's gut increased in intensity. He hoped that didn't mean she was planning on keeping the same schedule once she got to Teresina. He expected her to be an active partner in Cleo's care, not an absentee parent.

He forced a smile as he addressed Tracy. "Is there a problem?"

She shook her head. "No, we're just working out some details about the office."

That's not what it sounded like to him.

Moistening her lips, she leaned forward to give Pedro a quick hug. "It's going to be all right. Give me a call when you get in. I should have cellphone service once I get on the road."

"Speaking of roads," Ben said, his eyes locked on Pedro,

"we should all be heading in that direction. Do you need a ride anywhere?"

"Nope. I offered to help with the clean-up then I'll catch a ride to the airport."

Tracy smiled. "I thought you said the soldiers were 'scary dudes.'"

"They're not so bad once you get to know them. Other people…not so much."

Yeah, Ben could guess who that little jab was meant for. Luckily, his skin had grown pretty thick over the last several years. Not much got through.

Except maybe one hot-tub episode.

And a few hot tears that had splashed on his shoulder as Tracy had confessed her deepest, darkest secret. Oh, yeah, that had gotten through more than he cared to admit.

"I have a crate of embroidered linens that need to be boiled and then we can go."

Pedro, as if finally realizing she was serious about going to *Teresina*, spun on his heel and walked away.

Maybe he should give Tracy one more chance to walk away as well. But as much as he tried to summon up the strength, he couldn't. Not just yet.

He had two kids to worry about.

And maybe someday he could convince himself that was the real reason.

"Where are the beds?"

Ben found Daniel standing in the middle of his new room, the backpack with all his clothes still slung over one of his thin shoulders. At least the boy's cheeks had some color back in them. "It's right there against the wall."

And then he realized why the kid had asked that question. He'd probably never slept on a spring mattress in his life. The military had used canvas cots for sickbeds, while

most of the houses in São João dos Rios contained *redes*...
hammocks. Ben had nothing against sleeping in them. The
things were pretty comfortable, in fact. And making love
in one...

Yeah, better not to think about the times he and Tracy
had shared one on various trips in their past.

Ben moved past Daniel and sat on the double-sized bed.
"This is what we normally sleep on."

"But it's not hanging up. Doesn't it get hot?"

The kid had a point.

"That's why we have fans." He nodded at the ceiling
fan that was slowly spinning above them. "It goes at different speeds."

"I don't know..." Daniel looked dubious.

Ben smiled. "Tell you what. Try it for a week or so and
if you absolutely hate it, we'll go buy you a *rede*."

"My mom made mine herself. And Cleo's."

His throat tightening, Ben nodded. By now the military would have burned everything. Houses, most material possessions that could carry bacteria out of the city.
That included Daniel and Cleo's hammocks. "I know. I
wish we could have brought them, but there was no way
to boil them."

They'd been able to sterilize a few of Maria Eugênia's
aprons and embroidered towels, but hammocks had been
too unwieldy. They'd been forced to leave so much behind.

"I understand." He looked around again. "Why is there
only one bed, then?"

That was another thing. The siblings had shared a bedroom in their old house, but there were enough rooms here
that they wouldn't need to any more. But how to explain
that to a boy who'd never had a room of his own. "Cleo
will have her own bed, in the room next door to this one."

Tracy was currently in there with the girl, making up the

couch with sheets and pillows. He tried to look at his home through their eyes. He wasn't a wealthy man by American standards, but it would certainly seem that way to Cleo and Daniel. There was even an air-conditioner in each of the rooms for when things got unbearably hot. But he didn't mention that right now. He wanted to give them some time to adjust to their new surroundings before springing too much on them.

The local government had been overwhelmed, dealing with the aftermath of the outbreak, so when Ben had asked permission to take the kids with them, they'd made copies of Ben's and Tracy's identity papers, called in a quick background check, then promised a formal interview in the coming weeks. He knew it would only be a formality. And maybe some long-lost relative would come forward in the meantime and claim the children.

He wasn't sure how he felt about that. In just two weeks Ben had grown fond of the kids. Too fond, in fact.

What had he been thinking, agreeing to this? And what had Tracy been thinking, saying yes?

A question that made something in his chest shimmy to life.

As if she knew he'd been thinking about her, Tracy showed up at the doorway with Cleo in tow. "We're all set up. How are you doing in here?"

Daniel looked up at the sign Rosa had hung on the bedroom wall when Ben had called to tell her the news.

Bem Vindo, Daniel!

There was a matching "welcome home" sign in Cleo's room, with her name on it.

Giving the first tentative smile Ben had witnessed since he'd known the boy, Daniel nodded. "I think we will do very well here."

"So do I."

The soft words came from Tracy, who also had a ghost of a smile on her face. She walked over and took one of his hands, giving it a quick squeeze before releasing it. Then she whispered the two most beautiful words he'd ever heard. "Thank you."

CHAPTER SIXTEEN

"I HAVE A surprise for you outside."

Ben had rounded them all up in the living room.

A surprise—anything, in fact—was better than Tracy trying to avoid looking into the bedroom she'd once shared with Ben. The one that seemed to call to her, no matter where she was in the house.

Tracy glanced at Rosa to see if she knew anything, but she just shrugged.

If the housekeeper was surprised to see Tracy back in *Teresina*, she didn't show it. She'd just engulfed her in a hug so tight it had squeezed the air from her lungs. She'd then dabbed the corners of her eyes with her apron before embracing each of the children.

"A surprise?" asked Cleo. "What is it?"

Giving Ben a puzzled look, Tracy wondered what kind of surprise he could possibly have. They'd only arrived a few hours ago. The kids hadn't even had a chance to explore properly yet.

"I bought a water tank," he said in English. "I thought we could convert it into a makeshift pool for the kids. Maybe even sink it partway into the ground to make it easier to climb into. I had it delivered when you agreed to come to *Teresina*."

Heat suffused her face as she processed this, ignoring

the kids who were asking to know what he'd said. "Is it the one from São João dos Rios?" Lord, she hoped not. Those memories were even fresher than the ones from the bedroom down the hall.

"No. Bigger."

"We could have bought an inflatable pool."

"I figured this would be more permanent and less likely to rupture. I can't afford to have a built-in pool put in, but I figured the kids could help with the upkeep. It'll also give them a place to entertain any new friends they might make."

"That was nice, Ben." She refused to wonder what would happen to it once everyone went their separate ways. "I think they'll love it."

Tracy switched back to Portuguese and twitched her index finger back and forth at the kids' expectant glances. "I can't tell you what we said without spoiling the surprise."

Standing aside as Ben pushed the door open, she watched the kids lope into the back yard. A large oval water tank sat in a sandy area. Daniel's eyes touched it then skipped past, still looking for whatever the surprise was.

Ben was right, it was huge. The thing must hold a couple of thousand gallons. Why had they never thought of using one as a pool before? Perched on rooftops everywhere in Brazil, the blue fiberglass tanks came in various shapes and sizes. This one must have been meant for a commercial building.

Cleo seemed just as lost as Daniel was. "Where's the surprise?"

To them, evidently, a *caixa de água* was just that: a holding tank for water. They couldn't see the possibilities.

Ben walked over to it and put his hand on the curved rim. "This is it."

The way both kids' faces fell brought a laugh up from Tracy's chest. "What? You don't think this is a good surprise?"

Cleo shook her head, and Daniel said, "It's fine. I'm sure you needed a new one."

"Oh, it's not for our roof." Ben motioned them round to the other side of the tank. They followed him, Tracy wondering what he'd hidden over there.

Taped to the outside edge was a glossy magazine ad showing a family playing in an above-ground pool, an inflatable raft bouncing on happy waves.

"This…" Ben patted the side of the tank "…is going to be a pool once we're done with it."

"A *piscina*?" Cleo's voice held a note of awe. "We're going to have a pool?"

"We're going to use the tank as a pool." He ran a hand over the top edge. "You're going to have to help me get it ready. And you'll have to help take care of it once it's set up. But, yes, we're going to have a pool."

"Beleza!" The happy shout came from Daniel, who now walked around the tank with a completely different mindset. "The water will be almost up to my neck."

"Yes, and you'll have to be careful with your sister," Ben said, "because it'll be over her head. I don't want you guys using this without supervision. In fact, I'm going to have a cover installed when it's not in use."

Cleo's fingers trailed over the image of the raft on top of the water.

Catching Ben's grin, Tracy could guess what was coming. "There's a bag on the far side of the tank, Cleo. Why don't you go and look inside?"

The little girl raced around to the other side. They soon heard a squeal. "A float. Just like in the picture. And there are two!"

"One for each of them," Tracy murmured to Ben. "You thought of everything, didn't you?"

"No. Not everything." Something in the words had her gaze swiveling back to him.

"I don't understand."

"I don't imagine you do, but it doesn't matter." He moved away from her before she could really look at him. She heard him talking to the kids then they all came around and walked across the yard behind the house, trying to decide on the best place for the pool. They finally came up with a spot near the *acerola* tree, where they'd at least get some shade during the heat of the day.

As soon as the kids had uncovered all the secrets of the soon-to-be pool, they went off to explore the rest of the backyard, leaving Ben and Tracy alone together.

When her eyes met his, the look was soft and fluid, reminding him of days gone by when he'd brought her flowers unexpectedly or had taken her on a long walk in the park.

Hell, he'd missed that look. Placing his hand out, palm up, he held his breath and waited to see if she'd take it. She did, her cool skin sliding across his. He closed his fingers, his gaze holding hers. "Are you okay with all this?"

"I am."

He'd felt the stab of guilt more than once since she'd agreed to come back with him. Especially after the way they'd parted four years ago.

With a sigh he opened his hand and released her. He'd never really known what she'd been thinking during those last dark days of their marriage. And he wasn't sure he wanted to. Maybe it would just make the rift between them that much deeper.

"I guess I'd better go help Rosa with dinner." She

stepped up on tiptoe and gave him a soft kiss. "The kids love their surprise, I can tell. Thank you."

Tracy stood back with a smile, the corners of her eyes crinkling. Oh, how he loved seeing that. The urge to kiss her came and went without incident. After screwing up so badly in the past, he didn't want to do anything that would send them spinning back to uglier times just when he was beginning to feel he'd made up some ground with her. Maybe with time they'd be able to move past those days and become friends again.

At least that was his hope.

Dr. Crista Morena gently palpated Cleo's abdomen, her brow furrowed in concern. "You know that type-one diabetes can occur at any age." She glanced up at them, and Ben could see the curiosity in her eyes. "You know nothing of her background, her medical history?"

"Just what we observed during the plague outbreak," he said. "Could her pancreas have been affected by the illness?"

She stood and straightened the stethoscope around her neck. "Some cases may be triggered by a viral infection—something in the enterovirus family—that causes an auto-immune response." She helped Cleo sit up. "I want to get some bloodwork done on her, but the finger prick we did when you first came in is right around two-twenty. We'll need to do another with her fasting. I'll send some testers home with you."

Tracy nodded. "Her glucose levels seem to fluctuate for no apparent reason, just like they did while she was sick, so her pancreas must be producing some insulin."

"If it's type one, she could be in the honeymoon phase. You administered insulin to bring her levels back down, right?"

"Yes."

"Doing that can sometimes give the organ a rest, stimulating those last remaining beta cells, which then pump out small quantities of the hormone." She looked at each of them. "If it's type one, the honeymoon phase is only a temporary reprieve. Those cells will eventually stop producing all together."

Ben swallowed. If that was true, Cleo would need constant monitoring for the rest of her life. Temporary would become permanent. He glanced at Tracy to see if she'd come to the same conclusion he had.

Yep. Her hands were clasped tightly in her lap, fingers twisting around each other. Well, taking the kids had been her idea in the first place.

But you agreed.

Besides, it had done him a world of good to hear Cleo's happy laugh when she'd realized what the water tank in the backyard meant. How her eyes had widened when she'd discovered she was getting a room of her own with a new pink bedspread—once the bed they'd ordered for her arrived. He wouldn't trade those moments for anything.

Ben helped Cleo hop off the exam table and motioned to the chair he'd occupied moments earlier. She chose to go to Tracy instead, who opened her arms and hauled the child onto her lap, hugging her close.

His throat tightened further. Tracy looked so right holding a child. Would she have cut back on her traveling if their baby had been born?

If the evidence he'd seen was any indication, the answer to that was no. She'd rushed to São João dos Rios during the outbreak, and Pedro had indicated they'd made quite a few trips during the year.

She saved lives by being in that city.

But at what cost to herself?

None, evidently.

Dr. Morena looked up from Cleo's chart and focused on Tracy. "I understand you practiced pediatric medicine in the past. We could use another doctor here at the clinic. Would you be interested?"

"How did you know that?" She shot him a glance that he couldn't read.

"Ben mentioned you were a doctor when he called to make the appointment."

His heart sped up as he waited to see her reaction. Although his slip had been unintentional, when Dr. Morena had mentioned an opening, he'd wondered if she'd say anything to Tracy.

"I haven't practiced pediatric medicine in quite a few years. I've been dealing more with indigenous tribes so—"

"You treat children in those tribes, don't you?"

"Of course."

Dr. Morena closed the cover of the chart with a soft snap. "It's like riding a bicycle. You never really forget how to deal with those little ones. And you obviously have a knack with them." She nodded at Cleo, who was now snuggled into Tracy's lap. "Give me a call if you're interested."

CHAPTER SEVENTEEN

IT WAS LIKE riding a bicycle.

Dr. Morena's words rang through her head a few days later as she stood in the doorway of her old bedroom.

Being with Ben in that water tank had been like that. Remembered responses and emotions bubbling up to the surface. She ventured a little further into the room, sliding her hand across the bedspread. The same silky beige-striped one they'd had years ago. She was surprised he hadn't bought a new set.

She glanced at the door and then, on impulse, lay across the old mattress and stared up at the ceiling. No one would know. Ben was safely at work right now, and Daniel had taken Cleo to explore the neighborhood. Even Rosa was off shopping for groceries, which meant she had a couple of hours to herself.

She wouldn't stay long, just enough to satisfy her curiosity. She'd passed this room for the last couple of days and had wanted to step inside, but she'd resisted the temptation.

Until now.

So, what does it feel like to lie here?

Just like riding a bicycle.

That thought was both terrifying and exhilarating.

The only thing lacking was Ben. And if he could see her now, he'd probably hit the roof. They'd patched together an uneasy truce since arriving in the city, and she was loath to do anything to rock that particular boat. But the open bedroom door had winked at her, inviting her to step through and relive the past.

Rolling onto her stomach, she grabbed the pillow and buried her face into it, sucking down a deep breath of air.

Yep, Ben still slept on the right side of the bed. His warm masculine scent was imprinted on the soft cotton cover, despite Rosa fluffing the pillows to within an inch of their lives. She'd have to make sure she left things exactly like she'd found them.

Being here felt dangerous…voyeuristic. And incredibly erotic. They'd made love in this bed many, many times. All kinds of positions. Her on top. Him. Her hands trapped above her head. His hands molding her body…making her cry out when the time came.

Just that memory made her tingle, her skin responding to the sudden flurry of images that flashed through her head. Oh, Lord. This was bad.

So bad.

Just like riding a bike.

Sitting on a bicycle was one thing. Putting your feet on the pedals and making them go round and round was another thing entirely.

She knew she should get up. Now. But the temptation to linger and let her imagination run wild—to remember one of their lovemaking sessions—was too great. The one that came to mind was when Tracy had been lying on the bed much like she was now. Only she'd been naked.

Waiting.

The covers pulled down so that Ben would find her just like this when he came home from work.

And he had.

Her nipples drew up tight as she recalled the quiet click

of the front door closing. The sound of his indrawn breath as he'd stood in the doorway of this very room and spotted her. Without a word, warm lips had pressed against her neck. Just when she'd started to turn her head, eyelids fluttering open, she'd heard the low command, "Don't look.

She'd obeyed, letting him explore her body and whisper the things he wanted to do to her. His hands had slipped beneath her to cup her breasts, drawing a whimper from her when he'd found the sensitive peaks and gently squeezed.

Even now, Tracy couldn't stop her own hands from replaying the scene, burrowing between her body and the mattress.

"Mmm. Yes."

He'd touched her just like this. Her teeth had dug into her lower lip as she'd let the sensations spiral through her system. Just a hint of friction then more as he'd seemed to sense exactly what she was feeling.

"Ben." The whispered name was low, but in the silence of the house it carried. She let out another puff of breath between pursed lips, even as one hand trailed down her side, her legs opening just a bit.

It wouldn't take long. She was so turned on. Just a minute or two. And she'd relieve the ache that had been growing inside her since their time in the tub. She undid the button on her jeans and her fingers found the juncture at the top of her thighs, sweet, familiar heat rippling through her.

Maybe she should close the door. Just in case. Her head tilted in that direction.

Instead of empty space, her gaze met familiar broad shoulders, which now filled the doorway.

She yanked her hands from beneath her in the space of a nanosecond, molten lava rushing up her neck and scorching her face.

Oh, God! Had he heard her say his name?

"Wh-what are you doing here?"

"I would ask you the same thing, but I think it's fairly obvious from where I'm standing." He took a step closer, his eyes never leaving hers. And the heat contained in them nearly burned her alive.

The door closed. The lock snicked.

"I was just taking a…" She rolled onto her back and propped herself up on her elbows, realizing her mistake when his gaze trailed to her chest and saw the truth for himself. Even she could feel the desperate press of her nipples against her thin shirt.

He stood at the foot of the bed. "Nap?" He gave her a slow smile. "Must have been having quite some dream, then."

Oh, it was no dream. More like a wish. And Ben had been at the heart of it.

"Wh-why did you just lock the door?" Sick anticipation began strumming through her, even though she already knew the answer.

His hands wrapped around her ankles and hauled her down to the foot of the bed, giving her all the confirmation she needed. "Isn't it obvious, Trace? *I* intend to be the one to finish what you started."

Ben wasn't sure what he'd expected when he'd come home early to spend the weekend with Tracy and the kids, but he certainly hadn't expected to find her in his bed…face buried in his pillow, her hands sliding down her own body.

Then, when she'd said his name, he'd known. She'd been fantasizing about him. About them. About the way they used to be.

He'd gone instantly erect, instantly ready for business. And then she'd turned and looked into his eyes, and he'd seen the fire that had once burned just for him. She still felt it. Just like he did.

It inflamed him. Enticed him.

And he wasn't above taking full advantage of it.

Leaning over the bed and planting his hands on either side of her shoulders, he stared down at her, hungry for the sight of her, hair in gorgeous disarray from being dragged down the bed, her slender body encased in snug jeans and a thin cami top. "Tell me you want me."

She licked her lips. "We shouldn't…"

"Maybe not. But I want to know. Was it me you were imagining?"

"Yes." The airy sigh was all he needed.

He bent down and closed his lips over the nipple he could see so clearly through her shirt, his teeth gripping, loving the tight heat of her against his tongue. She whimpered when he raised his head. "Did you imagine me here?" His knee parted her legs and moved to press tightly against her. "Here?"

Tracy's throat moved as she swallowed. "Yes."

His breath huffed out, and he moved up to whisper in her ear, "Let me, then. We'll sort all the other stuff out later."

She didn't say anything, and he wondered if she might refuse. Then her hands went to the back of his head and pulled him down to her lips, which instantly parted the second their mouths met. He groaned low and long as he accepted the invitation, pushing his tongue inside, tasting, remembering, pressing deep and then withdrawing…only to repeat the act all over again—a mounting heat growing in another part of his body.

Desperation spread through his veins, and he tried to rein in his need, knowing that soon kissing her would no longer be enough. The tiny sound she made in the back of her throat said she felt the exact same way.

This was how it had always been with them. The flames burned higher and faster than either of them wanted, until they were writhing against each other, fighting off the inevitable—knowing it would be over far too soon.

He pulled away, his breath rasping in his lungs. "Take off your shirt," he whispered. "I want to see you."

Tracy's hands went to the bottom of her cami without hesitation and lifted it over her head in a graceful movement that made him want to tear off the rest of her clothing and bury himself deep inside her. But he knew it was better if he didn't touch her for the next couple of minutes.

He nodded at her undergarment. "Bra next."

"Say please."

He swallowed, knowing she was teasing, but at this point he'd say anything she wanted. "Please."

She unclipped the front of the thing and shimmied it off her shoulders, the jiggle of her breasts making his mouth water. God, he wanted her.

He drank in the sight and, just like she always had, she took his breath away. "Touch them. Like you were when I came in." He gave her a wolfish grin as he added, "Please."

Her face turned pink, and this time he wondered if she might leap off the bed and stomp out of the room, but her hands went to her breasts and covered them, her head falling back as she gently massaged them.

This woman got to him like no other ever had. He slid his hand into the tangle of her hair and kissed her long and deep, drinking in everything he could.

He stood again, watching her eyes open and meet his. "Slide your thumbs over your nipples. Slowly. Just like I'm aching to do."

Again she hesitated, but then her hands shifted, the pads of her thumbs skimming over the tight buds in perfect synchrony. She repeated the motion, her gaze never leaving his. "Like this?"

"Oh, exactly like that." His voice had gone slightly hoarse, and he knew no amount of clearing his throat would chase it away. "Don't stop."

Her low moan sent heat skimming down his stomach and beyond.

"Where are the kids?"

"Outside. Rosa's shopping."

"Ah, so that's why you were in here." He stepped between her legs, which were still dangling over the side of the bed. He slowly spread them wider with his stance. "You thought you wouldn't get caught."

"I—I didn't plan it."

"But the second you got on that bed you felt it, didn't you? The things we used to do. Imagined me right here—just like this."

"Ben—"

"Shh. Don't talk. We're alone. We both want this." His fingers moved down to the waistband of her jeans. Her teeth sank into her bottom lip, her hands going completely still. "Uh-uh. I didn't tell you you could stop." He placed his hands over hers and showed her how he wanted her to stroke her breasts.

She moaned again, her hips shifting restlessly on the bed. "I want *you* to do it. Please?"

"Soon." His fingers returned to her jeans and dragged them down her thighs, stepping back so he could tug them the rest of the way off. "I don't want to waste a second of this time."

"The kids—"

"Will find the door locked." He smiled at her. "And you're sleeping. You need your rest."

Her panties were black, just like her lacy bra had been.

His hand glided down her sternum, past her bellybutton and stopped, fingers trailing along the line formed by her underwear. He wanted to watch her do that too.

"Tracy." His eyes met hers, and he took her hands in his, running both sets down her stomach until he reached the satin band. "Take them off."

She hooked her thumbs around the elastic and eased them down her hips, over the curve of her butt. When she'd pushed them as far as she could go without sitting up, Ben slid them off the rest of the way.

She was naked. His hands curled around her thighs and pushed them apart, his thumbs caressing the soft inner surfaces, then shifted higher, watching her eyes darken with each excruciating inch he gained. When he reached her center, he found her wet…open. He delved inside, still holding her thighs apart. A low whimper erupted from her throat when he applied pressure to the inner surface, right at the spot she liked best.

Her flesh tightened around his thumb, and she raised her hips stroking herself on him.

"Please, Ben. Now."

He didn't want to. Not yet. But he couldn't hold off much longer. He was already shaking with need.

With one hand he reached for his zipper and yanked it down, freeing himself. They could take it slowly later. Gripping her thighs again, he pulled her closer before filling his hands with her luscious butt and lifting it off the bed. He sank into her, watching as she took him in inch by inch.

Buried inside her, he savored the tight heat, trying his best not to move for several seconds. Tracy had other ideas. She wrapped her legs around him, planting her heels against his lower back and pulled him closer, using the leverage to lift her hips up then let them slide back down, setting up a sensual circular rhythm that wouldn't let up. The result was that, although he held perfectly still, his flesh was gripped by her body, massaged and squeezed and rubbed and…

He gritted his teeth and tried desperately to hold on, but it was no use. Nothing could stop the avalanche once it began.

With a hoarse groan he grabbed her hips and thrust hard into her, riding her wildly, feeling her explode around him with an answering cry even as he emptied himself inside her.

Heart pounding in his chest, he continued to move until there was nothing left and his legs turned to jelly. Slowly lowering her to the bed, he followed her down, pulling her onto her side and gathering her close.

Her breath rasped past his cheek, slowing gradually.

The moment of truth. Was she going to bolt? Or accept what had happened between them?

He took a minute or two to get his bearings then kissed her forehead. "Was it as good as you imagined?"

"Better." Her soft laugh warmed his heart. "Only you had your clothes off in my imagination."

"We'll have to work on that."

"Mmm." She sighed against his throat then licked the moisture that had collected there. "Someone will be coming pretty soon."

"Exactly."

"I meant coming *home*."

Something in Ben's throat tightened at the sound of that word on her tongue. *Home*.

Was that what she considered this place? Or would she take off again the second she had the opportunity?

He'd better tread carefully. Not let himself get too comfortable. Because she considered this a temporary arrangement. And if not for the kids, Tracy wouldn't even be here right now. The fact that she hadn't automatically expected to share his bed spoke volumes. She hadn't planned on returning to their old relationship, no matter how good their little interlude in the water tank had been. Or how much she'd seemed to enjoy their time in this bed.

And she had enjoyed it.

Seeing her pleasuring herself on his bed...*their* bed... had done a number on his heart. As had her admission of fantasizing about him...not about Pedro or some other faceless man as she'd touched her body.

Yeah. He'd liked that a little too much.

Well, somehow he'd better drag himself back from the edge of insanity and grab hold of reality. Because it wasn't likely Tracy was going to change her mind about staying with him for ever. And, unfortunately, with each day that passed he found that's exactly what he wanted.

CHAPTER EIGHTEEN

TRACY DREW THE insulin into the syringe and gave Cleo a reassuring smile. "You're becoming a pro at these."

This was Cleo's tenth shot, but her glucose levels were still fluctuating all over the place. Whether it was the honeymoon phase that Dr. Morena had mentioned or whether her pancreas would again start pumping out its own supply of insulin was the big question. One no one could seem to answer.

"It still hurts."

"I know. It always will. But sometimes we have to be brave and do what we know is best—even if it hurts."

Like leaving had been four years ago? Because that had hurt more than anything else ever had—that and her miscarriage. Looking back, she knew all kinds of things had led to her flight from *Teresina*. Anger, grief, shock. If Ben hadn't done what he had, she might have stuck it out and tried to make things work. But his actions had been the proverbial last straw...her whole world had collapsed around her, unable to keep functioning under the load she'd placed on it.

And now?

She and Ben hadn't talked about what had happened between them two days ago. There was still a part of her that was mortified that he'd caught her on his bed, but the result had been something beyond her wildest dreams. He'd been arrogant—and sexy as hell—standing there at the foot of the bed, ordering her to touch herself.

If the front door hadn't clicked open and then shut again, they might have started all over again. But the second the sound had registered, there had been a mad dash of yanking on clothing interspersed with panicked giggles as they'd snuck out of his room to face Rosa and her armloads of groceries.

Ben had been a whole lot better at feigning nonchalance than she had as he'd taken the canvas sacks from the housekeeper and helped her put things away. But the burning glances he'd thrown her from time to time had told her he'd rather be right back in that bed with her.

Heat washed over her as she tried to corral her thoughts and keep them from straying any further down that dangerous path.

Tracy rolled up Cleo's shorts. "Ready?"

"I—I think so."

With a quick jab that was designed to cause as little pain as possible, she pushed the needle home and injected the medicine. Other than the quick intake of breath, the little girl didn't make a sound. As soon as Tracy withdrew and capped the syringe, she tossed the instrument into the mini medical waste container they'd set up.

Cleo's voice came from the stool where she was still seated. "Are you going to work for Dr. Morena?"

Ah, so she had heard the doctor as she'd talked to them in the exam room. Tracy didn't have an answer today any more than she'd had one for Ben when he'd asked her much the same question after making love.

They hadn't been together again since that night but he'd gotten into the habit of dropping a kiss on her cheek before he left for work each day. She probably should have moved away the first time he'd done it, but this morning she'd found herself lifting her cheek to him in anticipation. At this rate, she'd be puckering up and laying one right on his lips very soon.

Probably not a smart idea.

She'd never fooled herself into thinking she didn't love Ben. Of course she did. She'd never stopped. She had been furious with him after the yellow fever incident and had needed time to think about how to deal with everything that had been going on in her life. Only she'd taken too much time, and hiding her condition had become second nature—and had seemed easier than returning to *Teresina* to tell him the truth.

During all those years she'd been gone he'd never called her, never begged her to change her mind. Although she couldn't imagine Ben ever doing that. He was strong, stoic. He'd had to be self-sufficient as a child in order to cope, since his parents had rarely been there for him.

She hadn't been there for him either.

But now he knew why. Didn't that change everything? Wasn't that what those little pecks on the cheek had meant?

She could say she hoped so, but in reality she had no idea. He'd barely had any time to process the information, but how would he feel once he had? She knew she was more than just the sum of her parts, but Ben loved her breasts. That much had been obvious from the heat in his eyes as her hands had cupped them. Stroked over the tips.

And, yep...her mind was right back in the gutter, despite her best efforts.

With a start she realized she was still standing in front of the cabinet, and that Cleo was now frowning up at her with a look of concern. Oh, she'd asked about Dr. Morena and whether she was going to work for her.

"How do you feel about what the doctor said? About me working at the clinic?"

Cleo hopped down from the stool and unrolled the leg of the shorts. "Does that mean we'll keep on staying with you?"

Afraid to get the girl's hopes up too high, she said, "Why don't you leave the worrying about that to us, okay?" She dropped a quick kiss on her head. "Just know that you are loved."

Ben pushed through the front door, stopping short when the sounds of screaming came from the backyard. Dropping his briefcase on the floor, he yelled for Tracy, but other than those distant shouts his call was met by silence. A sense of weird *déjà vu* settled over him. This was much like the day he'd come home to find Tracy gone.

Except there'd been no shouting that day. Speaking of which…

Moving to the back of the house, he threw open the door that led to the patio. There, in the pool, were three bodies. Only they were very much alive.

In fact, it looked like he'd arrived in the middle of some kind of battle from the looks of the water guns in each person's hands. He walked up the steps to the top of the deck, which was still under construction, and all three pairs of eyes turned to him in a synchronized fashion. Too late, he realized his mistake when Daniel shouted, "*Atire-nele!*"

They all took aim and squeezed their triggers. Water came at him from three different angles, soaking his blue dress shirt and plastering it to his chest. "Hey! Enough already!"

No one listened, but then Tracy, clad in a cherry-red bikini that held his eyes prisoner for several long seconds, ran out of water first. As she was dunking her gun to reload, he pounced, going over the side of the water tank in one smooth move and capturing her gun hand as he hit the water—before she had time to bring it back up. She gave a startled scream when he wrapped his arms around her and took her with him beneath the water. Out of sight of the kids, who were bobbing around him, he planted his lips on Tracy's, a stream of bubbles rising as she laughed against her will. He let her up, where she coughed and spluttered. "Not fair!"

He slicked his hair out of his face, brows lifted. "And shooting me without any warning was?"

"You saw the water guns. We figured that was all the warning you deserved."

Ben stood there, dress shoes lying at the bottom of the pool, obviously ruined by now.

But he wouldn't change this scene for anything in the world. This was what he'd always dreamed of. Except in his daydreams Tracy had stayed by his side for ever. For a minute or two he allowed himself to mourn what might never be. But Tracy was here, right now. And all he wanted to do was pull the loose end on that bikini and see what happened. Only they weren't alone.

But at least she was playing. Laughing at his attempt to kiss her beneath the water. Maybe it was enough for now. He could wait and see how things went. If he didn't get his hopes up too high, they couldn't be dashed. Right?

"So. You planned to ambush me the minute I arrived, did you?"

Daniel gave him another squirt—which hit him squarely in the eye. "Ow!"

Another laugh from Tracy. When was the last time he'd heard her laugh with abandon? Far too long ago.

Her gun was still on the bottom of the pool. Diving beneath the water, he retrieved it and came back up, his head just barely above the surface as he let water fill the reservoir. Then he went on the attack, giving back as good as he got. Tracy stayed well out of the line of fire this time, double checking her bikini to make sure she was still in it. The act distracted him for a second and both the kids got him again.

He glared at his wife, mimicking her earlier words. "Not fair."

"Oh, but you know what they say. All's fair in…" Her voice trailed away, her smile dying with it.

He cursed himself, even though he knew it wasn't his fault. Instead, he waved the kids off for a minute and jogged over to her. Draping an arm around her waist, he whispered in her ear. "Let's just take it a day at a time, okay? No expectations."

The smile she gave him was tremulous. "I feel awful, Ben."

"Don't." He kissed her cheek. "Although I think you owe me a new pair of shoes."

"Done." She slid back beneath the water and leaned against the side. "This was a great idea. The kids love it. I'm thinking of enrolling Cleo in swimming lessons. Did you know she doesn't swim?"

Tracy had switched to English so the kids wouldn't understand her. He glanced at Cleo, who was hanging onto the side of the tank with one hand while maneuvering the water gun with the other. He answered her back in the same language. "She definitely needs to learn if the pool is going to stay up year round. How about Daniel?"

"He had lessons in school, but he's never had a place to practice. So it might not be a bad idea for him to brush up on his skills as well."

"Right." He leaned back beside her, stretching his legs out beneath the water. Tracy's limbs looked pale next to the black fabric of his slacks. "Did you put sunscreen on?"

"SPF sixty. The kids have some on as well."

He touched her nose, which, despite her sun protection, was slightly pink. "How long have you guys been in the water?"

"About an hour. We were making a list of recipes that the kids' mother used to fix, and I felt like we needed to do something fun afterwards. I don't want every memory of their mom to end on a sad note."

"Smart." Ben paused, wondering how to ask the question that had been bothering him for the last couple of days. His timing tended to suck, so why worry about that now? "Listen, I've been meaning to ask. About the other night…"

She tensed beside him. "I don't think now is the best time to talk about this."

"I haven't exactly been able to get you alone." Whether that had been on purpose or not, only Tracy could say. "I'll say it in English, so no one else will understand. Are you okay?"

"Okay?"

"Are you upset with me for the way I…?"

He didn't know how else to ask it. And he wasn't sure if he was asking if Tracy was okay, or if "they" were okay.

She shook her head, eyes softening. "No. Of course I'm not upset."

"You've been acting a little funny."

"This whole situation is a little funny." She sighed. "I never expected to be back in *Teresina*."

"Are you sorry you came?"

Ben wasn't sure why he was pushing so hard for reassurance, but he felt like he was slipping and sliding around, searching for something that might or might not be there.

"No. But I was going to tell you something later today. I made a phone call and talked to my old doctor here. She got me an appointment with a surgeon on Monday."

He froze, then a million and one questions immediately came to mind. She gave a quick nod at the kids, who, Ben realized, were both looking at them, trying to figure out what was being said. "Okay. Let's discuss it after dinner, okay?"

"Thank you." She switched back to Portuguese. "Is the military still monitoring your movements?"

He'd mentioned an unmarked vehicle parked in the lot at the hospital since they'd gotten back to *Teresina*. He hadn't recognized it and the driver was always the same person. It was either the military or a terrorist, Ben had told her with a rueful smile. The latter wasn't very likely in Brazil, since it was a pacifist country.

"The car hasn't been in the lot for the last two days so hopefully, if it was the General's doing, they've decided I'm too boring to keep tabs on." He pulled a face at the kids.

Tracy laughed. "Those guys don't know you very well, then, do they, Dr. Almeida? You're quite unpredictable."

The way she said it warmed his heart, despite the chill he'd felt when she'd mentioned the word "surgeon."

He planted a hand on his chest as if wounded and winked at Cleo. "You think I'm a pretty boring guy, don't you?"

The little girl giggled then shook her head.

"What about you?" he asked Daniel.

The boy scratched his head with the tip of his water gun. "I guess you're okay. Not too boring."

Tracy grinned then shot Ben a smug look. "See? Told you."

They were throwing playful barbs at each other again. His spine relaxed. How good it felt to be back on solid footing, instead of crashing around in a scary place where you couldn't see the bottom for the muck.

At least for today. Monday might bring something altogether different.

Ben had knocked on her door that night around midnight. She'd been half expecting him to come and see her out of earshot of the kids. What she hadn't expected was for him to push the door shut with his foot and stand there, staring at her.

Then he'd swept her in his arms and kissed her as if there was no tomorrow. They'd made love on her bed, and it had been as fresh and new as the other two times they'd been together. Afterwards, he'd held her in his arms.

"Whatever happens on Monday, we'll face it together, okay?"

A little sliver of doubt went through her chest. "Are you saying you want to go with me?"

"Would that be okay?"

Tracy had to decide to let him in completely or shut him out. "What about your work?"

"I can take off for a couple of hours." Ben caught a strand of her hair, rubbing it between his fingertips.

"Okay." Whew. Why did that feel so huge? "I won't make any firm decisions until Cleo's diabetes is under control, but I just need to see where I am. I've been neglecting my tests and want to get caught up with them."

"Why now?"

"I don't know. Maybe I've been running away from making a decision one way or the other."

He nodded and wrapped the lock of hair around his finger. "If I asked you to start sleeping in our old bed again, would you say yes?"

"Tonight? Or…?"

"Not just tonight. From now on."

Wow. This had gone from talking about her appointment to Ben asking her to make their marriage a real one. At least that's what she thought he was asking. "I assume by sleeping, you don't actually mean closing our eyes."

The right side of his mouth quirked up. "I definitely think there might be some eye closing going on, but it would take place well before any actual sleeping."

Tracy's body quickened despite having just made love with this man fifteen minutes ago. She tilted her head as if in deep thought. "Hmm. I don't know. Do you snore?"

"Interesting question. I do make sounds from time to time, but I don't know if I'd call them snoring." His fingers tunneled into her hair, massaging her head in tiny circles that made her shiver.

"I think I remember those sounds. I kind of liked them."

"Did you, now?" His thumb trailed down the side of her throat, stroking the spot where her pulse was beginning to pick up speed in response to his words and his touch.

"Mmm."

He leaned over and kissed the side of her jaw. "And I kind of like the little sound you just made."

"I'm glad, because if you keep that up, I'm going to be making a lot more of— Oh!" Her breath caught as his teeth nipped the crook of her neck, sucking the blood to the surface and then licking over it with his warm tongue.

"Say yes," he whispered.

"Yes." She wasn't sure what she was agreeing to, but it didn't really matter at this point. She wasn't about to hold anything back, and she trusted him enough to know he wouldn't ask her for more than she could give.

He moved to her lips. "Yes to sleeping in my bed?"

"I thought we'd already decided that."

"No, you were still questioning whether or not I snored." His tongue slowly licked across her mouth.

"No snoring. Just sounds." As she said each word, his tongue delved into her mouth before finally cutting off her speech altogether.

I didn't matter, though, because Tracy was already beyond rational thought, her arms winding around his neck.

She was ready to lose herself to him all over again—for as long as he wanted her.

CHAPTER NINETEEN

BEN WAS STILL groggy with sleep when he reached across the bed and realized Tracy was no longer there. He could hear her talking softly from somewhere nearby, and he woke up the rest of the way in a flash.

"But I have a doctor's appointment on Monday." There was a pause. "I suppose I could. It's not urgent."

Ben sat up in bed, looking for her. She must be in the bathroom.

He wasn't purposely trying to eavesdrop, but something about the way she kept her voice hushed said she wasn't anxious for anyone to hear the conversation.

"I don't want to be gone long. Cleo's still getting her shots regulated."

Climbing out of bed and reaching for his boxers, he padded to the door. "Pedro, I can't leave right this second. No, I know. I'm sure Rosa won't mind watching them while Ben is at work. She used to watch him when his parents were gone. I'd have to teach her how to give Cleo her insulin shots, though."

Rosa won't mind watching them.

The soft warmth he'd felt during the night evaporated. Why would Rosa need to watch the kids? Or give Cleo her shots?

Unless Tracy was planning to be gone for a while.

And why was she talking to Pedro in the bathroom, unless she was keeping something from him?

It wouldn't be the first time.

They'd been home less than a week, and she was already off somewhere?

A jumble of emotions spun up inside him like a tornado, anger being the first to reach the top.

No. He was not heading down this path again. He turned the knob and pushed the door open.

Tracy's mouth rounded in a perfect "O" that had looked incredibly sexy last night. But all he saw this morning was betrayal.

"Pedro, hold on just a second."

She put her hand over the phone, but Ben beat her to the punch. "You're leaving."

Licking her lips, she nodded. "Just for a few days. The medical boat docked at a flooded village. There are five cases of cholera and there's certain to be dozens more, as they've all been drinking from the same water source."

"Send someone else." His voice was cold and hard, but that's how he felt inside. "Let Pedro deal with it."

"He's not a doctor, Ben. I am. Matt called him, they're expecting to be overwhelmed by—"

"You're *a* doctor. Not the only doctor in the whole country. You have responsibilities here."

"Rosa can—"

Fury washed over him. "Rosa practically raised my brother and me. These kids need a steady presence in their lives, not be pushed off on someone else every time your assistant has a runny nose. You promised me at least six months."

"It's only this one time."

He closed his eyes for a second, his hand squeezing the doorknob for all he was worth. Then he took a deep breath.

"I'm going to lay it out for you, Tracy. Either you let some-one else handle this, and we start looking toward a future. Together. Or I'm filing for divorce. Even if I have to go all the way to New York to do it."

Every ounce of color drained from her face. "Wh-what about Daniel and Cleo? You said you couldn't do this alone."

"It doesn't look like I have much of a choice." He shot her a glance. "*I* made a promise that I intend to keep. Be-sides, I've been through the same rinse-and-spin cycle a couple of times already. I'm sure I can figure things out."

Just before he pulled the door shut he added, "Finish your conversation, then let me know what you decide."

Tracy draped a moist cloth over the forehead of the woman she was treating then used a gloved hand to check her vi-tals. They were through the worst of the cholera outbreak. There were several army doctors among their group, but this time they hadn't been sent at the request of her hus-band but were instead digging drain fields and latrines in an effort to prevent a recurrence.

Ben wouldn't send anyone for her this time, because he was through with her. He'd said as much.

She wasn't sure why Pedro's call had spurred her to ac-tion. Maybe her instincts were programmed to bolt at the first sign of trouble.

Like having an actual appointment with a doctor? Was she still running…still having to move and work to feel alive?

No, she'd felt alive with Ben as well. And this trip felt hollow. It didn't fulfill her the way it might have a few years ago. She missed the kids. Missed Ben.

Matt's wife sat down beside her on an intricately woven mat. "How are you holding up?"

Stevie had been with *Projeto Vida* for two years, working alongside her husband. They had a daughter as well, but she was confined to the boat this trip. Neither Matt nor Stevie wanted to run the risk of her becoming ill.

"As well as anyone."

Stevie gave her a keen look. "Are you sure about that?"

"We're all tired. I came here to help."

"And you have." Stevie touched her gloved hand to Tracy's. "How's Ben?"

She flashed the other woman a startled look. Word evidently traveled fast. "I wouldn't know. I won't be heading back there."

"I'm sorry."

"Me too." She gave her patient's shoulder a gentle squeeze and murmured that someone would check on her in just a little while then she stood with a sigh. "How do you do it?"

Stevie got to her feet as well. "What do you mean?"

"How do you keep your marriage together and travel on the boat?"

"We both believe in what we do." She stripped her gloves off and motioned for Tracy to follow her. Once outside the tent she leaned against a tree. "Sometimes I just need a breath of fresh air, you know?"

Tracy did know. The smells of illness got to you after a while.

Letting her head bump the bark of the tree trunk, Stevie swiveled her head toward her. "Matt wasn't sure he wanted to come back to Brazil after losing so much here. If he'd chosen to stay in the States, I would have stayed with him. Because that's the only important thing—that we're together."

"So you're saying I shouldn't have come."

"No." Stevie gave her a soft smile. "Only you know what's right...what's in your heart."

"I don't know any more. Ben never liked me traveling."

"I'm sure he missed you very much when you were gone."

"Yes, I suppose he did. But other wives travel."

"As much as you do?" Stevie paused for a moment or two. "I think you have to examine your heart and decide what it is you want out of life. Why you're so driven to do what you do."

Because she didn't have to think about anything else when she was helping people?

In the past she'd worked herself to exhaustion day after day—had fallen into bed at night, her eyes closing as soon as her head had hit the pillow.

Movement equaled life.

But was this really living? Was she doing this because she believed in her work or because she was afraid to stay in one place, where she might start feeling trapped—claustrophobic?

She'd missed her doctor's appointment to be here. Could she not have delayed her flight for a few hours? In reality, despite Pedro's dire predictions, there'd been enough hands to fight the cholera outbreak, even if she hadn't been here. She'd been living her whole life as if she were single with no commitments. Yes, she'd had this job before she'd met Ben. But in choosing it over him time and time again she'd been sending the message that he meant no more to her than he'd meant to his parents.

Lord, she'd made such a mess of things. Such a mess of her life.

And in staying so incredibly busy, she'd not only risked her long-term health but she'd also lost sight of the person she loved most: Ben.

Maybe it was time to start pulling away. Let someone else take the helm of her organization—Pedro maybe—and go back to practicing medicine in a clinic. She might not be able to help whole swaths of people but she could help them one at a time.

Which path was more valuable in the long run? Maybe it wasn't a question of either/or. Maybe each had its own place in the grand scheme of things. And there were two children who'd trusted her to be there for them.

She turned and hugged her friend. "Thank you. I think I've just realized where I should be."

"In *Teresina*?"

She nodded. "I don't know why I didn't see it before now."

"Maybe because 'now' was when you needed to see it." With a secretive smile Stevie waved to her husband, who was working off in the distance. He winked back.

And Tracy did what she should have done four years ago: she walked to the nearest soldier and asked if she could hitch a ride on the next boat out of the Amazon.

Ben sucked down a mouthful of tepid coffee and grimaced before going back to his microscope and glaring down at the slide beneath the lens. He had no business being here today. He'd had no business here all week.

Why had he drawn that ridiculous line in the sand and dared her to cross it? Maybe because he'd never forgiven his parents for withholding their affection when he'd been a child?

Yeah, well, he was an adult now. Well past the age of holding grudges.

He hadn't heard from Tracy since she'd left, and he'd cursed himself repeatedly for not being more sensitive the last time they'd talked…for not trying to really listen to what she'd been saying.

He wasn't the only one who was upset.

Rosa had chewed his butt up one side and down the other when she'd found out Tracy wasn't coming home.

"I used to think I raised you to be a smart boy, Benjamin Almeida. Now I'm not so sure."

"You shouldn't have had to raise me at all."

"Was it so bad? Your childhood?"

He thought back. No, his parents had been gone for months at a time, but when they had been there there'd been laughter…and then, when they'd left again there'd been tears. But through it all Rosa had been there. How many children grew up not even having a Rosa in their lives?

If he thought about it, he was damned lucky.

And if he'd given Tracy a little more time to settle in before jumping to conclusions at the first phone call she'd got from the office, maybe he could have done a better job at being a husband this time.

He rummaged around in his desk until he came up with an old tattered business card that he'd saved for years. Staring at the familiar name on the front, he turned it over and over between his fingers, battling with indecision. He knew from their time in São João dos Rios that the phone number was still the same. Finally, before he could change his mind, he dialed and swiveled around in his chair to face out the window.

Did she even have cellphone reception wherever she was?

He heard the phone ring through the handset, but there was something weird about it. Almost as if it was ringing in two places at once—inside his ear and somewhere off in the distance. On the second ring the sound outside his ear grew louder in steady increments, and he frowned, trying to figure out if he was just imagining it. On the third ring her voice came through. "Hello?"

Ben's breath seized in his lungs as he realized the greeting came not only from the handset pressed to his ear but from right behind him. He slowly swiveled and met sea-green eyes. They crinkled at the corners as they looked back at him.

Keeping the phone pressed to his ear, he gazed at her in disbelief, while she kept her phone against her own ear as well.

"Tracy?"

"Yes."

God, he could just jump up and crush her to him. But he didn't. He said the words he'd been rehearsing for the last half-hour. "I've missed you. Please come home."

Tears shimmered in her eyes, her throat moving in a quick jerking motion. "I've missed you too. I'll be there soon."

With that she clicked her phone shut and moved towards him. When she stood before his chair, he reached up and pulled her down onto his lap. "You're home."

"I am. I'm home." She wrapped her arms around his neck and pulled him against her. "And this time I'm here to stay."

One year later

Ben strode down the hallway of Einstein Hospital in São Paulo, Brazil, until he reached the surgical wing. Tracy's dad was already in the waiting room. He stood as he saw Ben heading his way. The two men shook hands, Sam taking it one step further and embracing his son-in-law.

Ben said, "I'm glad you were able to come, sir."

"How is she?"

"Still in surgery."

The months since Tracy had stood in his office and they'd shared declarations of love had passed in a flurry of medical tests for both Cleo and Tracy. Cleo's initial diagnosis of diabetes had been confirmed, but it was now under control. They'd even been granted custody of both children.

Tracy's mammogram had come back with an area of concern and whether it was cancer or not, they both knew it was time. They'd made this decision together soon after she'd come home. She'd shed tears while Ben had reassured her that he'd love her with breasts or without.

Nodding to the chair Sam had vacated, they both sat down.

"She did it, then," his father-in-law said.

"Yes." Ben leaned forward, elbows on his knees, clasped hands dangling between them. "She wanted to be proactive."

Tracy's dad nodded. "If her mother had known she carried this gene, I know in my heart she would have done the same thing. And I would have stood beside her." He dragged a forearm across his eyes, which Ben pretended he didn't see. "How long will she be back there?"

"Two to four hours." He glanced at his watch. "It's going on three hours now. We should be hearing something fairly soon."

Two to four hours. Such a short time. And yet it seemed like for ever.

Unable to sit still, he settled for pacing while Sam remained in his seat. Ben had already made all kinds of deals with God, so many he wasn't sure he'd be able to keep track. But Tracy had been so sure of this, so at peace with her decision in the past week.

A green-suited man came around the corner, a surgical mask dangling around his neck. "Mr. Almeida?"

Ben moved towards him, Sam following close behind. The surgeon frowned, but Ben nodded. "This is Tracy's dad. He's just arrived in town."

The man nodded. "The surgery went fine. I didn't see any definite areas of malignancy, but I'm sending everything off to pathology for testing just in case."

"Tracy's okay, then?" Ben didn't want to hear about malignancies or what they had or hadn't found.

"She's fine." The man hesitated. "Reconstruction shouldn't be a problem. We'd like to keep her here for a day or two to observe her, however. Will she have someone to help her at home afterwards?"

"Yes." Ben's and Sam's answers came on top of the other, causing all of them to smile.

Ben finished. "We'll make sure she gets everything she needs." He knew the kids would both be beside themselves, desperate for a chance to talk to Tracy. But he'd left them in *Teresina*, in Rosa's care—though he'd realized the irony of it. Kids survived. And these two kids had survived more than most...more than he'd ever had to, even on his worst days.

"Good," the surgeon said. "Give us a few minutes to get her settled then someone will come and get you. Please, don't stay long, though. She needs to rest."

Ben held out a hand. "Thank you. For everything."

The surgeon nodded then shook each of their hands and headed back in the direction from which he'd come. Before he rounded the corner, though, he turned and came back. "I wanted to tell you what a brave young woman Tracy is. I don't know how much you've talked about everything, but whether you agree with her decision or not it was ultimately up to her. Support her in it."

"Absolutely." Ben wasn't planning on doing anything else. He'd spend the rest of his days supporting whatever decisions she made. He was just grateful to have her back.

"Thanks again."

"You're welcome. Take care." This time the surgeon didn't look back but disappeared around the corner.

"Why don't you go back and see her first?" Ben told Sam.

"My face is not the one she'll want to see when she wakes up. There's plenty of time."

Yes, there was. Ben swallowed. "Thank you. I'll tell her you're here."

Sleep.

That's all Tracy wanted to do, but something warm curled around her hand and gave a soft squeeze. Someone said her name in a low, gravelly voice she should recognize.

Did recognize.

"Trace."

There it was again. Her heart warmed despite the long shivers taking hold of her body. She was cold. Freezing. Her body fought back, shuddering against the sensation.

Something settled over her. A blanket?

She focused on her eyelids, trying to convince them to part—wanted to put a hand to her chest to see if they were still there.

Oh, God. Moisture flared behind still closed lids and leaked out the sides.

"Tracy." Warm fingers threaded through her own. "You're okay. Safe. I'm here."

She wanted to believe. But she was afraid the last year had all been a dream. At least the blanket was starting to warm her just a bit.

Her throat ached. From the tube she'd had down her throat.

Wait. Tube?

Yes, from the surgery. Ben was here. Somewhere. He promised to be here when she woke up.

So why was she even doubting she'd heard his voice?

Okay. Moment of truth.

Eyelids...open.

As if by magic, they parted and the first thing she saw was the face. The gorgeous face that matched that low, sexy voice. Broad shoulders stretched wide against the fabric of his shirt. Ruffled brown hair that looked like he'd shoved fingers through it repeatedly, a piece in the back sticking straight up.

Long, dark lashes. Strong throat. Gentle hands.

Her husband.

"Ben?" The sound rasped out of her throat as if coated by rough sandpaper—and feeling like it as well.

"I'm here."

Yes, it was Ben. He was here. Crying?

Oh, God. He was crying because she no longer had breasts. No, that wasn't it. They'd made this decision together. Had they found something during the surgery?

She tried to glance down at herself, but everything was buried under a thick layer of blankets. But there was no pain. Could the surgeon not have taken them?

"Are they...?"

"Shh. You're fine."

Closing her eyes, she tried to clear her fuzzy head. "The kids?"

"I spoke to Rosa a few minutes ago. They're fine. They miss you."

I miss you.

Her lips curved as she remembered Ben saying those very words as she'd stood in the doorway of his office a year ago. That he'd actually called her—wanted her to come home—was a memory she'd treasure for ever.

Where was the pain? Shouldn't it hurt to have something sliced off your body?

"I miss the kids, too."

He smiled and smoothed strands of hair back from her face. "Your dad's here. They'll only let one of us in at a time, and he insisted you'd want to see me first."

"He was right."

Lifting her hand to his lips, he kissed the top of it. His touch was as warm as his voice. "I love you, Tracy. And I'm going to spend the rest of my life showing you how much."

She closed her eyes, only to have to force them open again. "I like the sound of that."

One of the nurses appeared in the doorway, leaning against the frame. "We probably need to let Mrs. Almeida get some sleep."

"Mrs. Almeida." Tracy murmured the words as her eyelids once again began to flicker shut. She loved having his name.

Almost as much as she loved the man who'd given it to her.

EPILOGUE

THE SUNRISE WAS gorgeous, a blazing red ball of fire tossed just above the horizon by the hand of God.

Today promised to be a scorcher—just like most days in *Teresina*. And she relished each and every one of them. Curling her hands around the railing of the deck off their bedroom, Tracy let the warmth of the wood sink into her palms and gave a quiet sigh of contentment. She loved these kinds of mornings.

Five years since her surgery and no sign of cancer.

Tracy was thrilled to be a part of Crista Morena's thriving pediatric practice. And twice a year she and Ben took a trip along the Amazon to do relief work. Together. Something that might have been impossible in the past.

A pair of arms wrapped around her from behind, sliding beneath the hem of her white camisole and tickling the skin of her tummy. She made a quiet sound, putting her hands over his and holding him close. Leaning her head against her husband's chest, she thought about how truly blessed she was.

Except for one thing.

"I miss Daniel." The wistfulness in her heart came through in her voice.

Their adopted son had left for college in the States last month and was busy studying to be a doctor—hoping to return to Brazil and help people in communities like São João dos Rios. His mother would be so very proud of the man her son had become. The four of them had made several trips back to the kids' home town, and although the razed village was sad testament to what had happened there, it was also a place of joy. A place of new beginnings.

They'd had a permanent stone marker made and had placed it on Maria Eugênia's grave—although both Daniel and Cleo had decided the crude rock Ben had carved should remain there as well.

They'd also made a pact to go back once a year to put flowers on her grave.

Cleo, now thirteen, was growing into a beautiful young woman who was sensitive and wise beyond her years. All too soon she'd be grown as well, leaving them to start a life of her own.

"We can always phone Daniel later this afternoon." Ben planted cool lips on her neck.

"We'll wait for Cleo to get home from school. I can't believe how fast time has gone by."

"I'm grateful for every moment." His lips continued to glide up her neck until he reached her earlobe, biting gently.

She shivered, her body reacting instantly, the way it always did for this man. "So am I."

A thin cry came from the back of the house. Tracy squinched her nose and sighed. "So is someone else."

Their baby girl, just three months old, was letting them know she was hungry. Although she would never replace the baby they'd lost all those years ago, trying to have another child had seemed the right thing to do. Tracy was grateful for second chances, no matter how they came.

Ben had taken a little more coaxing—a year to be exact. He'd been worried about the ramifications to her health, but in the end he'd agreed. And Grace Elizabeth Almeida had come into the world kicking and screaming.

Someone ready to take on the universe and everything it held.

"I guess we'd better go feed her before she gets really wound up." Ben turned her in his arms and nipped her lower lip. "Although I was hoping we might get a little alone time. Just this once."

"Don't worry, Ben. We have plenty of time. Our whole lives, in fact."

Tracy sighed, her happiness complete. She had everything she could possibly want out of life. She and Ben had found their middle ground, despite seemingly impossible odds. And she'd discovered there was more than one path to happiness, as long as the man she loved was by her side. And as her three children had taught her, there was definitely more than one way to make a family.

* * * * *